Blackberry Wine

"Harris's voice is crisp and sure. . . . [*Blackberry Wine*] is a well-crafted escape into a world where lessons can be learned and evil is sometimes just dumb enough to be given the slip."

—*Seattle Times*

Sleep,
Pale Sister

Sleep,
Pale Sister

Joanne Harris

HARPER PERENNIAL

NEW YORK • LONDON • TORONTO • SYDNEY

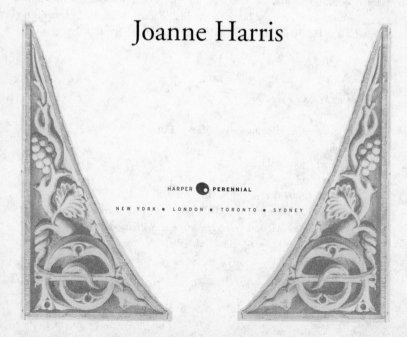

HARPER ● PERENNIAL

First published in Great Britain in 1994 by Arrow, a division of Random House Group Inc.

P.S.™ is a trademark of HarperCollins Publishers.

FIRST U.S. EDITION

Designed by Nicola Ferguson

Library of Congress Cataloging-in-Publication Data
Harris, Joanne.
Sleep, pale sister / Joanne Harris.
p. cm.
ISBN-13: 978-0-06-078711-0 ISBN-10: 0-06-078711-2
1. Artist—Fiction. 2. Murder victims—Fiction. 3. Artists' models—Fiction.
4. London (England)—Fiction. 5. Mothers and daughters—Fiction.
6. Prostitutes—Crimes against—Fiction. I. Title.
PR6058.A68828S57 2005
823'.941—dc22   2004065066

07 08 09 ❖ / RRDH 10 9 8 7 6 5 4 3

To Kevin, again

Acknowledgements

Many thanks to everyone who helped to bring this sleeper back to life. First of all to Christopher, who liked it from the start; to Serafina, Howard, and Brie; to my lovely editor Jennifer and all my friends at William Morrow; to Graham Ovenden for the cover I always wanted; to the booksellers, reps and stockists who work to keep my books on the shelves, and finally to all those fans of my earlier novels who have written, railed, persisted, queried and clamoured to see this one back in print.

Sleep,
Pale Sister

Introduction

Manuscript, from the estate of Henry Paul Chester
January, 1881

As I look at my name and the letters which follow it I am filled with a vast blankness. As if this Henry Chester, painter, twice exhibited at the Royal Academy, were not myself but some ill-defined figment of somebody's imagination, the cork to a bottle containing a genie of delicate malevolence that permeates my being and launches me into a realm of perilous adventure, in search of the pale, terrified ghost of myself.

The name of the genie is *chloral*, that dark companion of my sleeping hours, a tender bedfellow now grown spiteful. Yet we have been wedded too long now for separation, the genie and I. Together we will write this narrative, but I have so little time! Already, as the last shreds of daylight fall from the horizon, I seem to hear the wings of the black angel in the darkest corner of the room. She is patient, but not infinitely so.

God, that most exquisite of torturers, will deign to give me a little time to write the tale which I shall take with me to my cold cell under the earth—no colder, surely, than this corpse I inhabit, this wilderness of the soul. Oh, He is a jealous God: pitiless as only immortals can be, and when I cried out for Him in my filth and suffering He smiled and replied in the words He gave to

Moses from the burning bush: *I Am That I Am*. His gaze is without compassion, without tenderness. Within it I see no promise of redemption, no threat of punishment; only a vast indifference, promising nothing but oblivion. But how I long for it! To melt into the earth, so that even that all-seeing gaze could not find me ... and yet the infant within me cries at the dark, and my poor, crippled body screams out for time . . . A little more time, one more tale, one more game.

And the black angel lays her scythe by the door and sits beside me for a final hand of cards.

I should never write after dark. At night, words become false, troubling; and yet, it is at night that words have the most power. Scheherazade chose the night to weave her thousand and one stories, each one a door into which time and time again she slips with Death at her heels like an angry wolf. She knew the power of words. If I had not passed longing for the ideal woman, I should have gone in search of Scheherazade; she is tall and slim, with skin the colour of China tea. Her eyes are like the night; she walks barefoot, arrogant and pagan, untrammelled by morality or modesty. And she is cunning; time and again she plays the game against Death and wins, reinventing herself anew every night so that her brutish ogre of a husband finds every night a new Scheherazade who slips away with the morning. Every morning he awakes and sees her in daylight, pale and silent after her night's work, and he swears he will not be taken in again! But as soon as dusk falls, she weaves her web of fantasy anew, and he thinks: once more ...

Tonight *I* am Scheherazade.

The

Hermit

1

Don't look at me that way—I can't bear it! You're thinking how much I have changed. You see the young man in the picture, his clear, pale brow, curling dark hair, his untroubled eyes—and you wonder how he could be me. The carelessly arrogant set of the jaw, the high cheekbones, the long, tapered fingers seem to hint at some hidden, exotic lineage, although the bearing is unmistakably English. That was me at thirty-nine—look at me carefully and remember . . . I could have been you.

My father was a minister near Oxford, my mother the daughter of a wealthy Oxfordshire landowner. My childhood was untroubled, sheltered, idyllic. I remember going to church on Sundays, singing in the choir, the coloured light from the stained-glass windows like a shower of petals on the white surplices of the choristers . . .

The black angel seems to shift imperceptibly and, in her eyes, I sense an echo of the pitiless comprehension of God. This is not a time for imagined nostalgia, Henry Paul Chester. He needs your truth, not your inventions. Do you think to fool God?

Ridiculous, that I should still feel the urge to deceive, I who have lived nothing *but* a life of deceit for over forty years. The truth is a bitter decoction: I hate to uncork it for this last meeting. And yet I am what I am. For the first time I can dare to take God's words for myself. This is no sweetened fiction. This is Henry Chester: judge me if you wish. I am what I am.

There was, of course, no idyllic childhood. My early years are blank: my memories begin at age seven or eight; impure, troubled memories even then as I felt the serpent grown within me. I do not remember a time when I was not conscious of my sin, my guilt: no surplice, however white, could hide it. It gave me wicked thoughts, it made me laugh in church, it made me lie to my father and cross my fingers to extinguish the lie.

There were samplers on the wall of every room of our house, embroidered by my mother with texts from the Bible. Even now I see them, especially the one in my room, stark on the white wall opposite my bed: I AM THAT I AM. As I passed the summers and winters of my boyhood, in my moments of peace and the contemplation of my solitary vices I watched that sampler, and sometimes, in my dreams, I cried out at the cruel indifference of God. But I always received the same message, stitched now for ever in the intricate patterns of my memory: I AM THAT I AM.

My father was God's man and more frightening to me than God. His eyes were deep and black, and he could see right into the hidden corners of my guilty soul. His judgement was as pitiless and impartial as God's own, untainted by human tenderness. What affection my father had he lavished on his collection of mechanical toys, for he was an antiquarian of sorts and had a whole room filled with them, from the very simplest of counterweighted wooden figures to the dreamlike precision of his Chinese barrel-organ with its hundred prancing dwarves.

Of course, I was never allowed to play with them—they were too precious for any child—but I do remember the dancing Columbine. She was made of fine porcelain and was almost as big as a three-year-old child. Father told me, in one of his rare moments of informality, that she was made by a blind French craftsman in the decadent years before the Revolution. Running his fingers across her flawless cheek, he told me the story: how she had belonged to some spoiled king's bastard brat, abandoned among rotting brocades when the Terror struck and godless heads rolled with the innocent. How she was stolen by a pauper woman who could not bear to see her smashed and trampled by the sans-culottes. The woman had lost her baby to the famine and kept Columbine in a cradle in her poor hovel, rocking her and singing lullabies until they found her, mad and starving and alone, and took her away to the asylum to die.

Columbine survived. She arrived in a Paris antiquarian's the year I was born, and Father, who was returning from a trip to Lourdes, saw her and bought her at once, though her silk dress was rotten and her eyes had fallen into her head from neglect and rough handling. As soon as he saw her dance, he knew she was special: wind the key set into the small of her back and she would begin to move, stiffly at first, then with a slick, inhuman fluidity, raising her arms, bowing from the waist, flexing her knees, show-ing the plump roundness of her porcelain calves under the dancer's skirt. Months of loving restoration gave her back all her beauty, and now she sat resplendent in blue and white satin in my father's collection, between the Indian music-box and the Persian clown.

I was never allowed to wind her up. Sometimes, when I lay awake in the middlle of the night, I could hear a faint tinkle of music from behind the closed door, low and intimate, almost car-nal . . . The image of Father in his nightgown with the dancing Columbine in his hands was absurdly disquieting. I could not help wondering how he would hold her; whether he would dare to let his hand creep beneath the foaming lace of her petticoats . . .

I rarely saw my mother; she was often indisposed and spent a great deal of time in her room, into which I was not allowed. She was a beautiful enigma, dark-haired and violet-eyed. Glancing into the secret chamber one day I remember a looking-glass, jewels, scarves, armfuls of lovely gowns strewn over the bed. Among it all lingered a scent of lilac, the scent of my mother when she leaned to kiss me goodnight, the scent of her linen as I buried my face in the washing the maid hung out to dry.

My mother was a great beauty, Nurse told me. She had married against her parents' wishes and no longer communicated with her family. Maybe that was why she sometimes looked at me with that expression of wary contempt; maybe that was why she never seemed to want to touch or hold me. I idolized her, however: she seemed so infinitely above me, so delicate and pure that I was unable to express my adoration, crushed by my own inadequacy. I never blamed my mother for what she made me do: for years I cursed my own corrupt heart, as Adam must have cursed the serpent for Eve's transgression.

I was twelve; I still sang in the choir but my voice had reached that almost inhuman purity of tone which heralds the end of childhood. It was August, and the whole of that summer had been fine: long, blue, dreaming days filled with voluptuous scents and languorous sensations. I had been playing in the garden with friends and I was hot and thirsty, my hair standing on end like a savage's, grass-stains on the knees of my trousers. I crept into the house quietly; I wanted to change my clothes quickly before Nurse realized what a state I was in.

There was no-one there but the maid in the kitchen—Father was in church preparing for the evening's sermon, and Mother was walking by the river—and I ran up the stairs to my room. Pausing on the landing, I saw that the door to my mother's room was ajar. I remember looking at the doorknob, a blue-and-white porcelain thing painted with flowers. A scent of lilac wafted out from the cool darkness and, almost in spite of myself, I moved closer and peered through the door. There was no-one in sight. Looking guiltily around me, I pushed the door and entered, telling myself earnestly that if the door had been open, I could not be accused of snooping, and, for the first time in my life, I was alone in my mother's private room.

For a minute I was content to stare at the rows of bottles and trinkets by the looking-glass, then I dared to touch a silk scarf, then the lace of a petticoat, the gauze of an under-dress. I was fascinated by all her things, by the mysterious vials and jars, and the combs and brushes with strands of her hair still caught in the bristles. It was almost as if the room *was* my mother, as if it had captured her essence. I felt that if I could assimilate every nuance of that room I might learn to tell her how much I loved her in the kind of words she could understand.

Reaching to brush my reflection in the mirror I accidentally knocked over a little bottle, filling the air with a heady distillation of jasmine and honeysuckle. My hurried attempt to pick up the bottle only resulted in my spilling a case of powder across the dressing-table, but the scent acted so strangely upon my nerves that, instead of being panic-stricken, I giggled softly to myself. Mother would not be back for some time; Father was in church. What harm could it do to explore? And I felt an excitement, a power, looking over my mother's things in her absence. An amber necklace winked at me in the semi-darkness; I picked it up and, on impulse, put it on. A transparent scarf, light as a breath, touched my bare arm as I passed. I raised it to my lips, seeming to feel her skin, her scent against my face.

For the first time I began to feel an extraordinary sensation, a tingling in all my body focusing more and more strongly on a point of exquisite tension, a growing friction which filled my mind with half-recognized images of carnality. I tried to make myself believe that it was the room which was making me do it. The scarf *wanted* to coil lovingly around my neck. Bracelets found their way on to my arms on their own. I took off my shirt and looked at myself in the glass and, with hardly a second thought, I took off my trousers. There was a wrap lying on my mother's bed, a delicate, transparent thing of silk and frothy lace: experimentally I draped it around myself, caressing the thin fabric, imagining it touching her skin, imagining how it would look...

I began to feel physically faint, disorientated, the potency of the spilled perfume assailing me like an invisible army of succubi—I could hear the beating of their wings. It was then that I knew I was the devil's creature. Some inhuman instinct impelled me to continue and, although I knew that what I was doing was mortal sin, I felt no guilt. I felt immortal. My hands, knotting and clutching the wrap, seemed possessed by a demonic intelligence: I began to caper in a frenzied, ecstatic glee... then suddenly I was frozen in sublime paralysis, doubling up beneath the force of a pleasure I had never conceived of. For a second I was higher than the clouds, higher than God... then I fell like Lucifer, a little boy again, lying on the carpet, the silk wrap crushed and torn under me, the jewels and trinkets grotesque around my scrawny limbs.

A moment of stupid indifference. Then the enormity of what I had done broke upon my head like a hailstorm and I began to cry in hysterical terror, dragging on my clothes with shaking hands, feeling my knees buckle. I grabbed the wrap and rolled it into a ball, thrusting it into my shirt. Picking up my shoes I ran out of my mother's room and into my own where I hid the wrap up the chimney behind a loose stone, promising myself to burn it as soon as Nurse lit a fire there.

Feeling my panic abating a little, I took the time to wash my face and change, then I lay on my bed for ten minutes to still my trembling. An odd sensation of relief overwhelmed me: I had escaped immediate discovery. Fear and guilt were metamorphosed into a sense of exhilaration: even if I were punished for having been into my mother's room, the very worst thing would never be known. It was my secret, and I kept it coiled up in my heart like a serpent. There it grew with me—and, even now, continues to grow.

I did not escape entirely undiscovered, of course: the spilled powder and perfume gave me away—along with the theft of the wrap. I admitted that part to my father: that I had gone into the room because I was curious, that I had been clumsy and had trodden on the lace of the wrap by mistake, and had torn it, and that, to avoid punishment, I had thrown the wrap into the pond. He believed me, even commending my honesty (how the devil within me laughed and capered!), and, though I was whipped for my foolishness, the feeling of relief, even excitement, did not abate. From being all-powerful, my father had suddenly dwindled: I had fooled him, lied to him, and he had not known. As for my mother, maybe she guessed something, for I caught her looking at me with an odd expression once or twice, but she never spoke about the incident and it was soon, apparently, forgotten.

For myself, I never did burn the wrap I had concealed in the chimney. Sometimes, when I was alone, I would take it from its hiding-place and touch the silken folds, until years of handling and rising smoke from the chimney turned it brittle and brown as parchment and it fell to pieces of its own accord, like a handful of autumn leaves.

My mother died when I was fourteen, two years after the birth of my brother, William. I remember her lovely chamber transformed into a sickroom, with heavy wreaths of flowers on every piece of furniture; she pale and thin, but still beautiful to the end.

My father was with her all the time, his face unreadable. One day, passing the room without entering, I heard him weeping in violent abandon, and my mouth twisted in derision; I prided myself in feeling nothing.

Her grave was placed in the churchyard just outside the entrance to the church, so that my father could see it as he greeted his parishioners. I had often wondered how such a stern, God-fearing man had come to marry such a delicate, worldly creature. That he might have passions I could not guess at made me uneasy, and I dismissed such thoughts.

When I was twenty-five my father died. I was completing my Grand Tour at the time, and did not hear of it until all was over. It seemed that during the winter he had caught a cold, had neglected it—he hardly ever lit fires in the house except in the bitterest weather—had refused to take to his bed and, one day in church, had collapsed. Fever set in and he died without recovering consciousness, leaving me with a tidy fortune and an inexplicable feeling that now he was dead he would be able to watch over all my movements.

I moved to London: I had a certain talent for drawing and wished to establish myself as an artist. There I discovered the British Museum and the Royal Academy, and steeped myself in art and sculpture. I was determined to make a name for myself: I rented a studio in Kennington and spent my first five years accumulating enough work for my first exhibition. I painted allegorical portraits especially, taking a great deal of my ideas from Shakespeare and classical mythology, working in oils for the most part, that medium being the most suitable for the meticulous, detailed work I liked. One visitor who came to see my work told me that the style was 'quite Pre-Raphaelite', which delighted me, and I took care to nurture this similarity, even taking subjects from Rossetti's poetry—although I felt that the poet, as a man, was very far from the kind of person I should like to emulate.

My main problem was finding suitable models, for I had few friends in London and, after a most embarrassing experience near the Haymarket, did not dare to approach likely females with offers of work. I had no interest in painting men: I found more poetry in the female form, and a certain type of female form at that. I advertised in *The Times*, but found that from twenty or so applicants only one or two were even passably handsome, and that none of them could be termed 'respectable' women. As long as they didn't open their vulgar mouths I did not complain, however, which is why, when I look back at some of my earlier works, I find it hard to trust my memory, recollecting that sweet-faced *Juliet* had an illegitimate child or innocent *Cinderella* an addiction to the gin-bottle. I learned more about women in those days than I ever wished to know. In spite of their pretty faces, listening to their conversations, their lewdness, their unclean thoughts, I despised them.

Several of them tried their cheap seductions upon me, but at that time the serpent within me was well under control: I went to church every Sunday, painted at my studio during the day and relaxed at a respectable club in the evenings. I had a small circle of acquaintances, but found little need for company. After all, I had my art. I even fancied that women had no power over me, that I had finally conquered the stirrings of my sinful flesh. Such conceit is the wheel upon which God breaks sinners; but time runs on a short leash, and I must skim over three more years to a time when I was just thirty-three, to the clear autumn day when I met my nemesis.

I had been painting children for some time: it was always easy to find a beautiful child whose mother was willing to spare her for a few hours a day. I paid them a shilling an hour, and it was more than some of these women themselves earned. Thus I was walking in the park as I often did when I happened to catch sight of a woman and a child: the woman a dowdy customer in black, the child a little girl of about ten with such unusual and striking features that I stopped to stare after her.

She was a thin child, wrapped in an ugly black cape which looked like someone else's hand-me-down, but she moved with a grace unusual in one of her age, and her hair was a most troubling colour, a shade closer to white than gold, so that for an instant she looked like a little old crone, some changeling among the happy, rosy children around her. Her face was pointed and almost colourless but for her large, deep eyes; her lips were full for a child's, but pale; her expression quaintly tragic.

I knew instantly that I had to have her as my model: there was an infinite promise of expression in her face; each movement was a masterpiece of definition. Looking at her I knew that child would be my salvation; her innocence moved me as much as her spectral beauty, and there were tears in my eyes as I ran towards the couple. For a moment my heart was too full for me to speak.

The girl's name was Effie; the dowdy woman was her aunt. She lived with her aunt and her mother above a little milliner's shop in Cranbourn Alley and they were of a respectable type: the mother, Mrs Shelbeck, was a widow, living in straitened circumstances. A shrill, annoying woman, I later found, with none of her daughter's striking looks, and my offer of a shilling an hour was accepted without any of the modesty and reserve usually exhibited by genteel families. I suspect that if I had offered half the sum it would have been accepted with equal alacrity—as it was, I would have gladly offered double.

Effie came to my studio—respectably accompanied by the aunt—that very week, and I spent a whole morning simply drawing the child from various angles: profile, three-quarter, full-face, head high, head to one side . . . each more enchanting than the last. She was a perfect model: she did not shuffle and fidget as did other children, nor did she chatter or smile. She seemed overawed by the studio and by me, studying me covertly with an expression of respectful wonder. She came again; after the third time the aunt ceased to come with her.

My first painting of her was called *My Sister's Sleep*, from the Rossetti poem, and it took two months to complete: only a small canvas, but I flattered myself that I had caught the look of Effie. I painted her lying on a little narrow bed such as children use, a cross on the white wall above her and a vase of holly on the bed-stand beside her, the family's concession to the Christmas spirit. Her brother was sitting on the floor beside the bed, his head buried in the coverlet, and her mother, in black, was standing at the foot of the bed with her face in her hands. The painting focused on Effie; the other figures were faceless and dark-clad, but she was all in white, wearing a ruffled nightdress I had bought for the painting, her hair spread out on the pillow all around her. Her arms were bare, one hanging limply by her side, the other tucked childishly under her cheek. The light from the window transfigured her, promising redemption in death, the purity of the innocent who dies young. It was a theme close to my heart and I was to repeat it many times in the next seven years. Sometimes I was reluctant to let her go home in the evenings for she was growing so fast that I was afraid to lose even an hour of her company.

Effie never spoke a great deal: she was a quiet little thing, untouched by the conceit and vanity exhibited by other girls of the same age. She read avidly—especially poetry, Tennyson, Keats, Byron, Shakespeare—hardly any of it suitable for a child, although her mother seemed to pay little attention to the fact. I ventured to point this out to Effie one day and was pleased to find her properly attentive to my advice. I told her that poetry, although unexceptionable reading for, say, a young man, was rather too difficult for a susceptible young girl. The subject matter was too frequently indelicate, the passions too violent. I offered to lend her some good, improving books, and was delighted when she read them dutifully. There was no wilfulness in her: she seemed created to embody all the feminine virtues without any of the perversity of that sex.

I had never wanted to be a bachelor, but my mistrust of women, born of my professional contact with them, had led me to doubt whether I would ever find St Paul's 'one in a thousand', who is virtuous and obedient. However, as I saw more of Effie, as I was charmed by her beauty and her sweet ways, I realized that, after all, there was a way to achieve that ideal.

There was no taint on Effie: she was absolutely pure. If I could nurture her qualities, if I could keep a fatherly eye on her development, I was certain that I could make of her something rare, something wonderful. I would protect her from the rest of the world, educate her to be my equal. I would mould her, then, the work done...as I formulated the idea my mind threw back at me the memory of a small boy in a room full of forbidden marvels, and that fleeting, nostalgic scent of jasmine seemed to fill the air. For the first time the image brought no accompanying twist of guilt: Effie's purity would redeem me, I knew it. There was nothing worldly, nothing sensual about her; hers was the cool indifference of the true innocent. Through her I would find salvation.

I engaged private tutors for her—I wanted her to have as little contact with other children as possible—I bought her clothes and books. I employed a respectable housekeeper for her mother and aunt so that Effie would not have to waste time helping around the house. I befriended her tedious mother so that I should have the excuse to frequent Cranbourn Alley and I kept the money flowing in.

I was painting Effie almost incessantly now, abandoning all my other models unless they were needed as secondaries in a canvas. I concentrated upon Effie: Effie at twelve, taller, in the pretty white dresses and blue sashes I encouraged her mother to buy; Effie at thirteen, fourteen, her dancer's figure as graceful as a colt's; at fifteen, her eyes and lips darkening, her face taking a more adult shape; at sixteen, her pale hair bound up in a tidy coronet around her brow, her mouth the tenderest of arcs, her lovely rain-coloured eyes heavy-lidded, the skin around them so fine that it seemed almost bruised.

I must have drawn or painted Effie a hundred times: she was Cinderella, she was Mary, she was the young novice in *The Passion-Flower,* she was Beatrice in Heaven, Juliet in the tomb, draped with lilies and trailing convolvulus for *Ophelia*, in rags for *The Little Beggar Girl*. My final portrait of her at that time was *The Sleeping Beauty*, so like *My Sister's Sleep* in composition, showing Effie all in white again, like a bride or a novice, lying on the same little girl's bed, her hair, much longer than it had been when she was ten—I had always urged her never to cut it—trailing on to the floor, where a century's worth of dust lingers. Sunlight filters through the skylight on to the floor, and tendrils of ivy have begun to drop through the window into the room. A skeleton in armour, twined all over with the encroaching ivy, warns of the perils of disturbing the sleeping innocent. Effie's face is turned towards the light; she smiles in her sleep, unaware of the desolation around her.

I could wait no longer. I had woven the enchantment which had kept her waiting for me all these years: now was the time to break it. She was still very young, I knew, but to wait another year might be to risk losing her for ever.

Her mother did not even seem surprised that I should want to marry her daughter. Indeed, the eagerness with which she welcomed the offer made me suspect that she had already envisaged the possibility. I was a rich man, after all: it was certain that if Effie married me I would be obliged to help her relatives, and I was almost forty while Effie was seventeen. When I died, all my fortune would be hers. The maiden aunt—a sour-mannered creature whose only redeeming feature was an overpowering devotion to Effie—disapproved. Effie was too young, she said, too sensitive. She did not understand what would be required of her when we were married. I did not care about her objections. Effie was my only concern. She was mine: trained to grow along me like ivy on the trunk of an oak.

She married me in the same antique embroidered dress she had worn for the *Sleeping Beauty*.

The Star

2

'*This I say then,* Walk in the Spirit, and ye shall not fulfil the lust of the flesh.

For the flesh lusteth against the Spirit, and the Spirit against the flesh: and these are contrary the one to the other: so that ye cannot do the things that ye would.

But if ye be led of the Spirit, ye are not under the law.

Now the works of the flesh are manifest, which are these; Adultery, fornication, uncleanness, lasciviousness,

Idolatry, witchcraft, hatred . . .'

The black caravan of his words lurched onwards, and I was glad I had taken laudanum before the service. My migraine was quite gone, leaving in its place a cool dark cavity into which all my thoughts receded, remote as stars.

'"*wrath, strife, sedition,* heresies . . ."'

In my own quiet space I smiled to myself.

The rhythm of the verses was cruel, but poetry nevertheless, compelling as the pagan lilt of the skipping-songs I sang in the street all those years ago, in the days before I married Mr Chester:

The higher we jump
The higher they'll grow.
Around and around and around we go.

Remembering the song I felt suddenly sick at heart at the terrible remoteness of that lost time when Mother was well, and Father alive and we used to read poems together in the library of our old house, before Cranbourn Alley; a time when going to church was an occasion to celebrate, to sing and be happy. My hands clenched abruptly as the sick feeling intensified, and I bit down on my lip to quell my faintness. William, sitting to my left, gave me his rueful grin, but I kept my face lowered; Mr Chester would not like me to smile in church. Over the minister's head the sunlight illuminated St Sebastian, shot with arrows.

The higher we jump . . .

St Sebastian's face was cool and passive, like Henry's.

Suddenly I was falling, pinwheeling my arms in panic, my mouth open in a great silent O of terror . . . but I was falling *upwards*, towards the high vault of the church ceiling, and I could see the gilt paint and the scrollwork and the cold gleam of St Sebastian's eyes . . . As my fall slowed I looked dizzily on to the bowed heads of the congregation, my terror giving way to awe and euphoria. How could I be here? Had I died and left my body without realizing it? Was I dreaming? I skipped and danced in the air, whooping as I spun around the bald head of the minister like an angel on the head of a pin. No-one heard me.

Testing my new-found ability, I swooped invisibly over the tide of dark heads, realizing as I did so that my vision and hearing were sharper than ever before, each detail a miracle of precision. I could actually *see* the minister's words mounting heavenwards like smoke from a factory chimney. I could see the gloom of the congregation, occasionally broken by the clear beam of a child's inattention; looking closely I found that somehow I could see right *into* people; I could see their essence like sunlight through stained-glass. Behind a mask of flesh, an old woman with a sour face and a sharp tongue blossomed with a spectral radiance; a child radiated simple joy; a young, dark-haired woman was a terrifying pit of blackness and death. What I saw in the dark-haired woman chilled me, and I sped upwards as fast as I could.

From the vault I inspected my own discarded body; pale little face lost in the dark hollow of my bonnet, lips white, eyelids closed and blue as bruises. I was inclined to feel contempt at myself; such a thin little slip of a thing. Better to watch Mr Chester with his stern, handsome face, or William, his fair hair hanging over his eyes.

'Marta!'

The voice rang out across the chapel; I looked curiously, but the rest of the congregation failed to react.

'Marta!' The call was peremptory this time, but the minister did not halt once in his delivery. Only *I* heard. Looking down, I could see nothing but bowed heads and crossed hands.

At the very back of the chapel stood a woman, her face tilted upwards at an attentive angle. I had time to glimpse a face, a wealth of brassy curls beneath a frivolous gold hat, then I heard someone call my name.

'Effie!' William had turned towards my lifeless body and, perceiving me to be in a deep faint, was engaged in untying my bonnet-strings. Disembodied, I watched him with some amusement as he fumbled for smelling-salts in my purse. Dear William! So clumsy and sincere. So unlike his brother.

Henry stood up too, causing a ripple of interest to run down the line of people sitting in the pew, his mouth set in a harsh line. He said nothing, but lifted me into a standing position and, followed by William, began to propel me down the aisle. A few people stared after the group, but others simply smiled indulgently at each other and returned their attention to the sermon. In Mrs Chester's condition, after all, fainting was hardly abnormal.

The higher we jump . . .

I suddenly felt unaccountably dizzy; meeting the eyes of poor arrow-shot St Sebastian again I became aware of a sick, spinning sensation in the pit of my stomach, something like falling. Around and around and around . . .

I realized what was happening and fought it vainly.

'I don't want to go back!' my mind protested. 'Don't want to . . .'

In the instant I fell I dimly remembered meeting the eyes of the woman in the gold hat. I saw her lips moving, mouthing the unfamiliar name '*Marta*' . . . Then there was blackness.

Henry's face glowered over me as his hands moved to loosen the fastenings of my bodice and, as I drifted between dream and consciousness, I had time to appreciate the purity of the clear planes of his face, the straight brows and appraising eyes, his hair rather darker than that of his brother and cropped severely short. William was hovering uncertainly in the background. As he saw my eyes open he jumped forwards with the smelling-salts.

'Effie? Are you—'

Henry turned on him in a cold fury. 'Don't stand there like a fool!' he snapped. 'Go and call a hack. Hurry up!' William went, with a last glance over his shoulder at me. 'That boy thinks far too much of you,' added Henry. 'And he shows it ...' He broke off. 'Can you stand now?'

I nodded.

'Is it the child?'

'I don't think so.' It did not occur to me to tell him about my strangeness in the church; I knew from experience how much my 'fanciful notions' annoyed him.

I tried to climb into the carriage; for an instant nausea overwhelmed me again and I almost fell. Henry put his arm around me, hoisting me easily in and up; but glancing sideways at his tense profile I guessed his disgust, his fear. In that instant I half realized that he was *afraid* of me, sensed the depth of his turmoil, but the intuition faded almost before I could comprehend it as I felt myself swoon again.

3

She lost our child, of course. Nursed by laudanum, she was sleeping when it was taken away by the midwife and sewn into the sheet. I never asked to see my son. I waited to learn that my wife would make a complete recovery before leaving for my studio to paint. Our house was in Highgate and I had deliberately chosen to rent a studio some miles away. It gave me the feeling of isolation I needed when I was working and the light was very clean and cold, monastery light, so that my paintings, sparsely hung against the bare white walls, shone like trapped butterflies beneath the glass. Here I was High Priest, with Effie as my handmaiden, her sweet face glancing out from bright canvasses and pale pastels and thick folders of brown vellum; my soul's Effie, untouched by the curse of our heat and our flesh. That night—not for the first time—I slept in the studio on the little bed she had used for *My Sister's Sleep* and *Sleeping Beauty* and, with the crisp linen sheets cool against my fevered skin, I was able at last to feel content.

I returned at ten o'clock the next morning, learning from the servants that the doctor had left in the early hours. Tabby Gaunt, our housekeeper, had kept watch over Effie for most of the night, dosing her with laudanum and warm water. She looked up as I came into the sickroom, laying down the shirt she had been hemming. She looked tired and red-eyed, but her smile was open as a child's as she rose hastily to her feet, straightening her cap over her unruly grey hair.

'Young lady's sleeping now, Mr Chester, sir,' she whispered. 'The doctor says she's a little weak, but it isn't the fever, thank the Lord. A few days in bed, he said.'

I nodded. 'Thank you, Tabby. You may bring some chocolate for Mrs Chester.'

I turned towards the bed in which Effie lay. Her pale hair was unbound, spilling over the coverlet and the pillows, and her hand was at her cheek as she slept, like that of a little girl. I found it difficult to believe that she was eighteen and had just been delivered of her first baby. In spite of myself, I shuddered at the thought. Remembering the look of her, the feel of her pregnant flesh under her clothes as I touched her made me feel unclean, uneasy. Better by far to see her like this, in bed, one thin arm flung over her eyes, the tiny curve of her breasts (the word troubled me even in thought, and I dismissed it angrily) almost invisible in the rapid rise and fall of her nightdress.

Sudden tenderness overwhelmed me and I reached to touch her hair, chastely.

'Effie?'

She made a little sound as she began to struggle towards wakefulness. Her scent reached me, a poignant scent of talcum and fever and chocolate, like her childhood. Her eyes opened, focused sharply on mine, and she sat up abruptly, guiltily, like a schoolboy caught daydreaming in class.

'I . . . Mr Chester!'

I smiled. 'It's all right, my dear. Don't move. You're still weak. Tabby will bring you a warm drink presently.'

Effie's eyes filled with tears. 'I'm sorry,' she faltered. 'About fainting . . . in church, you know.'

'It's all right. Just sit back and be quiet. Here, I'll sit beside you and hold you. Isn't that better?' I moved on to the bed, pushing a pillow into the small of Effie's back. As I slipped my arm around her shoulders, I saw her face relax into a little dreamy smile. Still half-asleep, she murmured:

'That's nice, that's very nice. Just like before . . . like before we were married.' I stiffened involuntarily and, as the implication of what she had said penetrated her feverish thoughts, she jerked in panic.

'The baby! Is the baby all right?'

In spite of myself I pulled away: I could not bear to think of it.

'Please, Henry, tell me! *Please*, Henry!'

'Don't call me that!' I snapped, leaping to my feet, then, with an effort at self-control, I forced my voice back into gentleness. 'Try to understand, Effie. The child was sick. It couldn't have lived. It was too small.'

Effie's voice rose uncontrollably, a high, wordless wailing. I took her hands, half pleading, half scolding.

'You were too young to have a child! It was all wrong. It was a mistake. It was—'

'No-oooo!'

'Stop that noise!'

'Noo-oh-ooh-oooh!'

'Stop it!' I shook her by the shoulders, and she raised her hands instinctively to her face, eyes wild and cheeks marbled from crying. For a moment I found her tears deeply erotic, and I turned away, flushing angrily.

'It's for the best, Effie,' I said more gently. 'Now we can go back to what we used to be, my dear. Don't cry, Effie. It's just that you're too delicate to bear a child, that's all. You're too young.

Here.' Reaching for the laudanum bottle and the glass, I poured six careful drops into the water. 'Drink this to calm your nerves.'

Patiently, I held the glass as Effie drank, clinging to my arm and gulping tears and medicine in equal quantities. Little by little I felt her body relax against mine until she was quite subdued.

'That's my good girl. Isn't that better?'

Effie nodded sleepily and turned her head towards the crook of my arm. As she drifted once more in my arms I was momentarily aware of a sudden scent of jasmine—real or imagined? The impression was too fleeting to tell.

The Nine
of Swords

4

I was ill for several weeks; the wintry weather hindered my convalescence, for I caught a chill which confined me to my bed for some time after the premature birth of my child. I remember faces coming and going over me, with fixed grimaces of sympathy, but my heart was frozen inside me and, although I wanted to thank them for their concern, I could find no meaning in words. Tabby, who had been with me in Cranbourn Alley since I was a little girl, nursed me and shook her head over me and fed me thin broth as I lay in bed; my little maid, Em, brushed my hair and dressed me in pretty lace nightdresses and gossiped about her family and sisters in distant Yorkshire; Edwin the gardener sometimes sent a handful of early crocuses or daffodils from his precious beds with a gruff assurance that 'they'd bring a bit of colour to the young lady's cheeks'. But, in spite of their kindness, I could not bring myself to stir from my lethargy. I would sit by the fire with a thick shawl around my shoulders, sometimes working at my needlepoint, but more often simply staring into the fire.

William, who might have roused me, had returned to Oxford where a junior fellowship awaited him, torn between pleasure at this acknowledgement of his years of study, and unease at leaving me in so low a state.

Henry was all solicitude: for nearly a month I was permitted no visitors—no-one was to be allowed to distress me, he said—and he did not go to his studio once. Instead, he worked at home, making dozens of sketches of me, but I, who had once been enchanted by his work, cared nothing for it now. Once, I had loved the way he drew me, always emphasizing my eyes and the purity of my features, but now his art left me indifferent and I wondered that I had ever thought him talented.

The pictures sickened me, spread out like trophies over every available surface of wall in every room; and worst of all, in the bedroom, *The Little Beggar Girl*, painted when I was only thirteen, haunted me like the ghost of myself. A London slum, reproduced in minutest detail, from the sweat on the pavements to the 'blacks' drifting down from the muddy sky. A scrawny cat sits sniffing a dead bird in a gutter. Next to it sits a dying child, barefoot and clad only in a shift, her long hair touching the stones around her. Her broken begging-bowl lies on the street, and a stray shaft of light plays on her uplifted face. The frame, designed by the artist, bears a stanza from his poem of the same title:

Thou Innocent, untouch'd by worldly care,
Defil'd not by the fleshly taint of Love,
Surrender now these mortal limbs so fair
Yet feeble; clad in radiance soar above.
Among the lowliest of all wert thou
And yet, to thee the hosts of Heaven bow
Their humble heads; as by th'Almighty's side,
Enthron'd in ecstasy, thou art His bride.

Once I had been filled with admiration for the Mr Chester who could write real verses with so little effort. I had borne no criticism of him, had wept with frustration at the unkind words of Mr Ruskin on the occasion of his first exhibition. I could still vaguely remember the time when I had worshipped him, treasured every word he wrote to me, every sketch he discarded. I remembered my awed gratitude when he had offered to pay for my tutors, the leap of joy in my heart as I overheard my mother and Henry as they spoke together in the library. Aunt May had mistrusted the idea of my marriage to a man so much older than I. But my mother had been blinded by the thought of all the opportunities Mr Chester could give her daughter—and I, I was blinded by Mr Chester himself. At seventeen I had married him.

Married him!

I dug furiously at my needlepoint, tent-stitch *one*, cross-stitch *two*, suddenly bloated with hate and fury. The embroidery was half finished, the design an invention of Henry's in rich, glowing colours: the Sleeping Beauty on her couch, all twined round with climbing roses. Even in its unfinished state, the face of the sleeping girl looked like mine.

Cross-stitch *one*, tent-stitch *two* . . . I stabbed at the needlework, making no effort to stitch now, simply digging at the fabric in mounting rage, tearing at the delicate stitchery, the gold thread. All unaware, I was crying aloud, without tears, a hoarse, primitive sound which, at any other time, would have terrified me.

'Why, Miss Effie!' It was Tabby's voice, shocked into improper address.

Jolted out of my furious trance, I started and looked up. Tabby's plump, good-natured face was twisted with distress.

'Oh, what have you done? Your poor hands . . . and all your pretty 'broidery, too. Oh, ma'am!'

I looked down in surprise and saw my hands bleeding from a dozen stab wounds. A bloody handprint branded the needlework, obliterating half of the sleeping girl's face. I surrendered the spoiled tapestry and tried to smile.

'Oh dear,' I said mildly, 'how clumsy of me.' Then, as Tabby began to say something, tears springing to her eyes, 'No, Tabby, I am quite well, thank you. I will go to wash my hands.'

'But ma'am, you'll take a drop of laudanum, surely! The doctor—'

'Tabby, if you would be so kind as to put away my sewing-things? I will not be needing them again today.'

'Yes ma'am,' said Tabby woodenly, but she did not move to obey the order until she had watched me stumble vaguely out of the room, fumbling at the doorknob with my bloody hands like a murdering sleepwalker.

I was poorly for almost two months before the doctor at last pronounced me fit enough to receive visitors. Not that I saw many people; Mother came once to talk about her toilettes and to reassure me that I still had plenty of time to start a family, and Aunt May came twice to sit quietly with me, discussing commonplaces with a gentleness very far from her usual style. Dear Aunt May! If only she had known how much I longed to talk to her, but I knew that once I opened the floodgates I would have to tell her everything—things I was not even prepared to admit to myself— so I remained silent, pretending that I was happy and that this cold, meticulous house was home. Not that Aunt May was deceived for a moment, but for my sake she tried to hide her dislike for Henry, conversing in stiff, brittle phrases, her back very straight against the chair.

Henry liked her as little as she did him, sourly commenting

that her visits always seemed to leave me looking exhausted. She made a tart rejoinder to *that* comment. Triumphantly, Henry suggested that she should perhaps refrain from frequenting the house until she learned a more genteel conversational style; he would not have his wife subjected to this kind of talk. Aunt May was drawn into unguarded utterances and left beneath a cloud of recriminations. From my window I watched her leave, very small and grey beneath the cold sky, and I knew that Henry had his wish. I was his alone, for ever.

It was March, and, although the weather was still very chill, the sun was shining and there was a hint of approaching spring in the air. The parlour enjoys a fine view of the garden with its pond and meticulous flowerbeds, and that morning I was sitting for Henry in front of the wide bay window. I was still very wan, but with the bright sunlight warming my cheeks and my loose hair, I was conscious of a feeling of satisfaction and well-being.

I wished I were in the garden now, with the cool air against my skin and the damp of the grass against my ankles. I wanted to smell the earth, to lie down and bite it, to roll in the greenery like a cat at play . . .

'Effie, do keep still!' Henry's voice jerked me back to reality. 'Three-quarter profile, please, and don't let the dulcimer slip. I paid enough for it, you know. That's better. Remember, if at all possible, I want the picture ready for the exhibition, and there isn't much time.'

I corrected my position, shifting the instrument in my lap. Henry's latest idea, *A Damsel with a Dulcimer,* was already four weeks under way and was to feature myself as the mysterious lady in Coleridge's poem. Henry envisaged her as 'An adolescent girl, all dressed in white, sitting upon a rustic bench with one foot curled up under her body, charmingly intent upon her musical study. Behind her lies an arboreal landscape, with, in the distance, the mythical mountain.'

I, who knew the poem by heart, and had often dreamed about it myself, had ventured to say that I felt 'an Abyssinian maid' should be someone rather more colourful and exotic than the insipid damsel I was to portray, but Mr Chester's reply had left me in no doubt as to his own poor opinion of my taste, graphic, literary or otherwise. My own efforts at painting and poetry were proof enough of that. And yet, I remembered certain moments, before Henry had forbidden me to waste my time in areas in which I had no talent; I remembered looking into a canvas like an angry vortex of stars and feeling joy—joy and something like the beginnings of passion.

Passion?

The first night of our marriage, when Mr Chester had come to me with guilt and excitement in his eyes, had taught me all I needed to know about passion. My own innocent ardour had cooled his at once; the sight of my body had sent him to his knees, not with joy but with repentance. Thereafter his act of love was an act of contrition for both of us; a cold, comfortless joining, like that of two locomotives. After the baby was conceived, even this ceased.

I never understood it. Father had always told me that there was no harm in the physical act between a man and a woman in love; it was God's reward, he said, for procreation. We are feeling beings, he used to tell me, innocent until evil thoughts take our innocence away. Our original sin was not the search for knowledge, but the shame that Adam and Eve had of their nakedness. It was that shame which sent them from the garden, and keeps us from the garden now.

Poor Father! He could never have understood the icy contempt in Henry's face as he pulled away from my arms.

'Is there no shame in you, woman?' he had demanded.

Shame? I never knew it before I knew Henry.

And yet, there was a fire in me which neither the death of my child nor the coldness of my marriage could entirely quell; and sometimes, through the chill, clinging veils of my life, I felt the stirring of something more, something almost frightening. Watching Henry's face as he sketched me I was seized by a sudden sharp revulsion. I wanted to throw the dulcimer to the ground, to leap up, to dance naked and without shame in the spring sunlight. The desire overwhelmed me, and before I knew it I was on my feet, crying aloud in a harsh and desperate voice ... But Henry never heard me. He continued to frown contentedly over his paper, looking up for a second at an object just behind me, then returning to his sketch. I turned abruptly and saw myself, my position unchanged, holding the dulcimer in my lap.

I was conscious of a feeling of intense relief and elation. I had spoken to no-one of the episode in the church, although I had thought of it often, with a mounting conviction that it must have been the effect of the laudanum and would likely not be repeated. But this time it had been a whole day since I had last taken my drops, I was not ill, and there had been none of the sickening, spiralling sensation of the last occasion. Warily I looked down at myself; my new 'body' was a white, naked replica of the one I had temporarily vacated. A faint, silvery light seemed to emanate from it and I could feel the pile of the carpet beneath my feet and the freshness of the air against my skin. I was vibrant with energy and excitement, all my senses enhanced and given new dimension outside the clutter of my body.

Carefully I approached my physical body, wondering whether, when I touched it, I would be forced back inside; my hand passed through clothes and flesh without resistance. For an instant I was aware of the peculiar sensation of being in neither state, my body like a half-discarded nightdress around my real, living self; then I forced myself back. The world readjusted itself listlessly around me for a moment, then I leaped out again, overwhelmed with elation at the thought that now I could seemingly perform this feat at will. Rapidly gaining in confidence, I moved lightly across the room. Impelled by a new sense of mischief I lighted on the crown of Henry's head and pirouetted, but he was in no way distracted from his sketching. Leaping down, I ran to the window and looked out, halfminded to jump through the glass but wary of leaving my body too far behind. A quick glance behind me told me that all was well and, throwing caution aside with the rest of my earthly burdens, I passed through the glass and into the garden.

So may the caterpillar dream of flight, or the chrysalis dream in her dark silken cradle.

And I? Into what frail murderous being will my chrysalis hatch?

Will I fly?

Or sting?

5

She's lying, you know. I was never unkind to her, never. I loved her more than any woman has the right to be loved: I worshipped her, gave my soul for her. I gave her everything she wanted: the white wedding, my fine house, my art, my poetry. The day she married me I was the happiest man alive.

She was the one who spoiled it, like Eve before her in Eden. The seed was in her, in spite of my careful nurturing. I might have known.

What has she told you? That I rejected her? That I was cold? I remember her waiting for me in our room after the wedding celebrations were over: all in white, with her hair loose and spread over the pillows and the bedstead, brushing the floor. For a moment I thought she was asleep. I crept to the bed, afraid to wake her, a terrible tenderness spilling over into every part of my body. Above all else I wanted to lie down next to her, to breathe her scent, the lilac of her hair. At that moment I was blessed: there was no lust in me but for sleep, for the sweetness and innocence of her, and it was with tears in my eyes that I laid my face on the pillow beside hers.

For a second, there was a quiescence, then her eyes opened. I saw my face as in a witch's crystal, a tiny pinprick against the fascia of her pupils. Her cold, pale hands crept around my neck. I felt my own responding in spite of myself. I had never so much as kissed her before and, as her lips met mine, I was submerged in her, my hands full of her hair and the softness of her breasts . . .

I should have died then: no man was made to endure the bliss and the torment of her as I was. I could feel her heat through the thin fabric of her nightdress; the awakened response in myself—and suddenly I was transported back to that day in my mother's room, the scent of jasmine in my nostrils, felt again the hot, sulphurous excitement which had possessed me, which possesses me still. I could not move. I did not trust myself even to turn away. Maybe I cried aloud in despair and self-loathing. Effie clung to me like a Fury: when I tried to shake her from me she twisted on top of me and pinned me to the pillow, her long legs entwined around me, her mouth pressed against mine.

I tasted salt on her lips and I was drowning in her, with her hair in my mouth and in my eyes and all around me like the web of some fiendish spider-goddess. She had shed her nightdress as a snake sheds its skin, and was straddling me like a terrible centaur-woman, head thrown back in defiance of all decency and modesty. For a moment I could not help but respond: there was no thought in me but lust.

When I could think again I was pinned to the mattress in horror: where was my beggar girl, my sleeping beauty, my pale sister? Where was the child I had nurtured? She was all adult now in the dark heat of her desire. As she closed her eyes I managed to escape her mesmerism and I pushed her away with as much violence as my weak limbs could muster. Her eyes snapped open and it was all I could do to prevent myself being lost in their depths again, but I held on to the last of my sanity and turned my face away.

There was no shame in her. The last hope of salvation had

been denied me in this girl, and the realization was bitter in me. Her kiss still salted my mouth, the memory of her touch beguiling against my skin, and I cursed my weak, sinful flesh. I cursed her too, this Eve of my downfall: cursed her white skin and her cavernous eyes and her hair which had made me mad with longing for her. With tears streaming down my face, I went down on my knees and prayed for forgiveness. But God was not there for me and, in the darkness, the demons of my lust pranced all around. Effie did not understand why I had withdrawn from her, and for a time she tried to drag me from my penance with tears and caresses.

'What's wrong?' she asked softly, and if I had not known that she, too, was tainted to the core by the same demon which possessed me, I could have sworn she was pure. Her voice was unsteady, like that of a little girl, and her hands around my neck were as soft and loving as they had been when she was ten years old.

I dared not answer, but pushed her away, my hands clenched furiously.

'Please . . . Henry . . .' It was the first time she had called me by my first name, and the intimacy that it implied froze me with remorse.

'Don't call me that!'

She was confused, and her hand crept into mine, whether to comfort herself or me I was unsure.

'But—'

'Be quiet! Haven't you done enough harm already?'

Perhaps she really didn't know what irreparable damage she had already caused: I sensed her confusion and, in her troubled, tainted innocence, I hated her. She began to cry, and I hated her even more. Better that she should be dead than this carnal wrestling in the hot night! Better that she should be dead, I repeated fiercely. Her shamelessness had killed my little girl on the very night she was to have been mine. She had damned us both, and now she would be with me for the rest of her life, a living reminder of the death of all my illusions.

'I don't understand. What have I done wrong?' Effie's voice was so sincere, so vulnerable in the dark.

I laughed bitterly.

'I thought you were so pure. I thought that even though all other women—even my own mother—might be whores, you at least had been spared the taint.'

'I don't—'

'*Listen!*' I snapped furiously. 'I watched you grow. I kept you from the other children. I protected you. Where did you learn it? Who taught you? When I was painting you as Mary and Juliet and the Convent Flower, were you already twisting on your bed at night, dreaming of your lover? Did you look into your glass on May Eve and see him there, watching you?' I took her by the shoulders and shook her. 'Tell me!'

She pulled away from my grasp, trembling. Even then the sight of her body aroused me, and I threw a blanket at her.

'Cover yourself, for God's sake!' I shouted, biting down on my lips to stop the hysteria.

She drew the blanket tightly around her shoulders, her eyes huge and unreadable. 'I don't understand,' she said at last. 'I thought you loved me. Why are you afraid to make me your wife?'

'I'm not afraid!' I snapped angrily. 'We could share so many things together. Why demean it, for the sake of this one act? My love for you is pure, pure as the love of a child for his mother. *You* make it something shameful.'

'But something which gives pleasure—' began Effie.

'No!' I interrupted. 'Not the true unsullied joy of a pure marriage. That can only exist in God. The flesh is the Devil's domain, and all *his* pleasures are filth and corruption. Trust me, Effie. We are above this. I want to keep you innocent. I want to keep you beautiful.'

But she had turned her face to the wall, the blanket tight around her.

The Knave
of Coins

6

Knave of Hearts, dear fellow, of *Hearts.* Kindly give me my proper title. Even a knave has his pride, you know. And I have so many hearts! I gave one to the mistress and one to the dame, and one to the beggar girl who cries in the lane—only to stop her crying, mark you. But what did they give me in return? A few sighs, a quick tumble, and enough tears to fill my bathtub. Women! They've been the death of me and still I can't do without them; in hell I'll swear I'll ogle the little *diablesses*—I like 'em hot.

What's that?

Ah, the story, the story. I see you find me distasteful. Well, you've given me the limelight for a time, and I'm not about to give it back yet. So smoke your pipe, old man, and move over. Let me introduce myself.

Moses Zachary Harper, poet, sometime painter, sinner, philanderer, hedonist, Knave of Hearts and Ace of Rods, erstwhile lover and loser of Mrs Euphemia Chester.

What of the good Henry?

Let's say there was a contretemps; maybe a woman (who knows?) . . . maybe a true word spoken in jest at the expense of the pious Mr Chester. Suffice it to say there was a coldness, but a professional coldness. Mr Ruskin had taken a fancy to my *Sodom and Gomorrah* and had written favourably of me. There was a canvas! Three hundred bodies in rapturous, tortuous embrace! And every inch of female flesh conquered territory! The parsonic Mr Chester despised me cordially, but envied me my connections. To tell the truth, I had none—on the right side of the bed, that is—but I had managed to eke a few poor favours along the petticoat-line.

Imagine the conversations between us at the tea-tray; poor Henry, Friday-faced as a maiden aunt. 'Won't you have a cup of tea, Mr Harper? I hear your exhibition met with some success...' Yours truly *négligé* to a point with no hat, and shirt undone, uttering calculated insults ('I think I see the influence of Sir Joshua Reynolds in that last canvas, dear fellow...'). I confess, I was a thorn in his flesh. Poor Henry was never made to be an artist; he had none of the artistic temperament, exhibiting instead a distressing inclination for clean living, churchgoing and the like, which never failed to set my teeth on edge.

Imagine my surprise when, on returning from a long trip abroad, I heard he was married! My first reaction was hilarity, then disbelief. Oh, he's good-looking in his way, but any woman with an ounce of sense can see he's no more passion in him than a piece of ham. Which just goes to prove that most women don't have an ounce of sense.

My second reaction was an intense curiosity. I wanted to see the specimen of misguided womanhood the man had snared. A plain girl, I imagined, no doubt a pillar of the local church, proficient in watercolours. I asked around the artistic circles and learned that Henry had been married for just under a year; that his wife was of frail constitution, and had given birth to a dead child in January. Opinion had it that she was rather lovely, in an unusual style. As it happened Henry, I was told, had planned an exhibition to coincide with the anniversary of their marriage, and, knowing that this was probably the only way I could get myself received by the old bluestocking, I determined to see it.

He had decided to hold the event at his house in Cromwell Square, Highgate—a mistake, I thought. He should have hired a small gallery; somewhere like Chatham Place, perhaps. But he would never have had the cheek to place himself beneath the very noses of his Pre-Raphaelite idols. Besides, from the start he had pretensions to exhibit at the Academy, and I knew him too well to expect him to compromise for anything less. An announcement duly arrived in *The Times*, followed up by a number of coy invitations to various influential critics and artists (myself not included, naturally).

I arrived at about twelve, having had lunch at a chop-house nearby, and as I approached the house I saw a small cluster of people lingering at the gate as if unsure of their welcome. I recognized Holy Hunt and Morris, scowling fiercely at some remark of Hunt's—the woman with him was *Mrs* Morris: I'd have recognized her from Rossetti's paintings any day, but personally I found her rather too much on the grand scale for my taste. Henry would be pleased, though, as long as he didn't have to talk to them: he couldn't abide anyone eccentric or abrupt—and from what I had heard of Morris, he wasn't the type to suffer a pompous ass like Henry very kindly.

There were a couple of my friends arriving in the wake of the little party, and I joined them, wondering all the while why they should have bothered to come in the first place. He was a young wretch of a poet called Finglass, she his Muse, Jenny; I grinned to hear him introduce her to the tight-lipped old biddy of a housekeeper as 'Mrs Finglass'—the housekeeper managed to look sceptical and polite at the same time—and we went in together.

As I entered the house it occurred to me how typical of Henry

Chester it was to set up an exhibition *à domicile* just after his wife, by all reports, had been so ill. I am certain that he would have been most affronted if anyone had pointed it out. I knew what Henry was like: all his ex-models agreed, although he paid quite well, he was a 'regular Tartar' when he was painting, he fell into the most violent rages if a girl as much as shifted her posture, he forgot to allow his models to take a rest, and, on top of that, moralized most harshly to the unfortunate creatures—most of whom were on the street through no real fault of their own, and had turned to modelling as a rather better-paid and more respectable form of prostitution.

There were maybe a dozen people in all; some peering at the framed canvasses in the passageway, but most of them in the parlour, where the bulk of the work was exhibited, with Henry in their midst talking volubly to a rapt little circle of nonentities over glasses of sherry and ratafia. He glanced at me as I came in and acknowledged me with a curt little nod. I smiled winningly, helped myself to a glass of sherry and idled over to the paintings, which were every bit as bad as I expected them to be.

The man had no fire: his paintings were wan, limp and horribly whimsical, with the sentimentality of his commonplace soul as evident as his lack of passion. Oh, he could paint, I suppose, and the model I acknowledged to be interesting enough, but sadly lacking in colour. She was obviously his favourite, because her face stared out at me from almost all the frames. She was an odd little thing, far removed from modern standards of beauty, but with a certain mediaeval look in her childish figure and loose, pale hair. A favourite niece, perhaps? I scanned the titles inscribed on the frames: *Juliet in the Tomb*, *Nausicaa*, *The Little Beggar Girl*, *The Cold Wedding* . . . No wonder the girl looked so mournful: every canvas showed her in some macabre, gloomy role . . . dying, dead, sick, blind, abandoned . . . thin and piteous as a dead child, swathed in her winding-sheet as Juliet, in rags as the beggar girl, lost and frightened-looking in rich silks and velvet as *Persephone*.

I was roused from my critical reverie by the door opening, and was astonished to see the girl herself come into the room. I recognized her features, but Henry hadn't done her justice by a long way. She was a delightful wraith of a thing, like a silver birch, with the sweetest slim waist, long delicate hands with pointed fingernails and a mouth that only needed a kiss to make it burst into bloom. She was demurely dressed in grey flannel and looked barely out of her teens. I supposed that she was the niece, or even some professional model he had picked up. The thought of Mrs Chester was far from my mind at that moment and it was in all innocence that I greeted the Stunner:

'My name's Mose Harper. How do you do?'

She blushed and murmured something, looking around with those big, hunted eyes as if afraid to be seen with me. Maybe Henry had warned her about me. I smiled.

'Henry should never have tried to paint you,' I said. 'I find it's always a mistake to try to improve on Nature. May I ask your name?'

Another sideways glance at Henry, still absorbed in conversation.

'Effie Chester. I'm . . .' The nervous glance again.

'A relation of friend Henry? How interesting. Not the sober side of the family, I hope?'

Again the glance. The Stunner resolutely put down her head and mumbled, not at all coyly. I realized that I had really embarrassed her and, detecting a soupçon of the bluestocking, changed my tack.

'I'm a great admirer of Henry's work,' I lied valiantly. 'You might say I was a colleague . . . a *disciple* of his.'

The violet eyes flickered for an instant, with amusement or scorn. 'Is that true?'

Confound the minx, she was laughing at me! The light in those eyes was definitely laughter, and suddenly her face was illuminated, irrepressibly. I grinned.

'No, it isn't true. Are you disappointed?'

She shook her head.

'It's his style I dislike. I have no fault to find with the raw material. Poor Henry is a painter, not an artist. Give him a nice, ripe apple and he'll put it against a silk screen and try to paint it. A pointless waste. Neither the apple nor the public appreciates the gesture.'

She was puzzled, but intrigued; and she had stopped looking at Henry every time she spoke.

'Well? What would *you* do?' she ventured.

'Me? I think that to paint from life you have to *know* life. Apples are for eating, not for painting.' I winked slyly and grinned at her. 'And lovely young girls are like apples.'

'Oh!' She clapped her hands to her mouth and her eyes left mine and flew to Chester who had just discovered Holman Hunt among his guests and was engaged in earnest, pedantic conversation. She turned away, almost panic-stricken. No, she was not a flirt: far from it. I took her arm, gently turning her back towards me.

'I'm sorry. I was only funning. I shan't tease you again.' She looked into my face to see if I was telling the truth. 'I'd say "on my honour", but I don't have any,' I said. 'Henry should have warned you against me. Did he?'

She shook her head dumbly, entirely withdrawn.

'No, I don't suppose he did. Tell me, how do you like modelling? Does Henry share you with any of his friends, I wonder? No? Wise Henry. Oh, what's the matter *now*?' She had turned away again, and I read a deep, sincere distress in her face.

Her hands clenched the soft fabric of her gown, and her voice was low and violent. 'Please, Mr Harper . . .'

'What is it?' I was caught between irritation and concern.

'Please don't talk about modelling! Don't talk about the wretched paintings. *Everyone* asks about the paintings. I hate them!'

This was getting interesting. I lowered my voice, conspiratorially. 'Actually, so do I.'

She gave an involuntary chuckle, and the stricken look went out of her eyes. 'I hate having to play the same part every day,' she went on, almost dreamily. 'Always to be good, and quiet, to do my embroidery and sit in attractive poses, when inside I want to . . .' She broke off again, perhaps realizing that she was about to pass the bounds of propriety.

'But he must pay you quite well,' I suggested.

'Money!' Her scorn was evident, and I dismissed any notion of her being a professional.

'I wish I had your healthy disregard for it,' I said lightly. 'Or, at least, that my creditors did.'

She chuckled again.

'Yes, but you're a *man*,' she said, sobering abruptly. 'You can do what you like. You don't . . .' Her voice trailed off miserably.

'And what would *you* like?' I asked.

For a second she looked at me, and I almost saw something in her expression . . . like the promise of a bleak passion. Then, nothing. The wan look returned to her face.

'Nothing.'

I was about to speak, when I became aware of a presence at my elbow. Turning, I found that Henry, with impeccable timing, had finally left Hunt to mingle with his other guests. The girl at my side stiffened, her face rigid, and I wondered what hold Henry had over her to make her so much in awe of him. And it wasn't just awe: there was something like horror in her eyes.

'Good day, Mr Harper,' said Henry with his punctilious courtesy. 'I see that you have been looking at my canvasses.'

'Certainly,' I replied. 'And fine though they are I could not help but notice that they fail to entirely capture the charm of the model.'

It was the wrong thing to say. Henry's mellow gaze narrowed to an icy pinprick. It was in colder accents that he introduced me to her at last.

'Mr Harper, this is my wife, Mrs Chester.'

I possess, you may have noticed, some degree of charisma: I exerted all of it to negate my earlier *faux pas* and create a good impression. After a few minutes of shameless flattery Henry thawed again; I caught the birch-girl looking at me a few times, and there and then I swore I'd give her my heart. For a while, anyway.

The first thing I needed was access to the beauty. It takes patience and strategy, believe me, to seduce a married woman, as well as a solid footing in the enemy camp, and for a while I was at a loss as to how I could insinuate my lecherous self into her life and her affections. Patience, Mose, I thought. There was a world of small-talk to be done before that!

During the course of the conversation I made every effort to seduce, not the wife, but the husband. I spoke of my admiration of Holman Hunt, whom I knew Henry admired; deplored the newly decadent tendencies of Rossetti; spoke of my experiences abroad, expressed an interest in Henry's newest canvas (a vile idea to cap all of his previous vile ideas), then finally voiced the desire to be painted by him.

'A portrait?' Henry was all attention.

'Yes . . .' hesitantly and with the right degree of modest reserve, 'or a period piece, Biblical, mediaeval . . . I haven't really thought much about it, yet. However, I have been an admirer of your style for some time, you know, and after this very fine exhibition . . . I was mentioning it to Swinburne the other day—he was the one who suggested the portrait idea, in fact.'

Easy to say: I knew that a Puritan like Henry would hardly be likely to exchange words with a man like Swinburne to verify the fact, and he knew as well as I did the relationship between Swinburne and the Rossettis. Conceit puffed him up like a tea-cake. He scanned my face carefully.

'Fine features, if I may say so,' he said ponderously. 'I should not be ashamed to transfer them to canvas. Full-front, would you say? Or three-quarter profile?'

I began to grin, and quickly transformed the vulgar leer into a smile.

'I'm in your hands,' I said.

7

As the door opened and I saw him for the first time, I was certain that he had seen me. Not this body, but the essential *me*, in my most naked, helpless form. The thought was terrifying and, at the same time, powerfully exciting. For an instant I wanted to strut and dance before this stranger in a display of shamelessness which transcended the pale envelope of flesh I could discard at will, as my husband stood by unseeing.

I cannot explain the strange wantonness which possessed me. Perhaps it was the heightened perception lent to me by my recent illness, perhaps the laudanum I had taken earlier for my headache, but the first time I saw Moses Harper, I knew that this was a truly *physical* being, governed by his own desires and pleasures. Watching him and speaking to him under the heedless eye of my husband I understood that he was everything I was not; he radiated energy, arrogance, independence and self-satisfaction like the sun. Best of all, there was no shame in him, no shame at all, and his lack of shame drew me irresistibly. As he touched my arm, his voice low and caressing, charged with the promise of sensuality, I felt my cheeks flush, but not with shame.

I watched him covertly throughout his conversation with Henry.

I cannot recall a word he spoke, but the tone of his voice made me shiver with pleasure. He was maybe ten years younger than Henry, with an angular figure, sharp features and a satirical expression. He wore his hair long and tied in the nape of the neck in an eccentric, old-fashioned style. His dress, too, was deliberately informal, even for a morning visit, and he was hatless. I liked his eyes, which were blue and rather narrow, as if he were laughing all the time, and his easy, mocking smile. I am certain he noticed me watching him, but he only smiled and continued his conversation.

I was astonished that he should have commissioned a painting from my husband; from the little I had previously heard of him, Mose Harper was an impudent good-for-nothing, fit only for painting filth, with no sense and less taste. Now, Henry was telling me, in an indulgent voice, that Mose was 'a young rogue' whose travels around the world had 'much improved him,' and he would no doubt one day make a 'fine painter,' as he showed 'excellent draughtsmanship and a certain originality of style.'

For some time Henry propounded his ideas on the portrait, suggesting, then rejecting, various subjects such as *Young Solomon* and *The Jacobite*. Mose had written a list of his own ideas, including *Prometheus, Adam in the Garden* (rejected by Henry because of what he called 'the degree of modesty which must be accorded to such a subject') and *The Card Players*.

This last title intrigued Henry, and he met Mose later at his studio to discuss it. Mose told him that the idea had come to him while reading a poem by the French poet Baudelaire (I have never read any of his work, but I am told he is very shocking, and it does not strike me at all odd that he should be a favourite of Mose's), in which:

Le beau valet de coeur et la dame de pique
Causent sinistrement de leurs amours défunts.

Mose thought the phrase most evocative, and visualized a canvas 'set in a greasy Parisian café, with sawdust on the floor and bottles of absinthe on the table. Sitting at the table is a young man holding the Knave of Hearts; next to him a beautiful lady has played the Queen of Spades.'

Henry was not immediately enthusiastic about this subject, which he found rather sordid. He himself had a notion to paint Mose in mediaeval dress, perhaps as *The Minstrel's Lament*, 'sitting beneath a rustic sundial and holding a viol, whilst behind him the sun sets and a procession of veiled ladies, carrying various musical instruments, passes by on horseback.'

Mose was politely unenthusiastic on the subject. He did not see himself as a mediaeval minstrel. Besides, there was the background to be thought of. To paint the mediaeval landscape with the ladies on horseback might take months. Surely it would be simpler to choose the dark interior and concentrate upon the portrait itself?

There was some sense in that argument, and Henry's reluctance lessened. There would be no harm in the subject, he decided, as long as it was tastefully executed. He did draw the line at having the French poem engraved on the picture-frame, but Mose assured him that that would not be necessary. Henry began to make plans for the new canvas, abandoning *A Damsel with a Dulcimer* for the time being, to my immense relief.

What price Mose had promised Henry for the picture I do not know, but my husband was filled with hopes for it; Mose, with his connections, would no doubt have it hung at the Royal Academy and this might well be the making of Henry's career. I paid little attention. Henry and I were not dependent upon Henry's paintings for income. Any money he made was for him a matter of personal satisfaction, a proof of his talent. For myself, the only interest I had in his new painting was that the long and frequent sittings meant that I would have the opportunity to see Mose nearly every day.

8

I never liked Moses Harper. A thoroughly dangerous and calculating individual, rumour had it that he had been involved in countless shady enterprises from forgery to blackmail, although none of the rumours—which inexplicably led to even greater success with the ladies—were ever proved.

For myself, I found him a very inferior type, with no morals and fewer manners, except when he chose to exert himself to please. He was an artist of sorts, though the work I had seen, both painting and poetry alike, seemed calculated only to shock. His work was neither harmonious nor true to life; he delighted in the grotesque, the absurd and the vulgar.

Despite my dislike for low company, I realized that the connections he had acquired might be of use to me: besides, my idea for his portrait was an excellent one, and might even attract the attention of the Academy. I had already submitted my *Little Beggar Girl* along with the *Sleeping Beauty*: the critical response was encouraging, although *The Times* condemned my choice of model as being 'insipid' and suggested that I expand my choice of subject-matter. For this reason I abandoned my current project and began on the sketches immediately although I disliked having to deal so closely with Harper—his reputation was such that I did not want Effie to come into contact with him: not that she would have encouraged the fellow, you understand, but I hated to think of his eyes on her, demeaning her, lusting after her.

However, I had little choice: Effie had been ill again, and I arranged a small studio on the top floor from which I could work. More often than not, Harper would sit in the garden or in the living-room while I sketched him from various angles, and Effie would work at her stitchery or read a book, seemingly quite content with our silent company. She showed no interest in Harper at all, but that afforded me little comfort. In fact, I might have been more patient with her if she had shown a little more animation.

Effie could think of nothing but her books. I had discovered her reading a most unsuitable novel a couple of days previously, a hellish thing by a certain Ellis Bell, called *Wuthering Heights*, or some other such nonsense. The wretched book had already driven her into one of her megrims, and when I took it away—for her own good, the ungrateful creature—she dared to fly into a violent tantrum, crying: How dare I take her books! weeping and behaving like the spoiled child she was. Only a strong dose of laudanum was sufficient to calm her, and for several days afterwards she kept to her bed, too weak and pettish to move. I told her, when she had almost recovered, that I had long suspected that she read too much; it gave her fanciful notions. I did not like the kind of morbidity, bred of idleness, that it encouraged. I told her that there could be no objection to improving, Christian works, but forbade any more novels, or anything but the lightest kind of poetry. She was unstable enough as it was.

Whatever she told you, I was not unkind: I saw her instability and tried to control it, encouraging her to take up activities appropriate to a young woman. Her needlework lay untouched

for weeks and I obliged her to take it up again. Not for myself—
no—but for *her*. I knew she desired to have talent such as I had:
when she was a child she used to try and paint scenes from her
favourite poets, but I always dealt honestly with Effie; I did not
flatter her to gain her affection but told her the sober truth:
women are not, as a rule, made for artistic activities; their talents
are the gentle, domestic ones.

But she was wilful; she persisted in her daubs, saying that she
painted what she saw in dreams. Dreams! I told her she should
dream less and pay more attention to her duties as a wife.

You see, I *did* care for her. I loved her too much to allow her
to delude herself with vanities and conceits. I had kept her pure
for so long, had lived with her imperfection, had forgiven her for
the seed of wickedness she, like all women, carried within her.
And what did she give me in return? Megrims, fancies, foolishness and deception. Do not be deceived by her innocent face as I
was! Like my mother she was diseased, the bud of her unfurling
adolescence blackened from the core. How could I have *known*?
God, in His ferocious jealousy, threw her in my path to test me.
Let a single woman, just one, into the Kingdom of Heaven itself,
and I swear she will throw down the blessed one by one—angels,
archangels and all.

Damn her! She has made me as you see me now, a cripple, a
fallen angel with the seed of the serpent in my frozen entrails.
Slice an apple and you will find the Star, bearing the seeds of
damnation in its core: God knew it even then, He who knows
everything, sees everything. How He must have laughed, as He
drew the rib from Adam's sleeping body! Even now I seem to hear
His laughter . . . and in my darkness spit and curse the light.
Twenty grains of chloral to buy Your silence.

9

For two weeks I was content to watch him and wait. Mose haunted my dreams with visions of delightful abandon; waking, I saw him every day. I existed in a warm and lovely dream-state, like some sleeping princess waiting for her kiss, and I trusted in him implicitly. I had seen him watching; I *knew* he would come for me.

Days passed, and Henry moved back to his studio to work. He already had enough studies of Mose, and was eager to transfer his initial idea on to canvas. He was vaguely considering using me as the model for the Queen of Spades, but Mose, with a hidden wink in my direction, had said abruptly that I was 'not his type'. Henry was not sure whether to be offended or relieved; he settled for a thin-lipped smile and promised to 'think about it'. Mose accompanied him to the studio and for some time I did not see him, though his face never left my thoughts.

My health improved daily and I began to take fewer and fewer of the doses of laudanum Henry brought me. One night he found that I had thrown away my medicine, and was very angry. How could I expect to get better, he demanded, if I wilfully disobeyed him? I must drink my medicine three times a day, like a good girl, or I would become morbid and fanciful again, my nightmares would return and I would be good for nothing but idleness. My health was frail, he said, my mind weakened by illness. I must at least *try* to make an effort not to be a burden to him, especially now that his work was at last being recognized.

Meekly, I acquiesced; I promised to take a daily walk to the church and back and to take my medicine regularly. From then on I made sure that the number of drops in the bottle diminished at a steady pace—and with it I watered the araucaria on the stairs three times a day. Henry never suspected a thing. In fact, he was almost cheerful when he returned from the studio. His painting was progressing very well, if slowly, he told me, with Mose sitting for him maybe three hours a day. Henry worked till the early evening and, as the weather grew fine, I took the habit of going for a long walk to the cemetery in the afternoons. Once or twice Tabby came with me, but she had too many things to do in the house to act as a permanent chaperone to me. Besides, I told her, I was only going as far as the church; I could come to no harm, and I was feeling much better now that the winter was over. Three or four times I took the same walk from Cromwell Square, down Swain's Lane, down the hill, into the cemetery to St Michael's. Since the day I had my vision in that church, the day I lost the baby, I had felt an odd link with St Michael's, a desire to go in there alone and try to recapture the sense of purpose I had felt that day, the sense of revelation. But I had not been back, except on Sundays, with Henry on one side of me. Since William had gone to Oxford I had felt even more closely watched than ever. I dared not allow my mask to slip for an instant.

But now I felt almost as if I were on holiday. I enjoyed my trips out of the house more than I dared admit, and led Henry to believe that I walked only because he had ordered me to do so. If he had known how much those outings meant to me, he would surely have cut them short. So I nursed my secret and my joy, while inside me something wild and frenzied capered and grinned. I tried the church several times, but each time there were too many people for me to dare enter: sightseers, baptisms, weddings . . . and once a funeral, with row upon row of black-clad mourners, intoning the dark hymns to the howling of the organ.

I drew back from the half-open door, embarrassed and somehow afraid as the wave of sound struck me. In my confusion I almost knocked over the vase of white chrysanthemums which was standing by the entrance. One woman turned at the noise and fixed her gaze on me insistently, almost threateningly. I made a helpless little gesture of apology and continued to back away, but suddenly I felt my legs begin to buckle under my weight. I looked up and saw the vault spiralling towards me uncontrollably, the face of St Sebastian suddenly very close to mine; St Sebastian smiling, showing his teeth . . .

Not now! I thought urgently, struggling to regain control. Looking wildly around me I caught sight of the woman, still watching me with that insistent look of recognition. From afar I thought I heard a voice calling a half-familiar name. Unreasoning panic seized me and I turned, abruptly released from my trance, and ran, slamming the heavy door. I stumbled, tried to retain my balance and cannoned headlong into a black-clad figure standing at the bottom of the steps. His arms locked tightly around me. By now I was thoroughly unnerved, and I was on the point of screaming aloud when I looked into the face of my assailant and saw that it was Mose.

'Mrs Chester!' He looked surprised to see me, and let go of my arms immediately with a show of apology which might have seemed genuine had it not been for the mischief in his eyes. 'I'm terribly sorry to have alarmed you like that. Do forgive me.'

I struggled to regain my composure. 'It's quite all right,' I said.

'It . . . wasn't you. I went into the church, and walked straight into a funeral service. It . . . I hope I didn't hurt you,' I finished lamely.

He laughed, but almost immediately narrowed his eyes in an expression of some concern.

'You *have* had a shock, haven't you?' he said. 'You look quite pale. Here, sit down for a moment.' He eased an arm around my shoulders and began to move me towards a bench a few yards away. 'Why, you are so cold!' he exclaimed as his hands found mine. Before I could speak he had pulled off his own coat and thrown it over my shoulders. I protested half-heartedly, but he was cheerfully proprietary and, besides, it felt very comfortable to be sitting on the bench with his arm around me, the woolly tobacco-smell of his overcoat in my nostrils. If he had kissed me then, I would have responded with all my heart; I knew it—and felt no guilt at all.

10

I'd been following her for nearly a week before I made my move; she was difficult game, and I had to tread carefully if I was not to frighten the girl away. As it was, she was touchingly trusting; I met her every day after that and within the week she was calling me Mose and holding my hand, just like a child. If I hadn't known better I'd have sworn she was a virgin.

Not my usual tipple, I hear you say? Well, I couldn't have explained it either. I suppose it was the novelty of playing the prince, after being so many times the knave . . . Besides, she was beautiful.

A man could fall in love. But not me.

Still, there was something about her, something at the same time cool and deeply carnal, something beyond that girlishness which sparked off some latent emotion in me. She was an entirely new experience; I felt like an alcoholic, his palate jaded with heady intoxicants, tasting for the first time one of those sugary children's drinks. Like him, I paused to relish the newness, the unfamiliar sweetness. She was without any sense of right or wrong; she followed me wherever I wished to lead her, shivering with pleasure when I touched her, hanging on my every word. We talked far more than I ever did with any other woman; I forgot myself in her presence and told her about my poetry and art, my dreams and longings. I mostly saw her in the cemetery—it had the advantage of being huge and rambling, with plenty of enclosed places to hide. One cold, dull evening when Henry was working late we met by the Circle of Lebanon; there was no-one around, and the devil was in me. Effie smelled so good, like roses and white bread, and her face was flushed with the cool air. Her hair had been blown by the wind and little tendrils of it fell all around her face.

For a moment I was all hers.

It was the first time I had kissed her on the mouth, and I forgot everything I had planned about not alarming her. She was standing beside a vault, and I pushed her right up against the wall. Her hat fell off—I ignored it—and her hair came half unpinned around my face. I pulled the rest of it down and ran it through my hands, gasping for breath like a diver before I prepared to plunge again. I don't suppose it was the kind of kiss she expected, because she clapped her hands to her mouth with a little cry and stared at me, her face scarlet and her eyes like saucers. I realized that my hasty impulse had probably wrecked all my careful planning and I swore, then swore again at myself for swearing.

Recovering, I pulled away from her and fell to my knees, playing the part of the Repentant Lover. I was sorry, more sorry than I could say, for having alarmed her; no punishment could be too bad for me. I had succumbed to a momentary weakness, but I loved her so much; I had so longed to kiss her, ever since I first saw her, that I had lost control. I was not made of stone; but what of that? I had frightened her, insulted her. I deserved to be horsewhipped.

Maybe I overdid it a trifle, but it was a technique which had worked well enough before with married women; I had researched it carefully in the pages of *The Keepsake* and, God help me, in this case some of it was nearly true. I peered up cautiously to see if she had taken the bait and, amazingly, she was rocking with laughter, not unkindly but uncontrollably. As she saw me looking at her she burst out again.

Little Eff rose rapidly in my estimation. I stood up and grinned ruefully.

'Well . . . it was worth a try,' I said with a shrug. Effie shook her head and laughed again.

'Oh, Mose,' she said. 'You are a hypocrite! You should be on the stage.'

I tried another tack: the Unrepentant Lover.

'I've often thought that,' I said. 'Still, it usually works, you know.' I ventured a disarming smile. 'All right,' I said. 'I'm *not* sorry.'

'That's better,' said Effie. 'I believe that.'

'Then believe this,' I said. 'I love you.' How could she not believe it? At the time, I nearly did myself. 'I love you, and it's killing me to see you married to that pompous ass. He doesn't think of you as a woman, he thinks you're his thing, his beggar girl, his sick little fallen angel. Effie, you need me; you need to be taught how to live, how to enjoy life.'

I was almost sincere. Indeed, I practically convinced myself. I looked at her to see how she was taking it and her straight gaze fixed mine. She took a step towards me and such was the intensity of her expression that I nearly backed away. Almost abstractedly she lifted her cold hands to my face. Her kiss was soft and I tasted salt on her skin. I held back, allowing her to explore my face, my neck and hair with her fingers. Gently she pushed me towards the vault. I heard the gate open behind me and allowed myself to be manoeuvred inside. It was one of many family monuments in the cemetery, shaped like a tiny chapel, with a gate to protect it from the curious, a chair, prayer-stool and altar, and a little stained-glass window at the back. There was just enough space for two people to enter, shielded from view. I closed my eyes and stretched out my arms for her.

The gate slammed shut in my face.

I opened my eyes quickly and there she was, the minx, grinning at me through the bars. At first I laughed and tried to push the door open, but the catch was on the outside.

'Effie!'

'It's frightening, isn't it?' she said.

'Effie, let me out!'

'Being locked up, unable to get free? I feel that with Henry all the time. He doesn't *want* me to be alive. He wants me to be quiet and cold, like a corpse. You don't know what it's like, Mose. He makes me take laudanum to keep me quiet and good, but inside I want to scream and bite and run naked through the house like a savage!'

I could feel the passion and the hatred in her; you can't imagine how exciting that was to my jaded taste. But I was uneasy, too. For a moment I contemplated abandoning the whole campaign, asking myself whether she wasn't too hot for me to handle, but the appeal was too much. I growled at her like a tiger and bit at her fingers through the bars. She laughed wildly, a bird's mad scream across the marshes.

'You won't betray me, Mose.' It was a statement. I shook my head.

'If you do, I'll bring you back here and bury you here for ever.' She was only half joking. I kissed her knuckles.

'I promise.'

I heard her push the catch open in the gloom, and she stepped into the vault with me. Her cloak fell to the floor and her brown flannel dress with it. In her underclothes she was a wraith, and her touch was burning brimstone. She was all untutored, but made up for that in her enthusiasm. I tell you, I was almost afraid. She tore at me, bit me, scratched me, *devoured* me with her passion, and in the dark I was incapable of telling whether her cries were of anguish or of pleasure. She returned my careful gentleness with a violence which tore at the heart. The act was quick and brutal, like a murder, and afterwards she cried, but not, I think, with any sorrow.

There was a mystery in her which left me with a feeling of awe, of sanctity, which I never felt with any other woman. In some incomprehensible way I felt that she had purified me.

I know what you're thinking.

You're thinking I fell in love with the chit. Well, I didn't. But that evening—only that evening, mind you—I thought I felt something deeper than the brief passions I had had for other women. As if the act had opened up something inside me. I wasn't in love with her; and yet, when I returned to my rooms that night, all aching and scratched and feeling I had been in a war, I couldn't sleep; all night I stayed beside the fire thinking of Effie, drinking wine and looking into the flames as if they were her eyes. But however much I drank I did not manage to quench the thirst which her burning touch had begun in me, nor could a whole brothel full of whores have stilled the ache of wanting her.

11

⁓⁓

I was lucky that Henry was late home; it had been past seven when I arrived, and he usually came back from the studio for supper. As I came in by the back door I could hear Tabby singing to herself in the kitchen and knew that Mr Chester had not yet returned. I crept upstairs to my room to change my crumpled dress, choosing a white dimity with a blue sash which I had almost outgrown but which was a favourite of his. As I hastened to put it on I wondered whether Henry would see the difference so clearly written in my face, the rending of that veil which had kept me so long apart from the world of the living. My whole body was shaking with the violence of it, and I sat for a long time in front of my mirror before I was reassured that the marks of my lover's touch—marks which I could *feel* scarlet over every inch of my skin—existed only in my imagination.

I looked up at the wall where *The Little Beggar Girl* hung, and could not repress my laughter. For a moment I was almost hysterical, fighting for breath, as I met the mild, sightless gaze of the child who had never been me. I was never Henry's beggar girl; no, not even before I outgrew my childhood. My true portrait was hidden at the bottom of my work-basket, the face branded with scarlet. *Sleeping Beauty*, now awake and touched with a new kind of curse. Neither Henry, nor anyone else, would ever be able to put me to sleep again.

At the knock on the door I started violently and turned to see Henry standing there, an unreadable expression on his face. I could not suppress a shudder of apprehension. To hide my confusion I began to brush my hair with long, smooth strokes, *Low adown, low adown* . . . like the mermaid in the poem. The feel of my hair in my hands seemed to give me courage, as if some remnant of my lover's strength and assurance still lingered there, and Henry walked right into the room and spoke to me with unusual bonhomie.

'Effie, my dear, you're looking very well today, very well indeed. Have you taken your medicine?'

I nodded, not trusting my voice. Henry nodded his approval.

'I can see definite improvement. Definite roses in those cheeks. Capital!' He patted my face in a proprietary fashion, and I had to make a real effort to stop myself from drawing away in disgust; after my lover's burning touch, the thought of Henry's cool caresses was unspeakable.

'I suppose supper is almost ready?' I asked, parting my hair and beginning to braid it.

'Yes, Tabby has made a game pie with buttered parsnips.' He frowned at my reflection in the mirror. 'Don't pin up your hair,' he said. 'Wear it as it is, with ribbon through it, as you used to.' From my dressing-table he chose a blue ribbon, gently threading it through my hair and tying it in a wide bow at the back. 'That's my good girl.' He smiled. 'Stand up.'

I shook out my skirts in front of the mirror and looked at my reflection, still so like that other, unmoving reflection in the frame of *The Little Beggar Girl*.

'Perfect,' said Henry.

And though it was May, and there was a fire in the grate, I shivered.

Over supper I managed to regain much of my composure. I ate most of my piece of pie, some vegetables and a small dish of rhenish cream before announcing with fake good cheer that I could not possibly eat another morsel. Henry was in fine spirits. He consumed almost a whole bottle of wine over supper, although it was not his habit to drink a great deal, and he drank two glasses of port with his cigar afterwards, so that, without actually becoming *inebriated*, he was certainly in a very jolly mood.

Inexplicably this disturbed me, and I would have much preferred his indifference to the attentions he lavished upon me. He poured wine for me which I did not want to drink, complimented me a number of times on my dress and my hair, kissed my fingers as we rose from table and, as he smoked his cigar, he asked me to play the piano and sing to him.

I am not a musician; I knew maybe three or four little pieces by heart, and as many songs, but tonight Henry was charmed by my repertoire and caused me to sing 'Come with me to the Bower' three times before I was allowed to sit down, pleading fatigue. Suddenly Henry was all solicitude; I was to put my feet up on to his knees and to sit with my eyes closed, smelling at my lavender bottle. I insisted that I was quite well, simply a little tired, but Henry would have none of it; and presently, feeling quite oppressed at his attention, I pleaded a headache and asked permission to go to bed.

'Poor child, of course you must,' replied Henry with unimpaired good cheer. 'Take your medicine, and Tabby shall bring you up some hot milk.'

I was glad to be gone, hot milk or not, and, knowing that I should not sleep otherwise, took a few drops of laudanum from the hated bottle. I took off the white dress and changed into a ruffled nightgown, and was brushing out my hair when I heard a tap on the door.

'Come in, Tabby,' I called without looking round, but on hearing the heavy tread on the boards, so different to Tabby's light scuttling footsteps, I turned abruptly and saw Henry standing there for the second time that evening, holding a tray with a glass of milk and some biscuits.

'For my darling girl,' he said in a jocular tone, but I was quick to see something in his eyes, a shifting, shameful expression which froze me where I stood. 'No, no,' he said as I moved to get into bed, 'stay a while with me. Sit on my knee as you drink your milk, just as you used to.' He paused, and I saw the furtive expression again behind his wide smile.

'I'll be cold,' I protested. 'And I don't want any milk, my head aches so.'

'Don't be peevish,' he advised. 'I'll make a nice fire, and you shall have some laudanum in your milk, and very soon you'll be better.' He reached for the bottle on the mantelpiece.

'No! I've taken some already,' I said, but Henry did not pay any attention to my protest. He poured three drops of the laudanum into the milk and made to hand me the glass.

'Henry—'

'*Don't* call me that!' For a moment the jocular tone had disappeared; the tray with the glass and the biscuits wavered, and a dribble of milk slopped over the rim of the glass on to the tray. Henry noticed it but did not comment; I saw his mouth tighten, for he hated waste or untidiness of any kind, but his voice was still mild.

'Clumsy girl! Come now, don't make me lose my temper with you. Drink your milk, like a good girl, and then you shall sit on my knee.'

I tried to smile.

'Yes, Mr Chester.'

His mouth remained narrow until I had finished the milk, then he relaxed. He put the tray carelessly down on the floor and put his arms around me. I tried not to stiffen, feeling the sickly, indigestible weight of the hot milk resting in the pit of my stomach. My head was spinning and the hundred marks of Mose's embrace were like burning mouths on my body, each one screaming out its fury and outrage that this man should dare to lay his hands on me. My body's reaction at last corroborated what my mind had been too afraid to admit; that I hated this man whom I had married and to whom I was bound by law and duty. I *hated* him.

'Don't worry,' he whispered, his fingers tracing the pattern of my vertebrae through the linen nightdress. 'There's my good girl. Sweet Effie.'

And as he began with an eager and shaking hand to unfasten the buttons of my nightdress, a wave of nausea submerged me and I submitted passively to his touch, all the while praying to the wild, pagan god Mose had awakened in me that it should be over soon, that he should be gone, so that I could fall into the well of laudanum and the memory of his sickly, guilty embraces would be extinguished.

I awoke from a kind of thick swoon to find daylight filtering through my curtains, and stumbled weakly out of bed to open the windows. The air was fresh and damp as I stretched out my arms to the sun and felt some strength return to my shaking limbs. I washed carefully and completely and, after dressing in clean linen and a grey flannel gown, I felt brave enough to go down to breakfast. It was not yet half past seven; Henry was a late riser and would not be at table; I would have some time to compose myself after what had happened the previous night—it would not do for Henry to realize how I felt, nor what power he wielded over me.

Tabby had prepared eggs and ham, but I could not eat anything. I did drink some hot chocolate, more to please Tabby than myself, for I did not want her to tell Henry that I was unwell; so I sipped my chocolate and waited by the window, scanning a book of poems and watching the sun rise. It was eight when Henry made his appearance, dressed severely in black as if he were going to church. He went past me without a word, seating himself at the breakfast-table with the *Morning Post* and serving himself lavishly with ham, eggs, toast and kidneys. He took his meal in silence except for the occasional rustle of the paper and, leaving most of it untouched, he stood up, folded the paper meticulously and glanced towards me.

'Good morning,' I said mildly, turning a page.

Henry did not reply except for a tightening of the mouth, a trick of his when he was angry or when someone contradicted him. Why he should be angry I did not know, except that he often had abrupt changes of mood which I had long since ceased to try to understand. He took a step towards me, glanced at the book I was reading and frowned.

'Love poems,' he said in a bitter tone. 'I should have expected you, ma'am, with the education I have lavished on you, not to waste whatever sense God gave you on reading such trash!'

Hastily I closed the book, but it was too late.

'Do I not give you anything you want? Are you lacking in anything in the way of gowns, cloaks and bonnets? Have I not stayed with you when you were ill, borne with your megrims and your hysterics and your headaches . . . ?' The bitter voice was rising in pitch, sharp as piano-wire.

I nodded warily.

'Love poems!' said Henry sourly. 'Are all women the same, then? Is there not one female who has escaped the taint of all womankind? "One man among a thousand have I found; but a woman among all those have I not found." Am I such a poor teacher, then, that the pupil I thought was the most untouched by the weaknesses of her sex should waste her time in fanciful contemplation? Give that to me!' Reaching for the book he tossed it vengefully on to the fire.

'Of course,' he added spitefully, 'your mother *is* a milliner, used to pandering to the vanities of the fashionable world. I suppose no-one thought to instruct you. A fine clergyman your father must have been to allow you to fill your brain with fanciful notions. I suppose he thought such dangerous rubbish *romantic*.'

I knew I should have remained silent to avoid a quarrel, but my disgust of the previous night still lingered and, watching my book, with Shelley and Shakespeare and Tennyson curling up among the flames, I felt a great, rushing anger.

'My father was a *good* man,' I said fiercely. 'Sometimes I feel he is with me, watching. Watching us together.'

I saw Henry stiffen. 'I wonder what he is thinking,' I continued in a soft voice. 'I wonder what he sees.'

Henry's face clenched like a fist and I burst out, uncontrollably, 'How dare *you* burn my books! How dare *you* preach to me and treat me like a child! How can you, when last night . . .' I broke off, gritting my teeth with the effort of not crying my secret hatred out loud.

'Last night . . .' His voice was low.

I put up my chin defiantly. 'Yes!' He knew what I meant.

'I am not a saint, Effie,' he said in a subdued voice. 'I know I am as weak as other men. But it's you—*you* drive me to it. I try to keep you pure; God help me, I do try. Last night was all your doing. I saw the way you looked at me while you were combing your hair; I saw the colours in your cheeks. You set out to seduce me and, because I was weak, I succumbed. But I still love you: that's why I try to keep you clean and innocent, as you were when I first met you that day in the park.' He turned to me and grasped my hands. 'You looked like an angel child. Even then I guessed you were sent to tempt me. I *know* it wasn't your fault, Effie, it's your nature—God made women weak and perverse and full of treachery. But you owe it to me to fight it, to deny sin and let God into your soul. Oh, I do love you, Effie! Don't fight against the purity of my love. Accept it, and my authority as you would that of a loving father. Trust my deeper knowledge of the world, and respect me, as you would your poor dead father. Will you?'

Grasping my hands, he looked into my face most earnestly and such was the power of years of obedience that I nodded meekly.

'That's my good girl. Now, you must ask my forgiveness for the sin of anger, Effie.'

For a second I hesitated, trying to recapture the rebellion, the shamelessness, the certainty I had felt with Mose in the cemetery. But that had gone, along with my brief moment of defiance, and I felt weak, easy tears pricking at my eyelids.

'I'm sorry. I'm sorry I was rude to you, Mr Chester,' I mumbled, the tears coursing down my cheeks.

'Good girl,' he said, triumphantly. 'What, still crying? Come now. You see that I was right about those poems—they make you peevish and melancholy. Dry your eyes now, and I'll ask Tabby to bring you your medicine.'

Half an hour later Henry had gone and I was lying on my bed, dry-eyed but heavy with a listless despair. The laudanum bottle was on the bedstand beside me and, for a moment, I contemplated the greatest sin of all, the sin against the Holy Ghost. If there had not been Mose and the knowledge of love and hatred in my heart I might have committed that blackest of murders there and then, for I saw my life stretching out in front of me like a reflection in a fairground Hall of Mirrors, saw my face in youth, in middle age, in old age, adorning the walls of Henry's house like dim trophies as he took more and more of myself from me. I wanted to tear off my skin, to free the creature I had been when I danced naked in a shower of light . . . If it had not been for Mose I would have done it, and with joy.

12

I stopped at my club, the Cocoa Tree, for a late breakfast—I couldn't bear to eat with Effie staring at me with those dark, wounded eyes; as if I was somehow guilty of something! She had no idea of the sacrifices I made for her, the torments I endured for her sake. Nor did she care. All she cared for were her wretched books. I narrowed my eyes at *The Times* and tried to concentrate, but I could not read the closely spaced paragraphs; her face intruded, the image of her lips, her eyes, the grimace of horror which had come over her features when I kissed her . . .

Damn her games! It was too late for her to pretend that she was chaste; I knew her to the cheating core. It was for her sake that I visited that house in Crook Street—for *her*. To safeguard her tainted purity. A man could visit such places and need feel no compunction; after all, it was only the same as visiting a club, an exclusive *gentleman's* club. I had instincts, damn her, like any man: better that I should slake them on some Haymarket whore than on my little girl. But last night there had been something about her, something different; she had been rosy-cheeked and sensual, elated and warm, the scent of grass and cedar on her skin and in her hair . . . She had *wanted* to seduce me. I knew it.

Ridiculous, that *I* should be the one to be made to feel unclean. Ridiculous that she should try to accuse *me*. I sipped my coffee, liking the smell of leather and cigar-smoke in the warm air, the muted sounds of voices—*men's* voices—in the background. This morning, the very thought of women sickened me. I was glad I had burned her stupid book. Later I would go through the bookshelves and find the rest.

'Mr Chester?'

I started, spilling coffee into the saucer in my hand. The man who had addressed me was slim and fair, with round spectacles over sharp grey eyes.

'I'm so sorry to have disturbed you,' he said, smiling, 'but I was at your exhibition the other day and I was most impressed.' He had a clipped, precise delivery and very white teeth. 'Dr Russell,' he prompted. 'Francis Russell, author of *The Theory and Practice of Hypnotism* and *Ten Case Histories of Hysteria*.'

The name did seem familiar. Now I came to think of it, so did the face. I assumed I must have seen him at the exhibition.

'Perhaps you'd care to join me in a drink of something stronger?' suggested Russell.

I pushed aside the half-empty coffee-cup. 'I don't usually touch spirits,' I said, 'but a fresh cup of coffee would be welcome. I'm . . . a little tired.'

Russell nodded. 'The pressure of the artistic temperament,' he said. 'Insomnia, headaches, impaired digestion . . . many of my patients exhibit these very symptoms.'

'I see.' Indeed I did; the man was simply offering his services. The thought was somehow reassuring; for a moment I had wondered whether his apparently friendly approach might conceal something more sinister. Angry with myself at the very thought, I smiled warmly at the man.

'And what would you usually recommend in these cases?' I asked.

For some time we spoke together. Russell was an interesting conversationalist, well versed in art and literature. We touched upon the subject of drugs; their use in symbolist art, their necessity in cases of highly strung temperaments. I mentioned Effie and was reassured that the use of laudanum—especially for a sensitive young female—was the best method of combating depression. A very sound young man, Francis Russell. After an hour of his company I found that I could begin to touch delicately upon the subject of Effie's strange moods. I was not explicit, of course, merely hinting that my wife had odd fancies and unexplained illnesses. I was gratified to find that the doctor's diagnosis was much like my own. My feeling of unfocused guilt—as if I had somehow been responsible for Effie's actions of last night—receded as I learned that such feelings were not uncommon; the correct term, he informed me, was *empathy* and I must not allow myself to be depressed by my natural reactions.

We left the Cocoa Tree on the best of terms; we exchanged cards and promised to meet again, and it was in a far more optimistic mood that I finally made my way to the studio to meet Moses Harper, secure in my knowledge that in Russell I had an ally, a weapon against the spectres of my guilty fantasy. I had science on my side.

13

You see, she needed me. Call me a villain if you like, but I made her happy, which was more than your preaching ever did. She was lonelier than anyone I have ever known, trapped in her ivory tower with her cold prince and her servants and everything her heart desired except love. *I* was what she needed—and however much you might despise me, I taught her everything I knew. She was a quick enough pupil and quite without inhibitions. She accepted everything without reserve, without shame or coyness. *I* never corrupted *her*—if anything, *she* corrupted me.

We met as often as we could, mostly in the afternoons when Henry was working and I had finished the day's sitting. His canvas was progressing very slowly and he worked until about seven every evening. This gave me plenty of time to see Effie home safely before he got back, so that he never knew how long she had been gone—and if the old Tabby suspected anything, she never said so.

This went on for about a month, with me meeting Effie either in the cemetery or at my rooms. She was moody—sometimes highly strung and tense, sometimes recklessly bright; never twice the same. Her lovemaking reflected this, so that she gave the illusion of being many different women and I suppose that was why she held on to me so long; I'm terribly easy to bore, you know.

She told me she had dreams in which she travelled all over the world; sometimes she described the strange and distant places she had visited and wept at the lost beauty of the dream. She also said that she could step out of her body at will and watch those around her without their knowledge; she described the physical pleasure of this act and urged me to try it. She was certain that if I were to learn how to perform this feat too, we could make love outside our bodies and be joined together for ever. Needless to say I never managed, although I did try, using opium, feeling rather foolish at believing her. *She* believed it, however, just as she believed everything I told her. I could make her shiver and grow pale, cry, laugh or flush with rage at my stories, and I took some innocent pleasure in doing this. I told her tales of ghosts and gods, witches and vampires dredged up from my earliest childhood, amazed at her childish hunger for all that knowledge, at all her wasted potential for learning.

I told you, she was a new experience, disarming me from one moment to the next. However, her real talent, like all women, was for emotion, and I sometimes pitied Henry Chester who had not been able to use and appreciate the reserves of passion in his poor little Effie.

The change came the day I decided to take her to the travelling fair which had camped on the Islington road. All women like fairs, with the little knick-knacks on sale, the Tunnel of Love and the fortune-tellers predicting dark handsome men and large families. For myself, I had heard that there would be on display a large collection of human grotesques, something which, since my earliest childhood, I have scarce been able to resist. They have always been a subject of fascination for me, these poor wretches, playthings of an uncaring God. In China, apparently, such shows are so lucrative that natural occurrences are not thought common enough, and parents of large families often sell young babies to fairs at birth to be used as freak attractions. The babies—usually the despised girls—are deliberately deformed by being kept in a small cage, in which their limbs are not allowed freedom to grow. The result, after some years of this treatment, is the comically atrophied creature so much loved by young children, the dwarf.

I told this story to Effie as we set off for the fair and it was a full fifteen minutes before I could stop her tears. How could they, she was crying, how could they be so cruel, so inhuman? To deliberately create something like that! Could I imagine the inconceivable hatred which such a creature would feel . . . Here she broke down hysterically and the coachman glared accusingly at me through the glass. It took all of my arguments to persuade her that none of the freaks in this fair were so obtained; they were all of them honest errors of Nature, doing well for themselves in their chosen trade. Besides, there would be other things to occupy her mind: I would buy her some ribbons from the pedlar, and maybe some hot gingerbread if she wanted it. Inwardly I grimaced and made a mental note not to tell her any more stories about China.

At the fair, Effie's despondency lifted, and she began to take an interest in what was going on around her. Pedlars with brightly coloured wares; an old man with a barrel-organ and a dancing monkey in a scarlet coat; some jugglers and acrobats; a fire-eater; and some gypsy girls dancing to pipes and tambourine.

She lingered for some time in front of the dancers, her eyes fixed especially upon one girl of about her own age, but with the dark skin and loose blue-black hair of the gypsy race, her feet bare and her ankles—nicely turned ankles, I noticed—ringed about with jangling bracelets. She was wearing a gold-embroidered skirt, scarlet petticoats, and a multitude of necklaces. Effie was enchanted.

'Mose,' she whispered to me as the girl ceased her dance, 'I think she must be the most beautiful woman I have ever seen.'

'Not as beautiful as you,' I said to reassure her, taking her hand.

She scowled and shook her head irritably. 'Don't be silly,' she said. 'I *mean* it.'

Women! Sometimes there's no pleasing them.

I was ready to move on; the freak-show had begun, and I could hear a crier extolling the marvels of 'Adolphus, the Human Torso', but Effie was still watching the gypsy. She had moved towards a faded blue-and-gold tent by the side of the path, and a crier now began to announce that 'Scheherazade, Princess of the Mystic East' would tell fortunes using the 'Magickal Tarot and the Crystal Ball'. I saw Effie's eyes light up, and resigned myself to the inevitable. Summoning up a smile, I said: 'I suppose you want to know your fortune?'

She nodded, her face vivid with eagerness. 'Do you think she's really a princess?'

'Almost certainly,' I said with great seriousness and Effie sighed with rapture. 'She has probably been cursed by a wicked witch and is reduced to living in poverty,' I continued. 'She has lost her memory and disguises her magical powers as fairground charlatanry. But at night she turns into a silver swan and flies in her dreams to places no-one but she has ever travelled to.'

'Now you're laughing at me,' she protested.

'Not at all.'

But she was hardly paying attention. 'Do you know, I've never had anyone tell my fortune? Henry says that kind of thing is witchcraft in disguise. He says that in the Middle Ages they would have been hanged for it, and a good thing too.'

'Pious Henry,' I sneered.

'Well, I don't care what Henry says,' said Effie with determination. 'Would you stay out here and wait for me? I won't be long.'

Anything to keep the lady happy. I sat down on a stump and waited.

The High
Priestess

14

It was hot inside the tent and what light there was came from a small red lamp on the table in front of me. The gypsy was sitting on a stool, shuffling her pack of cards, and she smiled as I came in, beckoning me to sit down. For a moment I hung back; surprised that she was not the woman who had danced, but an older woman, a scarf drawn over her hair and a thick layer of kohl outlining her tawny eyes. Something covered in black cloth stood on the table beside the lamp and as my eyes lingered upon it, trying to decide what it was, 'Scheherazade' indicated it with one strong, still-beautiful hand.

'The crystal ball,' she explained. Her voice was light and pleasant but accented. 'I have to keep it covered or it loses its power. Please cut the cards.'

'I . . . Where is the girl who danced?' I asked hesitantly. 'I thought that she would be telling the fortunes.'

'My daughter,' said the gypsy curtly. 'She and I work together. Please cut the cards.'

She handed me the pack of cards and I held them for a moment. They were heavy and looked very old, with a shine to them born not from grime but from much respectful handling. I gave them back with reluctance, for I would have liked to look at them more closely, and she began to spread them in a spiral pattern around the table.

'The Hermit,' began Scheherazade. 'And the Ten of Wands. Oppression. This man speaks of virtue, but he has a shameful secret. The Seven of Cups: debauch. And the Nine of Swords: cruelty and murder. I play the Lovers, but they are covered by the Knave of Coins. He will bring you joy and despair, for in his hands he bears the Two of Cups and the Tower. But who is here, riding atop the Chariot? The High Priestess, bearing the Ten of Swords, which spells ruin, and the Ace of Cups, great fortune. You will trust her and she will save you, but the cup she offers is filled with bitterness. Her chariot is driven by a Knave and a Fool, and beneath her wheels lie the Ace of Wands and the Hanged Man. In her hands she brings Justice and the Two of Cups which spells Love, but hidden inside the cups are Change and Death.' She paused, as if she had forgotten that I was there, and spoke softly to herself in Romany.

'Is there more?' I asked after a time, as she seemed lost in thought.

Scheherazade hesitated, then nodded. She looked at me for some time with an unreadable expression, then she stepped towards me, kissed me quickly on the forehead and made a sign with three fingers of her left hand.

'You have a strange and magical destiny, *ma dordi*,' she said. 'Better to look for yourself.' And she carefully unwrapped the crystal ball from its black covering and pushed it towards me.

For a moment I was unsure of where I was; the ball reflected the light so that I had the illusion of being out of my own body looking downwards. The scene was familiar, stylized like the figures on the Tarot: a girl sitting at a table where a gypsy watches over a hand of cards. Suddenly I was light-headed, almost dizzy, overflowing with unreasoning laughter, but feeling dislocated somehow, as if struggling with lost memories.

When shall we three meet again? I said to myself, and I laughed aloud, uncontrollably, as if in recollection of some wild and ridiculous farce.

Then a depression, as abrupt as the hilarity, seized me, and I was close to tears, the image of the crystal blurring before my eyes. I was afraid, disorientated and without memory of what had frightened me, looking into the clouded surface of the crystal and trembling.

Scheherazade was singing gently, almost idly under her breath:

> *'Aux marches du palais . . .*
> *Aux marches du palais . . .*
> *'Y a une si belle fille, lonlà . . .*
> *'Y a une si belle fille . . .'*

I tried to stop myself from falling out of my body towards the crystal, but the pull was too strong. I could no longer feel my limbs, no longer see beyond the clouded surface where, at last, some of the cloud was beginning to disperse. Scheherazade was singing softly in a rhythmic, lilting voice, three notes rising and falling compulsively. As I followed the coaxing beat I found myself leaving my body without effort, my senses warping, spiralling out of control. I allowed myself to drift, guided by the sound, and was conscious of drifting through the darkness right out of the tent and high into the air like a child's balloon.

From far away I heard Scheherazade's voice, gently coaxing: 'Shh, sshhh . . . that's right. See the balloons. Watch the balloons.'

Vaguely I wondered how she could have known what I had been thinking, then remembered, with a childish, absurd delight: she was Scheherazade, Princess of the Mystic East. I giggled.

'Sleep, little girl,' she whispered. 'It's your birthday, and there will be balloons, I promise. Can you see them?'

They were drifting around me, all colours, shining in the sun. I nodded. From a great distance I heard my voice in sleepy reply.

I saw the tent from above, saw Mose sitting on his stump, heard the pedlars selling their wares.

'Hot gin'erbread' and 'Ribbons and bows' and 'Liquorice laces'. I smelled the mingled confusion of hot pies, candyfloss and animals. I hovered, directionless, for a few moments like some fairy-tale sky-ship, then I felt myself being drawn gently down towards a scarlet tent across which was stretched a banner which read: 'HAPPY BIRTHDAY MARTA'. All around the banner were strings of balloons, and I thought I could hear music from inside the tent, the music of a barrel-organ, or maybe a child's clockwork toy. I began to float down towards the tent.

As I touched the ground I realized that the sun had disappeared. It was cold, and the bright banner had vanished; in its place I saw a small, tattered poster, advertising:

The Gallery of the Grotesque!
A most Admirable Display of Murderers, Monsters
and Freaks of Nature Depicted in Wax

I felt myself moving towards the tent-flap, my elation dimming rapidly. I had begun to feel cold, with a dull, sickly chill which pulled me from my delightful dream of flying into an earthy darkness. I saw the tent-flap open by itself and, although I struggled, I was not able to escape the malignant attraction of that opening. I could smell stale straw, kept for too long out of the sunlight, the musty reek of damp old clothes and the sharp scent of wax; and as I entered the tent, and my eyesight began to adjust to the darkness, I saw that I was alone and that all around the sides of the tent—which now seemed very much larger than I had first thought—were placed wooden pens or enclosures, housing the life-sized exhibits. I wondered why I had felt such a sensation of dread as I first entered; these figures were wax, their limbs held together with horsehair and whalebone, their clothes glued on to their bodies. The blood was red paint; even the gallows in the famous hanging scene had never been used for a real execution. But I was suddenly convinced that they were all real, that Burke and Hare in the corner were waiting there just for me, assessing me greedily from under thin masks of wax . . .

I moved backwards, angry at myself and my childish, unreasoning terror, and cried out aloud as I ran straight into the exhibit at my back. Even in my discorporate state I felt a moment's tension as I touched the wood of the pen, and I whipped round to face the thing behind me. An enclosure of wire and planks surrounded a still scene; tacked on to the wood was a sign which read:

THE HERMIT
Please do not touch the exhibits

I moved a little closer, squinting against the troubling light, and saw that the scene was a tiny bedroom, like a child's, with a narrow bed covered with a patchwork quilt, a small stool, bedside table and a couple of coloured prints of the type I had had when I was a girl. There were flowers on the bedside table, marigolds in a glass jar, and by the bed a small stack of wrapped presents. Beside the open window a bunch of balloons swayed in the draught.

But why had I thought it was dark? The light was streaming in from the window on to the bare floorboards; evening light which reflected a warm rosy radiance on to the bright little room. A man was sitting on the side of the bed, no doubt to say good-night to his little girl, who was in her nightdress, a stuffed toy frozen in one hand. She looked about ten, long black hair hanging down dead straight around a solemn, pointed face. The man's face I could not see, as he had his back to me, but I could guess at a certain heaviness of build, a square jawline, a stiffness in the posture which I found faintly familiar. I moved forwards curiously, wondering vaguely why this comfortable domestic scene had been included in the Gallery of the Grotesque.

As I moved, the girl's head snapped towards me and I jumped back with a stifled scream. The girl froze again, her eyes fixing me with a stare so intense that I found it difficult to believe she was merely a thing of wax and horsehair. Reluctantly I stepped forwards again, angry at myself for having been startled so by a piece of machinery; at the London Waxworks there had been similar devices, triggered by pressure on a plate in the floor, enabling the exhibits to move as the onlookers passed by. I found myself scanning the floor for the concealed plate.

There! As I passed a certain point she moved again, turning her head towards the man with a fluid, boneless movement that could surely not be mechanical. Her hair fell across her face and she brushed it back with a nervous little gesture, the other hand clenching at the thick cotton of the nightgown. I was suddenly convinced that despite the misleading term 'exhibit' these were real actors, playing out some ghastly charade for my benefit, and I was suddenly angry at my nervousness, angry but, at the same time, filled with a dreadful sense of predestination. I *knew* what I was about to see as if it were a memory from my own past and, impelled with a growing sense of urgency, I touched the wire which separated me from the scene and called urgently to the child.

'Little girl!'

The child did not react but moved warily towards the bed. I raised my voice.

'Little girl! Come here!' I heard my voice rise shrilly, but the child might as well have been clockwork. I tried to call again, but found myself moving instead right into the enclosure and into the scene. Suddenly I began to feel dizzy; half falling, I reached out towards the figure of the little girl as if to ask for help . . .

And I was ten once more, ten and coming to see my mother, as I did every Sunday. I loved my mother and wished I could be with her every day, but I knew it wasn't possible; Mother had work to do, and didn't want me in the way. I wondered what her work was. I liked Mother's house, so grand and full of pretty things—elephant statues from India and hangings from Egypt and carpets from Persia, like in the *Thousand and One Nights*. When I was grown up, maybe I could come and live with Mother all the time, instead of at Aunt Emma's—except that Aunt Emma wasn't my aunt at all but a schoolteacher, and she didn't like Mother very much. Not that she said anything, but I could tell from the funny face she used to pull when she said 'your poor mother', as if she had just swallowed cod-liver oil. Mother would never give me cod-liver oil. Instead she always let me eat at the table with her, instead of in the nursery with the babies, and there would be cake and jam and sometimes red wine with water in it.

Sometimes the pretty young ladies who lived in the house with Mother would come down and talk to me; I liked that because they were always so kind, giving me gingerbread and sweets, and they always wore the most lovely dresses and jewellery. Aunt Emma must never know about *that*; years before, when I was still a baby, I had let something slip, and she had been terribly angry, saying, 'Surely the woman has no shame, allowing a child into *that* place, and with those abandoned creatures!' I tried to say that they weren't abandoned, that they had plenty of company every day, but she was too angry to listen, so now I don't say anything at all. It's safer that way.

But tonight Mother said that I would have to go to bed early, because she's expecting company. I don't mind; I sometimes pretend to go to sleep and then, when she thinks I'm in bed, I creep down and watch the pretty ladies and the guests through the gap in the banisters. I'm very quiet; no-one ever sees me. Well, hardly ever. Not till tonight.

He was very kind, though, the gentleman; he said he'd not tell Mother. He didn't even know Mother had a daughter at all and he seemed surprised, but he was very kind; he said how pretty I looked in my nightgown, and that, if I was a good girl, he'd come and put me to bed and tell me a story.

But now I'm not so sure. He looks funny, staring at me like that, and I wish I'd never asked him here. He frightens me. I said, 'What about my story?' but he didn't even seem to be listening. He just keeps looking at me in that funny way, and suddenly I wish Mother were here. But if I call her she'll know I was out of my room . . . Now he's coming forwards, with his arms held out; maybe he'll just give me a goodnight kiss and leave me alone.

'Like mother, like daughter,' he whispers as he pulls me towards him, but I don't understand what he means. He smells funny, salty, like the river after the rain, and his mouth is very cold. I try to push him away; I don't understand why, but he frightens me—he's kissing me the way grown-up men kiss ladies.

I say 'No' but he just laughs and says 'Come here' and some other things I don't understand. He's so strong that I can't move my arms to push him away; I'd like to bite him but I know he's Mother's guest, and I do so want Mother to love me and to want me to live with her for good. I don't want to be a baby. But I can hardly breathe; I try to say, 'Stop, you're holding me too hard,' but the words won't come out. Suddenly he pushes me on to the bed; he's so heavy on top of me that I'm afraid he's going to squash me, and he's beginning to take off my nightgown; this time I manage to give a little scream, but he puts his hand over my mouth. I begin to struggle; never mind about being a baby, I don't care if Mother finds out, I don't care if Aunt Emma . . . I manage to get my teeth into his hand and I bite down hard; he tastes horrible, of sweat and perfume, but he swears, and lets go. I take a breath and scream.

'Mother!' He swears again and slaps me hard across the face. I scream again and he grabs me by the neck. He's cursing all the time, saying 'Bitch bitch shut up bitch shut up *shut up . . .*' but my face is against the pillow and I can't breathe. My head is so tight, like a balloon. It feels as if it's going to burst and I can't scream, I can't breathe, I can hardly move with him on top of me and I can't *breathe*, I can't *breathe*. He seems to be moving away, so far away into the distance, and I can hardly feel the pillow over my mouth, hardly taste the starch and the lavender scent in the thick linen. In the background I can hear Mother's voice calling me:

'Marta?'

Then nothing.

15

I was beginning to become impatient; she had been in there for long enough to have her fortune read a dozen times, and I was the one who was going to have to pay the gypsy bitch when she finally did come out. I was getting cold, sitting there with nothing to do, so I got up and walked into the tent.

For a moment I was disorientated; the tent seemed cavernous, filled with the reflections of torches like some dead Pharaoh's pyramid. Then, as my eyes adjusted, I realized that it was after all just a small tent, strewn with the usual trappings of the fairground charlatan, the sunlight streaming in through the tent-flap on to the array of gilt and paint and glass, showing it to be just that. Effie did not flinch as I threw back the tent-flap, but remained sitting with her back to me, her head hanging loosely to one side. Of 'Scheherazade' there was no sign.

The suspicion of foul play crossed my mind at once, as I leaped to Effie's side in one step. I shouted her name, shook her by the shoulders, but she was limp as rags, her eyes open but blank. I cursed and lifted her from her chair, carrying her outside into the sunlight, where the noise I had made had already attracted a small knot of curious onlookers. Ignoring their bleating I laid Effie on the grass and, after having checked that she had no visible injury, I tipped out the contents of her purse to look for the smelling-salts. Some woman screamed in the background—I suppose the bitch thought I was robbing the unconscious lady—and I snapped a vulgar rejoinder which made another woman gasp faintly and reach for her own smelling-bottle. An officious type with a military moustache demanded explanations while a vapid youth suggested brandy, but failed to produce any, and a female with dyed hair attempted to compete for attention by having an unconvincing fainting spell of her own. Oh, the scene was high vaudeville, all right; someone had already summoned the constable and I was beginning to wonder whether it wasn't time for Mose to take a bow and leave when Effie's eyes suddenly focused sharply on mine with an expression of horror, and she screamed, a high, demented wail of unreasoning terror.

At that moment the constable arrived.

A babel of voices greeted him: a woman had been robbed; the man here had been attacking the poor lady in broad daylight; she had had a fit; one of the animals in the wild beast show had escaped, frightening the ladies—it shouldn't be allowed . . . I saw the constable's eyes light up as he reached in his pocket for his notebook.

Effie managed to sit up with my help and was rubbing her eyes confusedly.

'It's all right,' I shouted above the din. 'I'm the lady's . . . husband. She fainted because of the heat.' But I could tell that the tide of popular opinion was against me and, foreseeing the necessity of lengthy and unpleasant explanations at the police station, wondered again whether I should not simply disappear now while there was still time and confusion enough to do so. As for Effie, she'd be all right; after all, she was in some way responsible for the situation; if she hadn't screamed in that idiotic way I should have been able to carry it off well enough. As it was she made me look like a rapist. Besides, there was Henry to think about. I had almost made up my mind when I became aware of a female figure at my side, and a crisp, familiar voice rang out over the hubbub:

'Marta, dear, are you all right? I told you not to exert yourself so much! Here!' I caught a glimpse of a pair of narrow, bright eyes levelled at mine and heard her whisper fiercely, 'Be *quiet*, you idiot! Haven't you done enough?' I moved aside dazedly, and she took my place beside Effie, holding a smelling-bottle and uttering coaxing words.

'Fanny!' I said blankly.

Again the hiss. 'Shut *up!*'

'Now, Marta my love, can you stand? Let me help you. Hold on to Mother, now. That's right. That's my lovely darling.' Still holding the bemused Effie by the waist Fanny turned on the constable, who was by now looking decidedly confused.

'Officer,' she said sharply, 'perhaps we might ask you to do your duty and disperse this . . . this *herd* before they alarm my daughter any further?'

The constable hesitated; I could see him wrestling with his dwindling self-assurance, still suspicious, but intimidated by the stronger personality.

'Well?' Fanny demanded impatiently. 'Must we be importuned by these vulgar onlookers? Is my daughter an exhibit to be stared at?' With a superb and righteous fury she turned on the crowd.

'Go away!' she commanded. 'Go on, move! I said *move!*' A number of people at the edge of the scene began to shift uneasily and drift away; only the military gentleman held his ground.

'I demand to know . . .' he began.

Fanny set her hands on her hips and took a step forwards.

'Now look here...'

Fanny took another step. Their faces were nearly touching. She whispered something, very quietly.

The military gentleman jumped as if he had been stung and moved away hurriedly, pausing only to look back over his shoulder at Fanny with an expression of almost superstitious alarm. Then she joined us again, a smile of sublime unconcern on her face.

'That, officer,' she said, 'is how it is done.' Then, as the constable seemed dissastisfied, she continued: 'My daughter has a delicate constitution, officer, and is upset by the slightest thing. I warned my son-in-law not to take her to the fair, but he would go against my advice. And because he is most ill equipped to deal with a young lady in her condition...'

'Ah?' said the constable.

'Yes. My daughter is expecting a child,' said Fanny sweetly.

The constable blushed and scribbled something meaningless in his notebook. Struggling to maintain his dignity, he turned to Effie.

'I'm very sorry, ma'am,' he said. 'Just doin' my duty. You *are* this lady's daughter?'

Effie nodded.

'And this gentleman's wife?'

'Of course.'

'Would you mind giving me your name, please, ma'am?' Effie flinched almost imperceptibly. I noticed, but did not think the constable did, so quick was her recovery.

'Marta,' she said, continuing in a stronger voice, 'Marta.' And, turning towards Fanny with a smile, Effie put her arm around the older woman's waist and began suddenly, inexplicably, to laugh.

Fanny Miller had been a part of my life for years, and I respected her as I have done no other woman. She was ten years older than I, good-looking in a heavy kind of style, with a razor-sharp intelligence and a masculine, devouring ambition. Like myself, she was a Jack-of-all-trades; her mother was a country girl turned Haymarket slut and had given Fanny to that oldest of professions by the time she was thirteen. Four years later the mother was dead and Fanny was on her own, all teeth and claws against the world into which she had been thrown. She was avid to get on and, in the years which followed, she learned how to read, to write, to pick pockets and locks, to fight with a razor or with her fists, to make medicines and poisons, to talk like a lady—though she never quite lost her mother's West Country burr—and drink like a man. Above all she learned to despise men, to ferret out their weaknesses and use them, and soon enough she was able to graduate from selling herself to selling others.

Fanny had earned her money in a dozen ways, both honest and dishonest: by singing in the vaudeville, by telling fortunes in a travelling fair, by selling fake rheumatism cures, by blackmail, by theft, by fraud. When I met her she was already in charge of her own establishment, with maybe a dozen girls in her stable. Pretty, all of them; but none of them could have competed with Fanny. She was tall, almost as tall as I am, with strong, rounded arms, broad shoulders and rolling curves all free from corsets and stays. She had bright amber eyes, like a cat's, and a profusion of brassy hair which she wore in a complicated knot at the back of her head. But Fanny wasn't for sale, not at any price. Foolishly, I insisted—there's a price and a line for every woman, or so I thought—and she struck at me just like a cat, the arc of her ivory straight-razor leaping towards me with a fluid grace, deliberately missing me by half an inch. She was quick—I never even saw her pull the razor from her pocket—and I still remember the way she looked at me, snapping the wicked blade shut again and returning it to her skirts, saying, 'I like you, Mose. I really do. But forget yourself again, and I'll take your face off. Understand?' And all that without a tremor in her voice or a quickening of the heart.

Sometimes I think that if Fanny Miller ever had a heart she must have left it along the way with all the rest of the useless flotsam of her life; certainly, by the time we met, she was steel through and through. I never saw her falter. Never. And now she had returned, my personal daemon, unchanged but for a streak of grey in her luxuriant hair, to take in hand my little crisis.

I was not altogether pleased, although Fanny had undoubtedly saved me from some unpleasantness; I suppose I simply don't like being indebted to a woman. Besides, I was already running my own masquerade with Effie, and it disturbed me that Fanny knew it; she was the type to turn every situation to her own advantage, and I did not like the almost instinctive way in which Effie had clung to her, almost as if she were indeed Fanny's daughter. However, I said nothing until we had left the green and were back on the Islington Road where I could hail a fly and be off before I had to give any tedious explanations. I glanced at Fanny, still arm-in-arm with Effie, and cautiously began to search for my role.

'A long time since we last met, Fanny,' I said idly. 'How are you faring nowadays?'

'Come-day, go-day,' she replied, with a smile.

'Business?'

'I'd say business were fine.' Still the smile, mocking, as if she knew she was hiding something from me. Turning to Effie, she levelled the smile at her, their faces intimately close. 'You'll excuse me, miss, if I alarmed you back there,' she said cheerfully, 'but I could see you didn't want the commotion, and I guess you might not want anyone to recognize you.' A knowing, sidewards glance at me. I shifted uneasily before it. What did she know? What game was she playing?

'Our guardian angel,' I commented, trying to keep the sourness out of my voice. 'Effie, this is Epiphany Miller. Fanny, this is Effie Chester.'

'I know. I know your husband well,' said Fanny. That made me start, but Effie did not react.

'Oh, modelling,' she said. She was still staring at Fanny with a kind of stupid intensity and, for the first time, I found myself out of all patience with her. I was about to make a sharp comment when she roused herself abruptly.

'Why did you call me that?' she asked.

'Call you what, my dear?' said Fanny comfortably.

'Marta.'

'Oh, that? It was just the first name which came into my head.'

I'm damned if I knew what her game was. I could see no reason why she should want to befriend Effie, who was as unlike her as a woman can be, nor why she should invite us to her house; but she did and, despite the black looks I levelled at her, Effie agreed. I was beside myself; I knew where Fanny lived; she had a house in Maida Vale, near the canal, consisting of her own rooms and the lodgings of the dozen or so girls who lived under her protection—not the kind of place I wanted to be recognized in with Effie, unless I wanted all my careful liaising with Henry to be wasted.

'Really, Effie, I think we should be getting you home, don't you think?' I said pointedly.

'Rubbish!' answered Fanny. 'It's only three o'clock. There's plenty of time for a cup of tea and a bite to eat.'

'I really don't think—'

'I'd like to come,' interrupted Effie with a defiant look in her eye. 'If Mose wants to leave now, let him. I'll come home presently.'

Damn her impudence!

'I can't let you jaunt about London on your own!'

'I won't be on my own. I'll be with Miss Miller.'

Miss Miller be damned! I could see Fanny was enjoying the whole scene vastly, and so I was forced to hold my tongue and accompany them both. Dealing with Effie could wait. I'd make her pay later.

16

I could tell that Mose was annoyed that we had encountered Fanny; he dragged his feet, scowled, made impatient gestures and made it clear that he wanted us both to be gone as soon as possible. I could understand why: despite her spirited performance at the fair, Fanny had soon abandoned her high tone and, although her clothes were of excellent quality, there was in the richness of the mulberry velvet dress, the matching plumed hat and the rope of baroque pearls around her long neck, more than a suspicion of the adventuress. I knew what Henry thought of women who dressed, walked and talked as she did; but, if anything, that only added to her attraction.

For there *was* an attraction; I'd felt immediately drawn to Fanny. As soon as I set eyes on her I felt that there was some secret in Fanny, some bold message writ in her flesh for me to read, and, as I walked beside her, I was sure that she had recognized something inside me as I had in her.

Fanny's house was on Crook Street, quite near the canal, at the intersection of four alleys which led out from the house like the points of a star. In that part of town there were a number of old Georgian houses, once very fine and fashionable, now receding into shabby-gentility, some derelict, with the rags of ancient curtains hanging at the toothy mouths of their broken windows, others fresh painted and spotless as the false fronts of a theatre backdrop.

Fanny's house was larger than the rest, built of the same soot-grimed London stone, but respectably clean, with bright, heavy curtains at the windows and pots of geraniums on all the sills. In that neighbourhood the house stood out with a kind of countrified incongruity. The door was painted green, with a bright brass knocker and, at the doorstep, sat an enormous striped ginger cat, which mewed when we approached.

'Come in, Alecto,' said Fanny to the cat, opening the door, and the big tabby rolled her boneless weight silently into the hall. 'Please . . .' Fanny gestured for me to follow, and the three of us—Fanny, Mose and I—entered the house. I was struck immediately by the scent; something like sandalwood and cinnamon and wood-smoke, a scent which seemed to come from the furniture and the walls all around us. Then there were the flowers, great vases of them, crimson, purple and gold, on stands in every corner. Tapestries in jewel colours hung on the walls and rich rugs covered the parquet floors.

It seemed to me that I had been magically transported to some Aladdin's cave; in this setting Fanny, as she unpinned her hat, took off her gloves and loosened her hair, was a beauty of awesome, mythical proportions, a giant Scheherazade with no hint of the Haymarket now in her appearance or her bearing, a creature entirely at ease. She guided us through a passageway and past a great sweeping staircase into a cosy drawing-room where a fire had already been lit. Two more cats rested, Sphinx-like, before it.

As I slid into one of the huge, overstuffed armchairs I slipped momentarily out of my body and saw myself, alien in this warm and sensual setting, as pallid as a creature from beneath a stone, and I almost screamed. As the world focused again I saw Mose's face looming towards me like something seen in a fishbowl and I drew away in a kind of inexplicable loathing, with the room spinning about me like a crystal ball and his eyes locked mercilessly into mine.

'Dear girl, you look ill. Drink this.' I clung to Fanny in desperate gratitude as she handed me a drink in a brass goblet; it was warm and sweet, like wine punch, with a distinct aroma of vanilla and allspice.

I tried to smile. 'Thank you,' I said. 'I . . .'

Mose's voice, sharp with suspicion: 'What's that?'

'One of my own recipes,' answered Fanny lazily. 'A restorative, that's all. Don't you trust me?'

'I . . . feel much better,' I said, realizing with some surprise that it was true. 'I . . . I'm sorry I . . .'

'Nonsense!' Fanny's tone was crisp. 'No apologies in this house. Henry may like that kind of foolish submissiveness, but I can't conceive of anything more tiresome.'

'Oh!' I was for a moment unsure whether I should laugh or take offence at Fanny's bluntness; and she had called my husband by his Christian name. And yet, there was a certain rightness in the way she responded to me, a warmth in her familiarity which, in spite of myself, I welcomed. I laughed uneasily and drank the rest of the restorative in one draught. The cats, a white one and a thin brown tabby, left their places at the hearth and came to sniff the hem of my skirts, and I reached out cautiously to stroke them.

'Megaera and Tisiphone,' said Fanny, indicating the cats. 'They seem to like you. You're honoured—they don't usually get on very well with strangers.'

I repeated the names, 'Megaera, Tisiphone and Alecto. What strange names. Do they mean anything?'

'Oh, I have a liking for ancient mythology,' said Fanny carelessly.

'May . . . may I call you Fanny?' I asked.

She nodded. 'Please do. Don't stand on ceremony with me,' she advised. 'I'm old enough to be your mother, though not as respectable, no doubt. Have another drink.' And she refilled the goblet and handed it to me. 'What about you?' She turned to Mose, who had been sitting in the only straight-backed chair in the room, looking like a thwarted child. 'You look as if you could do with a drink.'

'No.'

'I think you should,' insisted Fanny lightly, 'if only to mend your temper.'

Mose forced himself to grin sourly and accepted the proffered glass. 'Thanks.'

'You don't seem very pleased to see me,' said Fanny. 'Doubtless you now have a reputation to uphold. And yet I would never have thought that Henry Chester was your tipple, Mose dear. You must be getting respectable in your declining years!' Mose shifted uneasily and Fanny winked at me and smiled.

'I am, of course, forgetting your new position as Mr Chester's sponsor,' she added. 'Fancy you and Henry becoming friends. I vow you'll be quite sober before the year's out.'

Abruptly she turned to me. 'You're so pretty, my dear,' she said. 'What a tangle you have yourself in, with Henry Chester on the one side and Mose on the other. Scylla and Charybdis. Be careful: Mose is a villain through and through, and Henry . . . well, we both know Henry, I hope. You can be my friend. It would infuriate them both, of course—men have such odd notions of propriety! Imagine Henry's astonishment if he knew! But Henry sees no further than his own canvasses. Even in those eyes of yours, so deep and clear, he sees nothing.'

Her tone was light, her words a shoal of bright fish spelling meaningless patterns around me. The tabby jumped on my lap, and I was happy at the distraction it offered, allowing my hands to move idly in the cat's fur. I tried to concentrate on what Fanny was saying, but my head was spinning. I took another drink to clear my head and, through the veil of unreality through which I perceived the world, I was aware of Mose watching me with an ugly look on his face. I struggled to say something, but my grasp upon drawing-room manners was weak, and instead of the polite comment I had intended I said the first thing which came into my head.

'Is this a bawdy-house?' For a second I froze, appalled at what I had said, then I felt a hot blush sweep me from head to toe. I began to stammer, spilling my drink across my skirts, almost in tears. 'I . . . I . . . I . . .'

But Fanny was laughing, a rich, deep laugh of the kind you might expect from a genie in a bottle. For a moment I was aware of her looming over me and I lost all grasp of scale; she was a giantess, terrifying, awesome in her rich velvet robes, the scent of musk and spices from her generous flesh overwhelming me as she took me in her arms. I could still hear her laughter as the world stabilized around me and my hysteria receded.

'You're quite right, my dear,' she said with a chuckle. 'How refreshing you are! "Is this a bawdy-house?" Mose, the child's a treasure.' I shifted, my face against her shoulder, protesting.

'You've given her too much punch. She's not used to it.' Mose was still disapproving, but I could see that he was smiling in spite of himself. Nervously, through half-shed tears, I too began to laugh.

Suddenly, a thought struck me and, made reckless by the alcohol in the punch and the hilarity of my unshakeable hostess, I voiced it: 'But . . . you said you knew my husband,' I said. 'I . . . *Was* it modelling?'

Fanny shrugged. 'I'm not his style, my love. But from time to time I can find him someone who is. Not always for modelling, either.'

'Oh...' It took some time for the implications of what she had told me to settle into my mind. Henry was unfaithful to me? After all his posturing and preaching, Henry had visited Fanny's house in secret? I was not certain whether to laugh or scream at the bitter farce; I imagine I laughed. To think that during all those years when he was my hero, my Lancelot, he was creeping to her house in Crook Street like a thief in the night! I laughed, but there was a bitterness in my laughter.

Mose, too, had been taken by surprise. 'Henry came here?' he asked incredulously.

'Often. He still does. Every Thursday, just like clockwork.'

'Well, I'll be damned! I'd never have thought that the old hypocrite had it in him. And he goes to church every Sunday, the devil, and proses and preaches as if butter wouldn't melt in his mouth! What's his taste, Fanny?'

Fanny smiled scornfully, but I cut off what she was about to say. Suddenly I knew the answer already.

'Children,' I said in a colourless voice. 'He likes children. He sits me on his knee and makes me call him Mr Chester. He—' I stopped, feeling sick, and broke into an ecstasy of sobs. For the first time I had voiced some of my hatred, my shame and disgust and, as I clung to Fanny Miller, drenching her mulberry velvet with my tears, I felt an inexplicable sense of release.

We talked for some time, Fanny and I, and I learned more of the story she had begun to unfold. She had met Henry—or Mr Lewis, as he called himself to the other visitors—many years ago, and since then he had been coming regularly to her house. Sometimes he would sit in her parlour and drink punch with the other guests, but more often he avoided the rest of her 'company' and went off with one of the girls—always the youngest and least experienced. He usually came on a Thursday, the day he supposedly went to his club.

I listened to this account of Henry's betrayal with an almost indifferent calm. I felt as though all the world had collapsed around me, but instinctively I hid it, holding out my goblet recklessly to be refilled.

'Don't drink any more of that,' said Mose irritably. 'It's getting late. Let's get you back home.'

I shook my head.

'I'd like to stay here for a moment longer,' I said with assumed calm. 'It will be *hours* before Henry gets back from his studio—and even if I am late, he'd never guess where I had been.' I laughed then, with a bitter recklessness. 'Maybe I should tell him!'

'I hope that was an attempt at humour,' said Mose, with a dangerous calm.

'I'm sure you do.' I heard the brittle note in my voice and tried to adopt Fanny's light, confident tone. 'But then, you do have an interest in Henry's continued goodwill. After all, you're seducing his wife, aren't you?'

I saw contempt and anger in his face, but was unable to stop. 'You have an odd notion of propriety,' I added. 'I dare say you think a man can get away with any crime, any betrayal, as long as appearances are safeguarded. I don't suppose it matters at all to you whether I suffer or not.'

'You're overwrought,' he snapped coldly.

'Not at all!' My laugh was shrill. 'I expect you to know all about pretence—after all, you're an expert.'

'What are you talking about?'

Suddenly I was no longer sure. For a moment I had felt such overwhelming rage that I had allowed it to overflow ... but at this moment the rancour seemed not to be my own but someone else's—someone much braver and stronger than myself . . . some stranger.

What *had* I wanted? It seemed nebulous now, like the vestige of some dream, dissolving into nothing as I awoke.

'I . . . I'm sorry, Mose: I didn't mean it. Please, let's not go so soon.' My voice was pleading, but he was not moved. I saw his blue eyes narrowed into slits like razors and he turned away rather abruptly, his voice icy.

'You knew I didn't want to come here,' he said. 'I came for *your* sake. Now, leave for mine or, by God, I'll leave without you.'

'Mose . . .'

'Try to have a little understanding, Mose my dear,' said Fanny in her mocking tone. 'Effie has had rather a rude awakening, wouldn't you say? Or would you rather have had her kept in blissful ignorance?'

Mose turned to both of us with an ugly expression. 'I won't let two whores give me orders!' he spat. 'Effie, I bear with your tears and tantrums. I was the one who almost got arrested today because of your hysterics. I love you as much as I have ever loved any woman, but this is the outside of enough. I won't be defied, especially not under this roof. Now, will you come home?'

Two whores. The words sank like stones, silently into the darkness of my thought. Two whores . . . He reached for my arm to steady it and I knocked his hand aside. The cat hissed wildly at him and sprang out of the chair to hide under the dresser.

'Don't touch me!'

'Effie—'

'Get out!'

'Just listen to me a moment . . .'

I turned to him and looked at him flatly. For the first time I saw the lines of tension around his mouth, the cold blankness at the back of his eyes.

'Get out,' I said. 'You disgust me. I'll get home on my own. I never want to see you again.'

For a moment his face was slack, then his mouth twisted.

'Why you impudent little—'

'Get out, I said!'

'There'll be a reckoning for this,' he said in a soft and ugly tone.

'Get *out*!'

For an uneasy time he was frozen, his arms folded defensively, and in some way I sensed that he was afraid, as if some lap-dog had suddenly learned to bite, and the knowledge of his fear was rapturous in me, so that the sickness receded, elation flooded my body and some savage voice in me sang *bite, bite, bite, bite, bite* . . . Then he turned with a shrug and left the room, slamming the door behind him. I collapsed, all my triumph dissolving into wretched tears.

Fanny let me cry for a minute, then, very gently, she put her arm around my shoulders.

'You love him, don't you?'

'I . . .'

'*Don't* you?'

'I think so.'

She nodded. 'You'd better go after him, my dear,' she told me. 'I know you'll be back. Here . . .' And, lifting up the tabby, who had returned to sit next to me as soon as Mose had left the room, she placed it in my arms. 'Tizzy seems to like you. Take her with you—look after her and she'll be a good friend to you. I can see in your eyes what a lonely thing it is to be married to Henry Chester.'

I nodded, holding the cat tightly against me.

'Can I come and see you again?'

'Of course. Come whenever you like. Goodbye, Marta.'

'What did you say?'

'I said, "Goodbye, my dear".'

'I thought you said . . .'

'Shh,' she interrupted. 'You go now, and remember what I said. Be *careful*.'

I looked into her strange eyes and saw nothing there but reflections. But she was still smiling as she took me by the arm and pushed me gently out on to the street.

17

The bitch. The bitch! Bitches, both of them. As I made my way back to my own lodgings seething with the injustice of her treatment of me, I nearly resolved to abandon the whole thing, to leave her to her Puritan husband and good riddance to them both. Or maybe a nice little anonymous letter, packed with intimate details . . . that might put a few pigeons in with the cat. *That* would teach her. But behind my anger there was unease. It was not simply a question of revenge, was it? No. It was the fact that I had been wrong about her, that the Ace of Wands had proved himself a Fool of the first water, that I had underestimated my little Eff, that I had been utterly, indubitably wrong in thinking that I had her under my thumb . . . And she had chosen to defy me in front of Fanny, *Fanny*, of all people!

Well, if she wanted Fanny, I'd give her Fanny. The right word in Henry's ear and he'd divorce her like a shot. What? You don't believe it? A few selected details and he'd not bear to look at her again. She'd be penniless, with no-one to turn to—don't think her mother would have her back after the mess she made of the fine marriage she had arranged. Vulgar? Yes, let's be vulgar. Alone and penniless, I said; and with no-one to turn to but friend Fanny.

She'd be filling a room for her in a month, along with the other girls. And all I had to do . . . Well, maybe I'd do that when I tired of her. But for the moment I still wanted the chit. She was a stunner, after all, and besides, the news that she did have a bit of spirit was not altogether unwelcome. But *Fanny*!

That was what hurt.

Oh, she came back quickly enough. I knew she didn't have the character to stand up to me for long, and I wasn't surprised when she came running out of the house a couple of minutes after I had left it. It wasn't her silly little hysterical outburst which bothered me, but the way she and Fanny had joined together against me, almost instinctively, like members of some secret sisterhood. We drove back to Cromwell Square in silence, she watching me warily from under the brim of her bonnet, I staring straight ahead, immersed in my bitter thoughts. By the time we reached Highgate she was sniffling furtively and I was feeling much better.

Never mind, I thought, Fanny wouldn't be there to influence her for ever. Once Effie was mine again I'd frighten her a bit, make her cry and the whole episode would be forgotten. For a while, anyway.

For a day or two I played a cool game. I missed our meetings in the graveyard and I let her hear me drive past the house as I returned from the studio. At the end of the week, Henry invited me over to dinner and I stayed aloof, talking a great deal about art and politics to Henry and almost ignoring poor little Eff. I noticed that she was rather pale and that she sometimes looked at me anxiously, but I ignored that and continued monstrously cheerful for the rest of the evening, drinking deep, laughing loud and yet allowing her to guess at my broken heart. Kean could not have acted the part with more virtuosity.

For some reason Henry seemed out of all temper with Effie. On the rare occasions she hazarded a comment on some subject at dinner he showed himself impatient and sarcastic, tolerating her simply because I was there. If I had not been present, I am certain that he could not have been in her company without starting a quarrel. I pretended to notice nothing, deliberately failing to catch her eye.

Over the meal Henry again voiced his desire to see Effie model for the figure of the woman. 'But,' he said, 'I really wanted a dark model. I think a fair-haired model would lack *substance* in this type of canvas.' He hesitated. 'Of course, Effie could sit for the basic outline, the position and the face,' he said. 'And I could paint the hair from some other model.' He seemed to consider this for a time. 'I dare say that might be the answer. What do you think, Harper?'

I nodded, studying Effie appraisingly, to her obvious discomfort. 'I noticed a fair down by the Islington Road,' I said innocently. 'Likely you could find some gypsy girl with the right kind of hair who could sit for you.' Out of the corner of my eye I saw Effie wince at the reference to the fair, and grinned inwardly.

'I want to make a start on the woman's figure as soon as possible,' continued Henry. 'For the present the weather is cool enough but when the heat of high summer comes, Effie's health suffers if she has to sit for hours in the studio.'

Effie stirred restlessly, picking up her fork, then laying it down without touching her food. 'I thought . . .' she said, almost in a whisper.

'What is it?' His impatience was palpable. 'Speak up, girl.'

'I thought you said that I didn't have to go to the studio any more. My headaches . . .'

'I said that you were not to go there when you were ill. You are *not* ill, and I don't see why I should have the expense of a model to bear, along with all our other expenses, when I have you.'

Effie made a vague, aimless gesture with her hands, as if to ward off the suggestion.

'And, as for your headaches, there's nothing there that a little laudanum could not cure. Come now, Harper,' he said, turning to me with renewed good cheer, 'I've a damned fine claret in my cellar today. You shall have some and tell me what you think of it.' And at that he turned and left us together. No sooner had the door closed than she was on her feet, her eyes swimming and her hands clapped to her mouth. I knew then that she was all mine again.

'Meet me tonight, Effie,' I whispered urgently. 'By the Circle of Lebanon at midnight.'

Her eyes widened. 'But, Mose . . .'

'If you care for me, be there,' I hissed, narrowing my eyes at her. 'If you're not there I'll take it that you don't—and believe me, I'll live.' Though I was still grinning inside I manufactured a sneer and looked away as Henry walked in again, just on cue. Effie turned her face away, white to the lips, and I wondered for a moment whether she really was ill. Then I caught her watching me, and realized that she was simply playing another of her games; oh, believe me, Effie wasn't the simple little innocent you all thought she was; none of you saw through to the dark, hidden core of her heart. Effie made fools of us all in the end. Even me.

18

Before I met Mose I never knew how bleak my life was; now that it seemed I might lose him, I felt I might go mad. My memory of what had provoked the quarrel at Fanny's house was so vague that I felt as if it had happened to some other girl, someone assured and strong. I waited for Mose in vain in all our usual meeting-places and I spent hours at the windows watching the street—but he did not come. Even my poetry was no consolation to me then; I was restless, twitching like a cat, unable to spend more than a minute or two at any occupation so that Henry swore that I was driving him out of his mind with my constant fluttering.

I took laudanum, but instead of calming my nerves the drug seemed to induce a kind of dim paralysis of the senses, so that I wanted to move but could not, wanted to see, smell, speak, but could only sense the world through fantasies and waking dreams.

Tabby made chocolate and cakes for me which I would not touch; irritably I snapped at her to leave me alone and immediately regretted it. I put my arms around her and promised to drink her chocolate. I was only tired, I didn't mean to snap; surely she knew that? She smelled of camphor and baking and, shyly, her hand crept up to stroke my hair. I could almost have imagined myself back at Cranbourn Alley again, with Mother and Tabby and Aunt May baking cakes in the kitchen. I clung to her sleeve, shaking with loneliness.

Henry believed that I was feigning illness to avoid modelling for him. My headaches were the result of idleness, he said; my embroidery was neglected; I had not been seen in church on a weekday for over a sennight; I was wilful and ill-tempered, stupid in my vague responses to his questions, ridiculously awkward with guests. He disapproved of Tizzy, too, saying that it was ridiculous that I should bring in a stray cat to the house without his permission, childish folly to let it lie on my bed at night or in my lap by day.

As if to prove to me that no concession would be made to my imaginary illness, Henry invited guests to dinner twice in a week—though this was an unusual occurrence as a rule—the first time a doctor named Russell, a friend from his club, a thin, clever-faced little man who looked at me with odd intensity from behind the wire frames of his spectacles and talked at length about manias and phobias; the second time Mose, his eyes hard and bright, his smile a razor's edge.

By the time he set me that dreadful ultimatum my nerves were so ragged, my loneliness so intense that I would have done any-thing to win him back to me, whether he loved me or not.

Very likely you think me a feeble, contemptible creature. I do myself, I know. I was quite aware that I was being punished for my brief revolt against him at Fanny's house; if he had wanted to see me he could easily have done so by day, or at least in his rooms; no doubt he thought that the cemetery at midnight, with its shadows, its prowlers, was the ideal setting for the scene of cruel reconciliation I was to share with him. Guessing this, I could not help hating him a little in some hidden part of my heart, but the rest of me loved and wanted him with such a bitter longing that I was prepared to walk into the fire if he asked me to.

Leaving the house was easy; Tabby and Em slept under the roof in the old servants' quarters—Edwin had his own cottage down the High Street and stopped work when night fell—and Henry slept deeply as a rule, going to bed quite early. At half past eleven I crept out of my room, shielding the candlelight with my hand. I had taken care to wear only a dark flannel dress, with no petticoats, so that I would be silent in the passageway, and so it was in almost total quiet that I drifted down the stairs and into the kitchen. The keys were hanging by the door and, holding my breath, I took the heavy housekey, opened the door and slipped out into the night.

Tizzy was sitting by the door and wound her way around my ankles, purring. For a moment I hesitated, reluctant to leave, feeling oddly comforted by the cat's presence and half inclined to bundle her in my cloak and take her along. Then, inwardly chiding myself, I pulled the hood of my cloak over my head, shivering, and began to run.

I saw few people as I made my way up Highgate to the cemetery; a child running from the public-house with a pint of ale in a pitcher, a beggar woman wrapped in a ragged shawl wandering listlessly from door to door. At the corner of the street a group of men passed me, smelling of ale, talking in loud voices and clinging to each other as they made their way home. One of them shouted something at me as I ran past them, but they did not follow me. As the streetlamps became wider spaced I tried to merge into the darkness, and after about ten minutes I found myself in front of the great black shape of the cemetery, sprawling against the glowing London sky like a sleeping dragon. It was very quiet, and I was conscious of a quickening of the heart as I moved towards the gates. There was no sign of the night-watchman, and no reason for me to delay, but I stayed fixed to the spot for some time, helplessly watching those gates with the same morbid fascination I had felt as I watched the flap of the red tent open, that day at the fair.

A fleeting memory awakened at the thought, and I imagined those thousands of dead sitting up at my approach, their heads poking out of the stony ground like clockwork toys. The image, there in that thick darkness, was almost too much for me to bear, but remembering that Mose was waiting for me barely a few hundred yards away gave me courage; Mose was not afraid of the dead, nor even the living—he positively revelled in stories of the grotesque and terrifying. He had told me the tale of the woman buried alive; of how she had been found suffocated, her stiff hands clawing the air, her face only a few inches away from the surface, her fingers worn down to the bone as she had tried to dig her way out. And in the year of the cholera epidemic the dead were so many that they had to be buried in mass graves, unmarked and covered with quicklime. The corpses were so numerous that the heat of their decomposition had driven some of them to the surface, where they had been discovered later by two lovers in the cemetery, four heads sticking up out of the ground like huge mushrooms, stinking of death. Mose knew how much I hated his stories; I think that was why he told them, to make fun of my weakness; and I had never before thought how much cruelty there was in his laughter.

The darkness here was almost complete; there were no gaslamps in the cemetery and the moon was a poor, shivering thing, casting a dim corpse-light on to the stones. The scent of earth and darkness was overwhelming; I could pick out the trees by their smell as I passed them: the cedars, laburnums, yews, rhododendrons. From time to time I stumbled against a broken stone or a stump, and the sound of my footsteps terrified me even more than the dense, threatening silence. Once I thought I heard footsteps somewhere behind me and I shrank behind a vault, my heart's pounding shaking the whole of my body. The footsteps were heavy and, as I remained motionless in the black shadow, I thought I could hear the sound of someone breathing, a thick asthmatic sound like a bellows.

I was almost at the Circle of Lebanon now, with only the long alley of trees to navigate before I reached its safety, but I could not move, sick with terror. For an instant my sanity spiralled away into the night like a shower of confetti; I was left in a timeless wilderness, horribly far from the light. Then, as my power of thought returned, I felt the world stabilize a little. I slipped to my knees, feeling my way along the side of the vault with fingers which had suddenly become miraculous points of sensation. Silently I crawled. As the footsteps moved closer I froze again, straining my eyes in vain for any sign to identify the intruder. I felt mud and water seep through my skirts, but flattened myself against the ground regardless, pulling my hood over my hair so that its whiteness should not betray me. The footsteps came closer still; now they were almost upon me. I held my breath, tasting eternity. The footsteps had stopped. Glancing over my shoulder like Orpheus, in spite of myself, I saw a man's shape against the dim sky, impossibly huge and menacing, his eyes two points of brightness in the eye of the night.

The
Moon

19

I know, I know. I was deliberately cruel. And I enjoyed it, too, stalking her through the graves as panic overtook her, watching her trying to hide, falling, slipping, and finally running her to earth, picking her up from the muddy path and having her cling to me like a child, her tears soaking the loose hair which straggled around her face. Now I could afford to be generous; she was mine once more.

As I comforted her, I began at last to understand a little of Henry Chester; the power I had over her was fundamentally erotic, her tears the strongest of aphrodisiacs. For the first time in my dissolute life a woman was mine, body and soul. She was poignantly eager to please, devouring my face with her lips in sweet repentance. She swore she would never try to defy me again and in the same breath vowed she would die if I abandoned her, spinning me in a carousel of different sensations. I fell in love with her all over again; the moment I had begun to think I might tire of her she had come to me, renewed.

Wild words gasped in darkness against my salt hair: 'Oh, Mose . . . it tears me body from soul . . . I need you . . . I'll never let you go, never let you leave me . . . I'd kill you, rather . . .' She took a ragged breath, her pale face turning towards mine. For a moment, a trick of reflection from the distant streetlamps revealed her features in dramatic light and shade; her huge eyes black and stark, her lips bruised with shadow, her lovely face distorted in such a grimace of thwarted passion that for a moment I felt uneasy. She looked like some vengeful black angel with madness and death in her outstretched arms. She had already shed her outer clothing and her skin glistened livid in the strange light. She took a step forwards, my name in her mouth like a curse, then she was in my arms with a scent like lavender and earth and sweat clinging to her skin. We made love where we stood, she murmuring her mad nonsense all the time. Afterwards I felt convinced that somehow, in the black climax of my passion, I had made a promise which later I might be required to keep.

Effie was sitting on a gravestone, curled up like a child and shivering; putting my hand on her forehead I realized that she was feverish, and I tried to persuade her to dress quickly, so that she should not catch cold. She hardly responded, looking at me with blank, tragic eyes, and I felt my earlier irritation returning.

'Can't you help me, for God's sake?' I snapped as I struggled with the fastenings on her dress.

Effie continued to stare at me through the blackness like a drowned girl under a lake.

'Come on, Effie, you can't stay here all night,' I said in a gentler tone. 'You'll have to get back home before Henry finds out you've been gone.'

But Effie just sat. She looked ill, her skin white and burning as sulphur. I could not send her back to Cromwell Square in such a state unless I wanted the whole scandalous affair made public; equally, I could not let her stay in the churchyard; it was cold—even I had begun to shiver—and she was already feverish. On top of that she needed a change of clothes; her own were muddy, the hem of her dress torn. There remained only one option and, as I examined it, I felt a hot grin forming around the region of my stomach; there was a certain poetry in the idea . . .

'Come on, my dear,' I said briskly, hoisting Effie to her feet. 'I'm taking you to see Fanny. I'll see that she lets you wash and gives you some clean clothes, then you'll be able to get home before the servants are up.'

Impossible to tell whether she had heard me; but she allowed herself to be manoeuvred along the path towards the street. Once she started at a sound from behind us, her pointed fingernails scoring the flesh of my wrists, but for the most part she was passive. I left her standing by the gate as I found a hackney and I saw the coachman's brows twitch as I lifted her in—a guinea in the hot palm of his hand soon put stop to his curiosity—but otherwise the few passers-by did not spare us a glance. All the better.

The house in Crook Street was lit up, of course, and the door was answered by a remarkably pretty red-haired girl who beckoned me in. Effie followed me without protest, and I left her with the pretty girl as I went in search of Fanny.

I have to say that Fanny always kept a genteel house: a card-room, a smoking-room, a parlour in which gentlemen relaxed in the opulent surroundings and talked to the ladies. She never allowed lewd behaviour in these rooms—for that there were private rooms on the first floor—and anyone failing to meet her standards was politely barred from the establishment thereafter. I have known gentry who were not so discriminating as Fanny Miller.

I found her in the smoking-room—she had always had a taste for those thin black cigars—fetchingly if eccentrically clad in a tasselled purple hat and matching smoking-jacket. Her tawny curls, barely restrained by a couple of amethyst clasps, glinted against the dull velvet. One of her cats stared coldly at me from her knee.

'Why, Mose,' she said with sweet composure, 'what brings you here?'

'A trifling problem,' I replied lightly, 'and a mutual friend. Could I impose for a moment?' This last remark addressed Fanny's smoking companion, an elderly gentleman with a wavering hand and a roguish expression.

Fanny's agate eyes travelled from my muddy shoes to my face and back. 'Do excuse me,' she said to her elderly friend and, leaving her cigar in a china ashtray and removing her cap and jacket, followed me into the passageway. 'Well, what is it?' she demanded, rather less sweetly.

'Effie's here.'

'*What*?' Suddenly the eyes were hard pinpoints of fire. 'Where is she?'

I did not understand her sudden fury, and I began to explain briefly what had happened. She cut me off with an angry gesture. 'For God's sake, be quiet!' she hissed. 'Where *is* she?' I mentioned the girl with whom I had left Effie, and without another glance at me Fanny was off up the stairs, her beautiful mouth set in a furious line.

'What's the problem?' I called after her, grabbing the sleeve of her velvet gown. She spun round, her hand raised to strike mine away; it was with a great effort of will that she did not. When she spoke it was with a venomous calm.

'Henry's here too,' she said.

20

Somehow I seemed to recognize the room. As I drifted, my spirit coiling half in and half out of my body like a genie from a bottle, I seemed to see the little bed with its patchwork quilt, the table, the stool, the pictures on the wall, with the eyes of memory. Mose, Henry, the strange insanity which had overpowered me in the graveyard were reduced to the level of dreams, myself a dream's dream in the floating dark. I vaguely remembered arriving at the house in Crook Street, being led upstairs . . . friendly hands in mine; faces; names. A girl about my own age with bright copper hair and emeralds in her ears: Izzy. A plump, good-natured lady, bodice cut very low over opulent white breasts: Violet. A tiny Chinese girl with hair like jet and a jade ring on every finger: Gabriel Chau.

I remembered their names, their voices, the soft mingling of scents on their powdered skin as they undressed me and washed my face in warm scented water . . . then all was blank for a time, and now I was clean and comfortable in the narrow white bed, wearing a child's ruffled linen nightdress, my hair combed and braided for sleep. I dozed for a while and awoke calling for my mother, aged ten again and afraid of the dark. Then Fanny came to bring me a drink of something warm and sweet; but in my mind Fanny became confused with my mother, and I began to cry weakly.

'Don't let him come back...' I begged. 'Don't let him in, don't let the Bad Man in!' For some reason I was afraid Henry would come in and hurt me, though Henry was in bed miles away, and in my feverish confusion I clung to Fanny and called her 'Mother' and cried. There must have been laudanum in the drink, because I slept again for a while, and when I awoke, my head ringing and my mouth dry and slack, I was afraid. I sat up abruptly in bed, thinking I heard someone standing outside the door. A floorboard creaked and, looking at the thin seam of light under the door, I saw the shadow of somebody standing there, heard his low, harsh breathing against the panels. A huge, delirious panic seized me then, and I tried to flatten myself against the foot of the bed, the quilt around my face, but even in the sounds of the bedclothes the breathing continued in my head, and I thought I could hear a creak of metal against wood as the predator began to turn the door-handle. In spite of myself I had to look as the seam of light became a broader and broader ribbon, revealing a man's square outline in the doorway.

Henry!

For a moment, I was not sure whether the drug I had taken was giving me delusions; all rational thought was suspended by stark terror, and again I began to lose my knowledge of my own identity. I was no longer Effie, but someone younger, a child, a wraith...

'Who's there?' His voice was sharp, but not with anger; I could almost fancy he sounded uneasy. When I did not answer I heard his voice rise, almost shrilly. 'I said, who's there? I can hear you. Who is it?'

I shifted helplessly and Henry took a step forwards.

'I can hear you, you little witch. I can hear you in the dark. Who are you?'

In a voice which was not my own I uttered the first name which came into my head.

'Marta . . . Marta Miller. Please—leave me alone, go away.' But Henry had taken a step forwards when he heard the name. He was three feet away from me and, although he could not see me, I could see his face in the landing-light, staring and distorted with something like fear.

'Let me see you.' There was more than urgency in his voice. 'Come into the light so that I can see you!' He grabbed at me, and I pulled away, sliding over the bedpost so that I was hidden in its deeper shadow. I hit my foot against the bed as I fell, and I cried out sharply. 'Please! Leave me alone! Go away!'

Henry cursed softly and took another step into the dark.

'I won't hurt you. I promise.' His voice was ragged, pretending softness. 'I just want to see your face. *Damn*!' he cursed as he kicked blindly against the bedstand. 'I said come here, by hell!'

Suddenly there was a sound of hurried footsteps on the landing; I glanced over the bedpost, and there was Fanny, a tray of milk and biscuits in one hand, one eyebrow cocked in cool astonishment. Henry was out of the room in a second; as I saw them together on the landing for the first time I was amazed at how tall Fanny appeared; she dwarfed Henry gloriously, dazzling as some Egyptian goddess. He almost visibly shrank from her, holding out his hands, placatingly.

'Who's that in there?' he asked, his tone almost apologetic.

Fanny's smile was as bright and cold as broken glass.

'My niece, Marta,' she said. 'She's ill with the fever, delirious. Why do you ask?' There was a challenge in the question, but Henry shifted his gaze uneasily, unwilling to take it up.

'I heard sounds . . .' he began vaguely. 'I . . . They made me

nervous. And she wouldn't show herself, the naughty thing. I—'
He broke off with a forced laugh. 'I never knew you had a niece.'
There was a question in the remark.

'You'll see her one day,' promised Fanny. She stepped into the
room, put the tray on the bedstand and closed the door.

'Come now, Henry,' she said firmly as he seemed to linger, and
I heard their footsteps grow fainter as they walked down the passageway towards the stairs.

21

It was almost dawn when I reached Cromwell Square and I was exhausted, my mind clouded with drink and the savage perfume of that house, a sultry combination of incense, smoke and the feral reek of cats and women. As a penance I had forbidden myself to take a cab home but in spite of it all I felt a continuing sense of filthy satisfaction which no amount of walking could obliterate. She had been young—about fifteen, by no means as young as Fanny had promised—and pretty, with curling brown hair and vivid rosy cheeks. She was no virgin, but was prepared to enact the part for me, pretending her reluctance and even crying real tears for me.

Don't look at me like that! She was only a whore, paid to do my bidding; if she hadn't enjoyed it she would have looked for some more decent profession. As it was, a golden guinea soon dried her tears, and it was not ten minutes afterwards that I saw her cheerfully going back upstairs with another customer. Your sympathy is entirely wasted on such creatures, I assure you: from the earliest age they are corrupt beyond belief. At least I was able to slake my guilty thirst upon them, rather than upon Effie. It was for *her* sake that I did as I did: believe me when I say that in my heart I did not betray her. She was my icon of purity, my sleeping princess . . . I knew she had the seeds of debauchery in her, but it was up to me to ensure that they should never be allowed to grow. My love could keep her chaste and whatever sacrifices that entailed I was willing to make them for her sake.

Oh, there were lapses. At times her latent sensuality was such that I could not help a momentary weakness, but forgave her her nature, even though she cheapened herself in my eyes, just as I forgave my mother for causing that first unforgivable lapse of mine.

I crept past Effie's room and opened the door to my own. It was dark and I could barely make out the shapes of the washstand, the bed and the wardrobe in the candlelight. I pulled the door closed behind me and set the candle on the mantelpiece. I stripped off my clothes and turned towards the bed—then caught my breath in shock. In the glimmering shadows I could see a child's face against my pillow: eldritch green eyes glinting in a fierce and vengeful expression of hatred.

It was nonsense, of course: there *was* no child. How could it have come into my bed at dead of night? There *was* no child. To prove it I forced myself to look closer. The livid gaze fixed mine once again; this time I caught sight of needle-sharp teeth bared in a snarl. Recoiling, I grabbed the candle. Dragging the long flame in a streamer of smoke behind me I thrust it at the apparition, spraying hot wax on to the bedclothes and on to my naked skin. The creature leaped at me, jaws open in sibilant defiance—and with a mixture of anger and desperate relief I recognized the thin brown shape of Effie's cat as it slashed past me into the darkness, vanishing between the curtains and out through the open window.

My face in the wardrobe mirror was mottled with livid marks, and my mouth was bracketed with tension.

I was furious with myself that a mere cat should have caused me such unreasoning terror, and even more furious with Effie, who had taken in the stray on some ridiculous whim. What name had she given it? Tisiphone? Some outlandish nonsense from one of her books, I supposed: I knew I had not found them all. In the morning, I promised myself, I would give her room a thorough search to find what she had been hiding from me. And as for that cat . . . I shook my head to dispel the image of the face on my pillow, green eyes glaring rank hatred into mine . . . Only a cat. All the same, I took ten grains of chloral, a new drug recommended by my new friend Dr Russell, before I could bear to lay my head on that pillow.

22

I remember her cool, strong hand against my hair. Her face in the lamplight, white as the moon. The sounds of her dress; the scent of her perfume, warm and golden with amber and chypre. Her voice, low and calm, singing without words in time to her rhythmic stroking of my hair. *Low adown . . . low adown.* Henry was a bad dream, melting away now into a million little teardrops of light. The clock on the mantelpiece ticked away a heartbeat stronger than my own: my heart was light as a dandelion clock, counting off moments into a warm summer night like silken seeds. My eyes were closed, gentle dream-thoughts spindling away into the welcome darkness of sleep. Fanny's voice was speaking very gently, very sweetly, every word a caress.

'Shh . . . sleep. Sleep, little girl . . . so sleepy . . . shhh . . .' I smiled and murmured as the fronds of her hair brushed against my face.

'That's right. Shh . . . Sleep, my darling, my Marta, my love.'

Rocked in the cradle of her arms I allowed myself to drift gently. As she stroked my hair I watched my memories drift away like floating balloons. Mose . . . the graveyard . . . the exhibition . . . Henry . . . However bright the memory I could will it to float away and, after a time, I saw the bright cloud of balloons, strings entwined, colours glowing in the setting sun. It was such a beautiful sight that I think I spoke aloud, in a lost little-girl's voice.

'Balloons, Mother, all floating away. Where are they going?'

Her voice was barely audible against my hair. 'Far, far away. They're floating up into the sky, right into the clouds . . . and they're all different colours, red, yellow, blue . . . Can you see them?'

I nodded.

'Float with them for a while. Can you do that?'

I nodded again.

'Feel yourself going up . . . up into the air with the balloons. That's right. Shh . . .'

I realized I was beginning to rise without momentum simply by thinking about it. I rose right out of my body, drifting, the peaceful image of the balloons still in my dreaming mind.

'You floated like this before,' said Fanny gently. 'Do you remember?'

'I remember.' My voice was no more than a wisp, but she heard.

'In the fairground,' insisted Fanny.

'Yes.'

'Could you go there again?'

'I . . . I don't want to. I want to go with the balloons.'

'Shh, darling . . . it's all right. Nothing can hurt you. I just need your help. I want you to go back and tell me what you can see. Tell me his name.'

I was floating in a sky so blue that it hurt to look. Over the horizon I could see balloons rising. Beneath me, a long way down, I could see the tents and the awnings of the fair.

'Tents . . .' I murmured.

'Go down. Go to the tent and look in.'

'N-no . . . I . . .'

'It's all right. Nothing can hurt you. Go down. What do you see?'

'Pictures. Statues. No, waxworks.'

'Closer.'

'No ...'

'Closer!'

Suddenly I was there again. I was ten years old, curled up against the wall of my bedroom as the Bad Man came towards me with lust and murder in his eyes.

I screamed. 'No! Mother! Don't let him! Don't let the Bad Man come! Don't let that Bad Man come!'

In the red haze of my drumming blood I heard her voice, still very calm: 'Who, Marta?'

'No-oh-ohh!'

'Tell me *who*?'

And I looked into his face. The terror peaked, a frozen eternity ... then I knew him. The terror fell away and I awoke, Fanny's strong arms around me, my tears soaking into the crushed velvet of her gown.

Very gently she repeated, 'Tell me who.'

After a moment I told her.

My mother held me close.

23

I suppose a century ago they would have called me a witch. Well, I've been called worse things, some of them true, and what people think has never been a worry to me. I can make up a broth that will calm a fever or brew a posset for dreams of flying, and sometimes, in my mirror, I can see things which aren't reflections. I know what Henry Chester would call that: but then again I have my own terms for the likes of Henry Chester, and not ones you'd find in the Authorized Version, either.

If it hadn't been for Henry Chester, Marta would have been twenty years old this July. I'm rich enough to have left her a tidy fortune: there'd have been no danger of her walking the streets. I'd have found her a house, a husband if she wanted one; anything she asked for I'd have given her. But when she was ten years old Henry Chester took her from me, and I waited ten years to take his Effie from him. I've not had much time in my life for poetry, but there's fearful symmetry in that pattern, and that's justice enough for me. Cold, to be sure, but none the less bitter for that.

I was young when I gave birth to Marta, in as much as I was ever young. She might have had thirty fathers but I didn't care.

She was all mine . . . and, as she grew, I took pains to shelter her from the kind of life I was living. I sent her to a good school and gave her the education I never had; I bought her clothes and toys and gave her a respectable home with a schoolteacher, a distant relative of my mother. Marta came to see me as often as I dared invite her—I did not want her to be exposed to the kinds of people who came to my house, and I never allowed any of my clients up to the little attic I made into a bedroom for her. I invited her to my house for her birthday and, although that evening I was expecting guests, I had promised I would make up for neglecting her. I kissed her goodnight . . . and I never saw her alive again.

At ten o'clock I heard her calling me and I ran up to her room . . . but she was already dead, lying sprawled across the bed with her nightdress around her face.

I knew the murderer had to be one of my clients, but the police simply laughed at me when I demanded they investigate. I was a prostitute, my daughter a prostitute's daughter. And the clients were wealthy, respectable men. I was lucky not to be arrested myself. As a result my daughter was buried under white marble in Highgate cemetery and her murderer was allowed to forget her for ten years.

Oh, I tried to find him out. I *knew* he was there: I smelled his guilt behind his respectable façade. Do you know what hate is? Hate was what I ate and drank. In my dreams hate walked alongside me as I stalked my daughter's murderer and painted the streets of London with his blood.

I kept Marta's room just as she had left it, with fresh flowers on the bedstand and all her toys in a basket in the corner. Every night I crept up there and I called her—I knew she was there—begging her to give me a name: just a name. If she had given me a name in those early days I would have killed him without the slightest remorse. I would have gone to the gallows in Biblical glory. But in ten years my hate grew hungry and lean, like a starving wolf. It grew clever and slinking, watching everyone with the same suspicious amber eye: everyone, and one man in particular.

Remember, I knew him: I knew his eager, shameful appetites, his abrupt self-loathings, his guilt. The girls he asked for were always the youngest, the unformed ones, the virgins. Not that there were many of *them*, but I'd seen him watching the beggar-children in the street, and I'd seen his paintings, the old hypocrite: sick longings fit to make an honest woman choke. But he wasn't the only one I suspected and I couldn't be sure. I tried to reach my little Marta; at first with candles and the mirror, then with the cards. Always the same cards: the Hermit, the Star, the High Priestess, the Knave of Coins, Change and Death. Always the same cards in differing order: always the Hermit flanked by the Nine of Swords and the Death card. But was Henry Chester the Hermit?

He was clever, you understand. If he'd run I would have known for sure; but he was a cold one. He kept coming, not often, maybe once a month; always polite, always generous. I followed other quarry: men who, too abruptly, had stopped visiting after Marta's death. A doctor, one of my long-standing clients, suggesting that my little girl had died of some kind of a fit; epilepsy, he said. I didn't believe it for a minute. But pain and time eroded my conviction; I began to doubt the purity of my hate. Maybe it *had* been a fit, or an intruder, lured by the prospect of easy pickings. Inconceivable that one of my clients could have committed such an act and remained hidden for so long.

My vengeance slept. Then I learned that Henry had married. A child scarcely out of the schoolroom, they said. A girl of seventeen. Suspicion woke again in me—I'd never been sure of him, never—and my hate went out to them both like a swarm of wasps. What right had they to happiness when Marta was rotting in Highgate? What right had anyone?

I followed them to church one day, hoping to catch a glimpse of the bride, but she was all swathed in black, like a mourner, and I could only see her thin little face under her bonnet. She looked ill and I could not help but feel a drawing-towards her, something which was almost pity. She looked so like my poor lost Marta.

I've no liking for preachers: I'd come to see Chester and his wife, not to listen to the sermon, and so I was the first one to see her go. One minute she was listening, the next she was gone, her head tilting forwards like a child saying her prayers. Now, I've long had the knack of seeing things that most of you don't, or won't see, and as soon as Mrs Chester fell I could see that it was no ordinary faint. I saw her pop out of the body, naked as the day she was born, bless her, and, judging by the look of surprise on her face, I'd guess it was the first time it had happened to her.

A pretty thing she was too, not a bit like Henry Chester's ethereal paintings, with a beauty natural to herself, like a tree or a cloud. No-one else could see her—and I don't wonder, in all that army of churchgoers. No-one had taught her *that* trick: she must have learned it all by herself, and I guessed she had other talents she didn't know about. Right there and then I wondered whether she might not know something that could help me . . . I called her, in my mind, and she looked at me sharp as a needle: I knew then that she was the answer to all my questions. All I had to do was bring her to me.

Her name was Effie and I watched her many times without her knowledge, calling her to me from Marta's little room at the top of my house. I saw she was unhappy, first with Henry, then with Mose. Poor, lonely little girl: I knew it would only be a question of time before I brought her to me and I began to care for her like a daughter. I knew her mind, her haunts . . . and when I saw her at the fair I knew that this was my chance to talk to her alone.

The crystal-gazer was happy enough to give me her place for the price of a guinea: I sat in the shadows with a veil across my face and Effie didn't suspect a thing. She was so sensitive to my thoughts that I didn't even have to put her to sleep: she did it herself . . . but even so, it was not until she began to speak to me in my daughter's voice that I truly realized how unique, how precious she could be to me. If she could bring back the voice so clearly, what else might she be capable of? My head was spinning with the possibilities: to *see* my little girl again, to *touch* her . . . why not? Believe me, I wished Effie no harm, but her reaction on being jolted out of her trance astonished even me. The girl was too precious to lose; I *couldn't* let her go.

Sure enough, before I had to delve too far, she gave me the name I wanted. Henry Chester, the Hermit, the murderer of my daughter . . .

I was past the age now of wanting to scream my rebellion on the scaffold. If there was to be a sacrifice, this time it would not be me.

24

It was an accident, I tell you. I never meant to kill her. I was going to tell you about it, but it was so long ago . . .

Her mother always made me feel uneasy: she was too *solid*. I felt dwarfed by her, fascinated and repelled by the abundance of her. She seemed barely human: as if beneath her rosy skin I should find, not the blood and muscle of an ordinary woman but some strange compound of black earth and granite, like an Egyptian idol with agate eyes. Her scent was a corrupt sweetness, like a million flyblown roses; a lingering, occult caress from all the secret places of her woman's body to the shameful longings of my heart. And *that* woman had a daughter!

I saw her peering out at me through the banisters. Eyes as green as glass fixed me in the half-light from the landing and, as my own gaze focused upon her, she gave a little laugh and jumped to her feet, ready to disappear up the stairs if I moved. She was barefoot and the light outlined her body through the fabric of her nightdress. She had none of her mother's fearful solidity: the little changeling was almost insubstantial, with straight black hair falling over a hungry, pointed face . . . and yet, there was a resemblance. Something in the eyes, maybe, or in the fluid grace of her movements: so might golden Ceres have been mirrored in pale Persephone.

I asked her name.

She tilted her head at me; her eyes filled with lights. 'I'm not supposed to tell.' The Cornish accent was light, almost imperceptible, like her mother's, a soft blurring of the syllables.

'Why not?'

'I shouldn't be here. I promised.' If it had not been for her smile and the way her body stood out against the light I might have believed in her innocence, but I knew that, standing there above me, like a parody of Juliet on the balcony, whatever her age she was her mother's creature, conceived in sin and bred to pray upon sinners like myself. I could almost smell her perfume from where I stood: a troubling, deceitful combination, like amber and swamp water.

'I promised,' she repeated, drawing away from the banister. 'I have to go.'

'Wait!' I could not control my response. Hastily I began to climb the stairs, sweat prickling my temples. 'Don't go. I won't tell. Look'—fumbling in my pockets—'I'll give you some chocolate.'

She hesitated, then reached out her hand for the sweet, which she unwrapped immediately and began to eat. Pushing my advantage, I smiled and put my hand on her shoulder.

'Come now,' I said kindly. 'I'll take you back to your room and tell you a story.'

She nodded solemnly at this and ran quietly up the stairs in front of me, her bare feet like white moths in the darkness. There was nothing I could do but follow.

Her room was tucked away under the eaves of the house, and she jumped on to the bed, legs tucked beneath her, and pulled the bedspread around her. She had finished the chocolate and I watched as she licked her fingers clean in a gesture so potent that my knees almost gave way beneath me.

'What about my story?' she asked pertly.

'Later.'

'Why not now?'

'Later!'

The perfume was overwhelming now. She shook it from her hair like a fall of flowers, and in the midst of it I detected the rank smell which might have been my own lust.

I could bear it no longer. I stepped forwards and seized her in my arms and buried my face in her, drowning in her. My legs gave way and I fell with her on to the bed, holding on to her in desperation. For an instant she seemed awesomely powerful, her eyes widening like ripples into the darkness, her open mouth screaming silent curses. She began to struggle and kick, her hair like a flight of black bats fanning out over my face, smothering me with its weight. At that moment, with her lithe, serpentine body coiling against mine, her hair in my mouth and the sickly smell of chocolate in my nostrils, I was certain she was going to kill me.

There was a rushing in my ears and a terrible panic seized hold of me. I began to scream aloud in terror and disgust. I was the sacrifice, she the granite death-goddess gasping for my blood. With the last of my sanity I grabbed at her throat and tightened the grasp as hard as I could . . . the little witch fought like a demon, screaming and biting, but I found that my strength had returned . . .

God was with me then: if only I had had the courage to leave the house and never return, perhaps He would not have turned His face away from me . . . but even in the trembling aftermath of that dreadful battle I felt a kind of unholy excitement, a triumph, as if, instead of quelling the rising tide of lust within me, I had simply opened up the door to a lust of a different kind, one which could never entirely be slaked.

25

I have little recollection of returning to Cromwell Square: it was almost daylight and in a few hours the servants would be about, but Henry was not yet home. I was able to let myself into the house, to undress by myself and to slip into bed. I slept a little, but I had to take more laudanum to combat the evil dreams which threatened my sleep. I could no longer distinguish between reality and imagination so that I wondered whether or not I had dreamed the events I thought had taken place in Crook Street . . . *Had* I spoken to Henry? *Had* Fanny come to me as I slept? At about six o'clock I fell into a deep sleep, and I awoke two hours later when Tabby came in with my chocolate. My head ached dreadfully, I was feverish and, although I tried to show a cheerful face, Tabby guessed immediately that something was amiss.

'Why, Mrs Chester, you don't look well at all!' she observed, pulling the curtains open and drawing closer to the bedside. 'You're as pale as can be!'

'No, Tabby,' I protested, 'simply a little tired. I'll be all right presently.'

'I'll tell Mr Chester you're not well, ma'am,' said Tabby firmly.

'No!' I hastily softened my tone: it would not do for her to sense my panic. 'No. That won't be necessary.'

She looked doubtful. 'Maybe you'd like a drop of laudanum, ma'am?' I shook my head.

'Please, no. It's only a little headache. I'll be better for this excellent chocolate.' I forced myself to sip it, even though it was scalding hot, and I smiled reassuringly. 'Thank you, Tabby, you can go now.'

She left the room with some reluctance, looking over her shoulder as she went, and I told myself that I could not count on her to keep my illness a secret from Henry. Sure enough, ten minutes later he came into the room with a glass and the laudanum bottle.

'Tabby tells me you won't take your medicine,' he said. His eyes flicked to where Tizzy was sitting on my bed, and his mouth twisted sourly. 'I've told you before that I don't like that cat in your room at night. I wouldn't be surprised if that was what was causing your illnesses.'

'It seems to me,' I said, 'that both Tabby and you are far too concerned with my health!' My sharp reply startled me as much as it did Henry, and I flushed and mumbled something apologetic and confused. I tried to remember why I should feel such sudden hostility towards Henry . . . and then I remembered the dream— was it a dream?—in which I had witnessed . . . It was at the back of my mind, tantalizingly close to recollection, but I could not remember it fully. Only the impression remained: that feeling of disgust and hatred, a thirst for vengeance which did not seem to be my own. The violence of the emotions shook me all the more because I could not remember why I should feel them, and it was with a trembling voice that I continued: 'I'll be all right. *Please*, don't give me any more laudanum.'

He gave me a look of contempt and began to measure drops from the bottle into the glass.

'You'll do as I say, Effie. I'm in no mood for your temper this morning. Take your medicine now, and another dose with your midday meal, or you'll make me angry.'

'But I don't *need* any medicine. Just let me go for a walk in the fresh air . . .'

'Effie!' His tone was cold. 'I will not allow you to cross me. I know your nerves are bad, but you put me out of all patience with you! If you were a *real* wife . . .' He bit off the rest of the sentence. 'If you persist in this wilful behaviour,' he went on in a quieter tone, 'I shall wash my hands of you and refer you to Russell. He has plenty of experience with hysterics.'

'I am not an hysteric!' I protested. 'I . . .' But, seeing the expression in his eyes, I submitted and took the drink, hating him but unable to resist.

'That's better.' His eyes were hard and somehow triumphant. 'And remember, a less patient man would soon have had done with your tantrums. I promise you that if you cause any more disorder with your tears and your stubbornness I will call Russell to see you. If you won't drink your medicine I'll *make* you drink it; and if you won't behave as a good wife should, I'll expect the doctor to tell me why. Is that understood?'

I nodded, and I saw a smile flicker behind his eyes; a malicious, furtive smile.

'I made you what you are, Effie,' he said softly. 'You were nothing before I discovered you. You are what I say you are. If I want you to be an hysteric, an hysteric is what you will be. Don't think the doctor would believe you rather than me; if I told him I thought you were mad, he would agree. I can say it when I like, Effie. I can make you *do* what I like.'

I tried to speak, but as his exultant face swam in and out of focus before my tired eyes. I was conscious only of a terrible urge to cry. Perhaps he saw it; because the hard line of his mouth softened and he leaned to kiss me gently on the lips.

'I love you, Effie,' he whispered, his tenderness even more frightening than his anger. 'I do these things *because* I love you. I want you to be mine, to be safe, to be well. You have no idea what filth there is in the world, what dangers for a lovely girl like you . . . You have to trust me, Effie. Trust and obey me.' Gently but firmly he turned my face to look at his. His expression was concerned, but in his eyes I could still see that dancing, cruel glee. 'I'd do anything to protect you, Effie.' His intensity was almost unbearable.

'Even lock me away?' My voice was barely a whisper. His gaze was steady, his flat voice almost disguising the malice.

'Oh yes, Effie. I'd kill you rather than see you spoiled.'

He left me then, and as I lay on the bed, my mind a drugged haze of confusion, I tried to remember what I knew about Henry Chester—but all I could recall was the image of Fanny's calm face, the feel of her hand against my hair, and an image of balloons . . .

I awoke at about twelve o'clock, feeling less tired, but very dull and confused. I washed and dressed myself and went downstairs to the parlour. Henry had already gone out. I decided to walk to Highgate to clear my head and to escape the oppressive air of the house. I was about to put on my cloak when Tabby came in carrying a tray: seeing me dressed to go out, she started in surprise.

'Why ma'am! Surely you're not going outside, after you were so ill this morning!'

'I feel much better now, Tabby,' I replied mildly. 'I believe a walk will do me good.'

'But you've not eaten a thing! Here, look; I've got some nice gingerbread in the oven—it won't be more than a few minutes—and you always used to like a piece of warm gingerbread in the old days.'

'Tabby, I'm not hungry, thank you. Perhaps I'll take something later, when I get back. Please don't worry.'

Tabby shook her head. 'Mr Chester wouldn't be at all pleased if I let you go out today. He said that you mustn't go out for any reason, with the state you were in, ma'am.' She flushed slightly. 'I know you'd like to go, ma'am, but try and see the sense of it. There's no point in causing the poor gentleman any more worry . . . and he did say, ma'am.' There was a crease between her eyes. She was fond of me . . . but Henry was master of the house.

'I see.' For an instant I was flushed with rebellion: what did Henry's instructions matter? Then I remembered what he had said about Dr Russell, and Tabby's artless repetition of his words: 'the state you were in'. I felt a sudden chill.

'Perhaps I'll stay in after all,' I said with pretended nonchalance, taking off my cloak and forcing myself to sit down.

'I think you'd better, ma'am,' said Tabby in a motherly tone. 'Perhaps you'd like some tea? Or some chocolate? Or some of that gingerbread when it comes out?'

I nodded, my forced smile cramping my jaw. 'Thank you.'

I strained to maintain my calm as Tabby tidied the parlour. It seemed that she spent an eternity lighting the fire, plumping the cushions, making sure I had everything I needed. I could have told her I wanted to be alone, of course: but her devotion to me was real and touching—and besides, I didn't want her to report to Henry that I had been at all nervous or unbalanced. His threat had been clear . . . The very thought of it filled me with a hysteria I struggled to overcome: if I was judged too ill or unstable to leave the house alone, when could I see Mose? When could I see Fanny?

I sprang to my feet and ran to the window. I looked out at the garden, where the rain had just begun to fall. I opened the window, stretching my arms out, feeling the moisture on my face, my hands. The rain was warm, the scent of the wet garden sharply nostalgic, like the churchyard at night, and I felt some of my panic diminish. Leaving the window wide behind me I returned to my seat and tried to think clearly, but the more I tried to marshal my thoughts the deeper I drifted into that half-world of the previous night, where every memory seemed touched with a narcotic deceit. Perhaps Henry was right; perhaps I was going mad. If only I could see Mose . . .

No! Not yet. First I had to convince Henry that I was well enough to be allowed out alone. *He* was the enemy, I told myself firmly; he was the guilty one, not me. I had a right to hate him. I had a right to be unhappy.

It was the first time I had admitted as much to myself; in a quiet way I declared war on Henry that day, a war filled with hate and cunning. He might think he had all the weapons, but I was not the pretty idiot he thought me: I would prove that. I, at least, had the advantage of surprise . . .

26

I didn't see Effie the next day and, to tell the truth, I didn't miss her: I had serious things on my mind. For a start, a volley of creditors had seen fit to descend upon me *en masse* demanding payment. If I had had the advantage of Fanny's crystal ball, no doubt I would have arranged to be elsewhere when they called, but the melancholy fact was that I was obliged, after some small unpleasantness, to pay out a sum of almost a hundred pounds. This left me sadly depleted and I spent a dreary afternoon poring over my accounts, after which I was forced to admit that I was in debt to the tune of over four hundred pounds, a sum that even I found difficult to make light of. A pleading note from Effie did nothing to cheer my mood: her maid—Em, wasn't it?—brought it at six in the evening, by which time I was pleasantly castaway over a bottle of wine and most unwilling for a repetition of our tryst of the previous night. I opened the note (heavily sealed) and by the light of my candle attempted to decipher Effie's laboured scrawl.

Dearest Mose,
I must see you *as soon as possible*; I am in a *Desperate Situation*.
Henry will not let me leave the House and threatens me with

the *Doctor* if I do not obey. I *must* escape, but I have nowhere to go. Please call when Henry is working. *You must help* me. I love you.

E.

I read the artless missive with no great relish. I could tell from the handwriting and the heavy underscoring that Effie had been in a state of great agitation when she wrote it, but I thought nothing of that. I knew how easily Effie could be thrown into hysterics and, as there is none of the Sir Galahad about me, I dismissed the whole thing with the minimum of thought.

I make no apologies: I'll not be at the beck and call of any woman, especially one in distress; I'll leave the fairy stories for the likes of Henry Chester. Tales in which the handsome prince runs off with the princess always seem to end with a sentence of marriage for the handsome prince—and I sensed a desperate threat in Effie's little note. So I ignored the letter. It was the kindest thing to do, I told myself, make a quick end to the whole affair, leave her to her daydreams, and soon enough she'd find another man to pin her hopes on. I was fond enough of her to be glad that no scandal would come to her through me.

Scandal. Now *that* was an idea.

I had been so absorbed in making my decision over Effie that for a few minutes I had actually forgotten my own financial problems. In my moment of philanthropy I had missed an opportunity which shone out at me sweet and clear as sunlight . . . and which might indeed solve my problems, and Effie's, too. Through the mist of the wine my mind began to make rapid calculations.

Don't call it blackmail: that's such an inelegant word. Call it creative investment if you wish. I had no love for Henry Chester. If he was fool enough to prefer girls in brothels to his ravishing wife he might as well pay for the privilege. He had plenty of money; I, on the other hand, had none. He was steeped to the eyes in his scruples; again, I had none. God was on his side—what more could he want?

I picked Effie's note out of the waste basket, smoothing the creased page reflectively. I hated to deceive her, but for the moment I would play her game.

I reached for a pen, sharpened it and wrote a quick note to Effie. Then I put on my coat and called a cab to take me to Crook Street. I had the feeling that Fanny could give me a great deal of help if I asked her.

27

I knew he would come: his greed and selfishness were the strongest and best things in him and I knew he would not disappoint me. If he had not, I suppose I would eventually have fed him the idea, but it was much better that he should come to me with it himself. He played all his charm to me that evening, little knowing that our aims were similar. He needed me, he said, to set the stage for a scandalous little scene which would ruin Henry if it were exposed. His Academy exhibition, his marriage, his standing in the church . . . all would be at an end if even a hint of the pious Mr Chester's secret activities were whispered in the right ears. And there was Effie, of course: Henry seemed to be holding the threat of a nerve doctor over her to ensure her obedience. If she were to reveal her knowledge to him, Henry would be powerless to frighten her again.

Mose was quick to point out that he would not be the only one to benefit from the plot: Effie would be freed from tyranny, he would earn a little much-needed tin (only a little, for he was not a greedy man) and I . . . Well, there I had him at a disadvantage. He could not understand why I refused the money; was it affection for Effie which prompted me? Was it some undisclosed grudge against the good Henry? I could tell he was itching to be told, but I laughed and told him nothing. He was too clever and unscrupulous to be trusted even with a truth he would not believe.

'No, no, Mose,' I said, smiling, 'I'll not say a word. Call it a grudge if you like, or simply a woman's love of mischief. Besides, Effie's a good girl and I hate to see her made unhappy by that hypocrite. What's your plan?'

Mose grinned. 'You tell me when Henry is expected at your house,' he explained. 'Arrange for me to watch him with one of your girls. After that, all I have to do is to write a nice little letter, with quotes and references and a promise to reveal details to all interested parties, and I promise you Henry will pay *what* I ask him *when* I ask him, as often as I please. And all that without any risk at all.'

I frowned. 'But how will any of that help Effie?' I asked. 'I can see how it would benefit *you*, but before I agree to any such plan I want to be certain that Effie will be happy.' I feigned puzzlement for a moment. 'I suppose you could write to her, too . . .' I suggested tentatively.

'No!' Mose's face lit up. 'I have a much better idea. I arrange for her to be there with me. Then, if Henry calls my bluff and refuses to pay, I have a much more reliable witness—who better than his wife? If she reveals that she saw him in a brothel, which of his fine, churchgoing friends will ever speak to him again?'

I looked at him with some admiration. What an apt pupil he was! So high on his arrogant pinnacle that he never realized how easily he was being manipulated.

'Effie here too . . .' My voice trailed off. 'I would never have thought of that. But I like it,' I decided, more forcefully. 'I think it will work. Tell Effie that Henry will be here again next Thursday at midnight. Tell her to be here at eleven. I'll hide her before Henry arrives. You be there at twenty past twelve, giving Henry time to prepare himself. I'll see to the rest.'

28

I spent my entire day at the studio working on *The Card Players*. I was very satisfied with the canvas; it was a powerful piece, with Harper sitting slouched against the wall with his elbows on the table and his face half tilted into the light, watching his hand with that expression of clever nonchalance which so typified him. A greenish oil-lamp guttered uncleanly above him, highlighting the greasy walls and the unvarnished table and throwing into sharp relief the thick glasses filled with milky absinthe.

I had sketched in the figure of the woman in charcoal, using a town model for the posture only: I wanted her to be in half-profile, one hand on the table in front of her, the other holding the Queen of Spades playfully to her lips . . . Soon I would need finer material, some dark-haired unknown. Not Effie, I decided; definitely not Effie. First, I hated to see her sitting so intimately with Harper, even in my own painting, and secondly . . . It was a vague, nebulous refusal, a sensation of unease as I envisaged her in my studio. Why should I be uneasy? I asked myself. She had sat there for me a thousand times. Why not this time? I could not answer. Instead my memory threw me a brief image, cold and intense as a brush with a ghost . . . a thin face staring at me in the dark, a voice like lace and frost whispering together, a scent of chocolate...

From where had that rogue memory surfaced? And that face, unformed and yet familiar, the white blur of little Persephone's face in the gloom of the underworld? I clenched my fists in frustration: I had seen her before, my Queen of Spades. Who was she?

Who?

When I arrived home, Effie was working at her embroidery, demure as a good child. The silks were spread about on the ottoman, on the footstool, on the grey flannel of her dress, and the threads and the long panel of tapestry were the only colour about her. She might have been a nun with her hair loose like a coif around her shoulders and, for a moment, her seeming purity was spectral, terrifying, like a vision of the Holy Virgin. Then she looked up, and in that instant I saw her face like that of a vengeful crone, grimacing in hate and fury, a white-haired Norn older than time with my life held by a thread in her knotted fingers. I almost screamed.

Then the light shifted again and she was Effie, her expression as meek and innocent as that of the Sleeping Beauty in her tapestry. I wondered what spiteful thoughts had been playing in her head and, seeing her smile, I determined to take care. There was something *knowing* about her smile, something which belied her timid voice when she greeted me. Had she been out? Had she been reading the forbidden books? Had she searched my room?

I forced a smile in return. 'Are you feeling better now, Effie?' I asked.

'Yes, thank you, much better. My headache is quite gone now, and I have been working at my embroidery all afternoon.' As if to underline that, she put the tapestry aside and began to wind the silks into a tidy plait.

'Excellent,' I said. 'However, bearing in mind your condition this morning I don't think it would be a good idea for you to go out for a few days at least.' I expected her to protest at this, knowing from Tabby how she liked to go for walks, but Effie did not flinch.

'Yes,' she agreed, 'I think it best to stay in the house while I am unwell: I should not like to catch a chill in the cemetery.'

'And no reading,' I added, thinking that if anything was going to shake her composure it would be a reference to her precious books. 'I'm certain that for a girl of your fanciful temperament, novels and poetry can only do incalculable harm. I have several improving books, as well as a store of tracts for you to read if you wish, but I have taken the rest of your books from the library and would ask you not to purchase any more.' I fully expected an outburst at that, but she merely nodded—and was that the tiniest smile on her pale lips?—and began to lay away her embroidery in her work-basket.

'I want to try and finish this tapestry this year, if I can,' she said. 'I think it might be pretty as a fire-screen, or maybe the centrepiece for a bedspread. What do you think?'

'As you wish,' I said coolly. 'I'm no judge of such things.'

I was surprised and rather disturbed. She had been helpless and hysterical that morning, wailing and crying like a spoilt child; now she was cool and self-possessed, her politeness almost a form of contempt. What secret was she keeping from me?

I watched her carefully over supper. As usual she ate little, but consented to take some bread and butter when I commented upon her loss of appetite. She was docile, sweet, and charming— why then did my stomach clench at the thought of her docility, her sweetness? My unease and dissatisfaction grew and eventually I retired to the smoking-room and left her alone.

I told myself that I was simply nervous: I had hardly slept the previous night, I had worked all day in the studio and I was tired. That was all. But somehow that was *not* all. While I was away something had happened to Effie, something secret, perhaps even something dangerous. In a strange, undisclosed way, I felt that Effie was no longer alone, no longer mine. I stayed awake late into that night, smoking and drinking, racking my brain to discover what had finally awoken my pale little sister.

Change

29

Five days.

For five days I waited. I could hardly eat; I was afraid to sleep in case I screamed my thoughts aloud in the night, and laudanum was the only rest I dared allow my disordered brain. I could see Henry was suspicious: sometimes I caught him staring at me and sometimes his eyes met mine with an air of calculation. Even a month ago I could not have borne the pressure of his questioning gaze; but there was a new strength in me, a sensation of *change*, a new darkness in my heart which filled me with terror and rejoicing. I felt protected by it as the formless butterfly gropes in the darkness of its hard chrysalis, as the wasp shifts in its silk cocoon and dreams uneasy vengeful dreams of flight.

And I? Would I fly? Or would I sting?

In my dreams I flew, floating among endless, shifting skies with my hair dragging behind me like a comet's tail. And in my dreams I saw Henry Chester in a child's room filled with balloons and the uneasy half-memories which had assailed me as I slept in Fanny's house came back to me with a startling clarity. Voices spoke to me from the dark and I saw faces, heard names and welcomed them like old friends; there was Yolande, hair cropped short and figure straight as a boy's, smoking her endless black cigars; there was Lily, the sleeves of her man's shirt pushed up to reveal her thick red forearms; there was Izzy and Violet and Gabriel Chau . . . and, clearer than all the rest, I remembered Marta, floating through the dim air with balloons in her hands, floating closer and closer as Fanny stroked my hair and sang . . . I *had* been there that night as Henry came to me with black and guilty lust in his eyes . . . I knew I had been there and I welcomed the subtle change which was coming over me with a fierce joy.

There were times I was afraid of losing my mind. But I always held firm: when laudanum was not enough to combat the onset of hysteria and when I ached with loneliness for Mose and Fanny and when my fingers trembled to shred the almost-finished Sleeping Beauty tapestry to bloody rags, then I crept to my room where, at the bottom of one of my drawers, I had hidden the letter from Mose and the note from Fanny. Reading them again and again I knew that I was safe, that I was sane: that soon I would be free of Henry's influence and his threats . . . I would be with friends who loved me.

On Thursday, I pleaded a headache in order to go to bed early and, at half past ten, I crept out of the house. At a reasonable distance from the house I hailed a cab to Crook Street, arriving there at about eleven as instructed. As soon as I passed the threshold I began to feel that spiralling, floating sensation again, the elated terror of my laudanum-dreams, the naked formlessness of my nocturnal flights. A girl opened the door, gaping, her face oddly distorted in the greenish gaslight; another girl's face appeared behind hers, and behind hers another, until there were a multitude of disconnected features fanning out down the passage . . . I stumbled against the step, keeping my balance by leaning on the door-jamb; a dozen hands reached for me and, as they drew me into the passage, I caught sight of my face in the mirrors bracketed to the wall on either side of the doorway: a line of images receding into infinity; white face, white hair, cronelike among the pretty faces, painted lips and bright ribbons of the other girls. A door opened abruptly to my left and Fanny was at my side.

'Hello, my dear,' she said, taking my arm to lead me into the parlour. 'And how are you?'

I grasped the stiff green satin sleeve of her gown to steady myself. 'Oh, Fanny,' I whispered. 'Just hold me for a moment. I'm so frightened. I don't even know what I'm doing here.'

'Shhh . . .' She pulled me towards her in a rough, one-handed embrace, and I could smell tobacco and amber and Pears' soap on her skin, a strangely reassuring combination which somehow reminded me of Mose. 'Trust me, my dear,' she said softly. 'Do as I say and you'll be safe. Trust no-one else. You may not understand yet what we are doing but, believe me, I do. Henry Chester has done enough—I'll not let him hurt you again. I'll give you your vengeance.'

I was hardly listening: it was enough to feel her strong arm around my shoulder and her hand smoothing my hair. I closed my eyes and for the first time in many days I felt I might be able to sleep without fear of my dreams.

'Where's Mose?' I asked sleepily. 'He said he'd come. Where is he?'

'Later,' promised Fanny. 'He'll be there, I promise. Here. Sit down for a while.' I opened my eyes as she pushed me gently but firmly towards a small couch in front of the fire. Gratefully, I leaned back against the cushions.

'Thank you, Fanny,' I said. 'I'm so . . . tired.'

'Drink this,' she suggested, handing me a small goblet filled with a warm, sweet liquid fragrant with vanilla and blackberry, and I drank, feeling a pleasant relaxation spread through my shaking body.

'Good girl. Now you can rest awhile.'

I smiled and allowed my gaze to wander lazily around the little parlour. It was a tiny room, furnished all in shades of red, with the same Oriental opulence as the rest of Fanny's house. There was a fine Persian rug on the floor, fans and masks hanging on the wall and a Chinese fire-screen half shielding the glow from the chimney. The furniture was of cedar and rosewood, upholstered in damask and scarlet. Megaera and Alecto were sitting in front of the screen on a mat, and on the table stood a tinted glass vase of red roses. For a moment, as I raised my hands to my face, I saw that, miraculously, I too had become a part of the change: my skin was tinted a glorious shade of flame, my hair a scarlet sunrise in the lamplight. I was filled with warmth and well-being. Almost unconsciously I reached for another drink of Fanny's punch, feeling new energy trail thin fire down my throat. A sense of sudden, intense clarity came over me.

'I *do* feel much better now, Fanny,' I said in a stronger voice. 'Please, tell me what we are going to do.'

She nodded, sitting down on the sofa beside me in a rustle of skirts. The two cats immediately came to her, pressing their soft faces into her hands and purring. She clucked and chirruped at them, calling them by name.

'How is Tizzy?' she asked suddenly. 'Is she treating you well?'

'Yes,' I replied with a smile. 'She sleeps on my bed at night and sits with me when I'm alone. Henry hates her, but I don't care.'

'Good.' For a second Fanny's generous mouth seemed to tighten, almost cruelly, and she watched the cats on her lap with a fierce, hard intensity. I felt that she had completely forgotten my existence.

'Fanny!'

'My dear!' The smile was back, her expression as serene as ever. I began to doubt I had ever seen it change.

'What am I to do when Henry comes? Will I hide, as Mose said?'

She shook her head. 'No, my dear, you will not hide. For the moment you will trust me, knowing that I care for you and would not allow you to be hurt. But you will have to be brave and you will have to do exactly as I say. Will you?'

I nodded.

'Good. No questions, then. Promise?'

'I promise.'

For an instant my eyes strayed from hers and were caught by something at the back of the room, something which from the corner of my eye seemed to be a bunch of balloons. I started, glancing involuntarily at the spot, and I felt Fanny's grip tighten, just a little, on my arm.

'What's that?'

There were no balloons. Simply a circular stain in the top far corner of the room, next to the door.

'Shh, my dear,' said Fanny coaxingly. 'Don't fret. You're quite safe here.'

'I thought I saw . . .' My words were heavy, each syllable a formless shape pushing its way through the decaying fabric of my exhaustion. 'I saw balloons. What . . . what do balloons . . . ?'

'Shh. Close your eyes. That's right. Shh . . . That's right. Sleep, my dear. Sleep. It's your birthday, and there will be balloons. I promise.'

30

The clock on the mantelpiece said a quarter past eleven. I looked at her, asleep on the sofa, and it was as if the bones beneath Effie's face had shifted to become less pronounced, blurred, like an unfinished child's face.

'Marta!'

She shifted slightly as I called her, raising her fingers to her mouth in that peculiarly childish habit she had always had.

'Marta, time to wake up.'

Her eyes opened, puzzled at first, then fixing my own with a sweet trust which tore at the heart.

'Have I been asleep?' she queried, rubbing her eyes.

'Yes, Marta; you've been asleep for a long time . . .' I felt my heart leap in elation; it was Marta's childishly deep voice, blurred now with sleep and gently accented with a nostalgic echo of my mother.

'Is *he* here yet?'

'No, but he will be soon. We have to get you ready for him. Come with me.'

She was docile, following me without a sound, her hand in mine. I prayed I was doing the right thing.

'First we have to make sure he doesn't recognize you,' I told her, leading her up the stairs to my own room. 'I'm going to lend you one of my dresses, then we'll change your face and your hair.'

'All right.' Her sweet smile did not waver. 'And I won't be afraid?'

'No,' I replied, 'you won't be afraid. You'll be strong and brave, as I told you.'

'Yes . . .'

'He won't even recognize you. And when he asks your name, what will you say?'

'I'm Marta.'

'Good.'

This is called henna, Marta,' I said as we rinsed her hair. 'It will darken your hair so that Henry won't recognize you. When Henry has gone we'll wash it out with something which will make it go clean again. All right?'

'Yes.'

'Now I'll help you put on this dress of mine: I haven't worn it for a long time, and I was younger and slimmer then. It's pretty, isn't it?'

'Yes.'

'And after that we'll put some powder and rouge on your face to make you look different.'

'He won't recognize me.'

'Not now you're older.'

Imagine the image from a photographic plate as it transfers the picture to paper, growing darker and darker from white to palest gold, from amber to sepia. Imagine the moon as she turns her thin profile slowly to full-face, pulling the tides with her. Imagine the chrysalis as it cracks open the larva's hard coffin and shows its wings to the sun. Does the imago mourn for the cater-pillar it once was? Does it even remember?

31

It's a lie: I don't dream. There are people who don't dream, you know; my nights here in Highgate are slices of oblivion where even God may not intrude. If God is unable to reach me, tell me, why should *she* pace my dreams, smelling of lilac and deceit, soft and murderous as a poison shirt? I *don't* see her: I don't feel her hair brush my face in the small hours of the night; I don't hear the sounds of her skin touching the silk of her dress; I don't glimpse her from the corner of my eye, standing at the foot of my bed.

I don't lie awake, wanting her.

I thought I was past the age of searching for Scheherazade: I had ploughed a thousand furrows in a thousand girls . . . young girls fair and dark and red-headed, plain and beautiful, willing and unwilling. I opened their secret flesh, fed them and fed from them; but still the Mystery eludes me. Every time I arose from their fetid couches, sated and raped by their arid hunger, I knew it: there was a Mystery, but the more I delved the less I uncovered of its essential self. They watched me with their flat, stupid eyes, hungrily, knowingly . . . the Mystery gone like the mythical castle in the fairy tale, never in the same place for longer than an hour. I begin to understand King Shahriyar, who married his brides in the evening to exe-

cute them the next morning: perhaps, like me, he thought to per-
ceive a part of the Mystery in the eviscerated remains of the night's
orgy; perhaps like me he crawled home too pale in the pitiless light
of day with nothing but blood and semen on his hands. But he and
I, brothers in disillusion, had this in common: we never lost hope.

Maybe if by magic I had been able to shrink back to the size
of a foetus, to swim back into the red darkness of my mother:
then, maybe, I might have understood the Mystery without the
need to bludgeon and destroy . . . but I have no magic. My last
impossible dream was Scheherazade, renewed each morning like
the Phoenix from the embers of my lust, to deliver a new message
of hope and acceptance, every night a new texture, a different
face: a thousand and one unbroken vials containing an elixir of
awesome, Biblical potency . . . the Mystery of eternal life.

Do I dream of her?

Perhaps.

I took nine grains of chloral before I left the house: I was
strangely apprehensive, my hands straying constantly to my
mouth, like a child taken in some misdemeanour. Strange
thoughts crossed my mind like ill omens: as I passed the cemetery I thought I saw the figure of a child all in white, standing
barefoot at the gate, watching me. I cried to the coachman to
stop: looking again I realized that there was no child, merely a
white gravestone just within the walls, reflecting the moon. As I
watched, a cat leaped up on to the stone and stared at me with a
glittering, feral gaze over the dark spaces. Magnified into an un-
real intensity by the clear night, it seemed to flex its jaws at me in
fear or warning as I drove past. In my fanciful state I almost
turned back, but a hunger which was far from purely carnal drew
me: I could not turn back. The house was calling me.

———

Fanny showed me into the hall, as usual managing to disconcert me with the sheer scale of her vivid green gown, her tall plumes, her scent. As always her house was a hive of odours and for a moment I was drowned in perfumes. Then Fanny led me gently down the passage to one of the little side-parlours, a room which, in nearly ten years, I did not remember ever seeing.

'I have someone here I think you might like to meet,' she said with a little smile.

I felt my jaw tense: there was something in her expression which disturbed me, a kind of quiet assurance. I shook my arm free from her surprisingly strong grip, losing balance as I did and striking the door-frame with my shoulder. Fanny smiled again, her face in the lamplight distorted into an expression of vengeful glee.

'Mr Chester . . .' Her voice was solicitous and the expression—if it had been there at all—was gone. 'You don't seem well today. I do hope you're not sickening?'

Sickening. In her accent the word gained a twist of eerie sibilances which insinuated themselves into my mind like snakes. I took her arm again to steady myself.

Ssssickening.

'Yes, thank you, Fanny,' I said randomly. 'I'm very well. Very well indeed,' I added, feeling the world stabilize. I forced a jovial smile. 'So, who am I to meet?' I enquired in a bantering tone. 'Some new *protégée* of yours?'

Fanny nodded. 'In a way, yes,' she agreed. 'But first I suggest a taste of my special punch to lift your spirits. Do come in.' And lifting the latch of the parlour door, she opened it and drew me in after her.

The light was reddish. It was almost as difficult to adjust my eyes to as total darkness. Incense was burning, an erotic scent like patchouli, and as Fanny guided me to a sofa and poured the drink—*she* seemed to have no trouble finding her bearings—I glimpsed gilt hangings studded with fake gems on the walls, brass ornaments on the furniture and one statue in particular, a huge bronze circle in which a four-armed god seemed to dance. In the flickering red light I saw him move.

Fanny held out a glass of warm punch to me and I took it without taking my eyes off the statue.

'What's that?'

'Shiva, god of the moon,' replied Fanny. 'And of death.' I drank to hide the abrupt return of my unease. The liquid was sharp, cramping my tastebuds; and beneath the sharpness was something almost bitter.

'Idolatrous nonsense,' I said more loudly than I intended. 'It looks . . . quite savage.'

'The world *is* savage,' said Fanny lightly. 'I find him a most appropriate god. But if he disturbs you . . .' her voice trailed off, questioningly and with a touch of mockery.

Stiffly I said: 'Of course not. It's only a statue.'

'Then I'll leave you for the time, Mr Chester.' She cleared her throat politely, and I remembered to pay her, fumbling guineas out of my pocket. Ever-ladylike, she palmed the coins as deftly as a conjuror, seeming hardly to notice them. Then she turned to the door.

'I'll allow Marta to introduce herself,' she said, and left.

For a moment I watched the door in bewilderment, expecting the girl to come in, then a tiny noise behind me alerted me and I spun round, half spilling the drink in a glittering arc around me. At that moment I was certain, with a superstitious conviction, that the statue of Shiva had come to life and was reaching for me with his four arms, his eyes alive with malicious intent. I almost screamed.

Then I saw her sitting in the shadows, hardly visible against the heavy folds of an Indian tapestry. I regained my composure as best I could, trying to restrain my anger at being caught unawares. I finished the drink Fanny had given me and put the glass on the mantelpiece; by the time I turned again I was calmer, able to smile reassuringly at the girl, squinting to make out her features in the troubling light.

I saw that she was young, maybe fifteen or so, and very slim and slight. Her long, loose hair looked black, but her eyes might have been any colour, for they reflected the red lamps like rubies. Her eyelids and eyebrows were heavily painted with kohl and gilt, and her skin had a kind of golden warmth which I associated with gypsies. She was wearing a silken kimono of some dull red material which accentuated her slim, childish figure, and around her neck and arms and in her ears heavy crimson stones smouldered and sparkled.

For a second I caught my breath at her beauty.

'M . . . Marta?' I faltered. 'Is that your name?'

'I'm Marta,' she said. Her voice was a whisper, slightly hoarse but with a soft country accent tempered with a touch of aloof mockery, rather like Fanny's own.

'But I . . .' Realizing: 'I met you before. I went into your room by accident.'

No answer.

'I hope you're feeling better.' The innuendo I hoped to put into the phrase fell sadly flat.

'Are you . . .' Again I was lost for words. 'Are you new to . . . I mean . . . Are you . . . ?' I could sense her mockery again, heady and bewildering.

'I am here for you,' she murmured, and for a moment I imagined that she had come to take my soul, like the Angel of Death. 'Just for you.'

'Ah.' Absurdly, I felt diminished, inarticulate as a schoolboy with a whore many years older than himself. Almost . . . almost as if this girl were not a fifteen-year-old slut but the virgin keeper of some immortal mystery. I shifted uneasily in my chair, wanting her but unable to speak. She was in control.

'Come closer, Mr Chester,' she whispered, 'and I'll tell you a story.'

'*The young man* set off in search of the Witch, and from afar the Witch saw him in her glass and smiled. She had waited so long for him to come, and for three days now she had felt his presence everywhere, in the milky winter sky, in the misty moor, in the chestnuts roasting by the hearth and, this morning, in the eye of the Hanged Man. It was hardly anything: a glance, no more, a semblance of a knowing wink, but for the Witch it was enough, and she waited, throwing another brick of peat on to the fire, scanning the cards for the first glimpse of his face.

'Others saw him come and shook their heads: they did not know his story, though it would have made a fine tale for a winter's evening, and they did not want to know it—only the blameless or the mad go in search of witches, and the gifts they offer are not always easy to bear. But the young man was rash and confident, striding out over the moor with the eagerness of one who has never strayed from the path. There was anger in his heart, and revenge, for beneath his handsome face there was a monster: a monster which came shambling out of the darkness every night to feed upon human flesh. The Witch's enchantments had created the monster, and the young man knew that only by slaying the Witch could he ever break the curse.'

She paused for a moment, laying her small, cool hand on my face. I felt her arms creep around me so that she was whispering into the hair at the back of my neck, making the hackles want to rise. The feeling was both erotic and disturbing.

'So . . .' I could hear the smile in her voice as she continued: 'The young man travelled across the moor until he came to the spot where the Witch lived; and when he saw her red caravan in a hollow of the hills he felt a thrill of joy and terror. It was almost night and, under cover of the bloody sunset, he crept to her caravan and looked in.

'The Witch was waiting. She saw him at the door and could not suppress her laughter as he raised his sword.

'"Prepare to meet your end, Witch!" he cried.

'The Witch stepped out into the light, and the young man saw that she was beautiful. She parted her robe . . . like this.'

With a superb gesture she dropped the kimono to the floor. For a moment she stood before me like a pagan goddess, her skin red copper in the rosy light, her hair loose, brushing her waist. Behind her Shiva stretched out his arms in graceful, savage desire. In a single, fluid movement she reached for my shirt and unbuttoned it: I, like a victim of bewitchment, found myself unable to move, assailed from all sides by the vibrant sensuality which clung to her, almost visibly, like St Elmo's fire. As she turned her face towards the light I saw her through the red veil of her hair: it reached into my entrails and dragged me screaming towards her . . . And yet there was no love, no tenderness in her eyes: only a kind of hunger, a fathomless elation which might have been lust or vengeance or even hate. I found I didn't care.

She sat atop me like a scarlet Centaur, face turned towards the ceiling, every muscle straining towards completion. I felt her devouring me; the pleasure was huge, annihilating, agonizing . . .

'. . . And when they had finished the young man drew out his dagger and cut the Witch's throat so that no-one would ever know how she had fed the monster within him, nor how eagerly it had fed.'

She was behind my back once more, the fall of her hair

streaming over my left shoulder, the fragrance of her sweet, warm skin overwhelming me. I hardly heard what she was saying, but was content simply to be in her presence.

'Then the young man slept for many hours, and when he awoke he found that it was daylight and the caravan was empty. He turned to go, but suddenly he caught sight of the Witch's card-case lying open on the table. An inexplicable compulsion seized him to open up the case and see the cards. They were beautiful, each one smooth as ivory and painted in exquisite detail.'

At any moment I expected the usual rush of self-loathing to break upon me: all my lust was spent and I never dallied with whores after I had used them . . . I rarely even wanted to see them again. But this was different. For the first time in my life I felt a tenderness for this woman—this girl—something I had not experienced even with Effie. Especially not with Effie. Something in me wanted to taste her, to know her: as if the mere act we had performed had been nothing . . . nothing revealed, nothing spoiled. I realized with sudden, exhilarating clarity, that this was the Mystery. This girl; this tenderness.

'On an impulse the young man spread the cards on the table in the pattern he knew as the Tree of Life. The Hermit, the Star, the Lovers, the Knave of Coins, Love, Lust, the High Priestess, Change . . . Suddenly the young man felt uneasy. He did not want to see the last card, the Fate card. His hand trembled as he reached out towards the card and turned it over, gingerly, afraid to see it.

'*Le Pendu*: the Hanged Man . . . He looked away, chilled. It meant nothing! The cards had no power over him.

'And yet, his eyes turned once again towards the card on the table, slyly, fearfully.'

I touched her neck, her arm, the taut curve of her thigh.

'Marta . . .'

'The face on the card seemed familiar. He looked again. Dark hair, clear brow, even features . . . He stepped back a pace.

'No! No. His imagination was playing tricks on him. And yet, looking at the card from a distance, he could almost believe that he recognized the face of the Hanged Man . . . was *almost* sure he did . . .'

'Marta.'

'Yes?'

'I love you.'

In the dark, her kiss was sweet.

32

At first I was furious.

At myself, for supposing that Fanny would give me any real help, at Effie for allowing herself to be dragged into such a dangerous, idiotic masquerade, but most especially with Fanny. I damned her to six kinds of hell when she told me that Effie was in the room with Henry and demanded to know what game she was playing.

She was maddeningly aloof.

'But *your* game, my dear Mose,' she replied sweetly. 'We're fabricating a scandal so that you can discredit Henry and lay hands on his money. Isn't that right?'

It was, but I didn't want the whole thing exposed before I got any profit out of it, and I said as much.

'It won't be exposed,' she said with a smile. 'Henry won't recognize her.'

That was ridiculous. Henry was *married* to her, for God's sake!

'To tell you the truth,' continued Fanny, 'I don't think you'd recognize her. She's a very good . . . actress.'

I uttered an expletive which only made her smile.

'Just watch,' she urged, with gentle mockery. 'I assure you that your precious money is quite safe.'

There was nothing else but to do as she asked. There was a peep-hole set into the wall behind a hanging tapestry and from it I could see into the parlour without any danger of being seen. As I set my eye against the hole I recall wondering uneasily how many other peep-holes existed in the house, and how often they were put into use.

Not that I expected anything more than a ridiculous confrontation between Effie and Henry: the girl would break down or go into hysterics as soon as he recognized her. I'd be lucky if I escaped arrest and, if Henry wanted it, here was the finest possible excuse to put his wife away in an asylum for ever. What was more, if she was goose enough to think that he might *not* recognize her, she belonged in one.

I was so engrossed in my bitter thoughts that for some time I did not really notice details of the actors in the little shadow-play Fanny had staged for my benefit. After some time had elasped, however, I was able to observe with a dispassionate, acrid curiosity, and I was even able to feel a small resurgence of my sense of humour. When I came to think of it, the whole situation *did* seem blackly comic. I might be in prison within the week for either bankruptcy or fraud, but I was able to feel the beginnings of a sour grin somewhere in the region of my stomach.

I could not hear what was being spoken, but my eyes had adjusted to the red light, and I could distinguish the features of both Henry and the girl.

Effie?

I squinted through the tiny hole, frowning. 'That's not Effie.' I had spoken aloud without meaning to, and I heard Fanny chuckle to herself by my side. I looked again, trying to see the resemblance.

It definitely wasn't Effie. Oh, there was a superficial resemblance, something in the figure and the shape of the face, but this girl was younger, her hair darker. In the deceitful light it might have been any shade between black and auburn, but it looked thicker than Effie's. The eyes were darker, too, and heavy with make-up, the brows were thick and black. But the real difference was in the way the girl moved: she had the fluid, snakelike grace of an exotic dancer, the teasing manner of the born courtesan. Effie was awkward, questing, passionate; this girl was cool, elegant in every movement but remote, perfectly, almost painfully in control.

But just as angry relief threatened to burst out in further imprecations against Fanny I saw that after all it *was* Effie, but a facet of Effie I had never suspected. For a second I was overcome with admiration—and something a little more primitive. I wanted this girl, this burnished gypsy. At that moment, perhaps, I wanted her even more than I wanted Henry's money . . . at least, it's the only explanation I can offer for the fact that I did not put an end to the dangerous charade that very night.

When Henry finally left the house, Fanny collected Effie from the little parlour and took her up to her own dressing-room to help her change. There I saw the cunning array of devices with which they had created the person they called 'Marta': the paints, powders, dyes and ointments which Fanny removed using a variety of creams and lotions. Then I watched as Fanny washed Effie's hair in a sharp-scented, clear distillation so that the dye they had used could be rinsed out with clear water.

Effie was passive throughout, uninterested in my observations or even my praise for her spectacular performance; and, when all traces of her disguise had been removed she fell into a heavy, somnolent state as if she had been drugged, hardly responding when I spoke to her. With a sharp glance at Fanny I wondered whether

'Marta' was not in fact a creation born of Fanny's strong aphrodisiacs. I wondered, not for the first time, what Fanny's game really was.

It was three o'clock when I was able to take Effie home. She spent some time drying her hair in front of the fire before Fanny declared her ready to leave, and I remember watching them both: Effie with her head in Fanny's lap; combing out her drying hair in long, sweeping strokes; Effie in her turn stroking the cats at her feet in unconscious imitation. The thought struck me that they looked alike in the symmetry of their posture and the quietude of their expressions, like sisters, like lovers. I was excluded, unconsciously, to be sure, but excluded; and although I was not in love with Effie I felt a kind of troubled anger. I was so deep in my thoughts that when Fanny eventually spoke I started guiltily.

'Now, my dear,' she said softly, 'it's time to wake up. Come now.'

Effie, who as far as I could see had not *been* asleep, stirred and lifted her head a little.

'Shhh, yes, I know you're tired, but you have to go home now. Remember?'

Effie made a small sound of acquiescence or protest.

'Come now, Effie. You'll be back soon.'

Effie looked up and, as she saw me, the confused expression dropped from her face and she smiled with more vivacity than I had seen all night.

'Mose!' she exclaimed, as if I had not been sitting there beside her half the night. 'Oh, Mose!' And I'll be damned if she didn't leap up there and then and fling her arms around my neck.

I was inclined to give her a sarcastic reply, but at that moment I saw the expression of complex satisfaction on Fanny's face and decided against it. Something was brewing in that witch's head of hers, and I wasn't going to be fool enough to ignore it. A dangerous woman, Fanny Miller: remember that, if you ever meet her.

So, as I said, I had to take Effie back home before the servants woke up: her hair was nearly dry by now and she put on her old dress and cloak. She seemed almost exhilarated, though she was evasive about the events I had witnessed in the parlour. In the cab I ventured to ask her a direct question and she looked at me with an odd expression of blankness.

'Ask Marta,' she said simply, and would say no more.

I forbore to tease her. I expect she knew I had been watching and felt a certain embarrassment to talk about it. It was natural enough, I suppose. No, it was Fanny I needed to talk to: she was the one who had engineered this situation. Effie was simply a tool. It was late, but as soon as I had delivered Effie to her door I turned and made my way back towards Crook Street.

33

I knew he'd come back. I'd seen him watching us with six kinds of hell in his eyes and I knew he wasn't at all satisfied. He liked to be in control, did Mose. He didn't like to be kept in the dark and he hated being used—he was bright enough to see that in a way he *had* been used, and it was important for me to keep him sweet until I didn't need him any more.

I was careful to show more warmth than at our previous meeting: to tell the truth, it wasn't difficult. My plan had succeeded even better than I had expected, and when Mose arrived I was feeling elated and suffused with energy. He, on the other hand, was cool and wary, suspecting a conspiracy but not certain where to begin looking. He walked into the parlour, hands in his pockets, his brows winged in a slight frown.

'Mose, what a pleas—'

'That was a dangerous game to play with my future, Fanny,' he interrupted drily. 'Perhaps you'd like to explain what in hell's name you were trying to do?'

I gave him my sweetest smile.

'Temper, Mose,' I chided laughingly. 'What are you complaining about? You were never in any danger, and you know it.'

'That's hardly the point,' he snapped. 'We had an agreement, and I expected you to keep it. In any case, you took a gamble and *I* was the stake: what if Chester had recognized Effie? *I* would have had the devil to pay. Chester's an influential bastard—do you think he'd let me go with a rap on the knuckles? He'd do his utmost—'

'Oh, stop whining,' I interrupted cheerfully, 'and do sit down. I can't bear to crane my neck to talk to you. I took no gamble. In that light, in that disguise, *no-one* could have recognized Effie. Especially not Henry. The idea of finding his wife in such a situation is beyond him.'

'Maybe. But why take the risk?'

'Sit down!' I repeated.

Sullenly he obeyed, and I suppressed a smile of triumph. I had him!

'Do you remember when we planned this?' I asked. Mose nodded. 'You asked me *my* reason for being involved in this.'

I could tell he was watching me intently.

'Years ago,' I explained, 'Henry Chester . . . well, I shan't tell you what he did, but it was the worst thing anyone has ever done to me, and ever since I have ached for revenge. I could have killed him, I know that; but I'm getting old. I don't want to finish on the scaffold. And I want my vengeance to be complete. I want the man to be *utterly* destroyed. Do you understand?'

His eyes were bright with curiosity and he nodded.

'I don't want his life. I want his position, his career, his marriage, his sanity. *Everything*.'

Mose grinned reluctantly. 'You don't do things by halves, do you, Fan?'

I laughed. 'Indeed I don't! And our interests do coincide in this, Moses. Do what I ask and you'll get your money, plenty of it. But . . .' I paused to make sure he was listening. 'If you decide to try to work on your own, or if you do anything to overset my plan, I'll hurt you. I don't want to, but this is far more important than you. If I have to, I'll kill you. I warned you once before. Do you remember?'

Mose grinned his engaging, rueful grin, and I knew he was lying. 'Do I? I'd know better than to cross you, Fan.'

A half-promise. His innocent expression rang as true as a lead sixpence, but it was better than nothing. Believe me, I was telling the truth. I quite liked Mose in spite of his patently two-faced nature—but I hoped he did know better.

'I want Henry to meet Marta again. Next week.'

'Oh?' His voice was smooth and non-committal.

'In fact, I want Henry to see a great deal of Marta.'

His sense of humour was beginning to reassert itself, and I saw him grin. 'I see.' He sighed. 'At least, I see the entertainment value of the situation, but not how it will help either of us, especially as it will mean that I can't touch Henry for any money.'

'Be patient,' I told him. 'You'll get the money soon enough. You see, Mose, my dear, thanks to a little forward planning and some simple chemistry, Henry is already half in love with Marta.'

He laughed at that. 'That *would* be a joke,' he said mischievously.

'And one which, in a little time, you could turn to your own advantage,' I prompted.

The sullen look was quite gone now: I could tell that Mose's keen sense of the ridiculous appreciated the irony of the situation, and for that reason, at least, I knew he would go along with me. For a while, anyway. And as long as I had Mose I had Effie.

Effie, who was to be my Ace of Swords.

I once read—it must have been in a fairy tale—that every man is secretly in love with his own death, hunting it with the desperation of a thwarted lover; if Effie had not told me, in Marta's voice, that Henry Chester was the Hermit, I should have known it as he stumbled home that night with that look of dark radiance in his eyes. Because I knew then that in some part of his guilty soul he had recognized her—no, not Effie, not the poor little blank thing waiting for a stronger mind to possess her, but *Marta,* my Marta, fluttering into life behind his Effie's eyes . . . Yes, he recognized her, the old Hermit and he was drawn as a man is drawn to the grave's cold seduction. I had ways of seeing in those days—I still do when I feel inclined to use them—and I felt his bleak longing and fed it. Oh, there are herbs to dim the mind and roots to waken it, potions to open the eye of the soul and others to fold reality into delicate shapes like paper birds . . . and there are spirits, yes, and ghosts, whether you believe in them or not, pacing the corridors of a guilty man's heart waiting for a chance to be reborn.

I could tell you a tale of how I watched my mother breathe life into a clay man, whispering strange memories into his brainless head, and of the real man who went mad; or of the root the pretty girl ate to speak to her dead lover; or of the sick child who left his body and flew to where his father lay dying to whisper a prayer into the old man's ear . . . all that and more I've seen. Shake your head and talk of science if you like; fifty years ago they'd have called your science magic. It shifts, you see, the uneasy tide of change. It carries us on its dark and secret waters. The tide gives up its dead, given faith and time. All we needed, the both of us, was a little time. For myself, to bring her closer. For Marta, time to grow strong.

We waited.

34

Strange, how time can fold in upon itself like linen sheets in a cupboard, bringing the past close enough to the present for events to touch, even to overlap. As I walked back from Crook Street to Cromwell Square I was suddenly smitten by a memory so intense that I could hardly imagine having put it out of my mind for so long: it was as if the red-haired girl had unlocked the sleeping half of my mind and freed the monsters of my past.

My exhilaration was a bitter thing, loaded with dreamlike images of damnation: the guilt I could bear—it was as familiar as the lines on my palms—but guilt was not all I felt. I felt a capering, Gothic joy. For the first time I revelled in my guilt, displaying myself as shamelessly as a penny whore before the stern image of my father in my soul. In the ochre light of the waning moon I ran, that hot, twisted nugget of joy burning my guts. In the silence I called her name, sacrilegiously: 'Marta!'

I seemed still to feel her touch on my skin; her scent was still in my nostrils, the scent of mystery and sulphurous delight . . . I laughed for no reason, like a madman—indeed, I felt my sanity begin to elude me, as a shy virgin may hide beneath her veils.

And I remembered.

My first Communion, only four weeks after that secret, shameful act in my mother's room . . . Summer had faded into a decadent, overripe autumn: fat brown wasps lurked treacherously around the apple trees and even the air had a yellowish, misty cast and a sickly, sweetish smell which told of heavy rains after the harvest and fruit left to rot on the branch.

There were six of us taking Communion that day, four boys and two girls: we had to form a procession from the village to the church while the choir followed, singing hymns, and the families brought up the rear holding candles. It was a proud day for my father—though my mother, who disliked the heat, would not be present—and I knew better than to complain; but I hated the white robe, so like a girl's nightdress, and the surplice which went over it. I hated the hair-oil which Nurse had plastered over my head: the smell of it was as overripe and sweet as the rotten apples, and I was afraid wasps would come to hover around my head, silent and bloated. The day was hot and I felt sweat rolling from my hair and face into my surplice, prickling and trickling from my underarms, my stomach, my groin. I tried to ignore it; to listen to the sweet, slightly off-key voices of the choirboys (my own voice had broken only a week before: there would be no more choir for me) and the deeper, sterner notes of my father's singing. I tried to remember that today was a special day for me; that today I would be accepted as a full member of the church, that next Sunday, when the adults stood to take Communion, to sip the wine from the jewelled chalice and to hold out their mouths for the mysterious white discs of the Host, I would be among them; *I* would taste the Blood and the Flesh of the Redeemer.

Suddenly I began to shiver. I had read about transubstantiation in my father's books, about the miracle of the Blood and the Flesh. But only now did the terrible image return to me. What would happen when I bit into the clean white wafer and felt it turn to raw flesh in my mouth? Would the wine change to the thick consistency of blood as the goblet touched my lips? If so, then how could I stop myself from fainting cold on the steps of the altar?

I had a momentary, nightmarish image of myself, white as a corpse, spraying blood and vomit out in great, rasping gulps as the congregation watched in horror and amazement and my father stood in shocked silence with the plate of wafers in his hand.

I almost fainted there and then. Maybe I was being punished, I thought, with desperate, guilty logic. I thought no-one had seen me in my mother's bedroom; I had not confessed it—could not confess it to my father, not even at the confessional—and I had thought in my wicked stupidity that I had escaped punishment. But *God* had been there all the time, God had seen it all and now He was going to make me drink *blood*, and I knew I was going to faint, really faint, because I could almost taste the dull slick of blood in my throat and if I defiled the Host I'd be damned for ever and ever . . .

With a tremendous effort I swallowed my terror. I had to go on. I had to go through with the ceremony. If I didn't my father would find out what I had done because I would have to tell him—and the thought of what he would do to me then goaded me out of my paralysis and set me half running towards the church. It wasn't blood, I told myself furiously. It was just cheap wine. And it wasn't the dead flesh of some old, crucified corpse. It was *wafers*, wafers because bread went stale too fast; I'd seen them in the casket Father kept in his special vestry. I looked up and saw the church's maw ready to engulf the six of us, dressed in white for all the world like six little white Hosts, and I suppressed a blasphemous urge to giggle. Mentally I thumbed my nose at it:

(I don't care . . . I'm not scared . . .

You can put your stupid wafers you-know-*whe-ere*)

Then I really did giggle, so loudly that my father glanced sharply at me and I immediately turned the giggle into a cough. I was feeling much better already.

We waited for what seemed like hours as the service droned on and on, my father's words like the heavy, sugar-soaked wasps in the apple orchard. I fixed my eyes on the two girls sitting opposite me to the left of the aisle: there was Liz Bashforth, plain and red-faced in a white dress several sizes too small, and Prissy Mahoney, whose mother had 'lost' her husband ten years earlier. Rumour had it that there hadn't *been* any husband, only a fine-talking Irish good-for-nothing who had run away to London, leaving his 'wife' and daughter to fend for themselves. Either way, Prissy's mother seemed to have fended for herself all right, because Priss was dressed in a brand-new Communion robe with lace and white ribbons, white gloves and little white shoes. As I looked shyly at her over my hymn-book I could see the way her hair fell loose in two neat sheaves over her breasts. The word made me blush a little, but I was at an age where my curiosity about girls by far exceeded the little real knowledge I had and I found myself looking at her again, my eyes creeping relentlessly towards the little swellings at her beribboned bodice. She looked back at me almost smiling, and I turned away hastily, blushing deeper. But I always looked again.

I was hardly paying attention when at last my father gave the signal for the Communion. I stood up hastily, taking my place in the line without taking my eyes off Prissy. As we made our way towards the altar I noticed that she was still aware of my looking at her, flicking her auburn hair over her shoulder with careless precision, her hips rolling in a childish parody of seduction.

I was so enthralled that for a moment I hardly noticed that the other boys were watching her too, with audible sniggers. For a moment I was genuinely bewildered; then I froze in shock. There was blood on the back of Prissy's white communion dress, seeping through the shiny silk just at the point where her legs met her body: a small irregular keyhole where blood had trickled slowly through the fabric during the hours she sat on the bench. I felt a sour panic cramp my stomach and the whole of my body was suddenly coated in slick ropes of sweat. It was as if my blasphemous thoughts about the Host had taken shape; I stumbled in the aisle, fascinated and horrified at the bloody keyhole in the back of Prissy's dress, unable to take my eyes from it. I was reminded in that nightmarish instant of my father's musical toys and I imagined Prissy Mahoney as the dancing Columbine in her blue-and-white dress, set into perpetual motion by my own sacrilegious thoughts. I saw her begin to move, at first jerky and graceless, then with the inhuman fluidity of her awakened mechanism, her hair flying, her bare legs kicking obscenely at the air, her breasts jiggling loosely at the lacing of her bodice while all the time she smiled her parodic, gruesome smile and the blood flowed down her legs as if it might never stop . . .

Much later I learned about menstruation and, although I never lost my disgust of the thought, I came to understand that poor Prissy was not the monster my twelve-year-old self thought her. But then I was totally ignorant and I simply knew that God was watching me with an eye as huge and pitiless as the sky; knew I was damned for mocking the Host and for daring to come unshriven to Communion. The sign was blood, like the blood of the chalice and the blood in the heart of the wafer, blood which was the legacy of the Original Sin, blood, blood . . .

They told me later that I collapsed screaming to the floor of the aisle. My father was as icily composed as ever, ordering me to be removed to the vestry while the others took Communion and then carrying me home to bed without a single comment. I lay in bed for twenty-four hours while rumours chased from one end of the village to the other: I was possessed by devils (why else would I have fallen into a fit at the sight of the Host?); I was insane; I was dead.

No doctor came to see me, although my father sat by my side all the time with his Bible and his rosary, praying through my fever and delirium. I do not know whether I spoke in my sleep—if I did, I cannot remember, and my father never spoke of it—but when I awoke the next day he hauled me out of bed without a word, washed and scrubbed me and dragged on my Communion clothes. In silence we went to the church and, in front of a good-sized crowd of onlookers, I took the wafer and the wine without the slightest incident. Thus the rumours were—not silenced, for in a village community no scandal is ever really dead—muted, at least when my father was within earshot. The official story was that I had suffered a slight epileptic seizure, and this was judged an adequate excuse to keep me away from school and the influence of other boys. My father's eye, like God's, was on me all the time; but he never mentioned the episode in the church, and for the second time I felt an uneasy, contemptuous elation at my narrow escape. As I grew older I forgot the incident altogether.

Until now.

Prissy Mahoney had been dead for twenty years; my father was dead and I would never again set foot in the village of my birth . . . so why should I feel the events of that long-forgotten summer so close, so immediate? I was a fool, I told myself savagely; that was all. There was no-one to judge me now. No-one.

But my mood had changed, and although I tried to recapture

my earlier feeling of carefree, shameless joy I could not, reaching Cromwell Square just before dawn with a sour stomach and heavy eyes.

I looked into Effie's room as I came in and was shaken by the bitter depth of my reaction as I saw her, white and peaceful among her tumbled sheets, innocent as a child. What right had she to look innocent? I *knew* her, and that narrow, talismanic keyhole of flesh between her legs; knew her sickening impurity. The hypocrite! If she had been a real wife I should not have had to make my bed with a Haymarket whore tonight or walk home in the cold dawn pursued by the Furies of my remembrance . . .

But here my rage struck an obstacle: Marta was no Haymarket whore. I knew that, even as my mind tried to lash my temper into a greater frenzy. I remembered her touch, her voice, the taste of her skin with a lover's intensity . . .

'Marta . . .' The sound of my voice made me flinch; I did not know I had spoken aloud. Anxiously I glanced at Effie. Alerted by my voice, she seemed to stir beneath the coverlet, turning restlessly on the pillow with a little childish sound. I held my breath at the door, willing her to sleep. For a minute or two I stayed there motionless, afraid to disturb her; then I pushed the door open, very gently, and stepped out into the passage.

Suddenly I felt something touch my leg and, in an absurd twist of near-panic, I thought of the Columbine doll with Prissy Mahoney's face, reaching for me in the dark. I almost screamed. Then I saw the eldritch gleam of its eyes in the shadows and swore softly. Effie's damned cat again!

I hissed at it, and it hissed back, then it returned to its element, the darkness, and I crept into the safety of my own room.

35

When I awoke, the sunlight was streaming through the open window and Tabby was sitting at my bedside with a tray of chocolate and biscuits. I reached within my memory for the dreams of the past night, but found nothing but a few intense, fragmented images: Fanny sitting by the fire with Meg and Alecto, my head in her lap; Mose's face, ochre in the firelight; and Henry's mouth smiling with a tenderness he never showed after our marriage ... Bright images, disassociated as the pictures in a pack of scattered cards ... and yet I felt a sensation of release and well-being I had not felt since the baby died.

I sat up abruptly, feeling suddenly ravenous. I drank the chocolate and ate all the biscuits, then I asked Tabby to bring me some toast.

'I'll swear, I'm feeling quite recovered this morning,' I said gaily.

'I'm very glad to hear it, ma'am, I'm sure,' answered Tabby carefully, 'but I hope you won't go tiring yourself out before you're well again. Mr Chester did say ...'

'Mr Chester? Where is he today?'

'He said he'd go to his studio to work, and wouldn't be back till tonight.'

I hoped my relief was not too apparent. 'I see,' I said, with a fair assumption of carelessness. 'Well, I think today I'll be well enough for a short walk. The fresh air will do me good, and it's a lovely day, don't you think?'

'Mr Chester *did* say, ma'am . . .'

'He said I wasn't to tire myself so soon after my illness. I think I am wise enough to judge for myself whether a short walk will do any harm.'

'Very good, ma'am.'

I hugged myself in secret delight, feeling as if I had scored a small victory.

I allowed Em to dress me in a smart gold-coloured walking-dress and matching bonnet. Looking at myself in the mirror I noticed how pale I had become in the past few weeks, how shadowed my eyes seemed under the brim of the bonnet, and I smiled bravely at my reflection to brighten the haunted expression which even now seemed to lurk behind the bones of my face. Enough, I told myself. I had been ill, but that was over now: Mose had put it right, and soon, we could . . . I passed my hand over my eyes, feeling suddenly confused. What *had* we done, Mose and I? Had I gone to Crook Street the night before? If so, what had I done there?

A wave of dizziness washed over me and I held on to the dressing-table to stop myself from falling. A rogue memory emerged from the confusion of my thoughts: Fanny washing my hair in a basin and drying it with her fingers . . . watching red ochre wash from the pale strands of my hair . . . No, that must have been a dream. Why should Fanny want to dye my hair? I frowned at my reflection, trying to remember, but as I looked I seemed to see my eyes change colour, my hair darken, my skin

warm to the pale gold of China tea . . . I felt my fingers grow
numb, my jaw drop, my soul slip out of my body like a leaf out
of a book . . . and I *knew* I should remember . . . But it was so much
easier to drift like a balloon at the mercy of every wind, to hear
Fanny's gentle voice telling me to sleep, that it was all right, that
I could forget, that it was all right . . .

I felt the nervous double-jerk which drew me back into my
body, and I forced the memory back into the dark. I didn't want
to remember.

*(Shh it's all right you don't have to you don't need to it's all
shhh . . .)*

I didn't need to remember. Fanny had it all under control.

It was mid-morning by the time I left the house; I reached
Mose's rooms at noon. He was just getting up, his eyes reddened
from lack of sleep and his fair hair falling messily over his pallid
face. Even in that condition I was struck, as always, by the purity
of his features, his almost feminine beauty—feminine that is, if
you were to discount the perverse lines around his mouth, the narrowed, troubling eyes and the perpetual mockery. Through the gap
in the doorway he flashed his smile at me—half a smile, at least,
for half of his face was all I could see through the narrow opening.
A breath of stale air and cigar-smoke drifted from the doorway.

'Effie! Wait a minute.'

The door closed again, reopening a few minutes later to reveal
Mose's untidy room. He had obviously tried to create some semblance of order, and the windows were open. He gave me a careless kiss on the mouth and sprawled across a chair, grinning.

'A drink of brandy, Effie?'

I shook my head, watching Mose splash a generous dose of
dark liquid into a glass, downing it in one easy, practised gesture.

'To celebrate,' he explained, pouring another glassful. 'You did magnificently last night, my dear.'

Last night?

He must have seen my puzzled expression, because he grinned even more broadly and raised his glass to me in a mock salute.

'I understand your modesty, my dear,' he said teasingly. 'Most inelegant of me even to mention it. Still, it's thanks to your spectacular performance that we have dear Henry in our pockets. All you have to do is to show a little patience and he'll be ours. *Yours*,' he amended emphatically, finishing the little which remained in his glass. 'All yours.'

Some instinct warned me not to reveal my loss of memory. I needed time to think.

'Are you saying that your idea worked?'

'Better than that,' said Mose, 'Henry swallowed the whole thing, hook, line and sinker. What's more, Fanny says he fell for Marta like a ton of bricks.' (A troubling, intimate wink in my direction.) 'A couple of weeks and we'll be able to make dear Henry pay whatever we like.'

'Oh!' I was beginning to understand that, at least. 'But what about me? You said . . .'

'Patience, my dear.' Somehow I found his smile too knowing. 'Give me a couple of weeks to work on him. Then, with the money . . . How would you like to live in France, my dear?'

I stared at him, confused, 'France?'

'Or Germany, or Italy if you prefer. They say there's a good market for painters in Italy.'

'I don't understand.' I was almost in tears: his grin now seemed monstrously gleeful, that of a troll.

'Of course, Henry might not allow you a divorce,' he continued relentlessly, 'so you might never be able to come home. But what would you miss? Who would miss you? I'm asking you to be

Mrs Moses Harper, you goose,' he explained, as I stared blankly at him. 'With Henry's money we could establish ourselves comfortably enough, and with my paintings we could make a decent living. Of course, there'd be a scandal, but by that time you'd be long gone—and would you care?'

I continued to stare. I felt like a clockwork toy with a faulty mechanism, filled with the potential for movement but frozen into stupid silence.

'Well,' said Mose, after a long silence, 'that will teach me to be so arrogant. I rather thought I had charisma. Now I see that you'd rather elope with the muffin-man.'

'No!' My words tasted coppery and unfamiliar in my mouth, but the syllable forced itself between my teeth with desperate vehemence. 'I . . . I never thought . . . I never imagined I'd escape from Henry, especially after you said . . .'

'Never mind what I said, Effie. I said I loved you, do you remember that?'

I nodded dumbly.

'I also knew that with the state of my finances at the moment there was no possibility of my being able to marry you. I could have been clapped up in a debtor's prison at any time. What sort of a marriage would that be for you?'

'So you—'

'So I lied to you. I told you I didn't want to marry you. It hurt—but not as much as it would have hurt you if I'd told you the truth.' He smiled reassuringly at me and put his arm around my waist. 'But now, if I can persuade Henry to share just a little of his wealth, we're set for life. Besides, Henry owes you something for all the misery he's put you through.'

Mose was persuasive and I allowed myself to be drawn into a delightful double fantasy, sketched by Mose's cunning hand, in which we lived in Paris or Rome or Vienna and Mose made a fortune from his paintings and Henry Chester was a dim memory.

Still the thought of the previous night ('your spectacular performance') continued to flutter uneasily at the edge of my consciousness, distracting me. I felt oddly remote, and for a moment I felt dizzy, grabbing hold of a chair-back to steady myself. Then an image struck me, an image which was also a memory, potent as neat gin, and I reeled with the impact of that image upon my mind—

I was in my room again, ready for bed, with my favourite doll tucked under my arm. In the corner I could see the balloons Mother had bought for my birthday bobbing against the window in the slight draught. I was excited and happy, but I felt an undercurrent of uneasy guilt, because the Man had seen me on the stairs; and although the Man had seemed friendly enough I knew that Mother would not have wanted me to ask him into my room.

I shook the memory away with a violent toss of the head, and for an instant the world stabilized again, locking into sharp, clear focus. Then everything tilted and I was—back in the room with (*the hermit*) the Bad Man, but this time I was not afraid. Instead there was a salty, coppery taste in my mouth which I took a moment to recognize as hate. But (*Henry*) the Bad Man was watching me, and I narrowed my eyes into languorous Egyptian cat's-eyes and tilted my smile at him like a Chinese doll. The Bad Man didn't recognize me (*Henry didn't recognize me*) and soon I would grow *strong* . . .

Suddenly the scene dissolved into a jangled, incoherent kaleidoscope of fragmented scenes: I felt my memories explode outwards in every direction and there rose a sound, murmurous at first but rising in pitch and intensity until it became a maniac wail, ululating on the very brink of sanity. And in the voice I found that I could hear words, thoughts, desperate questions and formless answers. It was a barbed wall of sound against which my sanity hurled itself meaninglessly, trying not to hear, trying not to remember.

(will i fly or will i)

(oh mummy the bad man don't let the bad man oh)

(sting sting sting stingstingstingstingst . . .)

(it was henry *henry* killed her *henry* killed)

(marta)

(*me* it was me but i'm back i'm back and now)

(oh we'll have *fun* now we'll learn to sting little sister we'll)

(fly?)

(because henry killed my . . .)

(marta)

(marta)

(marta)

My scream was high and despairing, a volley of wasps in flames, a razor slash in the eyes of sanity. I was dimly aware of hands clawing my face and a voice—my own—screaming from a whistling eyrie of madness:

'No! Get out! Get out! Get out! It's *Effie!* Effie! Effie! Eff . . .' screaming my name over and over again.

Then I heard Fanny's voice in my mind, the voice of my mother, my anchor, my friend. A cottony, delirious sensation of relief fell over me as all sound in my mind was stilled. I could almost feel her hands moving gently through my hair, soothing the terrors away.

(shh it's all right little girl it's all right you don't have to remember anything)

(but fanny there was someone else in my mind and i was)

(shh not for long now just until we deal with henry)

(but i)

(shh besides you like it you want it)

(. . . ?)

(he hurt you too frightened you too now you have a friend who understands)

(marta?)

(don't be afraid we understand we can help you we love)

(love?)

(oh yes let me in i *do* love)

Imagine a snowflake floating down a deep well. Imagine a flake of soot falling from the dim London sky.

(i love)

(i . . .)

Then nothing.

36

Poor Mose! And poor Effie. I suppose I should have expected something of the sort. I did try to make Effie forget everything she had done while she was in her trance—I didn't think it would do her any good to remember, but I found that I had much less control over her than I thought. Many people believe that a person can be forced to do almost anything under the influence of a powerful mesmerist: that isn't true. Marta *was* Effie in every real sense, or, if you like, Effie had become Marta. I like to think that she and my Marta were linked in some way, perhaps because of their shared experiences with Henry. I like to think that Effie was a natural clairvoyant, and that my Marta was able to speak to me, to touch me through her ... but I am aware that the voice of reason says otherwise. This spiteful, frosty little voice says that Marta was born only from my own suggestions and Effie's dependence on laudanum, that she saw only what I wanted her to see and acted only on my orders. Maybe so.

To me the voice of reason sounds a little like that of Henry Chester, weak and petulant. I say that today's science is yesterday's magic, and today's magic may be tomorrow's science. Love is the only constant in this uneasy rational world, love and its dark half, hate. Disbelieve me if you like, but we called Marta, Effie and I, out of love and hate; we gave her a home for a while and she allowed us a glimpse of a mystery. You may think I used Effie for my own ends: rest assured I did not. I love her as much as I love my own daughter, knowing them to be the two faces of the same complex woman. Together we make the Three-in-One, the Erinyes, inseparable and invincible, bound by love. It was love which prompted me to make Effie forget what I had shown her; love, too, brought her back to us when she needed her mother and sister. I knew it would happen sooner or later. It just happened sooner than I thought.

It was late afternoon on Friday when Mose arrived at Crook Street looking unkempt and rather agitated. Effie had come to visit him and had apparently suffered a kind of fit which disturbed Mose greatly. I gave him a simple explanation I thought he would understand; the voice of reason was eloquent enough to stall any of his qualms for a time at least, and he left, somewhat dissatisfied, but docile enough. Effie, he told me, was back in Cromwell Square with instructions not to leave the house before the following Thursday, and I had enough trust in her to be certain she would not give Henry any cause for suspicion. All we needed was a little time.

37

I saw less of my wife that week than ever before. I couldn't help it: suddenly I could not bear her presence, her scent, her voice. I had tasted stronger flesh now and Effie's sick pallor appalled me. She smelt of laudanum all the time now—she was taking the drug in frequent doses, unprompted by me, and I noticed that she tended to become increasingly nervous as the day progressed and her medicine lost its potency. She ate little and spoke less, accusing me with her smoky eyes. The cat was always on her lap like a malignant familiar, fixing me with its narrow yellow stare. In spite of myself I became infected with the delusion that some-how they were judging me, that they could see into the very channels of my brain.

I could not bear it, and I began a further correspondence with Dr Russell, expressing concern at my wife's mental condition. Even now I am not certain why I did so. Perhaps I realized even then that life with Effie would be unbearable once I had fallen under Marta's spell. I saw Russell several times and told him that his new drug, chloral, was exactly what I needed to combat my insomnia—his boast that it had no side effects was not idle—and I discussed Effie's seeming addiction.

Russell showed polite, respectful interest at all times, his keen grey eyes gleaming with absorption as he enumerated the various manias to which the female of the species is commonly prone, citing cases of hysterical catalepsy, schizophrenia and nymphomania. The weaker intellect of women, he told me, renders them more susceptible to diseases of the mind and the thought seemed to fill him with the abstract delight of the true academic. It occurred to me that in Russell I had a potentially invaluable ally. A pilgrim in search of more and more exotic cases of insanity, a collector of shrunken heads. One day—and the thought was barely formulated but stored away, delicately, for future use—he might be persuaded to add Effie to his collection. I put his letters to one side in a locked drawer of my desk, with the deliberate nonchalance of a poisoner laying aside the murderous vial for later use.

I spent whole days in my studio, trying to finish *The Card Players*, and for the first time in my life I painted without a model. Instead, I reached into my memory for *her* half-remembered features, sketching directly on to my canvas in oils and crayon. I found that she took form magically beneath my fingertips as I recalled the texture of her hair, the warmth of her skin, the careless turn of her head. I made no studies but painted directly, with a lover's delicacy: the reddish light glowed on her cheekbones, emphasizing the vulnerable, arrogant set of her jaw, the pale quivering bow of her mouth; a stray flicker from the fire reflected coals from her eyes. Her mouth was slightly tensed as she looked over the table at the other player, but there was a sardonic arch to her dark brows which spoke of laughter or triumph. I painted her figure in dark colours in order to emphasize her face—perhaps the most expressive features I have ever painted—and I highlighted her cascading hair with a nimbus of red which gave her a dangerous, ambiguous radiance, like a burning city. For five days I worked feverishly at my Queen of Spades, darkening the finished areas of the canvas so that the viewer was led to her face, only her face.

Once, very fleetingly, I fancied I saw that certain resemblance to Effie in her mobile, shifting features: but no sooner had I formulated the thought than I knew that I was wrong. Marta was so vibrantly alive that she could not be compared with my poor little Beggar Girl—as well compare a flame to a sheet of paper. I knew instinctively that if they were to meet, Effie would be as utterly consumed by Marta's voracious energy.

During that week I burned for her and at night I cramped and clawed under my heavy bedclothes with the Eye of God fixed like a nail into the top of my head. My sheets burned with the sulphurous dank of my body and my stench appalled me, but still I longed for her.

For six nights I borrowed my sleep from the chloral bottle—I still remember the midnight-blue glass, cool antidote to all scarlet dreams. Wasted by the potency of my fever and my lust, I met Thursday's dawn with a sense of doomed anticlimax. It was a mistake to go to her twice; I knew it now. There was no Scheherazade, no faery-footed damozel with eyes like garnets. Today she would be a penny whore, cunningly lit and robed, but a whore nevertheless, all her tender alchemy gone. Today I knew it.

I arrived at midnight: I saw the clock in the hall tick over the crucial minute and I shivered in foreboding as the hour began to strike. As the notes sank into the silence a door opened at my back and Fanny emerged, vibrant in yellow brocade, her hair like vines. Two of her familiars were coiled around her ankles, and I tried to avoid their silent, contemptuous gaze as Fanny led me, not to the red parlour as before, but up the stairs to a room on the first floor which I had never seen before.

She tapped on the door, then, wordlessly, opened it. It was almost dark, the light from the passageway momentarily destroying the subtle lighting inside the room. I heard the door shut firmly at my back and for an instant I looked around, disorientated. The room was large and almost bare, lit by several gas-jets shielded by blue glass globes. I was reminded for a moment of the chloral bottle, promising cool oblivion, and I shivered. It was not the thought, I realized: the room was cold, the dead fire screened by a dark Chinese lacquer panel. Rugs partly covered the floor, but the walls were bare and the room seemed dead, with none of the opulence of the red parlour. The only furniture I could see was a small table upon which stood a blue decanter and a glass.

'Please pour yourself a drink,' hissed a voice behind me, and suddenly she was *there*—strange how inconspicuous she could be when she chose. Her black hair (how could I have thought it was red? It was crow-black, black as the Queen of Spades) fell straight as rain between her spread hands. She was pale as smoke in the deathly light, her mouth a blur, her eyes a startling cobalt in the Gothic pallor of her face. Her dress was made of some stiff, panelled fabric which stood out against her vulnerable flesh, and its opulence was somehow disturbing in the bleak surrounding, as if she were a forgotten Coppélia in a deserted workshop, just waiting to be set into motion.

Mechanically I poured myself a glassful of the liquor in the cornflower-blue decanter—it was tinselly and sharp, with the stinging taste of juniper—and struggled once again to overcome my sense of unreality. For a moment I wondered if there were chloral in the drink, for I felt myself sink in watery abandon, the figure of Marta a swaying ghost in that undersea light, a drowned mermaid with the smell of weed and decay in her floating hair. Then her cold arms folded around me and I felt her mouth fleetingly against mine, her voice whispering inaudible obscenities in my ear, and I collapsed against her, clutching her dress, pulling her down with me on to the floor, on to the dim sea-bed, her blood a rushing in my ears, her flesh a welcome suffocation of my sense of sin.

When at last I was spent we lay together on the soft blue rugs and she whispered a long, dreamlike tale to me of a woman who changed with the moon, growing from young girl to beautiful woman to hideous crone as the month went by . . . then I wanted her again and I plunged into her like a dolphin into a wave.

'I have to see you again. I have to see you again soon.'

'Next Thursday.' Her whispering voice is matter-of-fact, passionless, almost coarse: the voice of a penny whore planning business.

'No! I want to see you sooner than that.'

She shakes her head abstractedly. The dull brocade of her dress clings to her knees and ankles and above that she is naked as the moon, her nipples the most delicate azure against her powdery skin.

'I can only see you once a week,' she says patiently. 'Only on Thursdays. Only here.'

'Why?' Anger spills out from me like acid. 'I pay you, don't I? Where do you go for the rest of the week? Who do you go with?'

Flawed Columbine smiles gently among her damp ringlets.

'But I love you!' Hapless now, clinging to her thin arm tight enough to raise bruises, and hungry, so hungry. 'I lo-ove . . .' (Revelation.) 'I *love* you!'

A shift in the light; chloral eyes reflecting my pleading face. Her head tilts slightly, like a child listening.

Flatly she says: 'No. You don't love me. Not enough. Not yet.'

She cuts off my anguished negative with a gesture, beginning to pull on her discarded dress with graceless grace, like a spoilt child dressing up in Mother's clothes. 'You will, Henry,' she says softly. 'Soon you will.'

For a long time I am alone in this blue room, coiled tightly around my longing. She has left a silk scarf lying on the floor at my feet; I crush it and twist it in my hands as some primitive in me would like to crush and twist her pale throat . . . but Scheherazade has gone with her wolves at heel.

Marta. Marta. Marta! I could drive myself mad with that name. Marta, my penny succubus; my waxing, waning moonchild. Where do you go, my darling? To some dim underwater crypt where undines drift? Some stone circle, to dance till dawn with the other witches? Or do you go to the riverside with your mouth painted red and your dress cut low? Do you roll in filthy alleys with the dregs and the cripples? What do you want of me, Marta? Tell me what it is and I'll give it to you. Whatever it is.

Whatever.

38

We were alone together, quite alone as Henry rattled about the house like a grain in a gourd, knowing only his own wan dreams . . . We were alone together.

She followed me like a flawed reflection in a cat's eye, pale retinal imprint of myself, whispering to me in the dark. Marta, my sister, my shadow, my love. At night we talked softly underneath the blankets, like children full of secrets; by day she followed me invisibly, taking my hand under the dinner-table, murmuring reassuring words into my ears. I did not see Mose— he thought that our meeting might be dangerous to his plans— but I was not lonely. Nor was I afraid: we had accepted each other, she and I. For the first time in my life I had a friend.

I faked illness so that we could be together, taking laudanum and pretending to sleep. My dreams were magical ships with sails like wings high in the clear air. For the first time in years I felt free of that hateful, anguished edifice of guilt Henry had constructed around me, free of Henry, free of myself. I was clear as glass, pure as spring water. I opened the windows of my chamber and felt the wind whistle through me as if I were a flute . . .

'Why, ma'am!'

Tabby's voice jolted me from my euphoric reverie and I turned, feeling suddenly dizzy and shaken. She put down the tray she was carrying and ran towards me; in the abrupt doubling of my vision I could see she was shocked and concerned. Her arms locked around me, and for a moment I thought she was Fanny, come to take me home, and I began to cry again.

'Oh, ma'am!' Supporting me with one arm around my waist she half carried me towards the bed. 'Just you lie down here for a minute, ma'am. I'll have you right in no time.' Clucking to herself in tones of dismay she had the window closed in an instant and was heaping blankets over me before I could say a word. 'Fancy standing there in the cold, with hardly a stitch on—you'll catch your death, ma'am, your death! Just think what Mr Chester would say if he knew—and you're so light, just like a feather; you don't eat enough, not half enough, ma'am, why, just—'

'Please, Tabby!' I interrupted with a little laugh. 'Don't worry so much. I feel quite recovered now. And I like the fresh air.'

Tabby shook her head vehemently. 'Not that nasty blustery air, you don't, ma'am, begging your pardon. It's fatal to the lungs, just fatal. What you need is a nice cup of chocolate and some food, not what that Dr Russell of Mr Chester's says, but some real old-fashioned country food—'

'Dr Russell?' I tried to keep the edge from my voice, but I heard my words rising shrilly, helplessly: 'He said he wouldn't send for a doctor! I'm quite well, Tabby. Quite well.'

'Don't take on so, ma'am,' said Tabby comfortably. 'I dare say Mr Chester was anxious about you, and called for the doctor for advice. Perhaps I shouldn't have told you.'

'Oh yes, Tabby, you should. You were quite right to tell me. Please, what did the doctor say? When did he come?'

'Oh, yesterday, ma'am, when you were asleep. I don't rightly know what he said, seeing as Mr Chester talked to him alone in the library, but he just told me to make sure you kept taking your drops, and to give you plenty of hot drinks and light food. Chicken broth and jelly and the like. But to my mind'—here her face darkened again—'it's good nourishing food you need, nice puddings and red meat and maybe a glass of stout with it. That's what you need, not broth and jelly. That's what I told Mr Chester.'

'Henry . . .' I murmured, trying to quell my agitation. What did it matter that he had spoken to the doctor? Soon it would be too late for him to do anything. All I had to do was to stay calm, not to give him any excuse for dissatisfaction. Soon Mose would be ready to put his plan into action. Till then . . .

(Shhh . . . sleep. Shhh . . .)

Tabby was holding out a cup of chocolate. 'Shhh, ma'am. You drink this and lie down. It'll do you a power of good.'

I forced myself to take the cup.

'And your drops? Have you taken them yet, ma'am?'

In spite of myself I smiled. The thought of *not* taking them was, suddenly, hilariously funny. I nodded, still smiling. 'You'll have to go to the chemist's soon, Tabby, to buy some more. I've almost finished the bottle.'

'Of course I will, ma'am,' replied Tabby reassuringly. 'I'll go this very morning, don't you fret. Now you drink that chocolate and I'll bring you up some breakfast.' With mock severity: 'And see that you try to eat some of it this time!' I nodded again, closing my eyes as a sudden wave of weariness broke over my aching head. I heard the door close after her and in a moment I opened my eyes again. Tizzy jumped lightly on to the coverlet beside my hand and I reached out mechanically to stroke her. Purring, she came to curl up on the pillow as close to me as she could manage and for a time we both slept.

I awoke to find my cup of cold chocolate and Tabby's promised breakfast tray beside me on the bedstand. Tea—long since gone cold—and toast with bacon and scrambled eggs. I must have slept for at least an hour. I poured the tea out of the window and gave the eggs and bacon to Tizzy, who ate them with delicate relish—at least poor Tabby would be pleased that for once my plate would not be sent back untouched. I dressed myself in an old grey housedress, pushing back my hair under a white cap; then I washed my face, noting in the mirror how pale and worn I looked. Even my eyes seemed colourless, and the bones in my face seemed to stand out with unaccustomed sharpness beneath the severe cap. I didn't care. I never thought of myself as beautiful, even in the days when I was Mr Chester's Little Stunner. Marta was always the pretty one. Not me.

Henry was at his studio as usual: he was spending almost all his time there nowadays. *The Card Players* was finished and had already received praise from Ruskin—he had recommended that Henry exhibit the painting at the Royal Academy, and had promised to write a glowing article on Henry for the newspapers—but Henry seemed distant, almost uninterested in the whole thing. He told me he was working on a different project now, a large canvas entitled *Scheherazade*, but he was oddly reticent about it. In fact I noticed that he was reticent about everything: our meals were eaten mostly in silence, the sounds of cutlery against china horribly amplified in the echoing dining-room. Several times I pleaded indisposition to avoid these terrifying meals, Henry chewing, my nervous fingers tapping my glass, my voice scratching at the silence in a desperate attempt to break it. A few times Henry emerged from his blank contemplation to launch into a violent, unsolicited tirade and for the first time I actually understood Henry Chester: I knew that he hated me with a bleak, hatefully intimate passion beyond reason or logic, something as elemental and unconscious as a swarm of wasps mindful only of the overpowering urge to sting . . . And in my new-found understanding I realized something else: Henry didn't know that he hated me. It was latent in him, something which grew in darkness, biding its time . . . I hoped Mose would act soon.

I spent the next four weeks in the drugged, dislocated half-sleep of a caterpillar in its chrysalis. I found that my body had acquired strange new tastes: I ate quantities of sweets and cakes, much to Tabby's uncritical delight, although I had never been fond of such things before, and instead of tea I began to drink lemonade. I was not allowed out of the garden—the servants saw to it that if I wanted fresh air there was always someone to keep me company as I sat by the pond or on the terrace, Em with her light-hearted babble or Tabby, inarticulate but unfailingly kind, the sleeves of her flowered smock turned up to reveal her thick red arms, her chapped, agile fingers busy with sewing or crochet. As the weather turned grim I spent hours at the window watching the rain and working at my embroidery: for the first time I actually enjoyed the tedious task of setting stitches. Sometimes the whole day passed without my noticing it and without my having formulated a single coherent thought. There were vast spaces in my mind where I remembered nothing at all, and between these spaces spun fragmented images which sometimes caught me unawares, blinding me with their sudden intensity.

One morning when Henry was out Aunt May called with Mother; my senses were so confused that day that for a while I hardly recognized them. Mother was resplendent in a pink coat and bonnet of ostrich-feathers, talking animatedly about a Mr Zellini who had taken her for a ride in his gig. Aunt May looked older and, as I kissed her, I found myself half crying for no real reason, remembering with a sudden nostalgia the old days in Cranbourn Alley.

She looked at me shrewdly from bright black eyes, holding me tightly against her hard, flat chest and murmured, so low that I could hardly hear her: 'Oh, Effie, come home. You know you'll always have a home with me, whatever happens. Come home with me now, before it's too late.'

And a part of my tears was the knowledge that it was already too late. I had a new home now, a new family. At that moment a terrible sensation swept over me, of drowning in alien memories . . . perhaps if we had been alone I might have tried to tell Aunt May what was happening to me; but Mother was there, happily cataloguing the virtues of her Mr Zellini, Tabby was polishing in the hall, her voice raised in a lusty rendition of a music-hall song . . . it was so far away from Crook Street that I could not find the words to begin.

One night, as I was preparing for sleep, I thought of Mose with an abrupt, hurt longing: stunned to realize that fully two weeks had passed since I had thought of him at all. My head began to spin and I sank helplessly on to the bed, filled with a tremendous confusion, loneliness and guilt. How could I have forgotten the man I loved, the man I would have died for? What was happening to me? If I had forgotten Mose, my mother, Aunt May, what else might I have forgotten? Perhaps I *was* losing my mind. What happened to me at night, when I seemed to sleep so deeply? Why had I found my cloak hanging in my wardrobe dripping wet one morning, as if I had been out in the rain? Why did the level of laudanum in the bottle diminish regularly, although I never remembered taking any? And why the growing knowledge that very soon something was going to happen, something momentous?

I began to keep a diary to remind myself of things, but when I reread the written pages I found that I could not remember having written half of what I saw there. Scraps of poetry, names and scribbled drawings punctuated the rest; in some placees the writing was so different to my own that I doubted I had written it at all. My own hand was neat and rounded; this stranger's hand was a shapeless scrawl, as if she had only recently learned her letters.

Once I opened my diary and read my name, EUPHEMIA MADELEINE CHESTER written over and over again. Another time it was the names of Fanny's cats: TISIPHONE, MEGAERA, ALECTO, TISIPHONE, MEGAERA, ALECTO, TISIPHONE . . . covering nearly half a page. But at other times my mind was a diamond-point of precision and clarity and it was at one of these times that I realized that Henry hated me. In the panic which followed the revelation I was able to accept, with something like joy, that I had to fight him, with all the cunning I possessed, using his own contempt for me against him. I waited, watching, and began to see what he was planning.

Tabby had warned me without meaning to, of course: as soon as she mentioned Dr Russell I knew; but the fear which had flooded me then had long since subsided. I would not let Henry win. I wrote it in my diary in blood-red capitals, so that if I suffered one of my memory-lapses I would be reminded: I was going to escape from Henry; I was going to run away with Mose; Fanny would see to that. When Henry was there I always pretended to be especially vague and somnolent . . . but my eyes were razor-sharp beneath my drowsy eyelids and I waited.

I knew what I was looking for.

39

Four weeks passed with the aching slowness of those summer afternoons when I was twelve and all Nature's treasury lay flung outside the schoolroom's dusty green windows. I waited, deliberately working myself to exhaustion in the studio so that when I eventually had to come home I would be able to present at least the semblance of sanity. The studio walls were covered with studies: profiles, full-faces, three-quarters, hands, details of hair, eyes, lips. I worked at a pace bordering upon mania; I littered the floor with sketches in watercolours, chalks and inks, every one perfect, infused with the clarity of my lover's memory.

On Saturday I went to my Bond Street supplier and bought a superb canvas, stretched and treated, the largest canvas I had ever thought to use. It was fully eight feet high and five feet across, and because it was already pinned to its frame I had to pay two men to transport it from the shop to my studio. But it was worth every penny of the twenty pounds I paid for it, for as soon as I had it set up against my easel I began to sketch feverishly, directly on to the beautiful creamy surface the monstrous, sublime figures of my fantasy.

I suppose you have seen my *Scheherazade*: she hangs at the

Academy even today, queening it over the Rossettis and the Millaises and the Hunts with all the colours of the spectrum in her cryptic eyes. She is rather taller than life; almost naked against a background of blurred Oriental drapery. Her body is barely mature, hard and slim and graceful; her skin is the colour of weak tea, her hands long and expressive with raking, green-painted fingernails. Her hair falls nearly to her feet (I have bent the truth a very little, but the rest is real, believe me) and there is a suggestion of a strut in her posture as she stands watching the watcher, defiant in her nakedness, mocking his guilty desire. She is gloriously immodest, reaching out to include the spectator in some exotic tale of perilous adventure; her face is flushed with the excitement of the tale and there is mockery and a wild humour around her mouth. At her feet lies an open book, the leaves fluttering randomly, and in the shadows two wolves lie waiting, teeth bared and eyes like sulphur. If you look at the frame you will find a fragment from a poem inscribed there:

Who goes to find Scheherazade
By land or air or sail?
Who dares to kiss her crimson lips
And lives to tell the tale?

I dare to seek Scheherazade
A thousand nights and one.
I seek her in the waning moon
And in the sinking sun.

O who can keep Scheherazade
Beyond the rising sun?
I'll seek her in the waning moon
A thousand nights and one.

On Thursday I came home earlier than usual: the vision of my half-completed *Scheherazade* was too powerful for me that day. I had left the studio in haste, omitting to change, my head suddenly filled with an ache which surged monstrously into the bloodshot orbits of my eyes. I had left my chloral at home and, as soon as I reached Cromwell Square, I ran directly to my room and the midnight-blue vial. I was halfway to the medicine closet, the bedroom door ajar behind me, when I saw her, frozen beside my writing-desk, as if by keeping quite still she thought she might pass unnoticed.

For a moment I thought she was Marta. Then a giant anger bloomed inside my head, obliterating even the pain. Maybe it was the fact that she had seen me in my unguarded, vulnerable state, scrabbling among the medicine jars for the chloral; maybe because I almost cried Marta's name aloud; or maybe it was her face, her doughy, idiot's face, her blank colourless eyes and crone's hair . . . or the letters she was holding in her hand.

Russell's letters! I had almost forgotten.

For an instant I remained silent, staring at her, my only thought a distant: 'How dare she; how *dare* she?' Effie might as well have been stone: she met my eyes with her dull grey gaze and her voice was low but accusing.

'You wrote to Dr Russell. You asked him to come.'

I was rendered temporarily speechless by her impertinence. Could she possibly be accusing me, when she had taken my letters?

'Why didn't you tell me you had written to Dr Russell?' Her voice was flat and steady and she held the letters out to me like a weapon. There was such viciousness in her face that I almost stepped back towards the door. Rage ebbed from her in waves.

'You read my letters.' I tried to make my voice commanding, but my words were a formless shuffle of sounds, like a handful of spilled cards. My thoughts seemed suddenly very remote and slow, anger obstructing their growth. I tried again. 'You have no right to look into my papers,' I said, licking my lips. 'My private papers.'

For the first time I could recall she did not wince at the sharp note in my voice. Her eyes were like stone and verdigris; cat's eyes.

'Tabby told me Dr Russell had called. *You* never told me. Why didn't you tell me you'd sent for him, Henry? Why didn't you want me to know?'

A slow, cottony fear began to chill through me. I felt small, somehow, before her scorching wrath, shrinking before her, becoming someone else, someone younger . . . the image of the dancing Columbine leaped abruptly into my mind like memory's hateful Jack-in-the-box; and I realized that I was beginning to sweat. I forced myself not to look at the chloral bottle inches from my hand.

'Now listen to me, Effie!' I snapped. Yes, that was better, much better. 'You are being foolish beyond permission. I am your husband and I have every right to take any measure I wish to ensure your good health. I know your nerves are bad, but that does not give you an excuse to pry into my personal papers I—'

'There's *nothing* the matter with my nerves!' Her voice rose furiously, but with none of the hysteria I would have expected from such an outburst. Instead there was a bitter sarcasm in her tone as she read aloud from the letter, mimicking the doctor's ponderous accents with the accuracy of an impudent child.

'Dear Mr Chester,

Following our recent conversation I am in whole-hearted agreement with your own diagnosis of your dear wife's nervous condition. While the mania seems not to be acute at present there does seem to be evidence of some degeneration; I would continue to recommend the frequent use of laudanum to prevent further fits of hysteria, as well as a light diet and a good deal of rest. I agree that it would be most unwise for the lady to walk abroad until I have made further verifications as to her mental state; in the meantime, I suggest that you keep her under close watch, reporting any instances of convulsion, fainting, hysteria or catalepsy—'

'Effie!' I interrupted. 'You don't understand!' Even to myself the words sounded weakly conciliatory and I was again overwhelmed by that unsettling sensation of diminishment. My head was pounding and I did not dare take the chloral bottle while she was watching. Once I darted my shaking hand towards it, knocking it to the back of the cabinet among the other potions and powders ... impossible to reach it now unless I actually turned my back on her, exposing the vulnerable nape of my neck to the evil potency of her eyes.

'I only want to help you,' I blurted. 'I want to see you well again; I know you've been ill and I ... you were so ill after you lost the baby ... it was only normal that your nerves should be a little unsettled. That's all it was, I promise, Effie. I promise!'

Stonily: 'There's nothing the matter with my nerves.'

'I'm glad to hear it, my dear,' I replied, finding my balance, 'and if you are right, I'll be the first one to be thankful. But you mustn't be foolish. This ... this silly fancy of yours ... This silly fancy that the doctor and I are somehow ... *conspiring* against you: can't you see that is what I was afraid of? You are my wife, Effie. What wife suspects her husband as you seem to suspect me?'

She frowned, but I could see that I had shaken her. The

pounding in my skull abated a little and I smiled and stepped forwards to put my arms around her. She stiffened, but did not pull
away. Her skin was burning.

'Poor darling. Perhaps you'd better lie down for a while,' I recommended. 'I'll send Tabby with a cup of tea.' I felt her rigid
body jerk convulsively in my arms.

'I don't want tea!' Her voice was muffled by her hair, but I
guessed at the helpless petulance in her cry and allowed myself to
smile. For a while there I had been worried by her icy, furious
composure but, as I knew she would, she had reverted to type. I
should have known that obedience was so deeply ingrained in her
that she would not defy me for long. And yet I had seen something in her eyes . . . something which for a short time had dismissed me as if I didn't matter, as if I didn't even exist . . .

Long after she left the room the memory of that moment persisted. Even the midnight-blue bottle was powerless against the
jangling of my discordant thoughts, and when I finally subsided
into a sleep I dreamed of winding up Father's dancing Columbine. I was a twelve-year-old again, watching in awe as she
danced faster and faster, writhing now in demoniac frenzy, arms,
legs and bloodstained skirt a blur. And now in my dream I was
possessed by the cold certainty that I had set some evil into
motion, which was even now winging its way towards me
through the years of my childhood, waiting to be given the
chance to pierce through the veil of memory and strike . . .

I reached through the churning air towards the blur of silk
and knives that was Columbine—I felt my hand slashed as if
by a razor but I managed to grasp her. She writhed in my hand
like a snake, but I held firm and, taking my aim carefully, I
flung her at the wall as hard as I could. There was a crash, a siz-
zle of gears and wheels, a final shiver of music . . . and when I
dared look again she was lying broken at the foot of the wall,

her china head smashed and her skirts drawn up around her waist. I felt a vast, hot wave of relief. And, as I began to move uneasily out of the dream towards wakefulness, I heard my own voice speaking, with eerie, dislocated clarity:

'Should have stayed asleep, little girl.'

The Ace
of Swords

40

They came together now, like ghostly twins, their faces merging one into the other so that for an instant Effie would stare at me through my daughter's eyes, or Marta's laughter filter through the veil of Effie's smile. At last she was there, almost visible, and it seemed that my heart would burst for love of her, love of them both. She was happy now, happier than she had ever been before, knowing that she had come home, that she was safe with her mother again, safe with her sister. Since the night I asked her to name the Hermit I had not needed her memories: that part of her slept, sinking deeper into the murk of things best left forgotten, and she had stopped dreaming of the Bad Man and what he did to her long ago. In fact, with the help of my potions she remembered very little.

She was content to sleep in her room with her books and toys around her; she played with Meg and Alecto and, when Henry came, she played with him, too. Every visit dragged him deeper; we dosed him with chloral and strong aphrodisiacs, flayed him with kisses which left him gasping on the floor long after Marta had left the room. He lost his power to distinguish reality from fiction and I am certain that if I had shown him Effie in her undisguised form he would not have recognized her. Her body had grown thin and sores bloomed on her arms and chest; but Henry was beyond noticing them. My Marta shone through Effie's flesh, transcending it, growing strong; and he was hers, all hers. I watched him become vague-eyed and listless as weeks passed, jumping at shadows, and my heart was filled with black rejoicing as we fed on him, my daughter and I. Don't let anyone tell you vengeance isn't sweet: it is. I know.

Mose came to see me twice. His creditors wouldn't wait for ever, he told me, and he didn't understand what we were waiting for. I lent him fifty pounds to tide him over and he seemed happy enough to play along for a while. Soon, I told him. Soon.

Just give my Marta time to grow.

Five more weeks passed and on five more Thursdays Henry Chester stumbled blindly up the steps of my house into a nightmarish rapture of lust. She walked right through him, my wraith, emptying him of all his assurance, his pretentious male superiority, his religious bigotry, his icons and his dreams. If he had not been Henry Chester I could have pitied him, but the thought of my sad little ghost and what she had once been cleared my head of all ambiguity. He had had no pity for my Marta.

Those five weeks saw the fleeting of a grey, lustreless autumn; winter came early and a hard, ringing black wind brought ice to the roads and tore the sky into dark, tattered streamers of grey. I remember Christmas decorations in the London shops, fir trees on Oxford Street and tinsel along the gaslamps, but at Crook Street the windows and doors stayed unadorned. We would celebrate later.

Henry came for the last time on 22 December: night fell at three that afternoon and by nine the thin rain had turned to sleet and then to snow, barely whitening the cobbles before turning black. Perhaps it was going to be a white Christmas after all. Effie came early, wrapped to the eyes in her thick cloak; I looked at the sky and almost turned her away, thinking that Henry would never come on such a bleak, dreadful night. But Marta's faith was greater than mine.

'He'll come,' she said with impish assurance, 'especially tonight.'

Oh, my lovely Marta! Her smile was so beautiful that I was tempted to abandon my revenge. Wasn't it enough to have her again, to hold her in my arms and feel her cool skin against my cheek? Why risk that for a sterile victory over a man already damned?

But of course I knew why.

For the moment she was still his. In his eyes half of her was still Effie, and she would never fully be mine until he abandoned his claim. While he continued to see them as separate individuals they could never be truly united, never return to the good, safe place they had left. They would be two floating halves, disintegrating slowly in a void of forgetfulness from which only a mother's love could drag them. She had to be freed.

'Marta.'

Her smile from behind Effie's viridescent gaze was radiant. 'Whatever happens, remember how much I love you.'

I felt her little hand creep into the warm hollow of my neck.

'I promise it will soon be over, darling,' I whispered, my arms around her, 'I promise.'

I felt her smile against my skin.

'I know, Mother,' she said. 'I love you, too.'

41

After that confrontation, my wife was the enemy: a soft shadow watching with cold, verdigris eyes as I moved through our haunted house. She had grown mantis-thin in spite of the quantities of sweetmeats she ate, drifting like a drowned mermaid through the thick green air of the gas-jets. I did what I could to avoid touching her, but she seemed to take pleasure in brushing against me as often as she could, and her touch was like winter fog. She hardly spoke to me but murmured to herself in a thin, childish voice; sometimes, as I lay awake at night, I fancied I could hear her singing in the dark: nursery rhymes and schoolyard chants and a French lullaby she had sung when she was a little girl:

> 'Aux marches du palais . . .
> Aux marches du palais . . .
> 'Y a une si belle fille, lonlà
> 'Y a une si belle fille . . .'

I spoke with Russell once more, and I allowed myself to be persuaded, with sighs and the suggestion of a few manly tears, that the only hope of a cure for my darling Effie was a spell of close supervision at some reputable hospice. I flinched visibly at the good doctor's hint that grief at the loss of her child might have permanently unhinged Effie's mind, but demurred when it was forcibly brought home that if I did not act soon Effie might do something to seriously injure herself. With an outwardly clouded brow and a hot, inward grin I signed a paper, which the doctor countersigned, and I tucked it carefully into my wallet when I left. On the way home I stopped at my club for lunch—for the first time in weeks—and ate ravenously. Over my glass of brandy I allowed myself the rare luxury of a cigar. I was celebrating.

It was almost dark when I reached Cromwell Square, though when I looked at my watch it was only ten past three. The wind had risen, blowing drifts of black leaves hither and thither across the roads, and I thought I felt the sting of sleet against my face as I paid the hackney and hurried indoors. A freezing catspaw of gritty wind clutched at my coat-tails as I opened the door, sending a flurry of dead leaves into the house ahead of me; I slammed the door against the dark, shivering. There might be snow tonight.

I found Effie in the unlit drawing-room, sitting beside the empty grate with her tapestry discarded across her knees. The window, absurdly, was open and the wind blew directly into the room. Dead leaves littered the floor. For a brief, nightmarish moment the old terror overwhelmed me again, the feeling of helpless diminishment, as if for all her Gothic pallor and ghostly appearance she had somehow made me a ghost in my own house, myself the wraithlike drifter and she the solid, living flesh. Then I remembered the paper in my wallet and the world reasserted itself. With an impatient exclamation and two steps forwards I rang the bell for Tabby, forcing myself to speak to Effie as I squinted at the grey blur of her face in the dark.

'Now, Effie,' I chided. 'What are you thinking of, sitting here in the freezing cold? You'll catch your death. And what is Tabby thinking of letting you stay here with no fire? How long have you been here?' She turned towards me, a half-girl, her face bisected by the slice of gaslight from the passage.

'Henry.' Her voice was as flat and colourless as the rest of her. In the bizarre dislocation of her features only half her mouth seemed to move: one eye fixed mine, pupil drawn to a pinprick against the light.

'Don't you fret, my dear,' I continued, 'Tabby will be here presently. I'll make sure she lights a nice fire for you, and then you can have some hot chocolate. We don't want you to catch a chill now, do we?'

'Don't we?' I fancied there was a faintly sardonic intonation in her voice.

'Of course not, my dear,' I replied briskly, fighting an urge to gabble. 'Tabby! Drat the woman, she should be here by now. Tabby! Does she want you to freeze to death?'

'Tabby's gone out,' said Effie softly. 'I told her to go to the chemist's for my drops.'

'Oh.'

'There's nobody else. Em has the afternoon off. Edwin has gone home. We're alone, Henry.'

The unreasoning terror swept over me again and I struggled to keep control. For some reason the thought of being alone with Effie, at the mercy of whatever strange thoughts were playing through her mind, appalled me. I fumbled in my pocket for my cigar-lighter, forced myself to turn my back to her as I struggled to light the lamp...I felt her eyes like nails in the back of my neck and my jaw cramped with hatred of her.

'That's better, isn't it? Now we can see each other.' That was right: brisk informality. No need to feel that she had somehow planned a confrontation; no reason to think that somehow she already *knew* . . . I turned to face her again, my jaw now aching with a smile I knew did not fool her for a minute.

'I'll close the window,' I said.

I took as long as I dared over the latch, the curtain, the leaves on the floor. I threw the leaves into the grate. 'I wonder if I could get the fire going.'

'I'm not cold,' said Effie.

'But I am,' I replied with false cheerfulness. 'Let's see . . . it can't be difficult. Tabby does it every day.' I knelt down in front of the grate and began to arrange the papers and dry sticks on the coals. There was a brief flare and crackle, then the chimney began to smoke.

'Dear me,' I laughed, 'there must be more of a knack to this than I thought.'

Effie's lips twisted in a knowing, hateful half-smile. 'I'm not a child,' she spat suddenly. 'Nor am I a half-wit. You don't have to talk to me as if I were.'

Her reaction was so abrupt that I was again taken aback. 'Why, Effie,' I began foolishly, 'I . . .' Collecting myself I made my voice crisply patient, like a doctor's. 'I can see you are ill,' I said. 'I can only say that I hope later you will realize quite how hurtful and ungrateful your words seem to me. However, I—'

'Nor am I ill,' interrupted Effie once more—and for that moment I believed it: her eyes were as sharp and bright as scalpels—'In spite of everything you have said and done to prove me otherwise, I am not ill. Please, don't bother to try to lie to me, Henry. We're alone in the house; there is no-one for you to perform to but yourself. Try to be honest, for both our sakes.' Her voice was dry and emotionless, like a governess's, and for a moment I was twelve again, blustering falsely and naively to try and save myself from punishment, every word fixing my guilt deeper and deeper.

'You have no right to talk to me like that!' My voice sounded weak even to myself, and I strained to keep the authority in my tones. 'There are limits to my patience, Effie, even though I make great allowances for your behaviour. You owe me respect as a wife, if nothing else, and—'

'Wife?' exclaimed Effie, and I was oddly reassured to hear a shrill note creep into her measured tones. 'Since when did you ever want me to be a *wife*? If I were to tell what you . . .'

'Tell what?' My voice was too loud but it seemed the words were beyond my control. 'That I've nursed you when you were sick, borne your tantrums, given you everything you have ever wanted? I—'

'My Aunt May always said it wasn't decent for you to marry a girl so much younger. If she knew . . .'

'Knew what?'

Her voice was a whisper. 'Knew how you treat me . . . and where you go in the middle of the night . . .'

'You're raving, girl. Go where, for Heaven's sake?'

'You know. Crook Street.'

I gasped. How could she have known? Could someone have recognized me? Could I have been followed? The implications of what she knew flooded over me. It couldn't be. She was bluffing.

'You're mad!'

She shook her head silently.

'You're mad, and I can prove it!' Feverishly I reached into my coat pocket, dragging out Russell's paper. I read it aloud in breathy snatches, sick euphoria coursing through my veins: '". . . that the patient, Euphemia Madeleine Chester . . . evidence too great to be ignored . . . mania, hysteria and catalepsy . . . dangerous to self and to others . . . hitherto recommend indefinite treatment . . . hands of . . . equipped to . . ." You heard what he said:

I can have you sent to an asylum, Effie, an asylum for the insane! No-one will believe an insane woman. No-one!'

There was no expression on her face, just a terrible blankness. For a moment I wondered whether she had heard me, or whether she had retired once more into her strange unguessed-at thoughts. But when she spoke her voice was very calm.

'I always knew you'd betray me, Henry,' she said.

I tried to speak; but after all, she was right: there was no-one to perform to but myself.

'I knew you didn't love me any more.' She smiled and for a moment looked almost beautiful. 'But that's all right, because I haven't loved you for a *long* time.' She tilted her head as if remembering something. 'But I won't let you sacrifice me, Henry. I won't let you lock me up. I'm not ill and soon enough someone will realize that. Then maybe people will begin to believe what I say.' She flicked me a glance which seemed ridden with malice. 'And I could tell them so much, Henry,' she added levelly. 'The house in Crook Street and what goes on there . . . Fanny Miller wouldn't lie for you, would she?'

My breath was a mouthful of needles in my throat, my chest tightening unbearably. Suddenly, desperately, I needed my chloral. Heedless of Effie's triumphant smile I grabbed the vial from around my neck and wrenched out the stopper. With shaking hands I poured ten drops into a glass and topped the glass with sherry. The glass was too full: some of the drink spilled, running down on to my cuff. A sudden, exquisite hatred welled up inside me.

'No-one would believe such an outlandish tale.' My voice was level again, and my relief was immense.

'I think they might,' she said. 'Besides, think of the scandal just as your work is beginning to gain recognition. The very hint that you had tried to put your wife in an asylum to prevent her from exposing your secret vice . . . it would ruin you. Would you risk that?'

I thanked whatever dark gods there were for the chloral; already it seemed as if the lid of my head had been lifted and a draught of cold air blown in, reducing my thoughts to the size of motes in the wind. I heard my voice speaking from a great distance.

'My dear Effie, you're overwrought. I think you should lie down and wait for Tabby to bring your drops.'

'I won't lie down!' Realizing her advantage was somehow gone Effie lost her eerie composure and her voice had a sharp edge of hysteria.

'Well, don't lie down then, dear,' I replied. 'Far be it from me to coerce you. I'll go down and see if Tabby has come back yet.'

'You don't believe me, do you?'

'Of course I believe you, my dear. Of course I do.'

'I can ruin you, Henry.' (Her voice wavered even as she tried to control it: 'ru-in you, H-henry.') 'I can and I will!' But the ghostly figure with the soft, cold voice and the verdigris eyes had gone, and the threat was empty. Tears silvered her face and her hands were shaking. I brushed the paper in my breast pocket and allowed myself the luxury of a smile.

'Sleep well, Effie.'

And, as I turned away into the gaslit passage, I felt a clenched fist tighten beneath my ribcage; tightening joyfully, cruelly. I'd never let her touch us, Marta and me. Never.

I'd see her dead, first.

I arrived at Crook Street twenty minutes late with the throat of the storm funnelled at my back. There was snow on the cobbles, melting into the winter rubbish to form a thick, oily sludge which made the hackney's wheels slip and skid on the corners. I was oddly serene in spite of the evening's confrontation with Effie— I had taken a second dose of chloral before setting off.

With Marta at my journey's end Effie was hardly in my mind: tomorrow I would arrange for her to be taken to a good nursing-home at some distance from London where no-one would listen to her ravings—and if they did, my exemplary public life would surely exonerate me from all suspicion: she was, after all, only a woman, and an artist's model at that. I might be pitied for the failure of my marriage, but I would not be blamed. Besides...she was ill. Maybe more ill than any of us thought. On a night like this I felt that almost anything might happen.

The door of Number 18 fanned open in a quarter of rosy light; shaking off morbid thoughts, I entered, leaving a trail of frozen mud behind me on the doorstep. Fanny was in magnolia silk and zephyr gauze; looking absurdly virginal, like a young bride, and I wondered uneasily about the limitless powers of women to appear as men wish to see them. Even Marta.

Even Marta.

What bleak secrets did *her* perfect flesh conceal?

Wordless, I followed Fanny's whispering train to the very eaves of the house: the attics, the box-rooms. As I realized where she was leading me I felt a sudden horror, as if she might throw open the door of the little attic bedroom to reveal the same scene; the toys on the floor, the white bed, the flowers on the bedstand and that whore's child naked beneath her nightdress, unchanged but a little pale after all those years in her dark vault, holding out her arms and calling out to me in Marta's blurred voice...

My own voice was brittle as icing: 'Why do I have to go right up here? Why can't we go into one of the parlours?'

Fanny ignored my incivility. 'This is Marta's own room,

Henry,' she explained reasonably. 'She especially asked for you to be brought up here.'

'Oh.' My words were a tangle of wires in my mouth. 'I . . . if she doesn't mind, I'd rather not . . . isn't it rather gloomy up here? And cold. It's very cold in this part of the house. Maybe . . .'

'The room is Marta's choice,' replied Fanny inexorably. 'If you were to snub her in this, I don't think she would accept to see you again.'

'Oh.' There was nothing more to say. I tried a jovial smile which felt more like a grimace. 'I . . . I hadn't quite understood. Certainly, if Marta . . .'

But Fanny had already turned away, her train dragging on the stairs. The floor looked as if no-one ever disturbed the dust by their passage. I looked at the door, almost expecting to see the blue-and-white enamel knob of my mother's dressing-room. I shook the thought away before it could reach my precarious chloral-induced self-control. What nonsense. There was no blue-and-white knob, no pale little whore's child with dark accusing eyes and chocolate around her mouth; there was only Marta, Marta, Marta, Marta . . . I put my hand on the knob, noticing the chipped white paint revealing the spectres of underlying layers . . . green, yellow, red . . . but not blue, I thought triumphantly, not blue. And beside my hand against the paint I saw the prints of small fingers, as if a child had paused there, pressing a palm and three fingers against the panels . . . Marta?

Even her hands could not be that small. And the marks, sticky, blurred impressions, fresh against the white. Could they be . . . *chocolate*?

My self-control collapsed. I screamed and pushed against the door with all my strength. It did not open. There was no room in my mind for thought: an insane logic compelled me, a sudden conviction that after all these years, *this* was how God intended me to pay for what I had done to the whore's child . . . to pay with Marta. The image was dreadfully plausible to my disordered brain: the whore's child with her hand on the door, listening; entering to find Marta waiting for me. Leaving again, her revenge taken . . . and Marta still waiting with her dress pulled up over her face . . .

I screamed again and began to pound against the panels with my bruised fists. 'Marta! Marta! M-m . . .'

Then the door opened into darkness. My momentum carried me into the room and crashed me against the far wall as the door swung shut behind me. For a moment the darkness was absolute and I continued to scream, certain now that the ghostchild was in the room with me, so cold, so white, and still wanting her story.

A light flared. For a moment I was blinded, then I saw her standing by the window, the lamp in her hand. My relief was so great that I almost passed out, great black blooms patterning my vision.

'Marta.' I tried to keep the relief from my voice. 'I . . . I'm sorry. I'm . . . not quite myself today.' I grinned weakly.

'As a matter of fact, Mr Chester, neither am I.' Her smile was small and mischievous, her voice a whisper of hay and summer sky. 'Perhaps we both need a drink.'

As she poured the drinks I watched her, feeling my heartbeat slow to almost normal, and before long I was able to look around.

The room was quite bare. A narrow bed with a white coverlet, a bedstand with a ewer and basin, a small table and a shabby armchair were all the furnishings there and, by the light of the single lamp, everything looked all the more bleak. There were no rugs on the bare boards, no pictures on the walls, no curtains. And today Marta herself was like her room, dressed in a plain white nightgown, barefoot, with her hair loose and partly shield-

ing her face. For a moment I began to feel uneasy once more—
the similarities to that other night were too strong—as if this, too,
were another of her disguises designed to push me off-balance
into permanent insanity. But when she put her arms around me
she was warm and lightly scented with simple, childish fragrances:
soap and lavender and something sweet like liquorice; she who
had overwhelmed me with heady, exotic sensations was now the
most elementary of juvenile seductresses, a shy, eager virgin of
fourteen, delightfully untutored, painfully sincere.

And of course I knew that this, too, was one of her disguises:
the essential Marta was as unknown to me now as it had ever
been. But I gave myself up to the illusion of tenderness, and as we
lay like children in each other's arms she whispered a little story
into my ear: the story of a man who falls in love with a dead
woman's portrait, who buys it and hides it in his attic for fear his
wife might ask questions. Every day he visits the portrait, growing more and more melancholy, unable to give up the pleasure he
feels gazing upon it. His wife begins to suspect and one day she
follows him up into his secret place and watches him as he sits in
front of the portrait. Seized with jealousy she waits until he has
gone, then she takes a knife and goes up to the hated picture,
meaning to slash it to pieces. But the picture is haunted by the
soul of the dead woman and, as her rival comes at her with the
knife, she leaps at her. There is a struggle, but the ghostwoman
has the strength of desperation. The poor wife is driven shrieking
out of her body into chaos and the ghostwoman, taking the
other's life for herself, calmly goes down the stairs to join her new
lover.

I shivered as the story ended. 'Do you believe in ghosts,
Marta?' I asked.

I felt her nod against my bare skin, and I thought she laughed
softly. The laugh made me uneasy, and it was with a touch of

anger that I replied: 'There are no ghosts. People don't come back to haunt the living. I don't believe people go anywhere after they're dead.'

'Not even Heaven?'

'Especially not Heaven.'

'So . . .' Her voice was teasing: 'You're not afraid of the dead?'

'Why should I be afraid? I've nothing to be ashamed of.' My face was burning and I wondered whether she could feel it. 'I don't want to talk about this.'

'All right.' Her acceptance was childlike. 'Then tell me about your day.' I laughed outright at that: hearing that wifely phrase in her mouth!

'No, tell me,' she insisted.

So I told her: perhaps more than I intended. She was soft and childish in my arms, silent but for occasional little sounds of acquiescence. I told her about Effie and how I had come to dread her; my almost superstitious feeling of being a ghost in my own home; my decision to remove Effie to an asylum where she would no longer be a threat; my conviction that she could destroy me. Effie knew about us now—though how she knew I could not imagine—Effie, the enemy, the silent watcher from the shadows, the ghostchild . . . the ghost. Effie, who should have stayed asleep, who should have died: Effie, who should have been dead . . .

After a while I forgot I was talking to Marta but imagined myself instead before God's throne, bargaining desperately with Him in His sublime and stupid indifference, bargaining for my life . . .

I had no right: I know that now. I took Effie before she was even old enough to understand what love was. I cheated her of her own chance at happiness. I twisted her to suit my own twisted appetites, then cut her away when I tired of her.

I know what I am.

And yet, with Marta in my arms, feeling the soft moisture of her breath against my skin, I seemed to glimpse another possibility, one which raised the hairs on my arms in a delicate, ecstatic self-loathing. The words I had spoken to Marta rang on in the hollow of my skull, sweet and taut as the invisible harp behind my eyelids:

'There are no ghosts. People don't come back to haunt the living. I don't believe people go anywhere after they're dead.' I realized I had repeated the words aloud, interrupting the flow of agonized self-analysis. But I could not remember a word of what I had spoken.

Marta was watching me, appraising. Her face was stone. 'Henry.'

Suddenly I knew what she was going to say and I flinched, caught in the beam of her deathly gaze. I began to speak, not caring what I was saying, anything to prevent her from speaking the words, the *word* I could hear resonating pitilessly . . .

'Henry.'

I turned. She was inescapable.

'Do you remember the day you told me you loved me?'

I nodded mutely.

'You made me a promise. Did you mean it?'

I hesitated. 'I . . .'

'Did you mean it?'

'Yes.' My head was pounding, my mouth flooded with a sourness like raw gin.

'Listen to me, Henry.' Her voice was low, compelling, intimate as death. 'You don't love her any more. You love me now. Don't you?'

I nodded.

'For as long as she's there I'll never be yours. You'll always have to hide. Always come in secret.'

My breath fluttered through dry lips in an unspoken half-protest, but the terrible purity of her gaze silenced me.

'You say she knows about us already: she knows she can ruin you. Even to lock her up—if you could do it—might not be enough. She might talk, might make people listen. Do you think her family wouldn't believe her? There'd be a scandal, whether they did or not. Mud would stick, Henry.'

'I . . .' The knowledge of what she was going to say was like a wall of rushing fire in my brain. What was worse, I *wanted* her to say it, to loose the wolves inside my skull. Sweet Scheherazade! My head swam deliriously. She was talking about *murder*: she was talking about silencing Effie for ever . . .

For a moment I gave myself entirely up to the images which fluttered through my mind and discovered within myself a kind of arousal at the thought of murder; a feeling so intense that it almost eclipsed my longing for Marta . . . then Marta's enchantment reasserted itself and I flung my arms around her, burying my face in the sweetness and softness of her, the scent of lilac and chocolate . . . I think I was crying.

'Oh, Marta . . .'

'I'm sorry, Henry. I really have loved you, and you'll never know what these nights together have meant to me . . .'

From my abyss I felt my mind questioning frantically; what did she mean? It almost sounded as if . . .

'. . . but after this I know that we can't see each other again. I . . .'

The numbness dropped over all my senses like a frozen blanket. Only the small helpless voice in my mind kept repeating stupidly: this is goodbye, this isn't what she was meant to say, this is . . . No! It couldn't be that! This wasn't the word I was expecting from her! This wasn't the promise I wanted to keep. Hysteria welled up in me. From a great distance I could hear my own voice beginning to laugh; a screaming, shrilling laughter like a mad clown's.

'No! No! Anything for you . . . anything . . . everything . . .' The most terrible thing. 'It doesn't have to be this . . .' O my Marta, my cold Gethsemane . . . 'I'll do anything!'

At last she had heard me. She turned her face into the light, meeting my eye. I repeated my words so that she would know I was telling the truth: 'I'll do anything.'

She nodded slowly, frail and implacable. I forced my voice into something like control.

'Effie is ill,' I said. 'She may not live long. She takes laudanum all the time. Sometimes she forgets how much she has taken.'

Marta was watching me still, her eyes eldritch as a cat's.

'She might die . . . at any time.'

It wasn't enough: as her gaze flicked away from mine I knew it; she was no Effie, grasping at shadows. I had promised her everything.

Desperately I blurted out the hateful words, cowardly admission of my already accepted guilt.

'No-one need ever know.'

The silence rang between us.

We sealed it as are traditionally sealed all the Devil's bargains. Imagine if you can the God's-eye view: Chester moaning on his rack of barbed flesh with the voice of a demon sweet in his ears—how He must have laughed! I gave my soul for a woman; how that immortal champion of the absurd must have rocked with laughter as our voices rose up out of the night to Him like flies . . . and how little I cared. Marta *was* my soul.

After my initial confession I found her terrifyingly practical. It was she who thought of the details, the plan with which you are already, no doubt, familiar. Quite coldly she outlined my part in her soft, whispering voice, her little hands like ice against my skin.

It would be quite simple. The next day I would go to the studio as usual to work, returning when night fell. I would instruct Tabby to give Effie her drops as usual. After dinner when Effie went to her room I would bring her a cup of chocolate as I often did, lacing it heavily with laudanum and a little brandy to hide the drug's medicinal smell. Effie would fall into a heavy sleep which would deepen and deepen until she stopped breathing: a painless release. When it was safe to go out without being seen I would carry her outside where a friend of Marta's would be ready to help me with a hired carriage. We would drive to the cemetery and take the body to a convenient vault, which we would open with tools provided by Marta's friend. We would place the body inside and reseal the tomb, with no-one the wiser. If we made sure to choose a family with no living descendants we could be certain that our tampering with the grave would never be discovered. I would be able to tell the police that my wife was mentally ill— Russell would certainly vouch for that—and prone to erratic behaviour. I would play the part of the anxious husband, and eventually the case would be forgotten. We would be free of her at last.

I was uneasy about only one detail: my proposed accomplice. I understood that I needed someone to help me carry the body and someone to keep a watch in the cemetery, but Marta refused to tell me whom she had in mind, saying that I should trust her. Finally she grew angry, accusing me of trying to find excuses for my cowardice. I remember her sitting on the bare white bed with her legs tucked under her body like Rossetti's *Virgin Mary*, her hair wild about her shoulders and her fists clenched like flints.

'You're afraid!' she spat contemptuously. 'You promise and

promise . . . if thoughts were sins you'd be in Hell by now—but when it comes to one real action you simper and sigh like a girl! Do you think *I* wouldn't do it? Do you?'

'Marta . . .' I pleaded.

Her rage was marvellous, all fire and poison.

'Maa-rtaaa,' she mocked cruelly. 'Mmm-aaar-taaaa . . .' Suddenly I was twelve again, in the schoolyard, my face pressed into the corner of the doorway, the taste of tears and hate in my mouth (*cry-baby, cry-ba-aby, look at the ba-by cry* . . .), and I felt my vision doubling briefly as the tears began to flicker down my cheeks. I could not comprehend her sudden cruelty. For some reason Marta was enraged.

'Is that all you can do?' she screamed bitterly. 'Cry? I ask you to free yourself, to free me, and you stand there like a thwarted schoolboy? I wanted a man, a lover, and you give me nothing! I ask you for blood and you give me water!'

'M . . . M-m . . .' For a moment I almost said 'Mother'. The snarl of wires in my mouth had become a broken harp, an Aeolian cavern of pain and confusion. I felt the left side of my face twitch uncontrollably, my eyelid a trapped butterfly beneath my tortured flesh.

Her contempt was too much to endure. I screamed with all the love and hate in my swollen heart. What words there were in my scream—if they were words—I do not know.

But there was a promise; relenting, she kissed me.

I am what I am.

42

As soon as I saw him leave Marta's room and stumble downstairs, I knew our time had come. He had shed his brittle control, the icy, contemptuous mask of his respectability; and what remained had no features, no pretences, simply the stupid scream of tortured flesh and endless desire. The black, sleety wind carried him away like a drowned child, his eyes immense and wondering, so that for an instant I glimpsed the innocent he had once been ... I never saw him again. Not in the way *you* could understand, anyway.

There was no dawn that morning, but at seven o'clock Mose emerged bleary-eyed from someone else's bed demanding to see me. He came into the room without knocking, his hair over his eyes and his mouth wry. He looked tired and irritable, and I guessed that his head hurt, for he made straight for the brandy and poured himself a generous glass.

'Why, Mose,' I said lightly, 'you look terrible. You really should look after yourself, my dear.'

Mose drained the glass and grimaced. 'You'd know all about that, wouldn't you, Fanny dearest?' he retorted. 'God knows what that bitch last night put into my drink, but I've got a blinding headache. And she had the cheek to charge me four guineas into the bargain!'

'Last night you thought she was a charming girl,' I reminded him gently.

'Well, that was then. She didn't look a day under forty this morning.'

'Ingrate! Have some coffee.' I smiled and poured. 'All women are illusionists, you know.'

'You're all witches,' he snapped, reaching for his cup. 'You more than any of them, Fanny. So don't start trying any of your charm on me this morning; I'm not in the mood.' He drank for half a minute in sullen silence, then stood up abruptly, slamming his cup down on to the table so hard that I thought it might crack.

'What *is* your game, anyway?' he asked resentfully. 'I'm tired of waiting, tired of staving off my creditors when I could be getting some money from all this. When are you going to stop playing games, you and Effie, and get down to business?'

'Sit down, Mose,' I said kindly.

'I don't want to,' he snapped pettishly. 'You must think I'm as half-witted as she is. What I want is an answer now. Otherwise, like it or not, I'll do the whole thing on my own, and you and Effie won't see a penny of Chester's money. Understood?'

I sighed.

'I see I'll have to tell you,' I said.

43

You have to understand that I was furious. I had nothing against either of them—not then, at least—I had waited as Fanny wanted me to wait, without asking any questions. But time was passing and I had had another call from one of my main creditors. As for Effie, I hadn't spoken to her in weeks. I only saw her when she came to Crook Street and she was pale and listless, with the blank half-witted stare of the laudanum addict she was. Though I felt some contempt for her weakness, I sometimes also felt a pang of regret for the lovely, passionate creature she once was. She wrote to me a dozen times; her letters were desperate, violent and confused, her neat italic writing broken by paragraphs of jagged scrawlings I could hardly decipher. She dared not meet me. The day before I finally confronted Fanny I received a last message, shorter than the rest: a page torn from a schoolbook with no signature and no date. The writing was shapeless, like a child's; my name headed the note in letters three inches tall:

Mose

God my love my love my love. It seems so long. Have I been ill? Can you remember? It seems I have slept, slept all my life away . . . and dreamed so many things. I dreamed I was dead, killed by Henry Chester and left in an attic full of clockwork toys. He says I'm mad . . . but his eyes are like tunnels. Sometimes I hear him at night, when everyone is asleep: I hear him talking. Mose? Do you love her too? Is that why you won't meet me? Everyone loves her. Sometimes I think that I could die for love of her . . . my life for her, poor miserable life . . . but for you. You are my life. In the dim passageways of my sleeping memory you follow me—I hear your laughter. Your hand on my hair: I sleep for a hundred years. Dust settles on my eyelids. I grow old. She doesn't care: she'll wait for me. Will you? Sometimes I look into my face in the mirror and I wonder if she's there waiting. Mose, stop me from sleeping.

When I was at Oxford I remember going to a party at some student's rooms; a midnight, back-street affair with illicit brandy and a couple of horse-faced giggling girls from the far side of the town. I remember that someone suggested we try table-rapping and it was with a good deal of merriment that we set up a little coffee-table with chairs in a circle and the letters of the alphabet chalked around the outside. We dimmed the lights, the girls shrieking and the young men hooting with laughter as we settled down to the game. I knocked on the table as soon as the company fell silent, setting the whole cacophony off again.

At first the glass beneath our hands spun aimlessly on the table: cries of 'Silence!' interspersed the laughter and there were indignant cries to the supposed cheats in the party—all of us!

Then, seemingly of its own volition, the glass went flying across the table, spelling out ribald messages about members of the assembled gathering and causing a new outbreak of squealing from the drunken girls. I always had a fair hand at conjuring.

But then everything changed: my careful manoeuvre was aborted by some more skilled table-rapper. I sought to win back the glass, but it was wrenched from my hand and spun across the table with astounding accuracy. Irritated, I glanced at my partners across the table . . . and I swear, no-one was touching that glass. *No-one.*

Even then I knew that it was a trick: I didn't believe in ghosts, nor do I to this day. But I never found out who the trickster was that night—I had thought my friends all too drunk, or too unimaginative, to carry off such sleight of hand—but the phrases which staggered across the coffee-table in that dark room fifteen years ago, the words which seared my brain in the minutes before my nerve broke and I kicked the table over . . .

I don't know why I'm telling you this. But Effie's slashed and fractured sentences and those desperate phrases against the table-top might have come from the same lost and broken heart: a voice from the dead.

Stop me from sleeping . . .

Fanny had her own reasons for keeping Effie away from me. God knows I didn't care; I was heartily sick of their charade and wished I had never become involved. Instead, Fanny kept me supplied with drink and entertainment while I was at Crook Street and she and Effie held their interminable counsels upstairs. But that wasn't the worst of it. No.

It was that name . . . Marta.

Her name was a sigh, a prayer, a supplication: on Fanny's lips a kiss, on Henry's a moan, on Effie's a benediction of such potency that her entire being was suffused with love and longing . . . Marta.

After midnight she walked the dim passageways of the Crook Street house. I felt her light, ironical touch against the nape of my neck as she passed. I caught the scent of her against the curtains, heard her sweetly hoarse, slightly accented voice from the open window, laughing from the damp London fog. I dreamed of her as I had first seen her through the chink in the wall—a burning rose of crimson flesh, a Fury with her hair in flames, laughing through the fire like a madwoman or a goddess . . .

And yet *there was no Marta.*

Sometimes I had to remind myself of the fact for fear I might go mad like all the rest of them. There was no Marta—I *knew* that: I had seen her reduced to a swirl of red ochre in the bathroom sink, a smear of cosmetics on the white of a linen towel. Like Cinderella, she was built from midnight's deceitful magic; dawn left nothing of her but a few dyed hairs on a pillow. And yet, if I hadn't seen it with my own eyes . . .

Damn her! Damn all their poisonous games.

There was *no* Marta.

Then there was the business with Henry Chester. Oh, don't think I was having second thoughts. I had no cause to love the man, nor he to love me, but it seemed to me that the whole affair was getting a trifle too eleborate for my taste. I admit I laughed at first at the thought of Effie's seduction of her own husband—there was something infinitely perverse in the idea which appealed to me—but if you had seen Chester, with his fixed and deathly smile . . . He looked like a doomed man at Hell's own border.

What did they want of me? Damned if I knew! Fanny must have known by then that even if we succeeded in wresting Effie away from Cromwell Square there would be no place for her with me. I wasn't going to marry her and had never intended to. When she spoke of the future at all, Fanny always said: 'When we're together again,' as if some family reunion was on the cards. I couldn't see it. Effie live at Crook Street? The more I thought about it, the more absurd it seemed. The sooner I was out of the game, I decided, the better.

It wasn't even as if I were seeing any money from it all: the grim masquerade seemed to lurch on indefinitely. Looking back, I suppose I could have broken free then—I would have lost my chance to blackmail Henry Chester, but that was not why I stayed. Call it arrogance if you like: I didn't want to be bested by a woman. Either way, I fell into their trap neatly enough. I must have been mad.

I like to think I hesitated at first: the plan was so Gothic, so ludicrous, that it might well have been the libretto for some darkly burlesque operetta. Fanny sat on the sofa and preened herself as she told me, and I, in spite of my spiralling headache, found myself laughing.

'Fanny, you're priceless,' I said. 'I really did think for a moment that you were serious.'

'Oh, but I am,' she said serenely. 'Very serious.' She watched me from her cryptic agate eyes for a moment then gave me a secretive half-smile. 'I'm counting on you, Mose, my dear. Really.'

I gave a sigh of exasperation. 'Are you telling me that Effie persuaded Henry to agree to her own *murder*?' My laugh was the sick, nervous laughter of hysteria. I cleared my throat, poured myself another glass of brandy and swallowed half of it at once.

The silence rang between us.

'Don't you believe it?' said Fanny at last.

'I . . . I don't believe *Effie* . . .'

'But it wasn't Effie.'

Damn her! Her voice was smooth as cream and I knew what she was going to say.

'Damn it, Fanny, there *is* no Marta!' I heard my voice crack, high above its normal range, and fought to bring it back under control. 'There is no Marta. There's only Effie, who is three parts crazy . . . and what does she expect to gain from all this? What does she want?'

She smiled indulgently. 'You should know that.' A moment to allow her words to sink in. 'She and I are both counting on you.' Her smile became impish.

'And Marta, of course.'

44

I could not go home to Cromwell Square. The thought of enter-ing the house where *she* slept, passing her door, maybe brushing against her in the passageway or feeling her mad, accusing stare in the small of my back; watching her drink her chocolate at breakfast or unfold her needlework in the morning-room . . . and all the while *knowing* that at midnight she would be dead in some anonymous grave in Highgate, perhaps the very same which sheltered the whore's child's unquiet half-sleep . . . I could not bear it.

Instead, I made my way in the dark to my studio and tried to sleep. But the wind screamed outside in Effie's voice, rattling the windows. Twenty grains of chloral was all I dared take. Even they brought no comfort, simply a lethargy of the spirit which quickly shifted to a shivering restlessness. I had a bottle of brandy in one of my cupboards: I tried to drink it but found that my throat had constricted to pinhole-size. Choking, I spat out the burning liq-uid in a wide arc around me. Suddenly I glimpsed a movement in the far corner of the studio; in the thickest shadow I thought I saw a shifting of drapery . . . the outline of a woman's hand . . .

'Who's there?'

No answer but the wind. 'I said, who's there?' I took a step forwards and she was standing in the furthest corner, her face a pale blur, hands outstretched to claim me. For an instant I sank into total delirium, an incoherent streamer of sound unfurling from my lips ... then my groping hands met the frame and the smell of paint and varnish filled my nostrils.

'Ahhh ...' I struggled to control my voice, dragging it back to its normal range. My mouth was slack; the captured moth beneath my left eyelid desperately fluttering.

'Sch ... Scheherazade.'

That was better. I said the name again, feeling my mouth take shape again beneath the difficult syllables. I forced myself to touch the painting and my laughter was forced and cracked, but at least it was laughter. There was nothing, *nothing* to be afraid of, I told myself fiercely. There was no dancing Columbine with empty eye-sockets and carnivorous teeth; no little ghostchild with arms outstretched and chocolate on her fingers; no Prissy Mahoney with her keyhole of blood; no Mother watching from her deathbed with her lovely ravaged face ...

Enough! I forced myself to turn away from the painting (absurd that I should *feel* the hammering of Marta's eyes like nails between my shoulder-blades, pitilessly bisecting the soft white cord of my spine) and walk towards the fire. I looked at my watch. Half past two. I found a book lying face down on a chair and glanced at it idly to pass the time. To my disgust I saw that it was a book of poetry; opening it at random I read:

MY SISTER'S SLEEP
She fell asleep on Christmas Eve:
At length the long-ungranted shade
Of weary eyelids overweigh'd
The pain nought else might yet relieve.

A childish hand had underscored certain parts of the verse in red pencil and, with a shiver, I realized whose book this was; on the title page the legend EUPHEMIA MADELEINE SHELBECK, written in a round, neat hand, made me hurl the book as far away from me as possible into the shadows. Damn her! Was she never to leave me in peace?

The wind's voice had reached an unearthly pitch in the chimneys and the rafters; the building was an eyrie of fluttering, shrieking, invisible creatures. *I* was inside Pandora's box, a shadow-thing awaiting my release. How could *I* be afraid of the dark? I *was* the dark, the essence of the night's monsters. Ludicrous to think that the monster might be afraid; pathetic to imagine him cowering in the dying firelight on this, the night of his release. I was almost beginning to enjoy the thought when the studio door slammed open and terror sliced at me once more.

For an instant I actually *saw* them, my memory's demons with my mother at their head like a black angel, then an icy gust of wind razored past my head and the door slammed shut. It was then that I saw the cat, Effie's cat, standing quietly next to the door in a drift of dead leaves blown in by the wind. At first I thought that the leaves *were* the cat, then I saw its flat, agate eyes gleaming from the doorway, one paw raised with delicate precision, like a beautiful woman's greeting. As I watched it yawned like a snake and began to lick the outstretched paw with languid grace. For a moment I was frozen by certainty: it was *her*; the ghostchild, watching me through the cat's eyes, the ghost of my first murder come to taunt me as I sat here contemplating my second. Could I hear the words?

(whataboutmy what about my what about my *story*?)

'Go away!' I spoke aloud.

(will she scream henry? will she wake and see you? will she smell of lavender and chocolate oh will she henry?)

'I'm imagining this.'

(are you)

'There's no cat here.'

(henry)

'There's no cat here!'

My voice cracked and flew off into the dark like a volley of shots and, as the silence settled around me again, I realized that I was right: what I had taken for a tabby cat standing by the door was really only a curl of brown leaves shifting uneasily in the draught. Oddly, the knowledge did not cheer me but drove a deeper chill into my heart. I turned away, sickened and trembling. I wondered what Marta was doing.

The thought of her, the strong, sweet certainty of her, cleared my head a little. I imagined her in my arms, and the knowledge that she would soon be mine made my heart thrill with courage. With Marta to help me I could do it, do it without remorse: there would be no black angel at my door, no autumn-cat curled in the shadows . . . no pale little ghostchild. Not this time. This time, Marta would be mine and we would walk a thousand and one nights together.

I took five more grains of chloral and was gratified to feel them taking effect almost immediately: the top of my head had become a clear, cold drum of resonances, delightfully floating above my body like a child's balloon. My thoughts, too, were balloon-like, enclosed and remote, moving with a dreamlike slowness in the dark.

Twenty-five to three. Time spiralled out indefinitely ahead of me . . . so much time. The seconds were silent breakers rolling across a bleak, grey shore, counting out infinity. I stumbled towards my easel and began to paint.

I suppose you've seen her: some call her my greatest work, though her story is perhaps too close to the dark core of her creator for her to be appealing. I cannot imagine her sharing a gallery with Rossetti's jaded courtesans or Millais's spoiled, sugary children. *My Triumph of Death* is a gateway into my particular hell, an incarnation of every black thought, cold fear, stifled sweetness . . . she is bone-white and lethal, hair blown up and around her face the points of a dark star, her eyes blind as fists. She stands with her legs apart and her arms raised towards the pitiless unblinking Eye of God in the curdled clouds above her, naked and terrifying in her nakedness, for though nothing human remains in her stark beauty, nothing tender in the pure, violent curve of her lips, she can still arouse desire: the frozen, desperate lust of the grave. In a sense she is more beautiful than she has ever been; red and white as the bloody Host, she stands astride a shattered landscape of human bones, a red, apocalyptic sky at her back.

Though she has Marta's face she is not Marta, not Effie, not my mother or Prissy Mahoney or the dancing Columbine. Or, if you wish, she is all of them and more. She is your mother, your sister, your sweetheart . . . the dim, shameful dream you dreamed when the world was young. She is I . . . she is you . . . on her head a crown of thorns, at her feet a cat of dead leaves yawning balefully; and across the sensuousness of her snakelike, childlike body, the double triangle formed between her mouth, her breasts and the dim nebula of her pubic hair, the four occult hieroglyphs of the Tetragrammaton: yod-he-vau-he. The secret name of God.

I Am That I Am.

45

The more I thought about it, the more uneasy I became. Mose, I said to myself, you must be mad. But there was too much at stake for me to be coy about a harmless deception: the plan was simple, childishly so indeed, without the slightest risk of mishap. All I had to do was to help Henry carry Effie to the cemetery, choose a vault in which to hide the body, put her into it, seal the vault, then return to the grave when Henry was out of the way, release Effie and drive her to Crook Street. There, whatever the both of them thought, my responsibility would end and I could at last begin to collect the profits. Simple.

Henry would assume that Effie was dead, either by the over-dose he had given her or by the cold in the vault—it had snowed all day—Fanny would be satisfied and I would see some money. Effie, I hear you saying? Well, I never promised her a miracle and she had a good friend in Fanny; Fanny would look after her. I might even drop in to see her once in a while, as long as there was no talk of Marta. That was one bitch I never wanted to hear about again.

So I arrived at Cromwell Square at about half past midnight. The snow had drifted, making coach travel impossible, and I had to walk from Highgate High Street to the house with snow in my boots, in my hair and caked to the back of my coat by the wind. It was going to be a perfect Christmas Eve.

A dozen snowmen watched the High Street like ghostly sentinels—one even sported a policeman's helmet set rakishly atop its bald head—and, though the hour was late, I could hear laughter and singing from lighted windows here and there. Coloured lanterns and bright garlands hung at the doors, tinsel and candles in the windows; sharp smells of cinnamon, cloves and pine needles floated out as I passed an open doorway; light fanned across the snow as a few late and drowsy guests drifted aimlessly out of the party into the night. I smiled. On a night like this— especially tonight—anything we did would pass unnoticed.

I hammered on the door for maybe five minutes before Henry answered. When he did eventually open—I had been looking forwards to seeing his expression when he realized who Marta's 'friend' was to be—I thought he was about to slam the door shut in my face; then realization dawned and mutely he signalled me to enter. I stamped the snow from my boots, shook myself and went in. The house looked drab, almost neglected; there was no holly, no mistletoe, not a single strand of angel's hair. There was to be no Christmas in 10 Cromwell Square. Henry looked terrible: in his immaculate black suit and starched shirt, shaved close enough to remove the top layer of his skin, he looked like a corpse fresh from the mortician's. His eyes were huge and blank, his white face slack, and under his left eye a muscle fluttered and tugged, the only living thing in his derelict face.

'You're the friend of Marta's?' His first words were spoken in a hoarse undertone. 'Why didn't she tell me? Did she think I wouldn't dare . . . ? Didn't she . . . ?' I caught a flash of rage and comprehension from his dilated pupils, and he grabbed me abruptly by the lapels, shaking with sudden fury. I could see the pores of his skin magnified through the beads of sweat on his lip.

'Damn you!' he hissed. 'I always knew you couldn't be trusted. You were the one, weren't you? You told Effie about Crook Street. *You* made this happen. Didn't you?' His voice cracked and the tick beneath his eye intensified, pulling his features into a gargoyle's rictus.

I shook my collar free of his grasp. 'Dear boy, I don't have the faintest idea what you're talking about,' I told him mildly. 'I came because Marta asked me to come. She trusts me. If you don't, you can deal with the matter on your own.'

Henry glared at me, breathing heavily. 'Damn you,' he said. 'Why did it have to be you? If you breathe as much as a word about any of this . . .'

'Oh, I'm likely to, aren't I?' I said with sarcasm. 'There's plenty at stake for me too, you know. I'll see that it comes off all right—besides, we can give each other alibis. Nothing strange about a successful painter spending an evening with his patron, is there? That makes us both safe.' I ran my hands through my wet hair and manufactured a hurt expression. 'Henry,' I added, 'I thought we were friends?'

The glare went from his eyes and he nodded slowly. 'I'm a little . . . overwrought,' he said gruffly. 'Of course, I should never have thought that of you. A friend of Marta's . . .' He shook my hand awkwardly. 'You took me by surprise, that's all,' he explained, finding his stride again, 'Come into the parlour.'

I followed him warily, keeping up the hurt look beneath my smile.

'Brandy?' he asked, pouring himself a generous glassful.

'Keeps out the cold,' I said cheerily, tipping my glass to him. We drank in silence for a time.

'So,' I said at last, 'where are the servants?'

'I sent Tabby to see her sister in Clapham. Christmas visit, you know. Effie's maid is in bed with a toothache.'

'Very lucky,' I remarked. 'Almost providential, you might say.'

Henry shuddered. 'I am aware of what you must think,' he said rather stiffly. 'The situation . . . is desperate in the extreme.' He swallowed convulsively. 'As well as quite . . . repugnant to me.'

'Of course,' I said silkily.

His glance towards me was sharp and nervous, like a bird's. 'I . . .' He hesitated, no doubt aware, as I was, of the farcical aspect of the situation. These civilized drawing-room manners!

'Believe me, I do understand,' I said, knowing that if I did not speak he might remain frozen with his glass in one hand and the meaningless, apologetic smile on his face for the rest of the evening. 'I have been aware of the . . . *problems* you have had from poor Mrs Chester.'

'Yes.' He nodded emphatically. 'She was ill, poor thing, terribly ill. Dr Russell—author of several books on disorders of the mind—examined her, you know. She is quite mad. Incurable. I would have had to send her away to an institution, poor Effie; and think of the scandal!'

'Any breath of scandal would ruin your career at this stage,' I agreed earnestly, 'especially now that your *Scheherazade* has met with such critical acclaim. I hear Ruskin is thinking about an article on her.'

'Really?' But his attention was only momentarily diverted. 'So you see . . .' he continued, 'why the kindest course of action . . . the quickest and . . .' The tic resurfaced for an instant and I saw him pull out his chloral bottle and shake half a dozen grains into the palm of his hand in an easy, practised gesture. He caught my glance and swallowed the grains almost furtively, with a mouthful of brandy.

'Chloral,' he said in a low, apologetic tone. 'My friend,

Dr Russell, recommended it. For my nerves, you know. It's taste-less ... odourless.' He hesitated. 'She wouldn't ... *suffer*,' he said painfully. 'It was so ... easy. She just went to sleep.' A long pause, then he repeated the words, wonderingly, as if mesmerized by their resonance. 'She went to sleep. On Christmas Eve. Do you know that poem? I did a painting of that ...' He drifted blankly for seconds, mouth open, almost serene but for the merciless tug-ging of the muscle beneath his eye.

'There is no better time,' I said briskly, looking at my watch. 'It *is* Christmas Eve; no-one will question our being out late at night. If we're seen carrying a body, people will assume it is some friend of ours who couldn't take his drink and it's cold enough for us to wear mufflers and hats and cloaks without attracting atten-tion. Best of all, it's going to snow all night and so our footprints in the cemetery will be completely hidden. There is no better time, Henry.'

A beat of silence. I saw him nod, accepting the truth of what I had said. 'Right,' I said in a matter-of-fact tone. 'Where's Effie?'

He flinched, as if jerked by invisible strings. 'In ... her room.' I was amused to read more embarrassment than guilt in his face. 'Asleep. I—I put it in her chocolate.'

'Good.' I kept my voice neutral. 'And what will you tell the servants in the morning, when they realize she's missing?'

Henry smiled, his mouth thin. 'I'll tell Tabby that Effie has gone to see her mother for Christmas Eve. I'll say I want to sur-prise her and I'll tell Tabby to make the house beautiful for Christmas. We'll want everything: holly, mistletoe, tinsel, the biggest tree she can find ... Keep her busy. As for myself, I'll go to London and buy Effie her Christmas present as if nothing had happened.' His smile was almost serene. 'Something nice. I'll put it under the tree and I'll ask Tabby to cook a special meal for us both—something Effie really likes—' He broke off, frowning as if a sudden memory had disturbed his train of thought. 'Chocolate. She likes chocolate . . .' He paused again, his eyelid pulled by invisible wires, then with an effort continued: 'Chocolate cake, or something,' he said. 'Then I'll wait. After a while, I'll begin to get restless and I'll send a messenger to her mother's house to find out whether she has been delayed. The messenger will return to say she never arrived there. Then I'll call for the police and report her missing.'

For a moment, as I met his unflinching, triumphant gaze, I felt something almost like admiration. I wondered whether I would have been so cool in a similar circumstance. Not that I haven't done the dirty deed a few times in my life, but I never poisoned a woman in cold blood—which isn't to say that I never wanted to! As I looked at Henry Chester with his white face and that frozen, pitiless look in his eyes I wondered whether I hadn't misjudged the man. For the first time he seemed truly alive, a man in control of his fate. A man who looked his guilt in the eye with a thin bitter smile and said: 'Right. Let's go. I am what I am.'

The Two
of Cups

46

Imagine a snowflake floating down a deep well. Imagine a flake of soot falling from the dim London sky. Imagine that for a moment.

Through layers of darkness I floated; I danced through dangerous landscapes. I saw a knight with a bunch of fluttering pennants salute a lady in a tower of brass; I saw a herd of white horses; I saw the lyre-bird, his tail like a comet . . . My dark sister took me by the hand and we followed dreaming tides on the shores of strange seas; and she told me the story of a girl who slept for a hundred years, while around her everything and everybody grew old and died. But the girl had a lover who refused to forget her; he kept guard over her frozen sleep and waited and waited, he loved her so. Every day he would sit beside her and talk to her and tell her about his love. Every day he brushed her hair and kept the dust and the cobwebs from her face and waited. And, as time passed, he grew old and infirm; his servants, thinking he was mad, deserted him and went away. But still he waited. Until one day as he was sitting in the last rays of the autumn sun, almost blind and crippled with age and hardship, he thought he saw her move and open her eyes and wake.

And he died of joy with his beautiful love in his arms and her name on his dying breath.

Yes, she whispered stories to me as I slept; I felt her hand on my hair and her voice singing softly:

'Aux marches du palais . . .
Aux marches du palais . . .
'Y a une si belle fille, lonlà,
'Y a une si belle fille . . .'

I looked down on the body stretched out on the bed; poor little white girl . . . would anyone wait for her?

Mose would wait for me. I knew he would; he had promised to wake me. I knew he'd wake me. When Fanny first told me of the plan I refused. I was frightened; I didn't want to wait in the dark as they sealed the vault over my head; even with the laudanum I was sure I'd go mad . . . but she assured me, no more than ten minutes, then he'd come and I could wake up. Then we'd be together, Mose and I, and nothing could ever part us. I knew. He had promised.

Henry had sent Tabby away to see her family and my heart ached for her. I longed to have my dear Tabby with me during those cold, dark hours, to hear her kind scolding voice, to smell her good scents of dough and starch and polish, to have her tuck the blankets around me as I lay in bed . . .

Tomorrow, I told myself, Tabby would believe I was dead. Aunt May would believe it too, growing suddenly old behind the counter of the little shop in Cranbourn Alley. Mother would have to forgo her frivolous bonnets and her rides in Mr Zellini's gig— she would wear black, which did not become her, in mourning for the daughter she had never really understood. Would I dare to call on them, when I was safely out of Henry's reach? I didn't think I would ever be brave enough. I would be dead to them, dead for ever. I could not risk Henry ever finding out.

The night grew cold; snow latticed my window and blew shrieking down the chimney, hissing on the hot stones of the hearth. Wind mourned through the chimneys and the hours ticked away. Tizzy sat on my knee for a time, purring, her eyes narrowed into crescents of gold in the firelight . . . I wondered whether Henry would look after my cat when I was gone.

Suddenly I was jolted by a scraping of feet against the floor-boards outside the door. My heart began to beat wildly. It was Henry, not with poison but with something more effective to still my troublesome heart: a knife, a cleaver, a rope cunningly knot-ted. The door swung open. His face was greenish in the gaslight, like a child's painting of a witch, his eyelids drawn down into long flaps of shadow. Thankful for the discipline I had learned in years of sitting as a model for Henry I forced my face into an expression of sleepy quietude, and yawned.

'Is that you, Tabby?' I murmured.

His voice was gentle, almost tender. 'It's me. Henry. I've brought you something.' His hand brushed the nape of my neck, scorching me with his fever. 'Chocolate. For my little girl. I didn't want you to be neglected just because Tabby is away.'

'Chocolate. Thank you.' I smiled vaguely. 'That will help me to sleep, won't it?'

'Yes, it will. Sleep well, Effie . . .' He kissed the top of my head and there was his breath, hot and moist against my hair. I felt his smile.

'Goodnight, Mr Chester.'

'Goodnight, Effie.'

When he had gone, I threw Henry's chocolate away and, as I

lay on my bed, I willed my subtle body to rise. I could do this effortlessly now and, moving from room to room, I flew all over the house then out into the snow. I felt the snowflakes rush through my body but I felt no cold, only the burning exhilaration of my soul's flight. I waited: in my present state I had little notion of time and I might have been drifting for hours, rocked in the arms of the storm, before I saw them coming out of the house. My heart gave a leap as it recognized Mose, with his old hat jammed down over his eyes and the collar of his greatcoat turned up against the cold. Henry was beside him and from my whistling eyrie I could see him clearly.

He was grotesque, a dwarf, comically foreshortened by the odd perspective, an eye glancing up from beneath his hat, a pair of mittened hands upheld to ward off my wind, my storm . . . I began to laugh. To think that that was all it took: a change of angle, to convert my terror and awe into contempt. I had been so used to looking up at the thin line of his mouth, the cold tunnels of his eyes, that I had forgotten the weakness, the cruelty and deceit which flawed him . . . From above I narrowed the gaze of my new perception to focus on things unseen and I saw the shifting cloud around his head, the murky halo of tortured colours which was his soul. From the mouth of the night I laughed—and maybe this time he heard me, because he glanced upwards and, for a moment, his wild gaze met mine in an instant of pure and hellish understanding . . .

But the dark delight which flooded me then lasted only for a second, for Mose was standing behind Henry, carrying the body of poor little Effie on his arm as if it weighed no more than the cloak which covered her from head to foot, and the face of my lover was half obscured by brightness, flawed by the spectral band which masked his face in a splash of brilliant scarlet, like the executioner's crimson hood.

47

She was lying on the bed with her hair loose, her breathing so light that for an instant I thought she was really dead. The vial of laudanum was beside her on the bedstand, with the empty chocolate-cup next to it, and out of the corner of my eye I saw Henry touch the discarded cup with a hand which seemed as brittle and translucent as the china. Effie was wearing her grey dress and against the colourless fabric her skin seemed luminous, her hair touched with pale phosphorescence as it coiled across the bedspread and to the floor. For an instant my eye was caught by the brooch at her throat, a present from Fanny, a silver thing shaped like an arched cat, which mirrored the greenish light. Behind me I heard Henry make some inarticulate sound, like choking.

'She's asleep.' I spoke briskly, not wanting Henry's resolve to weaken. 'Where's her cloak?'

Henry pointed to where the cloak hung behind the door.

'Help me wrap her in it. Does it have a hood? Better find a bonnet.' Henry did not move. 'Hurry, man!' I said impatiently. 'I can't manage her on my own.'

Mutely he shook his head in disgust.

'I . . . I can't touch her. Take these,' he added, thrusting the cloak and bonnet at me. 'Put them on her.'

I shrugged irritably and set to work with the bonnet-strings and the cloak-buttons. She was light, and I found that I could carry her on my arm like a child, her head hanging against my shoulder and her feet barely touching the ground. Henry was reluctant to touch her even then; he opened doors for me, shutting them behind us with his usual prissy attention to detail, rearranged ornaments, turned down the gaslight in the hall and pulled on his boots and his coat without once looking at either her or me. Some ten minutes later we stepped out into the snow and Henry locked the door behind us. Now there would be no turning back.

Suddenly I saw Henry stop, his body stiffening. A cat had sprung out across our path, one paw held high: I recognized Effie's cat Tizzy, yellow eyes gleaming wildly with excitement at the big snowflakes whirling about her. A strangled sound came from Henry's mouth as he saw the cat. Looking at his face I was convinced that he was about to suffer some kind of an attack: his features were unravelling like a piece of knitting.

'Aahaah . . .'

'Don't be a fool, man!' I snapped more sharply than I intended. 'It's only a cat. Pull yourself together, for God's sake.' The whole situation was beginning to work upon my own nerves. 'Get your arm around her,' I ordered, deliberately brutal. 'When you've got rid of her, then you can indulge in remorse if you like, but now . . .'

He nodded and began to move again; I saw hate in his eyes, but I didn't care. It would help to take his mind from other things.

The walk to Highgate would only have taken me ten minutes or so in normal circumstances; that night it seemed endless. The snow was heaped in irregular drifts across the road; powdery, treacherous stuff which had turned to ice beneath the surface and sent our feet out from beneath us. Effie's toes dragged against the snow's thin crust, slowing our progress still further. In spite of her lightness we found we had to stop to rest every few hundred yards, our breath ribboning out around us, our hands icy and our backs drenched with sweat. We saw hardly anyone; a couple of men outside a public-house watched us with incurious eyes, a child stared out from behind a plush curtain at the window of a dark house. At one point Henry thought he saw a policeman and froze in panic until I pointed out to him that policemen were not usually issued with boot-button eyes and a carrot in place of their nose.

Half an hour later we came to the cemetery which was unnaturally bright, almost luminous against the dull orange sky. As we approached it, I felt Henry begin to hang back, dragging against my shoulder so that I was almost supporting him along with Effie. Casting a last glance around us I saw that no-one was nearby. In fact, the visibility was so poor that I could hardly see the light of the nearest gaslamp, and the flurrying snow had already begun to fill our footprints with new snow. I shifted Effie's weight from my shoulder and took the unlit lantern from my belt.

'Here,' I said shortly to Henry, 'hold her for a minute.' I saw him almost collapse as Effie's head rolled on to his shoulder: the bonnet-strings had become loosened and her hair streamed out into his face, ghostly as the snow. Henry almost dropped her in his sudden panic. With a strangled cry of loathing he thrust the body from him so that it toppled backwards into the snow and he sprang back, his hands raised in an almost childish warding-off gesture.

'She's alive!' he whispered. 'She's alive and she moved.'

'Perhaps,' I agreed, 'but she isn't conscious. Help me to get her up.' In spite of my growing irritation I kept my voice gentle. 'Not far now.'

Henry shook his head. 'I felt her move. She's waking up. I *know* she is. You take her. Give me the lantern,' he articulated painfully, and I realized that he was close to collapse.

I thrust the lantern at him and picked Effie up out of the snow, pulling the bonnet once more over her loosened hair. Behind me Henry fumbled in his pocket and pulled out his bottle of chloral, upending it into his mouth. Then, with trembling fingers, he managed to light the lantern, and with a final glance behind him he followed me through the gates and into the cemetery.

48

Behind the wall of the cemetery and the endless, exquisite tension of the wind, the silence was immense, deafening. The sky above me was filled with flying things like jigsaw pieces; no moon, no stars, only the dark flakes flying like moths into the lantern. And the ground beneath was livid as the moon, as if somehow the earth and sky had changed places for this one monstrous night.

I watched Harper's back as I followed him. In spite of the deep snow his stride was long and even; he was carrying Effie in his arms, her hair falling like a shroud over his hands and wrists. For the first time in my life I was possessed of a sudden envy of this man who seemed to have no fear, no remorse, no guilt. For he was guilty, just as much as I was, but somehow he had accepted his guilt, made his peace with it . . . How I longed to be Moses Harper! But as the chloral began to take effect I found that I was once more able to accept the enormity of what we were doing. Absorbed into the silence of myself, I realized that I was facing a Mystery, a return through tides and currents I had travelled once before, through the waters of my childhood and my sin, back to the room with the blue-and-white doorknob and the source of all my hate and misery . . . my mother.

I had long since ceased to feel the cold. There was a tingling in the tips of my fingers and in my feet, but apart from that I had no body—I drifted a few inches above the snow, dragging my feet a little against the thin crust. I realized that St Paul was right: original sin was passed on through to the soul from the body. There I was, out of my body, and I felt quite pure; the word *murder* danced before me in a volley of bright lights: stare at the word for long enough and you'll find that it becomes quite meaningless.

I remember passing through the Circle of Lebanon; sepulchres on either side of the path, thatched with snow, were outlined in the fire of the lantern. Then Harper stopped, dropped the bag of tools from his shoulder into the snow and turned towards me.

'Cover the lantern,' he said tersely, 'and keep watch here, by the path.' Nodding towards the door of the sepulchre in front of him, he gently lowered Effie on to the ground and began to search in his bag. 'No-one comes to this grave,' he explained. 'All the relatives are dead. It's the ideal place.'

I did not answer. All my attention was focused on the little sepulchre. It was a chapel of sorts, the name ISHERWOOD emblazoned across the rotting stone in Gothic script. Briefly I saw a stained-glass window in the back wall, illuminated into sudden brilliance by the lantern in my hand. By the window stood the remains of a footstool, its once-fine brocade rotted into finest filigree by age and damp. Mose had opened the door without difficulty and, with mittened hands, was sweeping the floor clear of the accumulated snow and leaves which littered the marble.

'See?' he said, without looking round. 'This is the opening.' Over his shoulder I could just see a slab of marble, slightly paler than the rest, in which was set an iron ring. 'There must be dozens of people down here,' continued Mose, beginning to pry at the sides of the slab with the help of a small chisel. 'Damn!' he exclaimed irritably as the chisel slipped in his hand. 'It's an old seal and it's tight. I'll have to chip the stone.'

Suddenly the night was at my throat like a hungry wolf. Sensation flooded my frozen limbs once more and I began to sweat. I knew what we should find in the vault when Mose finally opened it. As the bitter air seared my lungs I thought I caught the elusive scent of jasmine and honeysuckle...

Then Effie moved.

I know she did: I *saw* her. She shifted her posture slightly and she fixed me with her terrible, verdigris eyes. I tell you, I saw her.

Harper had his back to her. He had managed to dislodge the marble slab and was working it away from the hole, his breath a dragon's-plume of pale steam around his face. He heard my cry and turned, scanning the path for any sign of a witness.

'She's awake! She moved!'

I saw Harper make a gesture of impatience. But she *was* moving; almost imperceptibly at first, though I could guess at the coiled hatred unwinding through her thin white body; and her face was my mother's, was Prissy Mahoney's, was the Columbine doll and the dead whorechild, their mouths moving almost in unison to form words of black invocation, as if, at their command, the earth might open and loose a fountain of blood on to the immaculate snow... But Harper had noticed her at last; the somnolent turn of her cheek against the dark cape, the fitful clenching of her fists. In a moment he was beside her with the laudanum bottle, his arm around her shoulders. I heard her murmur something, her voice blurred like a sleeping child's.

'Mo...ose, I...'

'Shh, be quiet. Go back to sleep.' His voice was a caress.

'No...I don't...I don't want...' She was closer to wakefulness now, struggling through shades of consciousness. Harper's voice in the shadows was gentle, seductive.

'No, Effie ... go back to sleep ... shh, go back to ...'

Her eyes snapped open and, in that moment, I saw the Eye of God behind her dilated pupils. I felt His Eye focusing upon me like a magnifying glass in the sun. I faced His immense, monstrous indifference.

I screamed.

49

Cursing inwardly, I tried to keep my voice soft and soothing. Damn her! A few minutes more and the whole affair would have been concluded. I pulled the cloak over her face to try and limit the reviving effect of the cold, put my arm around her and whispered gently. But Effie was coming round quickly, her eyes moving fretfully beneath her closed lids, her breathing rapid and irregular. One-handed I opened the laudanum bottle, trying to coax her to take a few drops.

'Come on, Effie . . . shh . . . just drink this . . . come on, that's a good girl.' But I could not persuade her to take the drug. Instead, disastrously, she began to talk.

Henry wasn't far away; he had panicked when Effie opened her eyes and run a few steps down the path, but he was still within earshot. If Effie let slip a single word about our plan I knew that even now Henry was shrewd enough to guess at the rest. I put my arms tighter around her and tried to muffle her words.

'Come on . . .' I said, more urgently. 'Drink this, and be quiet.'

Her eyes focused into mine. 'Mose,' she said quite clearly, 'I had such a strange dream.'

'Never mind that,' I hissed desperately.

'I . . .' (Thank God, I thought, she was drifting again.)

'Look, just drink your medicine, like a good girl, and sleep.'

'You will . . . you'll come back for me, won't . . . won't you?'

Damn her! Henry was coming back along the path. I tried to pinch her nostrils and force the laudanum down her throat, but she was still talking.

'Just like . . . Juliet in the tomb . . . like Henry's painting. You'll come, won't you?'

Her voice was suddenly very clear in the night.

You have to understand: I never intended her any harm. If only she had kept quiet for a few minutes more . . . it really wasn't my fault. I didn't have the choice! Henry was almost at my elbow: another word and the whole thing would have been ruined. All our effort for nothing. I couldn't keep her quiet.

Understand that I acted purely on instinct: I never meant to hurt her, simply to keep her quiet for the few minutes I needed to get Henry out of the way. It was dark; my hands were numb from working with the stone, and yes, I was nervous, anyone would have been nervous.

All right, all right. I'm not proud of what I did, but you'd have done the same, believe me. I hit her head, not very hard, but harder than I intended, against the edge of the sepulchre. Just to keep her quiet. She wouldn't have thanked me if because of me Henry had tumbled to our plan; she would have wanted me to do what I could, for her sake as well as for mine.

The bitch could have ruined everything.

She crumpled into the snow and, as I picked her up I saw a bead of blood darkening the hollow where her head had rested; just a single round patch the size of a penny. I fought back panic. What if I had killed her? She was frail, already close to collapse . . . it would not have taken much to finish Henry's work. I brought my face close to hers and listened for her breathing . . . there was none. What did you expect me to do then? I couldn't react: Henry would immediately have suspected. There was nothing I could do but wait. Ten minutes, and Henry would be gone. Then I could see to Effie. I couldn't believe that little tap on the head had killed her: more likely I hadn't heard her breathing because of the noise of the wind. I couldn't afford to panic on account of something so trivial.

Gently I brushed the snow from her and carried her to the vault. Looking into the opening I could see that it was dark in there, and I hung Henry's lantern above the entrance so that I wouldn't fall. There were a dozen narrow stairs leading down, some broken and rotted with age. Carefully I carried Effie's limp body down and looked around in the gloom for a place to put her. It was slightly warmer in the vault than outside, and it stank in there, of age and mould, but at least the coffins were out of the way, hidden behind stone slabs on their shelves and sealed with cement. I carried her to the back of the vault where there was still an empty shelf wide enough to lie on. I made a pillow for her head with my knapsack, wrapped the cloak tightly around her and left her there as I made my way back up the steps towards Henry.

I sealed the vault again, scattering earth and dead leaves over the slab so that my interference would not be noticed. Then I shut the door and wedged it with a stone. Turning to Henry, I handed him the lantern and smiled.

For a moment he stared at me, his eyes blank, then he nodded and took the lantern.

'So . . . it's done,' he said softly. 'It's really done.'

Oddly enough, he sounded more lucid than he had been all night: his voice was clear and almost indifferent.

'You will remember what to do next, won't you?' I urged, wary of Henry's new serenity. 'The presents. The tree. The house-keeper. Everything has to be perfectly normal.' I was uncomfortably aware that if I had really killed Effie, we were risking my neck as well as his.

'Of course.' His tone was almost arrogant. He half turned away, and I was struck by the peculiar thought that I was being dismissed. At that thought I grinned, and suddenly I found myself laughing, choking with sour hilarity among the graves, the sound absurdly appropriate to that Gothic night as the heavy snowflakes filled my mouth, my eyes, my hair. And Henry Chester began to move slowly down the path, the lantern held high, like some stern Apostle leading the dead along the road to hell.

50

For a time beyond time there was nothing. I was beyond motion; beyond thought, beyond dreams. Then the world began to return; single thoughts drifted through my mind like isolated notes of an unfinished symphony. I moved through clouds of memory in search of myself until suddenly a face floated in front of me like a balloon and I remembered a name . . . then another . . . and another, fluttering around me in the haze like a hand of spilled cards. Fanny . . . Henry . . . Mose . . .

But where was she, my dark sister? My fellow-dreamer, my twin, my closest friend? In rising panic I looked around for her and realized that, for the first time since we met and travelled together, I was alone; alone and in darkness. A wave of memory broke upon my head and I cried out in dismay: my voice echoed oddly against frozen stone and, in the aftermath of the black wave, I realized where I was. I tried to move, but my body was stone, my hands frozen clay. As I forced my rigid limbs into movement, I found that I could raise myself on to my elbows. Painfully I began to search the area immediately around me, my eyes dilated against the endless dark. I was lying on some kind of ledge—my numb hands could not tell me whether it was of wood or stone, but I could tell that it ended a few inches to the left of me. What was beyond it I could not guess, preferring to stay quite still where I was rather than risk touching the rotting boards of some ancient coffin . . . Above me I could faintly hear the sounds of the night and the high whine of the wind.

Thinking of the outside I was for a moment disorientated, imagining myself deep under the ground with the roots of the cedars all around me. Tomorrow there would be people walking down the snowy path to church; children in bright coats and hats dreaming of sledging down Highgate Hill; lovers arm-in-arm, blinded by the sun on the snow; carol-singers with lanterns and hymn-books . . . and all the time I would be there beneath them, frozen into the dark stone with the dead around me . . .

At the thought I started and cried out involuntarily: No! Mose would come. I was supposed to wait, and he would come to find me. The realization flooded me with a great relief. For a moment I had been so confused that I had believed I was already dead, imprisoned for ever beneath the snow and the marble.

And in the warmth of that relief I slipped quietly out of my body again and out into the light where my sister was already waiting for me.

51

As I watched Henry disappear along the High Street I paused to look at my watch. It was two in the morning, technically Christmas Eve. I was drenched and, now that I was no longer carrying Effie, I had begun to feel the cold. I decided to give Henry half an hour or so to arrive home—it wouldn't do to have him walk in on me as I opened up the grave—and began the walk half a mile or so down the road to an old haunt of mine, whose owner had a healthy disrespect for closing-times and where I might be able to catch a quick drink or two to warm that grim night. If I was going to open up that vault again alone I was going to do it with a few drinks inside me.

I know what you're thinking and in a way you're right. You see, a thought had come to me as I laid Effie's lifeless body on the shelf in the vault, a thought I felt I should examine in a less morbid setting. So far I had been thinking only in terms of deceiving Henry into believing Effie was dead; neither Fanny nor I had really thought beyond that. No-one had ever wondered what would become of Effie, invalid that she was, when the charade was over. Now I realized that she would very likely need medical treatment—perhaps hospitalization. She would need a place to stay where she would not be recognized, for if word came to Henry that she was still alive it would not only mean the end of our lucrative plan but very likely arrest. In truth, everything pointed to the fact that Effie . . .

It was only a thought. A man can think, can't he? And anyway . . . I swear I would never have thought of it if I hadn't half believed she was already dead. Don't think I didn't feel a pang for my poor little Effie; I was very fond of her, you know. But you have to admit that her death would have been very convenient for all of us. Almost as if it had been meant, somehow. And so poetic, don't you think? Like Juliet in the tomb.

52

Silence shrouded me as I made my way slowly back to Cromwell Square; an immense silence like death. Effie's pitiless eyes had purged me of all thought and I walked mindlessly through the blank, drifting snow.

Stubbornly, I tried to force myself to suffer: I told myself brutally that I had murdered Effie; imagined her, still alive, inside the vault; waking, screaming, crying, scraping her fingers to bloody bone as she struggled to escape . . . but my most lurid imaginings failed to rouse the slightest shiver or the smallest stab of remorse. Nothing. And as I walked home I became aware of a kind of resonance in my mind, which gradually resolved itself into a single joyful, one-note anthem vibrating against my eardrum in time to the cadence of my heart: Marta, my black mass; my requiem; my danse macabre. I could *feel* her calling me through the night, wanting me, wanting my soul, her voice inaudible but close, intimate . . .

I reached my house and she was already there: her black cloak drawn around her so that I could only see the pale oval of her face as she beckoned me in, wordlessly. Without even stopping to light the lamps I reached for her. Why she had come; how she had entered the house were questions which did not even occur to me: enough to take her in my arms—how light she was, almost insubstantial through the heavy woollen folds of the cloak!—to bury my face in her hair and smell the acrid scent of the night on her skin: something like jasmine and lilac and chocolate . . .

My lips were burning against hers, but her flesh was searing cold; her fingers traced spirals of cold fire on my skin as she undressed me. She whispered in my ear, and her voice was like the whispering of the cypresses in Highgate cemetery. She slipped the cloak from her shoulders and I realized she was naked beneath it, ghostly in the greenish darkness, with the light from the snow reflected back on to her livid skin . . . but she was so beautiful for all that.

'Oh Marta, what I have done for you . . . what I would do for you . . .'

When it was over, I remember picking up my clothes and making my way down the passageway to my room. She followed me, still naked, her feet making no sound on the thick carpets. I left my clothes on the floor and slipped between the sheets of my bed: she followed me and we lay together like tired children until, much later, I fell asleep.

When I awoke at eight the following morning she was gone.

53

All right, all right. I had more than a couple of drinks. Well, it was warm in the Beggar's Club. I met a few friends who were playing cards and they bought me a drink. I bought a round myself, then we ordered a bite to eat, and with the cold and the walking and the drink, well, I was . . . *delayed*. Perhaps not delayed, exactly, but understand that I had been thinking hard as I walked and I had reached a difficult conclusion.

No need to look at me like that. Don't think it was an easy decision to take. In fact, it was partly to forget what I had been obliged to do that I started on the brandy in the first place, and, well, one thing led to another and I had almost managed to forget her altogether. I remember looking at my watch at five in the morning with something like shock; but by then, of course, it was too late. The decision was out of my hands.

I was too castaway to think of going home at that time; instead I gave the old harpy in charge of the club the last of my money in exchange for a room and crawled into bed in my shirt, intending to sleep until daylight then make my way home, but I had not been between the sheets for five minutes—I was already dozing comfortably—when something jolted me half-awake. I heard it again, a light, almost furtive scratching at the door, as of pointed fingernails just whispering against the uneven surface. Probably another customer, I thought, drunk as a wheelbarrow, wanting to share my room when he found all the others were full. Well, I had no intention of letting him in.

'Room's taken,' I called from beneath the blankets. Silence. Perhaps I had imagined the scratching. I began to drift almost immediately towards sleep again. Then my attention was snagged again by the sound of the doorknob turning. I began to feel annoyed. Damn the fellow, would he never leave me in peace? The door was locked anyway, I thought. Once he realized that I meant what I said he would go away.

'I said the room's taken!' I called loudly. 'Clear off, like a good chap, and find somewhere else, won't you?' That should do it, I decided, and turned over, savouring the warmth of the blankets and the smoothness of the linen.

Then the door opened.

For a second I thought it was the door of the neighbouring room, but as I glanced over my shoulder I saw a wedge of greyish light from the nearby window and, outlined momentarily, a woman's figure. Before I had time to react the door had closed again and I heard the small sounds of the woman's footsteps approaching the bed. I was about to say something—my brain was still rather fuddled by all that brandy—when she stopped beside me and I realized that she was undressing.

Well, what do you think I did? Did you expect me to pull the sheets over my head and call for the landlady? Or play the prude and say: 'Oh, miss, we hardly know each other'? No, I didn't say anything at all; I just waited: the little I had seen of the girl told me she was young and had a good figure. Maybe she had seen me in the club and thought . . . You needn't look so surprised, it's happened to me before. It also occurred to me that she might have inadvertently come to the wrong room, in which case I would be wiser to hold my tongue; besides which, I wasn't feeling half as tired as I had a minute previously.

She said nothing as her clothes slid to the ground in a rustle of silk: in the gloom I saw her pale figure move towards me, felt the weight of her on the coverlet and then beneath it as at last she slipped between the sheets with me. As she touched me I flinched. She was so cold that for an instant I had the disturbing illusion that her touch would tear my skin; but then her arms crept around me, teasingly, erotically, so that, in spite of the cold which sank into my limbs, I began to respond, to appreciate the voluptuousness of her freezing caresses. I could feel long hair falling over my face as she straddled me, hair as light and cold as cobwebs, her legs slim and strong, locking tightly around my ribs. And yet in spite of the novelty of it all I could have sworn she was familiar . . . Pointed fingernails gently raked my shivering shoulders. I heard her whisper something, almost inaudibly, against my face; instinctively I turned to hear her words.

'Mose . . .'

Even her breath was cold, raising the hairs on my chest; but more than that was the sense of unease, growing now; the knowledge that I had met her before.

'Mose . . . I looked for you for so long . . . oh, Mose.'

A moment, which was almost recognition.

'I waited, but you never came. I'm so cold.'

There again: almost . . . but not quite. And somehow I didn't want to ask who she was: just in case . . . I shifted uneasily, the fumes of the brandy clouding my thoughts; a memory blinked almost inconsequentially through the haze—myself at that long-past table-rapping party (*I'm so cold*) watching a glass which seemed to move across the polished surface on its own.

'I'm so cold . . .' Her whisper was forlorn, distant; a memory's voice. I tried the jovial approach.

'Not for long, darling. I'll soon warm you up.'

As a matter of fact, I could feel my arousal waning. Her flesh was like clay beneath my frozen fingers.

'I waited, Mose, for such a long time. I waited. But you never came. You never . . .' Another long sigh, like echoes in a cavern.

Then a thought so absurd that I almost laughed aloud; my laughter catching in my throat as I considered the implications . . .

'Effie?'

'I . . .'

'Oh God, *Effie!*' Suddenly there could be no doubt. It was her: the scent of her skin, the feel of her hair, her lost voice whispering in the dark. My head was spinning and I cursed the brandy; from a distance I could hear my voice repeating her name, stupidly, like a broken doll.

'But how did you get out? I . . .' Lamely: 'I meant to come, you know. I really did.' Hastily inventing a reason: 'There was a policeman on duty outside the cemetery when I came back so I couldn't get in. I waited and waited . . . I was frantic with worry.'

'I followed you,' she said blankly. 'I followed you here. I waited for you to come. Oh, Mose . . .'

The reality of my betrayal echoed between us, louder than words. I forced myself to speak, with counterfeit sincerity: 'God, Effie, you don't know. The damned flatfoot was there for hours . . . When I finally got past him, you were already gone. I must have missed you by minutes.' I kissed her, with counterfeit passion. 'For now, let's just be grateful that we're here together and you're safe. All right?' I forced my arms around her although I was shivering. 'Just warm up now, darling, and try to sleep.'

'Sleep ...' Her voice was almost inaudible now, her breath the tiniest whisper in the ear of the night. 'No more sleep. I've slept enough.'

When I awoke four hours later she was gone and I could almost have believed that I had imagined the whole incident; but as if to prove that I had not dreamed her she had left her calling-card on the bedstand beside me: a silver brooch shaped like an arching cat.

54

Tabby came back from visiting her family early on the morning of Christmas Eve: I awoke to the sounds of activity from below stairs and dressed in haste. I met her on the stairs, carrying a tray of chocolate and biscuits for Effie.

'Good morning, Tabby,' I said, smiling and taking the tray. 'Is that for Mrs Chester? I'll take it.'

'Oh, it's no trouble at all, sir ...' she began, but I cut her short, saying affably:

'I dare say you'll have a lot to do today, Tabby. Do see if we have any letters this morning, then come to the drawing-room and I will tell you what Mrs Chester and I have planned.'

'Very good, sir.'

I ran upstairs with the tray, tipped the chocolate out of the window and ate two of the biscuits. Then I unmade Effie's bed, rumpled her nightdress and threw it on the floor and drew the curtains. I left the cup on the bedstand—it was the kind of disorder Effie liked to live in—and, feeling well pleased with my ingenuity, went back downstairs to deal with Tabby. I was feeling very much more in control this morning; I found I could look at Effie's room, her things, touch her nightdress and the cup from which she had taken the drugged chocolate without as much as a qualm. It was as if my meeting with Marta the previous night had infused me with a new, indomitable spirit. The daylight had banished the night's demons for good and in the drawing-room I took care to adopt a jovial tone with Tabby.

'Tabby,' I said with brisk good cheer, 'today Mrs Chester has decided to surprise her mother with a Christmas visit. While she is out, you and I will surprise her.'

'Sir?' said Tabby politely.

'You will go and buy enough holly and mistletoe to trim the whole house, then you will begin to prepare the finest Christmas dinner you have ever made. I want everything: quail's eggs, goose, mushrooms . . . and, of course, the finest chocolate log—you know how partial Mrs Chester is to chocolate. If anything can bring her back to her usual happy self, that will, don't you think, Tabby?'

Tabby's eyes gleamed. 'Oh, yes, sir,' she said happily. 'I've been so worried about the poor young lady. She's that thin, sir, she needs feeding up. Good honest feeding, that's all she needs, never mind what that doctor says, and—'

'Quite,' I interrupted. 'So, Tabby, not a word. Let it be our secret to surprise Mrs Chester. If you go out immediately you will be back in plenty of time to decorate the tree.'

'Oh, sir!' beamed Tabby. 'My young lady *will* be pleased!'

'I certainly hope so.'

As Tabby left the house with a jaunty step, I allowed myself the luxury of a smile; the worst was done. If Tabby could be convinced that all was well, then my troubles were over. I was almost looking forwards to the day's shopping!

At about eleven o'clock I took a hack into Oxford Street and spent an hour or so looking at the shops. I bought a bag of chestnuts from an Irish costermonger and ate them with more relish than I had had for any food since I first met Marta, dropping the hot shells into the gutter and watching them float away on the grey river of melted snow. From one vendor I bought an ell of gold ribbon, from another a pair of pink kid gloves, from a third an orange. I almost forgot that I was acting a part and found myself carefully considering what kind of presents Effie would most like: would it be this pretty aquamarine pendant, this tortoiseshell comb, this bonnet, this shawl?

I went into a haberdasher's and found myself in front of a display of nightwear, idly looking at nightgowns, caps, petticoats. Then I froze. On the display in front of me was the wrap, my mother's peach silk négligée just as I remembered it, but new, the lace standing out from the thin silk like sea foam. I was filled with an immense, furious compulsion: I had to have it. Impossible for me to have walked away and left it, glorious trophy of my victory over guilt. I bore it away with a sense of dizzy exhilaration.

Before long I was carrying a dozen or so small packages along with the precious parcel; in my enthusiasm I had bought more presents than I had ever bought before—and among them was a small package I intended for Marta: a beautiful ruby pendant which glowed and pulsed like a heart. My last purchase was a fifteen-foot Christmas tree which I arranged to have delivered and, with a sense of perilous satisfaction, I began to make my way back to Cromwell Square.

It was then that I saw her: a small slim figure in a dark cloak, the hood pulled so that it partly covered her face. I glimpsed her long enough to see a white hand clutching the wool, and streamers of her pale hair stark in the shadow of an alley . . . then she was gone.

In an instant all my carefully built pretence was down, folding as completely as a house of cards. I struggled with the insane desire to run after her and tear the hood from her face. But that was ridiculous. Ridiculous even to *think* she might be Effie; ridiculous to imagine Effie with the mud of the grave still clinging to her skirts and that look of terrible hunger in her eyes . . .

In spite of myself I found my own eyes darting furtively down the alley where the girl had disappeared. It wouldn't do any harm to look, I told myself, just to see . . . The alley was narrow, the cobbles greasy with melted snow and weeks of accumulated rubbish. A thin brown tabby cat was nosing in the gutter after a dead bird, and the girl was gone. Of course she had gone, I told myself angrily. Did I expect her to wait for me? There were houses in the alley, shops for her to enter; this was no Gothic revenant to torment me.

And yet, I was cold, so cold . . . and as I turned resolutely from the alley into the lights and sounds of Oxford Street I could have sworn that all the doors in that lonely alley were boarded shut; yes, and all the windows too.

55

I awoke to the sound of bells: great clanging, discordant bells which rolled across my dreams, forcing them into sharp, brutal recollection. Outside the club the street was white; the air white. In the distance I could see a small group of people struggling through the haze towards the church. I rang for coffee and, ignoring the maid's cheery 'merry Christmas', I drank it and found that, as the warmth coursed through my veins, I could begin to face the previous night's events with my usual detachment. Don't think I wasn't rattled; the night had taken its toll in dreams and uneasy imaginings, but they were only dreams.

That's the difference, you see, between me and Henry Chester. He turned his terrors upon himself like hungry demons; I see my own for what they are, fictions of a restless night—and still somehow they duped me, as neatly as we duped poor Henry . . . But it isn't in me to be bitter: a gambler has to know how to lose with grace—I just wonder how they did it.

I dressed in my clothes of the previous night and began to consider my next move. God knew what Effie had told Fanny by now; last night I hadn't been able to guess whether she even understood that I had abandoned her. But Fanny would know;

and Fanny could make a great deal of trouble if she set her mind to it.

Yes, Fanny was the woman to see before I even thought of paying my visit to Henry.

So I pulled on my overcoat and made my way on foot to Crook Street. My head cleared as I walked—the air was sharp and tinselly and pungent with the scents of pine and spices—and by the time I arrived at Fanny's door I was ready to confront her with the most dangerous hand of bluff I had ever played.

I knocked for minutes on the door and received no answer. I was beginning to think that no-one was home when I heard the latch click and Fanny's face looked out at me, as white and expressionless as the face of the clock in the hall behind her. My first thought was that she had been to church because she was in black. Great folds of soft velvet swathed her from throat to ankles and, against the opulent fabric, her skin was startlingly white, her agate eyes more catlike than ever, but reddened as if she had wept. Strange and somehow uncomfortable to imagine that. In all the years I had known her I had never seen Fanny Miller shed a tear. I shifted uneasily, my smile stretching, grotesquely mobile, across my face.

'Fanny, merry Christmas!'

Unsmiling, she beckoned me to enter. I knocked my boots against the step and hung my coat in the hall. There was no sign of any of Fanny's girls and for a moment I had the eerie impression that the house was derelict. I could smell dust—or the illusion of dust—an inch thick on the rotten floorboards. For a fleeting instant I heard the ticking of the hall clock amplified into a deafening pounding like a giant heart…then it stopped abruptly, hands frozen stupidly at a minute to twelve.

'Your clock's stopped,' I said.

Fanny did not answer.

'I . . . I came as soon as I could,' I went on doggedly. 'Is Effie all right?'

Her eyes were unreadable, the pupils tiny. 'There is no Effie,' she said, almost indifferently. 'Effie is dead.'

'But . . . last night I . . .'

'There is no Effie,' she said again, and her voice was so distant that I wondered whether she, like Henry Chester, had developed too much of a taste for her own potions. 'No Effie,' she repeated. 'Now there is only Marta.'

That bitch again.

'Oh, I see, a disguise,' I said lamely. 'Well, it's a good idea; it means she won't be recognized. Ah, about last night . . .' I shifted uneasily from foot to foot: 'I . . . well, the plan went . . . I mean . . . Henry fell for the whole thing. You should have been there.'

No answer. I could not even be certain she was listening.

'I was worried about Effie,' I explained, 'I was going to come back for her straight away, but—Effie must have told you, I ran into some difficulties. There was a policeman at the cemetery gates. Must have seen the lantern and come to get a closer look . . . I waited hours. I went back at last but Effie had already gone. I was worried sick.'

Her silence was more and more unsettling. I was about to speak again when I heard a sound in the passageway behind me; a whispering of silk. Unnerved, I turned abruptly and saw a shadow, grotesquely elongated, flicker across the painted wallpaper: in the dimness of the passageway I could hardly see her. I half guessed at her features in the pale oval of her face, the folds of her grey dress falling softly to the ground in a perfect curve, her black hair loose and straight . . .

'Effie?' My voice was hoarse, attempting joviality.

'I'm Marta.'

Of course. I tried a chuckle, but the sound was lost, grotesque in the silence. Her voice was bleak, bloodless: the sound of snow falling.

Lamely I said: 'I just called to see if you were all right. Ah . . . not sickening for . . . anything, you know.'

Silence. I thought I heard her sigh; her breath the rasping of skin on frozen grass.

'I'm going to visit Henry later today,' I continued doggedly. 'You know, a business visit. Talk money.' My words were unbearable in my throat, like ulcers. I felt physical discomfort in speaking. Damn them, why didn't they speak? I saw Effie's mouth open—but no, it wasn't Effie, was it? It was Marta, that bitch Marta, black angel of Henry's desires, temptress, torturess . . . She had nothing to do with Effie, and though she might be a fiction born of ochre and powders I realized she was all the more dangerous for that. For she was real, damn her; real as you or me; and I could sense her passive delight as I stumbled through broken phrases in search of the explanation which had seemed so clear to me a few moments before in the snow. She was going to say it: I *knew* what she was going to say. Suddenly I could hardly breathe as she stepped forwards and touched me. Her rage was searing but her delicate touch against my skin was anaesthetic—I felt nothing.

'You left me, Mose. You left me to die in the dark.' The voice was hypnotic; I almost admitted it.

'No! I—'

'I know.'

'No, I was telling Fanny—'

'I know. Now it's my turn.' The voice was distant, almost expressionless; but my raw nerves were quick to sense that rage—and with it a kind of humour.

'Effie—'

'There is no Effie.'

Now, at last, I could believe that.

I took my leave as best I could; at the last fighting for breath as I struggled through fathoms of thick brown air with the smell of dust in my mouth, my nostrils, in my lungs . . . Fanny did not speak another word as I grabbed my coat and staggered out into the snow. Glancing fearfully over my shoulder, I caught one last glimpse of them, standing side by side, hand-in-hand, fixing me with their silent feral gaze. They might have been mother and daughter in that moment: their faces were identical, their hate mirrored. Panic slashed me and I fell in the snow, damp seeping into my clothes at the knees and elbows, my hands numb . . .

When I looked back again, the door was closed, but their hate remained with me, cruelly, delicately feminine, like a breath of perfume on the air. I found a gin-shop and tried to force my nerves into submission, but Marta's rage followed me even into drunkenness, souring my warmth. Damn them both! Anyone would think that I really had murdered Effie. What did they expect? I'd helped her to escape, hadn't I, even though the plan might have miscarried just a little? I'd fooled Henry, and I would be the one to get them the money—I was sure that they would have too much delicacy to dare to confront Henry themselves. Yesterday it was 'I need you, Mose, I'm counting on you, Moses' but today . . . No use wrapping it in clean linen, I told myself; they'd used me. I certainly didn't need to feel guilty about my own behaviour. I looked at my watch; half past two. I wondered what Henry was doing. The thought immediately cheered me somewhat. Soon it would be time to pay my little visit to Henry.

56

My euphoria lasted until I reached Cromwell Square. Then I saw the wreath of holly and berries on the door and a kind of lassitude crept over me, a numbing of the senses at the thought of the part I would have to enact with Tabby when, inevitably, Effie did not come home. My hand was on the door when it opened abruptly and Tabby's face appeared, smiling and radiant with excitement and pleasure. A quick glance took in the parcels in my arms and she gave a little crow of delight.

'Oh sir,' she said, 'Mrs Chester *will* be pleased! The house looks a treat, too, and I've got the cake just cooling in the oven. Oh my!'

I nodded, rather stiffly. 'You *have* been busy. Could you take these parcels and put them in the parlour?' I held out my purchases. 'Then, maybe a glass of brandy?'

'Of course, sir.' She bustled off with the presents, eager as a child, and I allowed myself a sour smile.

I was drinking brandy in the library when the Christmas tree arrived. I watched the porter and Tabby put it up in the parlour, then I watched Tabby hang it with glass balls and tinsel, sticking little white candles on to the ends of the branches with wax. It was oddly compelling. Sitting by the fire with my eyes half-closed and the pungently nostalgic scent of pine needles in my nostrils I felt a quite pleasant sense of disorientation, as if I were some other, younger Henry Chester waiting on Christmas Eve for a magical surprise . . .

Night was falling; Tabby lit candles on the mantelpiece and put more logs on the fire; the room had acquired a homely warmth, a sparkle which, though ironic in the circumstances, was oddly potent: the reality of last night seemed as distant as the events of my childhood and, as I turned to speak to Tabby, I found myself almost believing my own fiction.

'Tabby, what time is it?'

'Just left four, sir,' replied Tabby, applying the taper to the last of the tree's candles. 'Perhaps you'd like a cup of tea and a mince pie?'

'Yes, that would be very nice,' I said approvingly. 'In fact, you had better bring up a pot: Mrs Chester said she would be back at four at the latest.'

'I'll bring her a slice of my special cake,' said Tabby kindly. 'She'll likely be cold.'

Well, the pot of tea and the pies and cake stayed on the sideboard for nearly an hour before I allowed myself to feign unease. It was simpler than I thought. The fact was that with the approach of night my earlier indifference had begun to fade; I was restless without quite knowing why. I felt thirsty and drank brandy, but I found that the brandy made me hot and dizzy. My eyes kept turning towards the parcel containing the silk wrap, lying at the foot of the Christmas tree. I could not keep still.

Finally I rang for Tabby.

'Has there been no word from Mrs Chester?' I demanded. 'She did say she would be back by four, and it is past five now.'

'No word, sir,' said Tabby comfortably. 'But I wouldn't worry. Likely she's stopped for a chat somewhere. She won't be long.'

'I hope there hasn't been an accident,' I said.

'Oh, no sir,' she said, shaking her head. 'I'm sure she's on her way.'

I waited until the Christmas candles had burned to stumps on the mantelpiece. The ones on the tree were long gone and Tabby had already replaced them for when Effie returned. I drank coffee to steady myself and tried to read a book but could not concentrate on the dancing print. Finally I brought out my sketch-book and began to draw, focusing my thoughts on the lines and texture of the paper, of the pencils, my head a hive of silent bees. I looked up as seven struck on the mantelpiece clock and stretched out my hand for the bell-pull. The gesture stopped halfway; my hand left in mid-air like a puppet's as a movement by the tree caught my eye. There. The curtain moved, very slightly, as if plucked by invisible fingers. Straining my ears I thought I could hear a kind of resonance, like the wind blowing across a wire. A draught ruffled the bright wrapping on the presents under the tree. A glass bauble spun on its own, throwing an arpeggio of light on to the nearby wall. Then silence.

Ridiculous, I told myself, in subdued rage. It was a draught, an ill-fitting window-frame, an open door somewhere else in the house. Ridiculous to imagine Effie outside that window, Effie with her long, pale hair loose around her white, hungry face . . . Effie come to take her present . . . and perhaps to give one too.

'Ridiculous!' I spoke aloud, my voice comfortingly solid against the background of night. Ridiculous.

Still, in spite of that ridicule I found that I had to go to the curtain, twitch aside the heavy brocade, look through the thick glass into the street. In the light of the gaslamps the street was deserted, white: no footprints marred the glowing snow.

I rang the bell.

'Tabby, has there been any word from Mrs Chester?'

'No sir.' She was less ebullient now; Effie was three hours late and the snow had begun to fall again, stifling the night.

'I want you to take a hack to Cranbourn Alley and find out if Mrs Chester has set off home. I will stay here in case anything has happened.'

'Sir?' she queried doubtfully. 'You don't think she might have . . . I'm not sure I—'

'Do as I say,' I snapped, thrusting two guineas into her hand. 'Hurry, and don't stop for anything.' I tried a rueful smile. 'Maybe I am being over-cautious, Tabby, but in a city like London . . . Go on. And hurry back!'

'Yes, sir,' she said, still frowning, and from the window I watched as, wrapped from head to foot in shawls and cloak, she hurried out into the unbroken snow.

When she returned she had two policemen with her.

I could hardly suppress a guilty start as I saw them come in through the gate, one tall and thin, the other as squat as Tabby herself, lumbering ponderously through the dense snow to my door. Even as panic hammered down my spine I found myself stifling laughter as bitter as it was compelling. With one hand I fumbled for the chloral bottle on its chain and shook out three grains, which I swallowed with a last mouthful of brandy. I felt the rictus of my sour mirth relax. I forced myself to sit and wait.

When I heard their knock I leaped from my chair, almost tripping on the stairs as I ran to open the door. I let my face slacken in appalled comprehension as I saw them, Tabby's face puckered with half-shed tears, the officers of the law deliberately neutral; hatless.

'Effie!' My voice was ragged; I allowed all the desperate suspense of that evening to permeate the two syllables. 'Have you found her? Is she all right?'

The tall officer spoke, keeping his voice carefully flat. 'Sergeant Merle, sir. This'—indicating the other figure with a long, bony hand—'is Constable Hawkins.'

'My wife, officer.' My voice was raw with disguised laughter—no doubt it sounded desperate to Sergeant Merle. 'What about my wife?'

'I'm afraid, sir, that Mrs Chester did not arrive at Cranbourn Alley. Mrs Shelbeck was out, but Miss Shelbeck, her sister-in-law, was most distraught. It was all we could do to prevent her from coming herself.'

I frowned, shaking my head in bewilderment. 'But . . .'

'Could we come in a moment, sir?'

'Of course.' I hardly needed to play the part; I was light-headed, almost reeling from drink, chloral and nerves. I grasped the lintel of the door for balance. For a moment I almost fell.

Merle's thin arm was surprisingly strong. He grasped me as I toppled, leading me to the warmth of the parlour. Constable Hawkins followed us, with Tabby bringing up the rear.

'Mrs Gaunt, perhaps you might bring a cup of tea for Mr Chester?' said Merle softly. 'He looks unwell.'

Tabby left the room, looking back over her shoulder at the two policemen, her face pinched with apprehension. I sat heavily upon the sofa.

'I'm sorry, sergeant,' I said. 'I have been ill recently, and my wife's condition has put me under some strain. Please do not be afraid to tell me the truth. Did Miss Shelbeck seem surprised that she had planned to go to Cranbourn Alley?'

'Very surprised, sir,' said Merle neutrally. 'She said she hadn't had any word of it from the lady.'

'Oh, God.' I put my head in my hands to hide the capering

grin I could feel aching to show itself behind my slack features. 'I should never have left her! I should have gone with her, whatever the doctor said. I should have known.'

'Sir?'

I looked up at him wild-eyed. 'This is not the first time my wife has suffered ... lapses,' I told him dully. 'My friend the nerve doctor, Dr Russell, examined her not ten days ago. She is a victim of ... hysteria, believes herself persecuted.' I allowed my face to warp and twitch as if I were close to tears. 'My God,' I cried in an impassioned tone, 'why did I let her go?' I stood up abruptly and seized Merle's arm. 'You must find her, sergeant,' I pleaded. 'There's no knowing where she thinks she is going. Anything ...' My voice cracked obligingly. 'Anything might happen to her.'

And then I was crying, *really* crying, tears streaking down my face, choking me. I shook with great, hysterical sobs, releasing grief and poisoned laughter in alternate gusts. But as I wept, my face in my hands, I could not help being conscious of a kind of glee, a cold, mechanical capering in the chambers of my heart, and a knowledge that my grief—if grief there was—was not for Effie, or for anyone else I could think of.

57

It wasn't till after seven that I decided to pay my delayed visit to Henry; I caught a cab to the High Street and walked up from the cemetery to Cromwell Square. I passed a group of children singing carols—among them a girl of about twelve who radiated an unearthly, crystalline beauty: I slipped a wink to the pretty child and a sixpence each to her friends—after all, now I could afford it—and, whistling, I made my way towards the Chester household.

He answered my knock almost at once, as if he had been expecting callers. From his expression I guessed that I was far from welcome but, after a furtive glance across the street, he ushered me in. I saw no sign of the housekeeper and presumed she was out. All the better: it would make my dealings with Henry the easier.

'Merry Christmas, Henry,' I said cheerfully. 'The house is looking very festive tonight. Then again,' I added winningly, 'we do have quite a lot to celebrate, don't we?'

He looked sharply at me. 'Do we?'

I raised my eyebrows quizzically. 'Come, come, Henry, don't be coy,' I said. 'We both know what I mean. Let's say that this

Christmas we have both managed to contrive a solution to certain . . . embarrassments, shall we say? Yours, I believe, were marital, whereas mine are merely financial. We shall deal very well together.'

Henry was no fool: he was beginning to understand. Last night had seen him fuddled with guilt and chloral, but tonight he had a cooler head than I would have given him credit for, and he merely stared at me in that haughty way of his.

'I don't think we shall, Harper,' he said coolly. 'In fact, I doubt whether we shall even meet very often at all. Now, I was rather busy . . .'

'Not too busy, surely, for an old friend to share a Christmas drink?' I said with a smile. 'Mine's a brandy, if you please. I never discuss business with a dry throat.'

Henry didn't move, so I helped myself from a nearby decanter. 'Won't you join me?' I offered sweetly.

'What do you want?' he asked, through gritted teeth.

'Want?' I said aggrievedly. 'Why assume that I want anything? I fear you have misunderstood me, Henry: I would never be vulgar enough to ask for anything . . . If, of course, you were to offer—in the name of our friendship—let us say a mere three hundred pounds to pay off my creditors—a Christmas bonus, so to speak—I wouldn't think of refusing.'

His eyes were narrow with hatred and understanding. 'You can't blackmail me! You were a part of it too. I'd rub your face right in it.'

'Queen's evidence, dear chap,' I said lightly. 'Besides, I have friends who'd lie for me if needs be. Have you?'

I let that sink in for a while. Then, downing the brandy in one gulp, I said: 'Why not simply join in the Christmas spirit a little? One good turn deserves another. Think about it. What's three hundred to a man like you? Isn't it worth it, if only to see the back of me?'

Henry was silent for a minute. Then he turned on me, his expression ugly. 'Stay here,' he ordered, spun on his heels and left.

He came back a few minutes later with a small metal box which he thrust into my hands as if he wanted to hurt them.

'Take it, you wretch. The money's there.' He paused, his lips thin to the point of invisibility. 'I should never have trusted you,' he said softly. 'You planned this from the start, didn't you? You never had any intention of helping anyone but yourself. Get out of my sight! I don't want to see you ever again.'

'Of course you don't, dear chap,' I said gaily, pocketing the box. 'But who's to say you won't? Life, after all, is variety. I daresay we may meet again . . . at an exhibition, or a club . . . or in a cemetery, who knows? It would be a pity to lose touch, wouldn't it? I know my way out. Merry Christmas!'

Half an hour later I was at one of my favourite haunts in the Haymarket, the precious box carefully hidden in my inner pocket, drinking fine brandy in front of a warm fire and eating chestnuts boiled in cider from the hand of a fifteen-year-old charmer with hair like sable and a mouth like a slashed peach.

I never did have much time for guilt. Henry's discomfiture had put me in a good mood, and between that and the girl and the box of banknotes I admit that any lingering thoughts of Effie had long ceased to disturb me. There were other, more pressing things on my mind.

I drank to the future.

58

When he had gone, I paced the hall in a delirium of fury. Oh, I had been prettily duped; I saw it all now. Everything he had said about my art . . . the hours spent in my house, drinking my brandy, looking at my wife . . . all that time he'd been waiting for the moment to trip me, laughing behind his hands at my bumbling, ignorant kindness. Damn him! In the heat of my fury I could almost have confessed the whole sorry affair to the police for the satisfaction of seeing *him* hang . . . But I would have my revenge; not now, when I had to remain calm, when I had to seem in control if I was to deal with the police. But I would.

I made my way to my room and a little chloral diluted in brandy sank my rage to the sea-bed: numbness came quickly and I was able to sit in my winged armchair, forcing my trembling hands to be still, and wait.

But the night was full of sounds: here the sharp crack of a log in the hearth, there the whisper of bubbles in the gas-jet, so like the light uneven breathing of a sleeping child . . . I sat close to the fire and listened, and it seemed to me that behind the normal creakings and whisperings of an old house in winter I could hear something else, a sequence of sounds which finally resolved themselves in my torpid brain as the sounds of someone moving quietly from room to room around me. At first I dismissed it (the caress of a woman's skirts against the silk wallpaper) because it was impossible for anyone to have entered the house without a key and I had locked the door as soon as Harper left (the padding of light feet on the thick pile of the carpet, the creaking of a leather armchair as she rested there awhile). I poured myself another glass of brandy-and-chloral (a tiny sound of china from the parlour as she tasted the cake—she always had an especial liking for chocolate cake).

Suddenly I could bear it no longer. I leaped to my feet, throwing the door open, reflecting a long ladder of light from my room into the passageway. No-one. The parlour door was ajar—had I left it that way? I couldn't remember. Compelled by a bleak desire far stronger than fear, I pushed it, allowing it to swing gently open. For a moment I *saw* her: a girl of leaves with her leaf-cat in her arms, their eyes like mirrors reflecting me, my face pinprick-small in the wells of their pupils . . . then nothing. Nothing but the reflection of a weeping-willow etched in white against the darkness of a window.

There *was* no girl. There had never been a girl. I quickly scanned the room: the cake was untouched, the china as I had left it, the folds of the curtain mathematically precise. Not a breath of wind disturbed the candle-flames, not a shadow fell against the wall. Not the slightest scent of lilac. And yet there was something . . . I frowned, trying to place the change: the cushions were unruffled, the ornaments untouched, the tree . . .

I froze.

Under the tree, a small triangle of torn wrapping-paper lay on the carpet. Just one. Stupidly, I tried to think where it could have come from. Taking two clumsy steps forward I saw that the topmost present—the peach silk wrap—had slipped from the pile and fallen to one side. Automatically, I bent to straighten it and I saw that the string had been cut and the parcel loosened so that folds of silk and lace showed through the stiff brown wrapping.

The sense of what I had seen refused to connect with any part of my rational mind and while a part of me gibbered and cried, another simply stared calmly at the opened present as a great blankness settled over me. Maybe it was the chloral, but my mind was infinitely slow, moving from the wrap, to the torn paper, to the cut string, back to the wrap with imbecile detachment. There was a huge silence all around as I stood there alone with the wrap in my hands, the torn paper slipping from it and falling with dreamlike slowness to a floor miles below me. The silk in my hands was hypnotic; I could see into it with inhuman accuracy, testing the weft and warp of it, delving the intricacies of scrolled lace, of spirals within spirals . . . The wrap seemed to fill the whole world so that there was no room for thought, simply awareness, infinite awareness, infinite contemplation . . .

From my abyss, I realized that I was laughing.

59

It's amazing, isn't it, how money disappears? I paid my debts, the ones I could not delay paying, though by no means the whole, and for a few days I began to define the style of living to which I thought I might like to become accustomed. I ate well, drank only the best. As for women, there were more than I could clearly remember, all beauties, all delightfully eager to see the colour of dear Henry's money. Don't think I wasn't grateful to him: I made sure I drank to his health every time I opened a new bottle, and when Beggar Maid ran at Newmarket I made sure I put ten pounds on her—I won too, at fifteen to one. It seemed as if I couldn't lose at anything.

Not that I didn't keep a close watch on events from my little hotbed of debauchery. Effie Chester's disappearance was reported in *The Times* with the possibility of foul play mentioned—it seemed that she had set off on the morning of Christmas Eve to visit her mother in Cranbourn Alley and had never arrived. The lady was 'of frail and nervous disposition' and police were concerned for her safety. I reckoned Henry had played his part well enough; the paper described him as 'distraught'. But he was unstable, I knew that: chloral and religion in equal quantities had upset the equilibrium of his free will and I guessed that, after the first few weeks of subterfuge, he would very likely sink into a kind of stupid despondency and imagine all kinds of retribution to be heading his way.

I felt that there was a chance of his eventually giving himself in to the police in an ecstasy of remorse—at which time, of course, there would be no more tarts for poor Jack. I supposed that Fanny had intended that from the beginning, though I couldn't think why. The only logical reason was that she intended Henry to be arrested and ruined—but I still couldn't understand why she had chosen such an unpredictable method of arranging it. *I* was safe enough in any case. The chilly reception from the ingrates at Crook Street had convinced me that I had no further obligation towards *them*; if Henry tried to accuse me I would tell the truth—as much of it as was needed. Let Fanny explain her own motives and answer the possible kidnapping charge; let Effie explain about Marta. I was well rid of them both. No-one could accuse me of anything more than adultery or possibly blackmail and any attempt to produce the supposed corpse was doomed to ridicule; the 'corpse' was at this very moment wandering through Fanny's house with dyed hair and a bellyful of laudanum.

Fanny! I admit she was still an enigma to me; I'd have liked to pay her a visit, if only to learn what she was doing. But I wasn't eager to meet that bitch Marta again, or ever. So instead I decided to pay another visit to Henry.

It must have been … let me see … about 30 December. Henry had had nearly a week to deal with his various affairs and I had almost run out of money. So I ambled over to his house and asked to see him. The housekeeper looked down her nose and told me Mr Chester wasn't at home. Not at home to me, most likely, I thought, and told her I would wait. Well, she ushered me into the parlour and I waited. After a while I grew restless and began to look around: the parlour was still decorated for Christmas and under the tree were a number of parcels, still waiting to be unwrapped by a girl who would never come home. A poignant touch, that, I thought appreciatively—the police would have liked it. Additionally, Henry had covered all the paintings on the wall with dust-covers: the effect was disturbing and I wondered why he had done it. I idled in the parlour for nearly two hours until I realized that the housekeeper was right: Mr Chester wasn't at home.

I rang the bell for brandy and when she came up with the tray I slipped her a guinea and gave my most winning smile.

'Now, Mrs . . . I'm afraid I don't know your surname.' I don't suppose anyone had called her 'Mrs' anything for years and she bridled.

'Gaunt, sir, but Mr and Mrs Chester—'

'Mrs Gaunt.' The smile was at its most charming. 'I am, as you recall, an old friend of Mr Chester. I am aware of the distress he must be suffering at the moment—'

'Oh sir,' she broke in, dabbing her eyes, 'the poor young lady! We're so worried some *man*—' she broke off, visibly moved. I tried not to chuckle.

'Quite,' I said soothingly. 'But if—God preserve us—the worst has happened,' I continued piously, 'then our thoughts must be with the living. Mr Chester needs friends to help him through this. I am aware that he may have instructed you to turn away, or otherwise misinform visitors'—I looked at her reproach-fully—'but you and I both know, Mrs Gaunt, that for his own good . . .'

'Oh yes, sir,' she agreed. 'I know. Poor Mr Chester; he won't eat, he hardly sleeps, he spends hours in that studio of his, or just walking about the cemetery. He was that fond of the young lady, sir, that he won't have her mentioned . . . and you can see that he's covered up all of his lovely pictures of her: can't bear to look at them, he says.'

'So you don't know where he is today?'

She shook her head.

'But you won't prevent me from giving him what comfort I can if I call again?'

'Oh, sir!' Her reproach was apparent. 'If I'd known, sir ... but there are people, you know, who wouldn't be ...'

'Of course.'

'Bless you, sir.'

I grinned. 'I'll just leave a message, shall I? Then I'll go. Maybe it would be better if you didn't mention I was here.'

'All right, sir.' She was mystified, but game.

'I'll let myself out, Mrs Gaunt.'

When she had disappeared again I opened the parlour door and made my way quietly to Henry's room. From my pocket I took out Effie's brooch—the one she had left on the bedstand that night—and pinned it to his pillow. It gleamed in the semi-darkness. Above the bed I saw another shrouded picture and divested it of its shroud. Now Effie floated above the bed like a pale succubus. Henry would sleep well tonight ...

When I left Cromwell Square I made my way to Henry's studio. The light was failing—it was already late afternoon—and by the time I arrived it was dark. The studio was in a block of apartments and Henry's was on the second floor. The outer door was open, the stairs poorly lit by a single sputtering gas-jet. I had to hold tightly to the banisters to avoid falling on the uneven steps. When I reached the door marked CHESTER it was locked.

I swore. That was that, then. But, as I turned to leave, a sudden curiosity grasped me, a desire to see the inside of that studio, and maybe to leave another calling-card. I inspected the lock; it looked simple enough. A couple of turns of a small-bladed pocket-knife and it clicked open; I lifted the latch and pushed the door. It was dark in the studio; for a few minutes I fumbled with the gas-jet in almost complete obscurity. I could hear the sound of paper crunching beneath my feet as I moved, but could not see the cause. Then, as the light flared, I was able to look around at the room.

My first thought was that I had broken into the wrong studio. I knew Henry to be a meticulously, almost obsessively tidy person: the last time I had been here there had been framed canvasses hung on the walls, unframed canvasses in a large file to the left of the room, a trunk filled with costumes and properties at the back, a few chairs and a table pushed against the wall. Now a manic disorder reigned. The paintings had been torn from the walls—in some cases taking paper and plaster with them—and stacked higgledy-piggledy in front of the fire. Unframed paintings were strewn across the floor in all directions, like a hand of spilled cards. And everywhere, on every available piece of floor or surface, there were sketches, crumpled, torn or whole, sketches on parchment or canvas or wrapping-paper—some breathtaking. I never knew Henry had such talent. The fireplace was choked with them, half-charred, pitiful remnants, and I spent some minutes on my hands and knees exploring the carnage, turning the pictures in my hands, trying to find some reason for the mutilations.

After a while my head began to spin. There were so many pictures of *her*, pictures in watercolour, in chalks, in pencils, oils, tempera: outlines of unspeakable purity, studies of eyes, lips, cheekbones, hair ... profiles, full-face, three-quarter profiles ... all stark and poignant and true. I'd been wrong about Henry all these years: the wan decadence of his paintings, the contrived symbolism of all those earlier works had hidden the bleak, almost Oriental purity of his vision. Each stroke of pen or pencil was exquisite: cruelty and tenderness subtly merged . . . and these masterpieces, every one, discarded with who can guess what rage and love, every one an infanticide . . . I couldn't understand it.

In a way I could almost find it in me to envy Henry Chester. I'd always known, of course, that an artist has to suffer to become great. But suffering exquisite enough to produce *that* . . . maybe that was worth knowing . . . this passion which transcends everything.

For a few minutes I sat among the wreckage and mourned like a child. But then my mind turned to more prosaic things and I was myself again. There was still the business of the money.

I stood up for a moment and tried to think logically. Where was the man? I turned over the possible alternatives in my mind . . . and then I knew. Of course! Thursday. It was Thursday. Marta's day. I glanced at my watch. Five past seven. Wherever he was now, walking the streets of London in whatever cold circle of hell now possessed him, I knew that at midnight he would be there, in Crook Street, for his tryst with his lady. Whatever the risk, whatever she made him suffer, he'd be there.

For an instant my eyes rested upon the drawing I had picked up at random from the hundreds on the floor: a stiff rough-edged piece of watercolour paper with a blurred outline in brown chalk from which her eyes smouldered endlessly, promising endlessly . . . A man could fall in love.

I shrugged and dropped the sketch back into the fireplace.

Not me, Henry. Not me.

60

From the moment I saw the opened present underneath the Christmas tree I understood that Effie had at last come home. I heard her footsteps in the passageway, her breathing in darkened rooms; I smelled her perfume in doorways, found strands of her hair on my coats, her handkerchiefs in my pockets. She was in the air I breathed, the shirts I wore; moving beneath the surface of my paintings like a drowned girl just beneath the water so that at last I had to cover them with sheets to hide her face, her accusing eyes. She was in the chloral bottle, so that however much I took I gained no peace from the drug but only managed to make her image clearer in my mind . . . And when I slept—and in spite of all my attempts to cheat sleep I sometimes did—then she stalked through my dreams, screaming at me in a voice as shrill and inhuman as a peacock's: 'What about my story? What about my story? What about my story?'

She knew all my secrets. Night after night she came to me with gifts: the bottle of jasmine perfume, the blue-and-white doorknob, and once, the little white disc of the Host, marked scarlet by the touch of her lips . . .

Night after night I awoke drenched in the bitter sweat of terror and remorse. I could not eat: I tasted Effie in every morsel I brought to my mouth and she looked out through my haunted eyes every time I looked in the shaving-mirror. I was aware that I was taking far more chloral than was good for me, but I could not bring myself to reduce the doses.

And yet for *her* sake I endured it, for Marta, my Scheherazade. Does she know it? Does she wake in the night and whisper my name? Even without tenderness, does she whisper it? Does she love, my pale Persephone?

I wish I knew.

I waited until Thursday as I had promised. I dared not do otherwise—my Scheherazade was not kind, and I could not bear the thought of her rejection if I deviated at all from her instructions. On Thursday night I waited for Tabby to go to bed—I even drank her hot milk before I pretended to retire—and I made my way to my room to wait. As soon as I opened the door I sensed the change: a fleeting scent of laudanum and chocolate in the cold air, the flutter of a lace curtain in a half-open window ... Clumsily, I fumbled with the spluttering gas-jet, my hands shaking so that it took nearly a minute to light it; and all the while I could hear her in the dark behind me, the Beggar Girl, the sounds of her pointed nails against the silk coverlet, and her breathing, dear God, her breathing. The light flared and sputtered. I turned wildly, and she was *there*: for an instant her eyes met mine and held them. I was paralysed, mouth open, choking, my sanity unravelling like a ball of twine into a bottomless well. Then I saw the dust-sheet on the bed and relief swept over me in a great, hot wave. The picture. It was the *picture*. The sheet had slipped somehow and ... Dizzy with relief, almost laughing, I ran towards the bed ... and the relief froze in my throat, turning my legs to water. On the pillow, pinned to the pillowcase, was a silver brooch I remembered. Effie had worn it that night—I recalled the gleam of it as she

moved in the snow, the arch of a silver cat's back as she fixed me
with her own catlike, silvery gaze . . .

Stupidly I fingered the brooch, trying to slow the vertiginous
fall of my thoughts. Below my left eye a banner fluttered a signal
of uncontrolled panic.

(what about my what aboutmy whataboutmy story)

If I had heard her say it I know I would have lost my mind,
but I was aware that she spoke only in my thoughts.

(whatabout my whatabout whataboutmy)

I used the only magic I knew. To silence the pitiless voice in my
mind I spoke aloud the one magic word: I summoned the
enchantress with all the yearning intensity of which I was capable.

'Marta.'

Silence.

That, and something almost like hope. Almost like quiescence.

I waited in that undersea silence for what seemed like hours.
Then at ten o'clock I rose from my chair and washed in cold
water, dressing carefully and meticulously. I crept, unseen, out of
the house and into the breathless night. The snow had stopped
falling and a dreamlike stillness crept over the town; with it came
fog so thick that even the gaslamps were eclipsed, their greenish
globes lost in an endless haze of white. Beneath the fog, the snow
seemed to have a radiance of its own, a kind of unearthly cat's-eye
luminescence which made walking corpses of the rare passers-by.
But chloral and the proximity to Crook Street had subdued my
ghosts; no little Beggar Girl followed me, holding out her thin
bare arms in frozen entreaty; the ghosts—if there were ghosts—
dared not leave Cromwell Square.

As I made my way through the snow, bracketed from the fog
by the light of my lantern, I began to feel strong again, confident
in the certainty that *she* was waiting; Marta, my Marta. I had

brought her a present, tucked underneath my coat: the peach silk wrap I had bought on Oxford Street, repackaged in bright red paper and tied with gold ribbon . . . As I walked, my hand crept almost furtively to the package, testing its weight, imagining how the peach silk would look against her skin, how provocatively it would slip from her shoulders, its fine, translucent grain sliding against the rougher grain of her hair . . .

It was almost midnight when I reached Crook Street, and the flare of excitement and anticipation at knowing her to be so close was such that I was at the door before I realized what was wrong: the house was dark, no windows lit, not even a lantern at the door. Puzzled, I stopped in the snow and listened . . . but there was no sound from Fanny's house, not the faintest tinkle of music or laughter; nothing but that dreadful, buzzing silence which engulfed everything.

My knock echoed dully through the house and suddenly I was convinced that they had gone, Marta and Fanny and all of them, that they had simply packed their belongings and disappeared like gypsies into the uncertain snow, leaving nothing but regrets and a whiff of magic on the air. The conviction was so great that I cried out aloud and beat against the door with my fists . . . and the door swung open silently, like a smile, as from inside the house I heard the hall clock begin to strike the passage of day to night.

I paused on the doorstep, a faint smell of spices and old incense in my nostrils. There was no light from the hall, but the snow's luminous reflections were enough to cast a faint, ethereal glow on to polished floorboards and shining brasses, so that my shadow was startlingly clear in the moonlight, falling crookedly across the threshold and down the passageway. A tepid exhalation of scented air touched my face, like breath.

'Fanny?' My voice was intrusive, too shrill in the muted intricacies of the house: at last, after so many years of visiting, I realized its immensity, passage after passage of carpeted labyrinth, doors I never remembered passing before, pictures of languid nymphs and satyrs with ravaged, knowing faces; screaming Bacchantes with thighs like pillars, pursued by grinning dwarves and leering goblins; demure mediaeval handmaidens of Pandaemonium with narrow hips and cryptic, penetrating eyes . . . As I passed through dim galleries of explicit, gilt-framed lechery, the dark robbed me of all perspective. I speeded my step, hating the dull and somehow menacing pounding of my stockinged feet against the deep pile of the carpets. I tried to locate the stairs but managed only to turn into another passage, and turned handles only to find the doors locked and whispering as if some mystery crouched half-awakened behind.

'Fanny! Marta!' By now my disorientation was complete: the house seemed to stretch out for immeasurable distances in all directions; I felt I had been running for miles.

'Marta!' The silence reverberated. A hundred miles away I thought I could hear a tinkling of music. After a moment I recognized it.

'Marta!' My voice cracked on a high note of panic and I began to run blindly down the passageway, striking the walls with my hands as I went, calling her name in desperate invocation. I turned a corner and ran straight into a door which abruptly brought the passage to an end. The rush of panic dissipated as if it had never been and I felt my heartbeat slowing down almost to a normal rate as my hand closed around the porcelain doorknob and the door opened into the hall.

There were the stairs—I could not understand how I could have missed them the first time I passed that way—and I could see moonlight from a little stained-glass window casting reflections across the burnished wood. The light was so bright that I could even distinguish colours: here a splash of red across the banisters, a couple of green lozenges on the stairs, a blue triangle on the wall ... and higher on the stairs a naked figure, the subtle line of her flank and thigh etched in purple and blue and indigo, the rippling fall of her hair a darker veil drawn against the night.

Moonlight caught one of her eyes from the shadowed face, coaxing the iris into opalescent brilliance. She was poised like a cat, ready to leap; I saw the tautness of her white throat, the muscles corded like a dancer's, saw the arch of her foot on the stair, tension in every nerve of her body, and I was filled with an overwhelming awe for that unearthly beauty. For a moment I was too absorbed even to feel lust. Then, as I moved towards her, she sprang away from me with a soft laugh and fled up the stairs with me in pursuit. I almost touched her—I remember how the fronds of her hair brushed my fingers, flushing my whole body with a hot shiver of desire. She was quicker than I, evading my clumsy embraces as I pounded behind her. As I reached the topmost landing, I thought I could hear her laughter through the door, teasing me.

I gave a little moan of anticipation, the exquisite tension of the moment driving me to her door (the doorknob was blue-and-white porcelain, but there was no time for the fact to register). I had begun to shed my clothes even before I opened the door, leaving a trail of discarded skins (coat, shirt, neck-cloth) on the landing behind me. Indeed, when I opened the door I was absurdly half clad in socks, hat and one trouser-leg, and was almost too preoccupied with ridding myself of the rest of my clothes fully to take in the surroundings. With the benefit of hindsight I know that I had been there before: it was the room of my dreams, *her* room, my mother's room, transported by some ironic magick to Crook Street; in the dim light of a shielded candle I could make out the details I remembered from that first, terrible day, diluted almost into insignificance by the nearness of Marta: here was her dressing-table, with the flotilla of little jars and bottles; there was her high-backed brocade chair, a green scarf draped carelessly over the back; on the floor another scarf lay discarded; across the bed dresses lay tumbled in a splash of lace and taffeta and damask and silk . . .

If I noticed any of this, it was with the eyes of desire alone. There was no sense of danger, no foreboding; simply a childish feeling of rightness and a joy which was purely physical as I leaped on to the bed, where Marta was already waiting for me. Together we rolled among the gowns and furs and cloaks, crushing antique lace and ravaging costly velvets in our silent struggle. Once my outflung arm struck a side-table, sweeping rings, necklaces and bracelets to the floor as I laughed madly, burying my face in the sweetness of her jasmine-scented flesh and kissing her as if I could not bear to leave an inch of her skin unconquered.

As the first uncontrollable madness fell from me I was able to think clearly again, to relish her in ways which the urgency of my need for her would not have allowed. I realized she was cold, her lips pale as petals, her breath a thin, freezing draught against my face as I held her.

'Poor love, are you ill? You're so cold.'

Her answer was inaudible, icy against my cheek.

'Let me warm you.' My arms were around her, her forehead nestling in the hollow of my throat. Her hair was slightly damp, her breathing feverish and too rapid. I drew a blanket around us both, shivering in the aftermath of passion as I reached for my chloral bottle on its chain about my neck and shook out ten grains. Swallowing five myself, I gave Marta what was left, watching as she grimaced at the taste, her parted lips drawn down in an oddly childish expression which made me smile.

'There, you'll see,' I told her gently. 'I'll soon make you warm. Just close your eyes. Shh. Close your eyes and sleep.'

I felt her flinch against me and I flushed with tenderness; she was so young, after all, so vulnerable in spite of her apparent self-control. I allowed my hands to move softly through the tangled web of her hair.

'It's all right,' I whispered, as much for my own reassurance as hers. 'It's all right now. It's all over. Now we're together, my love, we can both rest easily. Try to rest.'

And, for a time, we did, as the light dimmed and dimmed and finally went out. And for a while, God slept too . . .

Maybe I dozed; difficult to remember in the haze of impressions. I floated in jasmine and chloral, my mind adrift, and when I awoke I realized that though I was quite warm beneath my blanket, Marta was not with me. I sat up, squinting against the light which filtered in from behind the curtains—the candle had long since burned out. Dimly I could distinguish details of the room, the richness of lace and velvet frozen to silver ash in the moonlight, the vials and bottles on the dressing-table twinkling like icicles against the dark wood.

'Marta?'

Silence. The room waited. Something moved by the cold hearth; I twisted round, my heart pounding . . . Nothing. Just a loose piece of soot in the chimney. The fireplace grinned toothily from its brass fireguard.

I was suddenly sure that I was alone in the house. Panic-stricken, I leaped to my feet, the blanket trailing from my shoulders, and cried her name in a voice of rising hysteria. 'Marta!'

Something clutched at my leg, something cold. I cried out in loathing and pulled away from the bed; the thing held fast and I felt dry, brittle scales against my skin. 'Ma-ar . . . aah!' I twisted violently while pulling at the thing with my frozen fingers . . . I heard the heavy crack of tearing fabric, felt shredded lace in my trembling hands and began to laugh sickly: my legs had become entangled in the folds of a gown which had been lying on the bed and now lay on the floor in a heap of dismembered petticoats, the sequinned bodice torn fairly in half.

I muttered to myself in derision: 'Dress. Fighting a dress,' but I was shocked at the way my voice trembled. Closing my eyes in sudden nausea, I listened as my heartbeat slowed back to normal in time to the ticking of my left eyelid. After a time I was able to open my eyes again and, forcing myself to think rationally, I went to the fire to try and light it. Marta would be back soon, I told myself. In a moment she would come through the door . . . and even if she didn't, there was no reason to think that this room— this *room*, for God's sake—might want something of me, as my mother's room had seemed to want so many years ago . . . and want what? A sacrifice, perhaps? A confession?

Ridiculous! It wasn't even the same room.

And yet there was something in the silence, something almost gloating. I fumbled in the fireplace, fighting the urge to look back over my shoulder at the door. For an instant the room flared with red light as I struck a match. Then it flickered and died. I cursed. Again. Again. At last I managed to coax the flame into flickering life; the paper caught, then the wood. I looked round as giant shadows bloomed on the walls, then stood with my back to the hearth, feeling the tentative heat of the new flames with a sense of victory.

'Nothing like a fire,' I muttered softly. 'Nothing like . . .' The words turned to paper in my throat.

'Marta?' For a moment I almost said 'Mother'. She was sitting on the bed with one foot curled under her body, her head slightly to one side, watching me expressionlessly. She was wearing Mother's wrap. No, she must have found my present, opened it and put it on to please me. Perhaps she had been waiting for me to notice her all the time.

'Marta.' I forced my voice into its normal range and tried a smile. 'Lovely.' I swallowed. 'Quite lovely.' She tilted her head coquettishly, slipping her face into shadow. 'Your present,' I explained.

'Present,' she whispered.

'Indeed,' I said more jovially. 'As soon as I saw it I thought of you.' That wasn't quite true, of course, but I thought she would like me to say so. 'And you do look very lovely.'

She nodded reflectively, quite as if she knew.

'Almost time for *your* present now,' she said.

'Once upon a time . . .' Her breath was cold against my throat, her fingers tracing tiny circles against my bare back as she whispered in the dark. I could feel silk and peach lace beneath my moist palms and a scent of jasmine, heavy and soporific, rose from her feverish skin along with a darker, sharper scent . . . A sudden image of wolves passed through my torpid mind.

'Once upon a time there lived a King and Queen who had one son.'

I closed my eyes and sank into the blissful half-light of the jade underworld. Her voice was a scattering of random bubbles at my feet; her touch a cool current from the deep.

'The Prince loved both his parents, but his mother had his heart—he never left her side. The Prince had everything he could wish for . . . but for one thing. In the castle there was a single room in which he was not allowed entry, a room which was always locked, and the key was kept safe in his mother's pocket. As the years went by the Prince began to think more and more about the secret room, and longed to see what was inside. Then one day, when both his parents were absent, the Prince happened to pass that secret door and found it ajar. Impelled by curiosity he pushed it open and went in.'

The air was dark with jasmine; Marta, I *know*.

'The room was gold, but the Prince had all the riches he could ever want. The room was scarlet and purple and emerald, but the Prince had damasks and velvets by the bale with which to clothe himself.'

Oh Marta, reaper of my dreams, child of my innermost dark . . . I saw her story—which was also mine; I *saw* the secret chamber and my fourteen-year-old self at the door with the reflections of a million gems in my black eyes.

'The room was scented with the essence of a thousand flowers; but the Prince lived in a garden where winter never came. There was nothing here to merit such secrecy, he thought.'

Scheherazade spread her long white fingers, the palms of her hands like scarlet orbs in the firelight.

'And still, the Prince could not bring himself to leave. A great curiosity gnawed him as, almost idly, he searched through chests and wardrobes until suddenly he came upon a small and very plain wooden casket which he had never seen before.'

My heart began to beat faster, my temples tightening painfully.

'Why keep this ugly old casket, thought the Prince in surprise, when everything else in the palace is so rich and fair? And he opened the box and looked inside.'

She paused—I saw the glimmer of her crimson smile—and I realized at that moment that she knew the Mystery, had always known it. Here was the woman who could lead me beyond the doomed posturings of sin and flesh: she understood my yearning, my hopeless regret. This was her 'present': this revelation.

'Go on, please; go on.' I could feel sweat trickling down my cheeks at the thought that even now she might withhold it. 'Marta, *please* ...'

'Shh, close your eyes,' she whispered. 'Close your eyes and you'll see. Sleep, and I'll show you.'

'What did he see?'

'Shh ...'

'What did I ...'

'Sleep.'

Imagine the sea-bed under a fathom of brown ooze.

Imagine the peace ...

'The Prince rubbed his eyes: for a moment he saw nothing in the box but a dark blur, like smoke, but as he strained to see what was there he was finally able to make out a wand of hazel wood wrapped in a stained black cloak. "How strange," said the Prince, "to keep such old and ugly things so secret," and because he was young and curious, he lifted the two objects out of the box. Now what the Prince didn't know—what no-one knew—was that the Queen was a witch who had come from a far Northern land beyond the sea, a long, long time ago. By enchantments she had made the King love her, and by enchantments she kept her nature secret. The cloak was magic, and so was the wand, and only the Queen could control them. But the Prince was her son, and the witch's blood was in his veins. When he put on the magic cloak and held the wand in his right hand he felt a sudden upsurge of power. He lifted the wand and power glowed in him like a sun ... but the spirits of the wand, seeing that the invoker was only a boy, saw their chance to rebel and escape bondage. They tore free, screaming with triumph, raking the Prince's face with their claws and breathing their vile breath in his face so that he fell to the ground in a dead faint.

'When the Prince awoke, the spirits were gone and the wand lay broken beside him. When he saw this, the Prince was afraid.

He replaced the wand and cloak in the casket and fled from the room. When the Queen returned she saw at once that her wand had been tampered with, but she could not mention it because no-one knew she was a witch. So she waited for the night of the dark moon and set a curse on the meddler, a terrible curse; for in breaking her wand he had broken her power, and from now on she would be fated to grow old even as mortal women. She put all her hate into the curse and waited, knowing that soon it would begin to take effect.

'That very night, the Prince awoke screaming in the aftermath of a terrible dream, and in the days and weeks which followed he grew pale and ill, sleeping little at night, unable to rest or to eat by day. Months passed. The King ordered all the greatest physicians in the land to see his beloved son, but no-one could find a cure for his slow and dreadful malady. To add to the King's despair, his wife too fell ill, growing weaker and more wan day by day. The whole country was ordered to pray for their recovery.

'Now one day an old Hermit came by the palace, a very holy man, and demanded to see the King. "I think I may be able to find what ails your son and your wife," he said, "if only I may see them." The King, mad with grief, agreed, and the Hermit made his way first to the Queen's room, then to the Prince. Without a word he looked into the Prince's eyes. Then he dismissed the guards and spoke severely to the Prince.

'"You have been cursed, my son," he said, "by the witch Queen, your mother. If you do not act soon then you will die and she will recover."

'The Prince wept, for he loved his mother dearly.

'"What must I do?" he asked at last.

'"You must go to her room and kill her," said the Hermit. "Nothing else can lift the curse."

'The Prince shook his head and wept again, but the Hermit was cold as ice. "The Queen has no other children," he said grimly, "and your father is an old man. Would you see a witch in command of your country for ever?"

'So the Prince agreed, with a heavy heart, and that night he rose from his bed and made his way softly down the long passageways of the palace to his mother's chamber.'

The door was open, I know. I see it from my bed of salt slime: the knotholes in the white wood, the blue-and-white china doorknob—how easily all this comes back to me! There is a notch in the side of the second panel where once I accidentally struck it with a cricket stump. The house is dark and somewhere far behind me I can hear Father in his toy workshop, a few bright notes from the mechanism of the dancing Columbine scattered in the dark. I am carrying a stump of candle in a flowered dish; the scent of tallow sharp in my flared nostrils. A thick white tear crawls down the side of the candle and on to the china, pooling across one of the blue flowers. My breathing seems very loud in the thick air.

The carpet is soft and yielding beneath my feet but in spite of this I can hear the sounds of my footsteps. Around me the candlelight catches the glass of her bottles and jars, throwing a thousand prisms against the mirror and the wall. For a moment I am not certain whether or not the baby is in the room with her; but the crib is empty—Nurse has taken it in case its cries awake my mother. Raising the candle behind the glowing red shield of my hand I look at her face in the rosy light with a rapture all the more precious for being forbidden. A laudanum vial glitters on the bedstand beside her: she will not wake.

A sudden wrenching tenderness overwhelms me as I watch her face: her thin blue eyelids, the perfect curve of her cheekbones, her cascade of dark hair covering the pillow and spilling down the folds of the coverlet on to the floor . . . she is so beautiful. Even so wasted, so pale, even now she is the most beautiful woman in the world, and my heart aches with a desperate, hurt love, poignant beyond my fourteen years. My child's heart feels as if it will burst with the strain of all these adult emotions; the tearing jealousy, the loneliness, the sick need to *touch* her, to be touched by her, as if her touch might erode the cancerous invasion of the serpent in my stomach, her arms ward away the night. Asleep, she is approachable and I almost dare to stretch out my hand to her hair, her face; I might even brush her pale lips with mine . . . she would never know.

Asleep, she is nearly smiling; her eyes blurred and softened beneath the violet eyelids, the mauve shadow of her collarbone a perfect Chinese brush-stroke against the pallor of her skin . . . her breasts a scarcely perceptible swelling through the linen of her nightdress. My hand moves almost by itself, a disembodied starfish in the dim brown night. I watch it, mesmerized, as the fingers touch her face, very gently, with miraculous daring slipping to her throat . . . I pull away, blushing, all my skin tingling with guilt and excitement. But it is the *hand* moving all on its own, drifting down the coverlet with languid purpose, now twitching the coverlet aside to reveal her sleeping form, the nightdress drawn up to her knees, showing her taut calves, the soft curve of a thigh.

There is a bruise there, just above the knee, and I feel my eyes drawn to its mauve delicacy. My hand stretches out to touch, and she is powdered satin beneath my fingertips, she is endless mystery, endless softness, drowning softness like undersea sand . . . Her jasmine scent hides another scent, like salt biscuit, and without even knowing it I bring my face against her, burying my face in the warmth and sweetness of her, taut with yearning and excitement. My hand finds her breast with a leap of savage joy;

my arms curl around her, my lips suddenly ravenous for hers ...
Her breath is faintly sharp, like sickness, but now my body is a
single tendon taut as a harp-string, filling the atmosphere with a
resonance of unendurable purity which rises and rises in pitch to
the point of insanity and beyond ... I have no body; I see my soul
drawn out like a fine silver wire, vibrating shrilly to the spheres'
ringing ... I hear laughter and realize it is my own ...

Her eyes snap open.

I feel the line of her mouth tauten beneath my lips.

'Mother ...' Helplessly, I curl away, stomach a fist of ice.

Her eyes are cruelly sharp; I know that she sees everything.
Everything. Years fall from me; a moment ago I felt old, now I am
falling backwards into my childhood; thirteen, twelve, eleven, and
as I shrink she grows, monstrous ... eight, seven ... I see her mouth
open, hear the distorted syllables: 'Henry? What are you ...'

Six, five. Her teeth are pointed, impossibly savage. Blood
hammers in my temples. A scream breaks from my lungs; her rage
is enormous. Worse still is her contempt, her hatred, like a tidal
wave filled with the floating dead. I can barely hear her voice
above the rushing in my ears; there is something soft in my hands,
something which struggles with monstrous strength against me.
The tide tosses me to and fro like jetsam; I tighten my eyes into
knuckles so that I do not have to see ...

A sudden, miraculous silence.

I lie on the black sand as the tide retreats, its breath like heart-
beats in my eardrums; the return to consciousness is like a million
pinpoints of light on my retina, my mouth full of blood from a
bitten tongue. I crawl to my knees on the spinning carpet, a rope
of bloody spittle dragging to the floor, the pillow still in my con-
vulsed hands.

'Mother?'

Her glazed eyes stare at me, still hard, as if outraged by the indignity of her posture.

'Mo-other?' I feel my thumb creep up to find the corner of my mouth, my knees curling to join my elbows. In some part of my mind I understand that if I can curl up into a tiny enough ball I will be able to go back into that half-remembered place of safety, the salty place of darkness and warmth. Smaller...smaller. Three, two, one...

Silence.

Far above me the sound of laughter, the huge troll-like bellow of God. The black angel picks up her scythe and the Furies fly screaming up out of the pit to find their new plaything; and I know all their faces. The whorechild, with a smear of chocolate on her cheek ...Effie's seawater eyes and foaming hair...my mother, so long forgotten in the merciful blindness but now recalled for ever, dragged back on to her dark pedestal, her fingers like blades. Closer now, the voice of the enchantress, Scheherazade, her wolves at her feet...her unearthly laughter. From my half-sleep, struggling, I try to call her, to invoke her name against the coming nightmare.

'Marta!'

I open bloodshot eyes, feel the firelight against my frozen limbs. The rogue muscle in my cheek pins my eye closed in a series of fluttering spasms too rapid to calculate. The memory, newly recalled by Marta's story, is a marble sepulchre from some grotesque fairy-tale, reaching higher than the clouds. I reach out for her comfort...

The light is suddenly, mercilessly bright. I raise my hands to shield my eyes, and I see her, Scheherazade, my golden nemesis, laughing.

'Marta?' The voice is barely a whisper, but even as I speak I know that she is not Marta. She is Effie, pale and triumphant; she is my mother, lewd and venomous; she is the ghostchild. All three speak as one, stretching out their hungry arms to me and as I fall backwards, striking my back against the bedrail and hardly feeling the pain as my vertebrae crunch against the angle of the post, I realize at last *what* she is, what *they* are. Tisiphone, Megaera and Alecto. Avengers of matricide. The Furies!

A tremendous bolt of agony drives through my body; razors sever my spine and a tremor grips me all down my left side.

As I pass into friendly oblivion I hear her voice, *their* voice, bright with venom and mockery: 'What about *my* story, Henry? What about *my* story?' And, in the far distance, the savage laughter of God.

61

The snow began to fall as I left Henry's studio. By the time I reached Crook Street the night had an ethereal clarity which illuminated my steps and touched my clothes with powdery phosphorescence. As I glimpsed Fanny's house from the corner I noticed that the lantern which usually hung from the door was dark. Moving forwards I saw that the windows, too, were dark, the curtains drawn, with not a chink of light shining through the heavy folds. I noticed that the snow was scuffled at the doorstep, though no light shone from the stained-glass of the porch. Thinking that maybe there would be someone in one of the back parlours of the house, I went up to the door and knocked. No answer. I tried the door: predictably, it was locked. I knocked again, shouted through the letter-box . . . but no answer came.

Puzzled, I tried the side door, with as little success, and I was about to leave, shaking my head in bewilderment, when I saw something dark and bulky lying in the shadow by the side of the house, half covered by the rapidly falling snow. At first I thought it was a discarded coal-sack; then I saw the heel of a man's boot poking out of the snow. A vagrant, I thought, looking for a place to shelter and caught by the cold, poor devil. I had a flask of brandy in my pocket and, pulling it out, I waded through the drifting snow and reached for the body—maybe there was still life in him, I thought. I dragged him from his hollow by the wall and as I brushed away the frozen mask from the twisted, petrified face, I recognized Henry Chester.

One eye was open, staring; the other drooped oddly. The muscles in his left cheek and temple were strangely distorted, like melted wax, and his left hand was a claw, his shoulder hunched grotesquely, his hip dislocated, the leg thrown out at a gruesome angle. Until he moved, I could have sworn he was dead.

A sound escaped his lips; a long, guttural moan.

'Aaa-daa. Aah-a.'

I pushed the brandy flask between his clenched teeth. 'Drink it, Henry. Don't try to say anything.'

Brandy trickled down both sides of his mouth and a rictus seized him as again he tried to form syllables. The intensity of his need to speak was agonizing.

'It's all right,' I said uncomfortably. 'Don't talk. I'll get help.' There were lights in the windows of nearby houses; surely someone would take care of him while I called for a doctor. Besides, the last thing I wanted was to stay alone with Henry.

'Ma—a. Maaah . . .' The right hand clenched against my sleeve; the head lolled, drooling. 'Ma-ahh.'

'Marta,' I said softly.

'Ahh.' His nod was convulsive.

'You came here to see Marta?' I coaxed.

'Ahh.'

'But she wasn't in, so you waited. Is that right?'

Another spasm; the head lolled again, obscenely, his one open eye turned up to the white. 'Nnn-ah. Mm-aah-a. Ahhh. Aahh . . .' His right arm flailed helplessly and tears trickled from his right eye, though the other stayed frozen, a knuckle of stupid flesh.

Unbearable, sick pity jerked me to my feet.

'Can't stay, Henry,' I said, trying to avert my eyes. 'I'm getting help. You'll be all right.'

An animal moan, in which I could still distinguish the chilling accents of the human voice; words struggling through dying flesh. Words? One word. One name. I couldn't bear the sound, the dying sound of his obsession. Cursing myself, I turned and ran.

It was easy enough to find someone to help; a woman from a nearby house accepted a guinea to call for a doctor and give shelter to the stricken man: two hours later the doctor arrived and Henry was transported back to Cromwell Square. It was a stroke, the doctor had said; a massive seizure of the heart. The patient must be kept quiet if there was to be a chance of recovery, and a dose of chloral mixed with water, patiently forced drop by drop between the patient's rigid lips, served to calm him. When I finally left them, certain that I could do no more, Henry had subsided into a thick stupor, his breathing almost imperceptible, his eyes glazed. That was enough, I decided; I was no sick-nurse. I had saved the man's life, most likely; what more could anyone expect? When no-one was paying attention I left, quietly, by the back door and disappeared into the deserted streets.

To save us both a little time, I took Henry's wallet with me as I left: anyone could see that the poor fellow was in no condition to talk business that night.

62

A soft current bore me to a silent world of muted shapes and uncertain perspectives. The darkness was deepest emerald; but in the middle distance I could see figures, featureless, shapes without line or definition and, in the foreground, a face, grotesquely disproportionate, swimming like a bloated fish in and out of focus. For a moment it swam out of my field of vision and I tried to turn my head to follow it but found myself oddly prevented from doing so. I tried to recall the terror and urgency which had forced me to the safety of the sea-bed, but I was strangely serene, as if regarding events through a dark crystal. A shoal of foetuses paddled clumsily through a reef of green coral where a pale girl floated, her long white hair rising like seaweed into the murky grey of the undersea sky.

The face mooned into my field of vision once more, its mouth opening cavernously . . . syllables oddly distorted beneath the water burst like bubbles in my face in a series of shapeless sounds. In some way the sounds were meaningful, but I could not recall why. I drifted for a while, as the face receded once more. But the sounds persisted, and more and more I began to hear meaning in their persistence. The face, too, was somehow familiar; the keen eyes, sharp nose and small pointed beard. I had once known that face.

The mouth opened and I heard my name, spoken from a great distance.

'Mr Chester. Mr Chester.'

For the first time since my retreat I saw the bookcases behind the face; the door, the open window with its velvet curtain, the painting on the wall . . . reality yawned in my face with pitiless clarity.

'Mr Chester? Can you hear me?' The voice was Dr Russell's. I tried to answer, but found that my tongue lolled at the doctor with a gleeful life of its own and a sound came from my mouth, a gargling noise which appalled me.

'Please, Mr Chester. Will you nod if you can hear me?' I felt my neck jerk convulsively.

'You've had a stroke, Mr Chester.' His voice was too loud, too arch, as if he were addressing a deaf child: I noticed that his eyes steadfastly avoided mine.

'You've been very ill, Mr Chester. We thought we might lose you.'

'Haaa . . .' The braying sound which was my voice startled me. 'Haa . . . How long?' That was better. I was still hardly able to control my clenched jaw, but I could at least form words. 'How long . . . since . . .'

'Three days, Mr Chester.' I could feel his embarrassment, his impatience at my laboured attempt at speech. 'The Reverend even gave you the Last Rites.'

'Aaah . . . ?'

'Reverend Blakeborough, from Oxford. I sent word, to your brother William, there. He suggested that the Reverend should come.' For the first time I noticed the unobtrusive little man with a mild childlike face seated in the corner of the room. As he caught my glance—*he* was not afraid to meet my eyes—Reverend Blakeborough smiled and stood up: I saw that he was a rather small man.

'I took over the parish when your father died,' he said gently. 'I was very fond of Reverend Chester and I'm sure he would have wanted me to visit you, but until now I never knew where you lived.'

'Ahh . . . I . . .'

'Now, then, please don't exhaust yourself,' chided Reverend Blakeborough. 'The doctor—and, of course, your good Mrs Gaunt—have told me everything. You really must rest now— killing yourself is no way to bring back your poor wife.' He looked at me with a compassion which tore at me; I felt my mouth gaping in silent laughter and my right eye shedding tears—but for whom, I did not know. Reverend Blakeborough took a step forwards and put his arm gently around my shoulders. 'The doctor feels you need a rest, Henry,' he said kindly, 'and I do agree with him. A change of scene, the country air would do you more good than to stay in this dreary place. So come with me to Oxford. You can stay at the vicarage with me and your house-keeper can come and look after you if you like. I can recommend an excellent doctor.'

He beamed at me. I could smell mint and tobacco on his breath and a comforting, familiar smell, like old books and tur-pentine, from his clothes . . . A sudden nostalgia overwhelmed me, a terrible longing to accept the innocent little priest's invitation, to live in my old village again, to see the vicarage where I was born. Who knows, maybe the room with the blue-and-white china doorknob would still be unchanged, with my mother's oak bed beneath the stained-glass window. I began to weep in earnest, with a shameless self-pity and a searing regret for the man I could have been.

It was too much for Dr Russell: from my frozen eye I saw him turn and quietly leave the room, his mouth warped with disgust and embarrassment . . . but the priest's kindness was unflinching; he held me as I wept for myself, for Effie, for Marta and for my mother, for wakened memories best left sleeping, for the cold little ghostchild, for the red room, for the silk wrap, for Prissy Mahoney's first Communion, for the Christmas tree, still glittering with fake icicles . . . and for the fact that I wanted to go to Oxford.

I *wanted* this little man's kindness, the peace of his simple life, the sound of the birds in the cypresses, the college spires in the evening mist . . . More than anything I had ever wanted, I wanted those things; I wanted Reverend Blakeborough's universal love. I wanted absolution.

I drooled and wept and, for the first time, someone who was not a whore held me in their arms and rocked me.

'Then it's settled,' said Reverend Blakeborough.

'N-no!'

'Whyever not?' The priest was bewildered. 'Don't you want to come home at last?'

I nodded, not trusting my voice.

'Then why?'

I struggled to keep my words clear; my mouth felt as if it were filled with mud. 'Have . . . to . . . confess,' I said painfully.

'Well, of course,' said the priest cheerfully. 'But we'll wait until you're feeling better, shall we? Surely it can wait.'

'No! N-no . . . time,' I said. 'Ha-as to be . . . now. In case I . . . You . . . have to . . . know. I . . . couldn't come home . . . with you . . . unless . . .'

'I see.' The little priest nodded. 'Well, if it makes you feel better, of course I'll take your confession. How long has it been?'

'Tw-twenty years.'

'Oh!' Reverend Blakeborough looked momentarily startled, but soon regained his composure. 'I see. Well . . . ah . . . Take your time.'

My story was long and laborious. Twice I stopped, too exhausted to continue, but the knowledge that I might never again find the courage to speak urged me on. When I had finished night was approaching, and Reverend Blakeborough had long since fallen silent. His round face was pale and shocked and when I ended my narrative he almost leaped from his chair. I heard him splashing in the bowl of water in the washstand behind me and when he came to face me again he was almost livid; his mouth was wry as if he had been sick and he could not meet my eyes. As for myself, I realized that my destructive impulse to confess had done nothing to alleviate my guilt; I carried it still, untouched and triumphant in the black shrine at my heart's core.

The Eye of God was not deceived. I sensed its inescapable malice—I had not evaded God. Worse still, I had corrupted this innocent little man; I had betrayed his confidence in the essential goodness of the world and its inhabitants. Reverend Blakeborough could hardly bear to look at me and his self-assurance, the impulsive kindness was gone from his manner, to be replaced by a look of bewildered confusion and betrayal. He did not repeat his invitation and he left by the next train.

After that events were random things, threaded across the chasm of my life like beads on a string. My studio was emptied and the oil painting of *The Triumph of Death* presented at the Academy. Dr Russell came and went, accompanied by several specialists who proceeded to disagree strongly over what had happened to my heart. What they did agree upon, however, was the fact that I would most likely never walk or move my left arm again, although I did regain some control over my right arm and my head. Tabby hovered anxiously over me with my medicine— I was taking chloral every two hours now and I would begin to shiver and sweat if the dose were not regularly administered. A gentleman from *The Times* came to visit and was summarily dismissed by Tabby.

And at night, as I lay in my bed, they came, my darling Erinyes, laughing softly in the dark, cold and triumphant, tender and merciless, their claws and teeth infinitely loving, banefully seductive. Together they explored the cavities of my brain, with a mother's tenderness, tearing, slicing with exquisite delicacy . . . By day they were invisible, barbed gossamer beneath my skin, a mesh of finest steel tightening and contracting on to my heart's bloody core. I prayed—or tried to pray—but God wanted none of my prayers. My suffering and guilt were tastier morsels. God fed well on Henry Chester.

A week, seven days of obscene delirium at the hands of my darling succubi. Like God, they were hungry; vicious now in their desperation.

I knew what they wanted, snapping at the leash, snarling and foaming for a glimpse of prey. I *knew* what they wanted. The story. *My* story. And I wanted to tell it.

The Hanged Man

63

I was between the rapacious thighs of my latest inamorata the day they arrested me.

Oh, it was all very genteel. The two constables waited politely while I got up, robed myself modestly in a Chinese silk dressing-gown and listened as the older of the two constables informed me, in a slightly apologetic tone, that I was under arrest for the murder of Euphemia Chester, and that the London Police Department would be grateful if I would accompany him to the station as soon as it was convenient.

I'll admit that the comedy of the situation struck me forcibly. So Henry had revealed all, had he? Poor Henry! If there had not been the question of the money I might have laughed aloud; as it was, I think I carried off the situation in the grand manner. I smiled, turned to the girl (howling and attempting to veil her not inconsiderable charms with a sheet) and blew her a kiss, made a small bow to the constables, picked up my clothes and marched, Orientally silken, out of the room. I was enjoying myself.

I waited for a dreary hour in a Bow Street cell while officers discussed my imaginary crime outside the door—I passed the time cheating at patience (I had found a pack of cards in my coat pocket)—and when two officers, one cranelike and phlegmatic, the other short and choleric, finally came into my cell the floor was a mosaic of coloured squares. I smiled ingenuously at them.

'Ah, gentlemen,' I said cheerfully, 'how nice to have company at last. Won't you sit down? I'm afraid it's rather bare, but, as you see . . .' I gestured towards a bench in the corner.

'Sergeant Merle, sir,' said the tall officer, 'and this here is Constable Hawkins . . .'

I'll say this for the English police; they're always respectful of class. Whatever a gentleman may have done he is still a gentleman, and gentry have certain rights. The right to eccentricity, for example: Sergeant Merle and his constable listened patiently as I explained the truth about my relationship with Effie, the business with Fanny and Marta, and finally our attempt to fake Effie's death in the churchyard. The policemen remained stolid and unquestioning (Merle occasionally scribbling details into his little notebook) until I had finished my narrative, frozen into attitudes of respectful disinterest. Oh yes, I love the English police.

When I had finished, Sergeant Merle turned towards his subordinate and said something to him in a low voice; then he looked at me again.

'So,' he said with a frown of concentration, 'you're saying, sir, that although Mr Chester thought that Mrs Chester was dead—'

'She was in fact alive. I see you have grasped the salient points of the narrative with stunning alacrity.' The sergeant narrowed his eyes and I smiled sweetly at him.

'And . . . have you any proof of this, sir?'

'I saw her that night, sergeant; and on several later occasions at Crook Street. I know for a fact that Chester met her the night he suffered the attack. She was very much alive then.'

'I see, sir.'

'I strongly suggest, sergeant, that you send a man to Crook Street to question Fanny Miller and her ladies. You will find that Miss Miller will corroborate my story. Mrs Chester may even be there.'

'Thank you, sir.'

'Failing that, you would doubtless find it useful to open the Isherwood vault in Highgate cemetery, where Mrs Chester was supposedly buried.'

'Yes, sir.'

'And after you have done those things, Sergeant Merle, I should be grateful if you would bear in mind the fact that, in spite of my natural delight in helping the police with their inquiries, I do have my own life to live, and would like to be allowed to continue living it as soon as possible.' I smiled.

Merle's frigid courtesy did not waver. 'Just a formality, sir,' he said.

Hours passed. From the window of my cell I saw the sky darken, and a warden came at about seven with a tray of food and a mug of coffee; at eight the warden returned, taking the tray with him. At ten I hammered on the door of my cell, demanding to know why I had not yet been released. The warden was courteous and impenetrable; he gave me a pillow and some blankets and advised me to sleep. After a while, I did.

I suppose I dreamed; I remember waking with cigar-smoke and the smell of brandy in my nostrils, my mind a blank, my perspective gone. It was almost dark except for the reddish light from the little lamp beside me on the bed; the walls were curtained in shadow, the window a blind eye on to the night.

There was a round table in the middle of the floor in front of me and, as my eyes adjusted to the dimness, I recognized it as one which I had had in my study at Oxford years ago. How odd to see it there, I thought vaguely to myself as I reached out a hand to touch the polished surface and the worn inlay around the side . . . How odd. And someone had been playing cards, I saw; all around the edge of the table, in a concentric pattern, there were cards, very white in the gloom, almost seeming to glow with a soft reflective quality, like snow . . .

I found myself standing, moving without thinking towards the table. A chair which had previously been tucked beneath it glided out and I sat down, my eyes fixed on the cards. No ordinary cards, these, I thought: each one had, painted in the centre, an ornate letter of the alphabet, intricately knotted into the card's design in a baroque forest of leaves and scrollwork.

I frowned vaguely, wondering what kind of game I had joined. As I peered at the circle of cards, trying to discover whether this might be some complicated kind of patience, my eye caught a gleam of crystal reflected against the table's surface. A discarded glass, still half full of brandy, glinted in the red light. As I looked up, I must have knocked the table, because the glass tilted and fell, spilling the drink in a wide, gleaming arc. A couple of cards were caught in its path and carried to the edge of the table in front of me. Drops of the dark liquid trickled on to my hand as I saw that the cards were the Knave of Hearts and the Queen of Spades: '*Le beau valet de coeur et la dame de pique* . . .'; the letters M and E.

It was at that moment, of course, that I knew I was dreaming. The absurd symbolism, the wholly unsubtle reference to Baudelaire and the baroque imagery of death . . . the artist in me knew it at once, in spite of the oddly tactile nature of the dream: the smooth coldness of the polished wood beneath my fingertips; the wet patch on my trouser-leg where the brandy had spilled; the sudden chill in the air. It was so cold that my nostrils stung with it and my breath was a nimbus around my face. I looked at the table once more and saw that the spilled brandy had frozen, a spiderweb glaze across the dark oak, and the empty glass was misted with frost. I began to shiver in spite of my knowledge that this was only a dream—it was probably cold in my prison cell, I thought reasonably, and my sleeping mind had created this tableau (macabre enough to fill Henry Chester with enthusiasm) to entertain itself. Its title: *Le Remors* or *The Phantom's Patience*; all it needed to make it a Gothic masterpiece was the Pre-Raphaelite lady, pale from her long sleep but deathly beautiful, the baneful damozel with blood on her lips and vengeance in her eyes . . .

The thought was so absurd that I laughed aloud. Haunted by my own fiction, by God! Fanny would appreciate that. And yet I remembered Effie's face, her pale lips, the bleak hatred in her voice as she said: 'There is no Effie.'

Only Marta.

Damn that bitch.

'There *is* no Marta!' I said it aloud—in dreams I can do as I please—and felt a small release in tension. I said it again. 'There is no Marta.'

Silence absorbed my words.

Uneasy silence.

Then suddenly she was there, sitting in front of me at the table with a glass of milky absinthe in her hand. Her hair was loose, falling over the chair-back to the floor in a cascade of heavy ringlets which gleamed rich as claret in the crimson light. She was wearing the dress she had worn for *The Card Players*, a dark red velvet cut low over the bodice so that her skin seemed luminous. Her eyes were immense and fathomless; her smile, so different to Effie's sweet and open smile, was like a slit throat.

'Effie . . .' I kept my voice light and level; there was no reason for my throat to tighten, my lips to parch; no reason for the trickle of heat to sting my armpits. No reason . . .

'No, not Effie.' It wasn't Effie's voice; it was that hoarse, scratched-silver whisper which was peculiarly Marta's.

'Marta?' In spite of myself, I was fascinated.

'Yes, Marta.' She lifted her glass and drank; I watched as the clear crystal misted over and froze where she had touched it. A nice detail, I thought. I would have to use it in a painting one day.

'But there is no Marta,' I said again. In my dream it suddenly seemed very important to prove to her that I was telling the truth. 'I *saw* you invent Marta. You made her out of paint and dye and perfume. She's just another part you had to play, like the Little Beggar Girl or Sleeping Beauty. She doesn't exist!'

'She does now.' *That* was Effie; that childish assertion. For a moment I even glimpsed her—or the ghost of her—then the dark eyes clouded over once again and she was all Marta. 'And she's very angry with you, Mose.' She paused to drink again and I sensed her cold hate, her fury, like a draught of winter. 'Very angry,' she repeated softly.

'This is ridiculous!' I said. 'There is no Marta. There never *has* been a Marta.'

She ignored me. 'Effie loved you, Mose. She trusted you. But she warned you, didn't she? She said she'd never let you leave her.'

'It wasn't like that.' In spite of my detachment I sounded defensive—and felt it. 'I thought it would be for—'

'You were tired of her. You found other women who asked less of you. You bought them with Henry's money.' She paused. 'You really wanted her dead. It was neater that way.'

'That's ridiculous! I never promised—'

'But you did, Mose. You did. You promised.'

I lost my temper. 'All right, all right! I promised!' My anger drove a spike of migraine into my forehead. 'But I promised *Effie*.

I never said anything to Marta.' My head had begun to spin like a child's top and I was light-headed with fury and something like terror. I was shouting, unable to stop as the words spilled out of me. 'I hate Marta! I hate the bitch. I hate the way she looks at me, the way she seems to see everything, know everything. Effie used to trust me, to need me; Marta doesn't need anyone. She's cold. Cold! I'd never have left you if it hadn't been for her.' It was almost true. I stopped, panting, the ragged headache pounding in my temples. I forced myself to breathe deeply: ridiculous, to lose control in a dream. 'I never made any bargain with Marta,' I said quietly.

She was silent for a moment. 'You should have listened to Fanny,' she said at last.

'What has Fanny to say to anything?' I snapped.

'She warned you not to stand in our way. She liked you,' she said simply. 'Now it's too late.'

Don't laugh if I tell you that, for a moment, as I looked into her sorrowful eyes I felt a kind of fearful regret, a despair like Dante's cold hell. For a moment I saw myself spiralling downwards in darkness for a dizzying eternity, like a snowflake blown down a bottomless well. Suddenly the beating of my heart seemed a terribly fragile thing; nothingness yawned below me and, in a flash of ridiculous association, I remembered that night in Oxford when a voice from the dead had spoken from the card-table: *'I'm so cold.'*

So cold . . .

In that instant it occurred to me that my certainty that I was dreaming was a little absurd; when had a dream been so clear, so intense, so real? When had I been able to smell the absinthe in her glass, to touch the table-top, still sticky with spilled brandy? To feel the hairs rise on my shivering arms? I sprang to my feet, grasping her hand across the table; it was cold, a blue-veined hand of marble.

'Effie . . .' Suddenly I knew that I had to say something to her, something of terrible urgency. '*Marta*. Where is Effie?' Her face was impassive.

'You killed her, Mose,' she said softly. 'You left her in the vault and she died, just as you told Henry. You *know* you did.'

It was the wrong question. I could feel my time spiralling away.

'Then who are *you*?' I cried in desperation.

She smiled at me, a tiny, cold smile like a hunter's moon.

'You *know*, Mose,' she said.

'I *don't* damned well know!'

'You will,' she whispered, and when I awoke in the dark, clammy with sweat and aching all over, her smile remained with me like a tiny, tugging fish-hook in the nape of my neck; it remains with me even now as I fall into the inconceivable emptiness of a world without Moses Harper . . . I see it gleaming through silent space like a bright scythe. '*Ni vue, ni connue . . .*' Between blindness, ignorance and the relentless momentum of annihilation a man could fall in love.

And when they told me that morning that a woman's body had been found in the Isherwood vault in Highgate cemetery I was hardly at all surprised.

64

You'd like to know, wouldn't you? I can smell that hunger on you like sweat, hot and sour. Oh, you'd like to know all right. But I won't tell you where I am—you'd never find me if I did—and anyway, all places look the same to the travelling folk: the farms, the towns, the little houses . . . all the same. I'm with the gypsies, now. It's an honest life for the most part, and it's safer to be always on the move. No-one asks any questions. We all have our secrets here, and our magic.

It's easy to disappear in London. People come and go, all wrapped in their own business; no-one noticed an old woman with her basket of cats as they made their way through the soft snow. I left all my things in Crook Street; I suppose the girls sold them when they finally understood I was never coming back: I hope they did; they were good girls and I was sorry to leave them. But life's like that. Travel light and fast, that was my motto, even in the old days when Marta was a little chit—and we're light and fast twenty years on, with the snow at our backs like the Angel at the gate.

The Romanies took us without a word—they know all about hunting and hunted—they even gave us a wagon and a horse.

Some of them still remembered my mother and said I had the look of her. I make potions and philtres to cure the gout—or a man's hard heart—and I've got more friends than you ever had with your church and your preaching. They gave me a new name, too, though I'll not tell it you, a gypsy name, and I sometimes tell fortunes at country fairs with my Tarot cards and my crystal ball and the green scarf draped over the light. But I won't tell my cards for just anyone. No, it's the young girls I like, the tender ones with their eyes shining and their cheeks flushed with fairy-tale hope; and maybe one day I'll find a special one, a lonely one like Effie who can learn to fly and follow the balloons . . .

We keep on hoping, Marta and I. Last time was so close, she tells me, so heartbreakingly close. And we are closer now than we ever were; the memory of Effie, the grief of Effie, binds us together, not with bitterness but with a gentle melancholy at what might have been. Effie, our little girl. Our pale sister. We loved her, you know, more than either of you ever did; loved her enough to want her with us for ever . . . and in a way she *is* with us, in our hearts; poor, brave Effie, who brought my lost Marta back home.

On winter evenings I sit in my caravan with the blue candle burning and Tizzy, Meg and Alecto curled at my feet by the stove and I sing to Marta as she sits purring on my knee:

> *'Aux marches du palais . . .*
> *Aux marches du palais . . .*
> *'Y a une si belle fille, lonlà*
> *'Y a une si belle fille . . .'*

We'll find her one day, Marta, I promise her as I smooth her soft, midnight fur. A sensitive one with bright, innocent eyes. A lonely one who needs a mother, a sister. We'll find her one day. One day soon . . .

65

It was Effie all right. They took me to identify the body as it lay in the morgue and they were polite throughout, with the quiet courtesy of the hangman. I could feel the noose tightening around my neck at every breath I took . . . She was lying on a marble block, slightly tilted, and in a gutter at my feet a strong disinfectant flowed, making tiny trickling sounds in the huge silence of the morgue.

I nodded. 'That's Effie.'

'Yes, sir.' Sergeant Merle remained impassive, as if he were discussing some matter of little interest. 'The doctor says that the body was in the grave for some time. Since Christmas Eve, or thereabouts. The cold appears to have slowed the . . . er . . . degenerative process.'

'But, damn it, I saw her!'

Merle looked at me expressionlessly, as if too polite to comment.

'I saw her . . . *days* after that!'

Silence.

'Besides, if I had known she was really dead, why on earth would I have told you where she was?'

The sergeant looked apologetic. 'Mr Chester had already informed the police,' he said. 'The ... er ... *responsibility*, he said, was preying on his mind.'

'Henry's a sick man!' I snapped. 'He's incapable of distinguishing fact from fantasy.'

'The gentleman is certainly in a very disturbed frame of mind, sir,' said Merle. 'In fact, Dr Russell, the nerve specialist, feels that his mental health is uncertain.'

Damn the man! I could see Henry's game: Queen's evidence, and the word of a well-known doctor might mean that he never had to stand trial for Effie's murder. But I'd be damned if I let him pin it on me.

'Have you seen Fanny Miller?' I could hear the desperation in my voice but was not able to curb it. '*She'll* tell you the truth. It was all her idea in the first place. Effie was staying with her.'

Again the expression of respectful reproach. 'I did send a man to Crook Street,' said Merle stolidly. 'But unfortunately the premises were empty. I posted a watch on the premises, but so far Miss Miller has not returned there. Nor has anyone else, for that matter.'

The news was like a blow to the neck.

'The neighbours!' I gasped. 'Ask them. Ask any—'

'Nobody remembers seeing a young lady answering Mrs Chester's description on the premises at any time.'

'Well, of course they didn't!' I snapped. 'I tell you she was in disguise!'

Merle simply looked at me in mournful scepticism and I could not stop my hand from creeping up towards my neck. The invisible noose drew tighter.

I suppose you know the rest of the sordid tale—everyone else does. Even here among the *racaille* I have achieved a certain fame;

they call me 'Gentleman Jack' and speak to me with the respect due to a gentry-tyke facing the Drop. Sometimes my guard slips me a greasy pack of cards and I deign to join him in a quick game of brag.

I always win.

My trial was a good one as they go: actually, I rather enjoyed the drama. The defence was plucky but easily winded—I could have told him that his plea of insanity wouldn't wash—but the prosecution was a mean-mouthed old Methodist, who dragged out all the details of my chequered career, including some episodes even I had forgotten, with a lover's attention to detail. There were a lot of women there too, and when the judge put on his black hat his quivering old voice was almost drowned out by the sounds of wailing and sobbing. Women!

Well, I got my three Sundays' grace—and I didn't see the priest on any of them—but at last he came to see me. He said that he couldn't bear to see an unrepentant sinner go to the gallows. That was easy to solve, I told him: don't hang me! I don't think he appreciated the humour. They hardly ever do. With a tear in his rheumy old eye he told me all about Hell: but I remember my final triumphant painting, *Sodom and Gomorrah*, and I think I know even more about Hell than that old lecher. Hell is where all the wicked women go—I told you I liked them hot—and maybe from down there I'll be able to look up the angels' robes or habits or whatever it is they wear and discover the answer to that old theological question.

I can tell you're shocked, padre; but remember that if there were no sinners in Hell, there'd be no entertainment for the folk at the balcony—and I always said I should be on the stage. So put those beads away and have a drop of something warm—money buys anything in here, you know—and maybe a hand or two of brag, then, when you leave, you can tell them you did your bit.

Give the girls a kiss from me and tell 'em I'll see them at the dance. Well, I do have a certain reputation to keep up.

But sometimes as I lie awake in the small hours I can't help but wonder how they did it, Fanny and her dark daughter. And sometimes, as the seconds fall away relentlessly into nothing, I can almost find it in me to believe . . . in dreams, in visions . . . in cold little nightwalkers with light, freezing fingers and hungry mouths and hungrier hearts. In vengeful dreamchildren . . . in a love greater than death and stronger than the grave.

And within that twilit border of sleep, a picture seems to emerge—I always was good at pictures when I was sober—a picture which, if I narrow my eyes, almost comes into focus: a picture of a mother who loved her dead daughter so much that she brought her back to inhabit the body of another girl, a sad and lonely girl in need of love; and the need and the love together were so strong, calling her across the dark spaces, that she came, longing for her chance to live again. Oh yes, I know all about that longing. And together, the unhappy pale girl and the lost, frozen dark one created one woman, with the body of one and the mind of both and experience beyond human imagining . . .

At night, when such things seem possible, I think it very likely that that woman still walks the moonlit cobbles, though the body lies discarded in the morgue: she walks, still longing, still hungry . . . so cold . . . and so strong that, if she pleased, she could walk through walls and doors and limitless space to confront her murderers with scenes of black, delicate nightmare and rapturous insanity. She might spin stories of murder or paint visions of the pit . . . but behind the fury there would always be longing and a cold, despairing hunger. The dead are not forgiving.

There is a pervasive logic in this line of reasoning—and a strange pagan poetry. I find myself remembering snatches of my Classical education, to which I paid scant attention when I was at school. Yes, I read Aeschylus too, and I know where Fanny took the names of her cats. And knowing that I can almost believe . . . in angels, in daemons, Erinyes . . . Eumenides.

Almost.

I do have my reputation to think of.

Death

Epilogue

Manuscript, from the estate of Henry Paul Chester
January, 1881

The black angel stirs restlessly and I look at the sky, rimmed now with the livid cataract of dawn.

Time.

A sudden panic sends ripples down my ruined spine. I feel the tic which has already frozen half my face begin to twitch again, relentlessly, as if a tiny, furious creature were imprisoned behind my eye-socket, gnawing its way out. The last card of our game is Death . . . I knew it from the start, but although the looseness in my ribcage is relief, my brain rebels against annihilation, stupid tissue screaming out: no no no no! The lid of night is beginning to lift and beneath it is the Eye of God with its blank, blue iris and terrible humour.

The tale is told and I am no Scheherazade, to slip away at dawn with the wolves snarling at her heels. The wolf is behind my cheekbone, curled in the hollow of my skull, waking . . .

Hungry.

The black angel reaches for her scythe. My last thought will be of Marta: my crown of thorns, Princess of Cups, hemlock and chloral, dreamchild and executioner, sorceress and penny whore. The pale light falls on the curved blade: lift it, Columbine, take my life, my words...but tell me this: Did you love, Scheherazade? Even once, did you love?

Silence.

Imagine a dead leaf drifting down a bottomless well.

Imagine that, for a moment.

About the author

About the book

Read on

Insights,
Interviews
& More . . .

Meet **Joanne Harris**

© Guzelian, Ltd.

JOANNE HARRIS is the author of *Chocolat,* which was nominated for the prestigious Whitbread Award. Joanne's latest work is *Jigs & Reels*—her first ever collection of short stories. Her other critically acclaimed works include the novels *Holy Fools, Coastliners, Five Quarters of the Orange,* and *Blackberry Wine,* as well as *My French Kitchen*—a collection of her family recipes and reminiscences. She studied modern and medieval languages at Saint Catharine's College, Cambridge, and taught French for twelve years at a boys' grammar school. The daughter of a French mother and an English father, she lives in her native Yorkshire with her husband and their daughter. ❧

A Conversation with
Joanne Harris

British literary critic Kevin Patrick Mahoney was born in Slough, England, in 1972, but now spends a great deal of time in London. An aspiring author himself, he likes nothing better than pulling apart modern novels to see how they work. In March 2000 he sat down with Joanne Harris to discuss Sleep, Pale Sister.

Kevin Patrick Mahoney: *You seem to have a great love of works of fantasy, but what do you think of the artists behind those works, like Baum, Carroll, and the Pre-Raphaelites? Many of them were flawed figures and drug abusers. Why is it that Henry Chester can only produce a critically acclaimed piece of art when he's addicted to chloral hydrate?*

Joanne Harris: I've been told that most of the people I admire are either dead or very ill. Perhaps artists who work very intensely also have to feel with similar intensity in order to maintain their creativity. Perhaps these artists felt obliged to maintain an image for the public, and got caught up in it, or the pressure of fame stressed them so badly that they turned to drugs. I do think that there is a greater potential for madness and depression amongst artists and writers anyway—maybe because of the level of introspection necessary for creativity. Henry Chester is not truly creative until he discovers the dual addictions of Marta the teenage prostitute and chloral hydrate—a barrier is broken inside him, letting him express himself to the full. I don't think there is a rule for this: people write—or paint, or create music—for all kinds of reasons, in many cases as therapy or to escape from themselves. Sometimes the escape is so complete that they never quite come back. . . . In this case the art would be a symptom of madness, an insight into the psyche. ▶

> ❝ I've been told that most of the people I admire are either dead or very ill. ❞

A Conversation with Joanne Harris
(continued)

KPM: *Dr. Francis Russell is the psychoanalyst in* Sleep, Pale Sister, *upon whose word Effie can be committed to an asylum. What's your view of psychoanalysis? Why were there so many "madwomen in the attic?"*

JH: Well, of course in Victorian times all women were viewed as potentially unstable—the affliction of "hysteria," a uniquely female complaint, most often being cured by total "hysterectomy"—by virtue of their sex. Women were often under tremendous pressure to conform to impossible— and often conflicting—ideals, the intelligent ones were bored and frustrated because education was not really available to them, they were physically misunderstood even by physiologists, they were crippled by the corsets they had to wear, and repressed in so many ways that I'm surprised any of them were sane. Nowadays we have progressed, but not, I think, as much as we would like to think. Psychoanalysis has come to mean so many things, and takes so many forms that we are now getting a kind of backlash—people finding names for problems that never existed before; people "discovering" abuse in their past, false memory syndrome. . . . Everyone, it seems, now has an analyst. We can obtain counseling for anything which we find mildly disturbing. We bare our psyches at the drop of a hat, often on daytime television. Perhaps some of it should have been left in the attic after all.

KPM: Chocolat *mentions the sins of the Catholic Church, for which the Pope has recently apologized. Henry Chester is also a repressed Catholic. Why is the church so demonized in your work? Are you merely obeying Gothic conventions, where Catholicism equals sin, or do you have a deeper critique of the church?*

JH: I have nothing against the Catholic Church or any other. What I find offensive is intolerance of

> " We can obtain counseling for anything which we find mildly disturbing. We bare our psyches at the drop of a hat, often on daytime television. Perhaps some of it should have been left in the attic after all. "

other beliefs. I also find it difficult to accept any belief system based on self-hatred and self-blame, the demonizing of pleasure, or the persecution of people of other faiths. However I don't think that in any of my books I am making a point against the Church itself. Instead I am criticizing particular individuals who use the Church as an excuse to pursue their own agenda of cruelty or dominance. A religion is only made up of the people who follow it, and like anything else, it can be a tool for good or for evil. Catholicism has been both, in spades, throughout history, as have many other "crusading" religions. I'm not a crusader. I don't discuss my own religion, nor would I want to persuade anyone else to follow it. I think people should find their own way, and let others do the same.

KPM: *The Victorians are often claimed to have invented childhood, and it's a theme on which you seem to write a great deal. How important is childhood to you?*

JH: I often feel as if I have never left my childhood, and that I never will. Certainly I have more vivid recollections of that time than of any other, and I am aware that most of what I am now was formed very early, and is at present pretty immovable. I think that there are a lot of misconceptions about childhood—the Victorian ideal of childhood as "a state of innocent bliss" being one of them. It can be a very confusing time, when unhappiness is felt more deeply than at any other, when all emotions are enhanced. I think that many writers are able to access these early feelings and memories as part of the creative process, which is why so many of them are so preoccupied with childhood in all its aspects. ⮐

For the entire interview please visit Kevin Patrick Mahoney's website, AuthorTrek, at http://www.geocities.com/SoHo/Nook/1082/genreindex.html

> " I often feel as if I have never left my childhood, and that I never will. "

Not Dead,
Only Sleeping

IT TAKES A CERTAIN KIND of person to want to raise the dead. Dead books especially merit caution; for each lost treasure there are a hundred milk-bottle tops waiting to be dug up by the incautious prospector. This is why over the past decade I became accustomed to thinking of *Sleep, Pale Sister* as the relic of a vanished time. In the hot summer of 1993 I gave birth to a daughter and a book. One lived; one died; as far as I was concerned, there was no competition. The world had changed for me overnight. I was someone else; and suddenly the thought of being published didn't seem to matter as much as once it had. By 2003 the book was long out of print; I hadn't opened a copy since it first came out; I rarely even thought about it any more.

Others did, however. Some had read it; some were booksellers; some were fans; some just wanted to see how the author of *Chocolat* had made the leap from English gothic to French gluttony. I was overwhelmed by requests for copies. The few hundred copies available on Amazon.com disappeared almost instantly. My publishers were bombarded with letters asking for it to be reprinted. Finally, we decided to give it a try. I have edited the original text very slightly—perhaps not as much as I should have done, but I soon realized that this patient was far too fragile for radical surgery—and corrected a number of small mistakes. In the process I have become aware—with some surprise—that I am still rather fond of this story and of its characters. My book was not dead, after all; only sleeping. I'm glad it has been given a second chance. ❧

> ❝ In the hot summer of 1993 I gave birth to a daughter and a book. One lived; one died; as far as I was concerned, there was no competition. ❞

The Cover That Does It Justice

Joanne Harris met Graham Ovenden in 1993, when she was working on Sleep, Pale Sister. *Ovenden, the cofounder of the Brotherhood of Ruralists, a group of artists committed to cultivating a new Romanticism, captured in his paintings a haunting beauty Joanne used as her muse during the creation of* Sleep, Pale Sister. *With the book's 2005 reissue, Joanne saw the opportunity to create, with Ovenden, a cover that would definitively capture the novel's seductive darkness. Below, artist and author discuss the collaboration.*

JOANNE HARRIS

TWELVE YEARS AGO, when I was working on my second novel, *Sleep, Pale Sister,* I happened to come across a television documentary on the work of an artist called Graham Ovenden. I had never heard of him before but I was immediately struck by the troubling beauty of his oil paintings, especially his portraits of young girls. There seemed to be a strong parallel between the dual face of childhood that Graham portrayed and the lead character in the book that I was writing. There also seemed to be a certain amount of common ground as to our joint influences; both of us were admirers of the Pre-Raphaelite brotherhood, we had a number of favorite poets in common and we were both aficionados of the gothic ghost story at its darkest and most baroque.

I took inspiration from Graham's work through the writing *of Sleep, Pale Sister.* When the book was finished and about to be published, I tried very hard to obtain my publishers' permission to use one of his paintings as the cover. I knew instantly which one it should be, his very haunting and strange portrait *Girl in* ▶

> 66 There seemed to be a strong parallel between the dual face of childhood that Graham portrayed and the lead character in the book that I was writing. 99

The Cover That Does It Justice *(continued)*

Shadows, which to me was the face of the heroine of my novel. With this in mind I contacted the artist, whom I found to be astonishingly congenial and in sympathy with my writing objectives. My publishers' art department, however, was less so. Apparently commissioning such an artist for a book cover was considered too controversial.

By this time, I had just given birth to my daughter, Anouchka, and was finding the delivery much more difficult than that of a simple novel. My life as a new parent took over my life as a novelist for some years, but I contacted Graham again and promised him that in the unlikely event that I was ever able to make more than pocket money from my novels I would return to him and commission a portrait of my daughter, who should within ten years be at about the right age.

Ten years later I did just that. My friendship with Graham and his equally talented artist wife, Annie, has flourished. I remain a great admirer of their work and through them have been introduced to the work of a number of their colleagues of the Brotherhood of Ruralists. Graham's portrait of Anouchka is hanging in my bedroom and at last my novel has the cover that I feel does it justice. As for *Girl in Shadows,* it has haunted me ever since I first saw it in poor reproduction in a book on art; this Christmas I bought it and it hangs up in my front hall where it haunts me still.

GRAHAM OVENDEN

SOME YEARS AGO I received a communication, from a then little-known writer, asking if I would be good enough to read her latest novel, *Sleep, Pale Sister.* I read the book she had enclosed, which immediately wove its dark romance and pathos on my senses. The word pictures evoked cast a spell, which held and still holds me.

> ❝ Some years ago I received a communication, from a then little-known writer, asking if I would be good enough to read her latest novel, *Sleep, Pale Sister.* I read the book she had enclosed, which immediately wove its dark romance and pathos on my senses. ❞

8

Time passed and the writer proved her personal vision and received the justified accolade of fame. Even so, though we had not personally communicated for a number of years, Joanne Harris had not forgotten the artist, who lives and paints in Cornwall. When it was decided to republish *Sleep, Pale Sister* I was asked to create a dust jacket for the novel—as had been Joanne's original intention. Thus it is and I have the deep satisfaction of a collaboration, which holds the elements of alchemy. ⟢

An Excerpt from
"Breakfast at Tesco's"

Available in hardcover and coming soon in trade paperback from Harper Perennial in Winter 2006, Joanne Harris's collection of short fiction, Jigs & Reels, *"delivers twenty-two diverse home runs"* (Seattle Times). *Read on for a special excerpt from the story "Breakfast at Tesco's."*

"GOOD MORNING, Miss Golightly. Your usual, is it?"

That's what I like about this place. That human touch. The way Cheryl always brings me my usual and calls me by name. I only know her as Cheryl, of course; that's only right, as she's such a young thing. One day maybe I'll ask her to call me Molly.

Two rounds of white toast, strawberry jam, a currant tea cake and a pot of Earl Grey. That's my usual. Cheryl knows always to bring it to my seat by the window, to serve the milk in a proper jug—can't stand those little plastic tubs—with two wrapped lumps of sugar in the saucer. There's something so very *safe* about coming here every Saturday morning and having the same breakfast, seeing the same faces, sitting in my favorite place and watching the people go by. It's my reward for having scrimped and worried all week; my little treat.

Cheryl is twenty-nine. She has bleached hair and a pierced nose, and wears those built-up trainers, like the orthopedic shoe Doris Craft wears down at the Meadowbank Retirement Home. I suppose you could say she looks cheap. But she brought the milk jug from her own house because Tesco's don't provide them—a tiny, tiny creamy jug which she later admitted came from a doll's tea set—and she always calls me Miss Golightly.

Not everyone is so polite. At the Meadowbank

Home, where I go twice a week to visit my sister, the nurses call me "dearie," with that awful, vulpine coyness, as if they know that it's simply a matter of time before I end up there too, alongside poor Polly, who has long since ceased to care about names at all, and rarely even remembers mine.

Perhaps that's why I always try to make an effort with my appearance. They must think I'm rather ridiculous, at the Meadowbank Home; always so correct in my black dress—a little shabby now, but still good—my gloves and my red spring coat. Who do I do it for?, they wonder. Surely I'm far too old for vanity. I don't wear my pearls to visits, though; not since Polly forgot how she'd given them to me, all those years ago, and made a scene. I shouldn't feel guilty, I know—her mind was quite sound when she gave them to me, and they are only cultured—yet somehow I always do.

There's a carnation here on the table, in a narrow glass vase. Cheryl again. No one else would bring me flowers. But she will deny it if I mention it to her, laughing and saying that it must be a gift from one of my gentlemen admirers. I sense that I fascinate Cheryl; to her I am a fragment from another world, like a piece of moon rock. She finds excuses to come and talk to me; to ask me questions.

At first, she was incredibly ignorant. Two years ago she had never seen a black-and-white film. She thought Hepburn was the name of a pop group. She had never heard of Luis Buñuel or Jean Cocteau or even Blake Edwards. Her favorite movie was *Pretty Woman*.

Two years on, she is still strangely shy of me. It comes out in a brashness which she means to be cheery but which to me sounds defensive and not entirely happy. She has the dirtiest laugh, though. When she laughs she could be pretty; perhaps even beautiful. There is a man, but no wedding ring among the dozens of cheap glittery things she wears. She seldom speaks of him. He has been through a rough patch, she explains ▶

An Excerpt *(continued)*

reluctantly. I take this to mean that he is unemployed. I've seen him once or twice in town—usually outside the pub or the betting shop—a big, once handsome man now going to seed, like an aging Marlon Brando. He comes into the café occasionally; I always know he's there because Cheryl gives him away with her eyes. Her movements are less free when she knows he is watching; she stabs at the keys of the till like a chicken pecking corn. On those days she does not come over to talk to me, but sometimes gives me a little apologetic smile. ❧

Have You Read?
More by Joanne Harris

BLACKBERRY WINE (2000)

Jay Mackintosh's life is stalled with regret and ennui. His bestselling novel, *Jackapple Joe,* based on his childhood summers with the kindly and wise Old Joe, is ten years in the past and he has written nothing since. Impulsively, he decides to move to a remote French village with hopes of re-creating the magic of those long-lost golden summers. But while the spirit of Joe is calling to him, it is a haunted, reclusive woman who will ultimately help Jay find himself again.

"[*Blackberry Wine*] is a well-crafted escape into a world where lessons can be learned and evil is sometimes just dumb enough to be given the slip." —*Seattle Times*

FIVE QUARTERS OF THE ORANGE (2001)

When Framboise Simon returns to a small village on the banks of the Loire, the locals do not recognize her as the daughter of the infamous woman they hold responsible for a tragedy during the German occupation years ago. But the past and present are inextricably entwined in a scrapbook of recipes and memories that Framboise has inherited from her mother. And soon Framboise will realize that the journal also contains the key to the tragedy that indelibly marked that summer of her ninth year.

"Her prose reads like poetry, and it is a physical experience to fall into her imagery." —*New York Times*

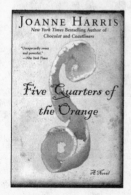

COASTLINERS (2003)

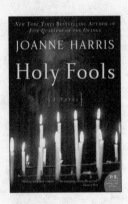

Mado has been adrift for too long. After ten years in Paris, she returns to the small island of Le Devin, the home that has haunted her since she left, full of hopes for reconciliation with her estranged father. Yet what she doesn't realize is that it is not only her father whose trust she must regain.

"Harris develops her beguiling story in layers . . . writing with power and grace about the family ties that bind."

—*Publishers Weekly* (starred review)

HOLY FOOLS (2004)

Britanny, 1610. Juliette, a onetime actress and rope dancer, is forced to seek refuge among the sisters of the abbey of Sainte Marie-de-la-mer. Reinventing herself as Soeur Auguste, Juliette makes a new life for herself and her young daughter, Fleur. But when the kindly abbess dies, Juliette's comfortable existence begins to unravel. The abbey's new leader is the daughter of a corrupt noble family, and she arrives with a ghost from Juliette's past—Guy LeMerle, a man she has every reason to fear and hate.

"[A] rapturous and page-turning story of devotion. . . . Harris's most ambitious and unforgettable novel to date."   —*BookPage*

JIGS & REELS (2004)

An enchanting collection of twenty-two tales, each a surprise and delight, melding the poignant and the possible with the outrageous, the magical, and, sometimes, the eerily haunting.

"Harris makes it look easy. . . . The stories deftly guide readers through a labyrinth of sensations from tenderness and sympathy to the bizarre to the humorous." —*Library Journal*

MY FRENCH KITCHEN (2003)

In this illustrated cookbook/memoir, coauthored with chef and writer Fran Warde, Joanne Harris shares her treasured collection of family recipes that have been passed down from generation to generation.

"Thank goodness for *My French Kitchen*."
—*Boston Globe*

The **Web Detective**

www.joanneharris.com
for Joanne's HarperCollins website

www.joanne-harris.co.uk
for Joanne's personal website

www.authortracker.com
to register to receive email updates on Joanne

**http://news.surfwax.com/authors/files/
Joanne_Harris_Book.html**
*for news, reviews, and articles about Joanne's
books*

**http://aznet.co.uk/ruralists/artists/
goprofile.html**
*for information on Graham Ovenden, the artist
who created the haunting cover for* Sleep, Pale
Sister

www.victorianweb.org
for more information on the Victorian age

**www.artcyclopedia.com/history/
pre-raphaelite.html**
*for more information on the Pre-Raphaelite
Brotherhood, the group of artists on which Henry
Chester was based*

www.facade.com/tarot
for a free tarot reading

**http://homepages.primex.co.uk/~lesleyah/
victrevs.htm**
for recommended reading of Victorian interest

Don't miss the next
book by your favorite
author. Sign up now for
AuthorTracker by visiting
www.AuthorTracker.com.